Holding Their Own III.
Pedestals of Ash

By

Joe Nobody

ISBN 978-0615708560

Edited by:
E. T. Ivester
Contributors:
D. A. Hall
D. Allen
T. Baughman

www.HoldingYourGround.com

Published by

www.PrepperPress.com

Other Books by Joe Nobody:

- Holding Your Ground: Preparing for Defense if it All Falls Apart

- The TEOTWAWKI Tuxedo: Formal Survival Attire

- Without Rule of Law: Advanced Skill to Help You Survive

- Holding Their Own: A Story of Survival

- Holding Their Own II: The Independents

- The Home Schooled Shootist: Training to Fight with a Carbine

Prologue

Julian Alvin Penderhurst shifted his weight, leaning back in the well-worn chair. He reached with one hand and tugged slightly on his jeans, before raising his feet to rest on the large oak desk. His intense, black eyes matched his hair, short beard, and much of the tattoo ink covering his arms. There was no mistaking the dark core of the man or his mood. His posture displayed an honest disregard for the myriad of files and documents scattered on the desk's surface. Sitting directly in front of the worn soles of his work boots was a sign that read "City of Alpha, Texas – Chief of Police." Julian was not the Chief of Police, nor had he ever met the man face to face. This was a rare circumstance, as Julian was no stranger to law enforcement. The majority of his adult life had been spent in the company of men such as the chief.

Julian had been arrested the first time at 12 years of age for petty shoplifting. His latest detention, just a few months ago, had been for armed robbery and assault with a deadly weapon. There had been so many arrests, warrants and convictions, Julian couldn't remember them all. He had spent more of his 32 years incarcerated, than free.

A lifetime of experience in the criminal justice system allowed Julian to develop a multitude of skills and some very unique habits. For starters, anyone who called him "Julian," risked being assaulted. His first prison experience as an adult taught him that the name Julian quickly became Julie, and that was definitely of the feminine persuasion. Not a positive situation for an 18-year old boy of average build, surrounded by larger men who had little hope, few options, and even less scruples. Over the years, the name Julian faded away, and Mr. Penderhurst had become known to everyone as Smokey.

The two men standing in front of Smokey were shifting their feet and moving their bodies as if they were scared. Smokey took a deep draw from the cheap cigar held between his thumb and forefinger and blew a perfect oval-shaped ring. The cloud formation drifted toward the man on the right, surrounding his face before dissolving into a greyish blue haze encircling the fellow's head. Smokey's lips curled just slightly at the corners in what amounted to more of a disapproving smirk than any resemblance of a smile.

"So," his gravelly voice sounded, "this *one* man killed nine of our guys and wounded three others. We lost three trucks, wasted 300 rounds of ammunition, and a motorcycle to boot. You dipshits also pissed away what…20 gallons of gasoline?"

The target of the smoke ring hesitated. "Umm ... uh ... yeah ... something like that. But I'm here to tell ya, he was like a Green Beret or something. I've never seen anybody shoot and move like that."

Smokey pondered the response. In a single motion, he lifted his boots off the desk and stood quickly. His unpleasant stare focused on the second man. "He was only one man – right? I mean, you guys had him outnumbered what – 20 to 1? Was he Superman or some shit? The caped crusader? Did bullets bounce off him or something? Do I need to give you clowns kryptonite or what?"

Small streaks of sweat streamed down the forehead of the man being grilled. Rather than answer, he used his shirtsleeve to wipe the perspiration from his brow. His partner couldn't leave well enough alone and added fuel to Smokey's fire. "We think it was the same guy who took out the sentries. He matched the description of the guy Hawk called 'Bishop.' He's the same dude who busted up the ambush the night before at the carwash. The good news is he's gone now."

Smokey's brow furrowed, and his gaze turned toward the ceiling as if to verify God heard the gentlemen's recount of events. After receiving no comment from the heavens, Smokey shook his head and exhaled loudly. Moving like a striking snake, both of Smokey's fists slammed down on the desk, causing the two men to jump and turn pale. Smokey roared, "Before we took over this town, all of you assholes were locked in your cells! None of you would have gotten out if I hadn't set you free! When the man who owned this desk tried to lock us back up, I was the one who took him out. I was the one who led the fight. Do I have to do every fucking thing around here myself?"

Smokey stopped his tirade for a moment, his expression showing contempt for both men. The only reaction he received was two pairs of eyes shifting their focus to the floor. This didn't please Smokey, and his speech became even more vehement. "Whose idea was it to bring every morsel of food you could find back here to the jail where we could protect it? Who was it that started recruiting all of those starving college kids? Who organized the kidnapping teams? Who had the idea to empty out the pharmacy and the liquor stores first? No wonder you two got busted – you are so fucking stupid. You two are no higher on the evolutionary scale than pond scum, and I'm surprised your cells can divide. Please...please tell me neither of you ever fathered children. No wonder the damn country collapsed with idiots like you two walking around."

The boss' temper was legendary. When he paused, both convicts believed the scolding was over, and they relaxed.

Smokey smiled, spreading his arms in a gesture of "*What the hell?*" The two men glanced at each other with relief, believing the storm had passed.

Smokey acted as if he were rubbing his lower back, and instantly a .357 Magnum revolver appeared in his hand. Before either man could protest, a moist, crimson dot appeared on each of their foreheads. The two bodies slumped to the floor with a solid thud while the room echoed with the thunder of the pistol's discharge.

Smokey turned back toward his desk as the door burst open, and several men came pouring in. The first one through was Hawk. He had known Smokey since their time together at the Terre Haute Federal Penitentiary. Hawk was Smokey's right hand man and was clearly relieved to see his boss was the man still standing.

Smokey looked at the men crowding the doorway and motioned to the bodies on the floor. "Get those worthless, incompetent carcasses out of my sight. Dump 'em along the road somewhere, and the feral hogs will eat 'em. They ain't worth a minute of shovel time."

As the two dead men were dragged from the room, Smokey motioned to Hawk and said, "Get everyone together, and I mean everybody. That bitch over at the church is behind all this, and I'm sick and tired of messing around with those holy rollers. We are going to storm that compound and take over this town once and for all. Is the tank ready?"

Hawk looked at his boss and calmly replied, "Just about. We're still working on the driver's compartment, but other than that, it's all ready."

Smokey didn't hesitate, "Finish up as much as you can. We're going to use it today and get this thing over with."

Hawk could tell his boss wasn't in the mood to debate tactics. Like his fearless leader, he was pissed that someone had invaded their territory and gotten away with it. He didn't know for sure what Bishop had taken, but everyone believed he had pilfered some pretty valuable medical supplies and equipment. There was probably some great prescription drugs heisted as well. All that medical stuff should have been theirs to use. No matter, Smokey was right. There weren't enough resources in the town for two different camps. The people at the church had to go.

"You got it, boss."

Chapter 1

Bishop's Trek

The West
Cracks and channels, craters and crevices,
Mark her ancient face.
Veins of color cross her surface
And yet display such grace.
Dry and yellowed,
Dusty from age.
Swirled and straightened,
Brushed with sage.
Widened, flattened,
Peaked and troughed,
A vast expanse of space so rough with age.

DALH, 2010

Bishop was having trouble maintaining focus. The inside of his mouth and throat felt like he had swallowed a handful of talcum powder. The lining of his nose was so dry it bled. He couldn't make spit, and his tongue kept sticking to his teeth. The last few precious drops of water had been sucked through the tube of his camelback hours ago, and that hadn't exactly been a geyser of refreshment. He started cursing himself for not refilling it before leaving Alpha, but then stopped. *No,* he thought; *don't be too harsh on yourself. You were a little preoccupied.* As he replayed the last 48 hours in his mind, the irony of it all dawned on him. Surviving four exhausting skirmishes and a minor concussion didn't mean squat now. Now the desert air was the reaper, and she was a dangerous, merciless bitch. A passing impulse to grimace was stopped cold, the effort sending pain shooting across dry, blistered lips. *All those dudes were wasting their time trying to kill me,* he thought. *They should've saved their energy and let the desert do the job.*

He paused to look at his surroundings for what had to be the tenth time in the last hour. It wasn't so much in anticipation that anything had changed, but rather an excuse to give his aching knees and sore feet a break.

As he sluggishly shifted his gaze across the desert terrain in front of him, he struggled to think of a more desolate place. He'd never felt any desire to visit Death Valley or the Bonneville Salt Flats – being raised in west Texas, he'd seen

1

enough scorched landscape for a lifetime of memories. Perhaps those places were as void of feature as the ground ahead. The moon, no doubt, was just as lacking of vegetation and life. He'd worked in Afghanistan, both in the pine-infested hills of the north and the destitute, parched south. Even the deserts of the Kandahar Province were graced with the occasional splotch of green here and there. In this place, he was completely surrounded by sterile and ugly.

Bishop was more aware than ever of the weight of the rifle slung across his chest. His movements were uncharacteristically slow, as he unhooked the sling and propped the weapon against his leg. He glanced down at the normally spotless carbine and grunted. A thin layer of crusty sand covered the rifle like the crystalline topping of a sugar cookie. Bishop had escaped from Alpha via a hijacked off-road motorcycle, and the weapon had been swung around to his back. The rooster tail of dust created by the bike's rear wheel left a coating of gritty earth that he hoped wouldn't cause a firing malfunction. *Not that there was anything to shoot at,* Bishop mused.

He sighed and continued scanning the surrounding area. To the west were barren foothills, colored mostly in a depressed and faded hue of yellow, accented with the occasional blotch of sun-blanched grey. Too steep to climb, but not commanding enough slope to provide shade, Bishop considered the mounds as something God had left unfinished, incomplete, and without purpose. The land directly in front of him was flat and just as worthless. There wasn't a serious undulation as far as he could see. Broken hunks of sandstone, both the color and size of his boots, littered the ground everywhere. He hadn't seen a single living thing for the past three hours – not even the small lizards so common in the southwest could survive here. He could see the floor of the valley spread out far to the east until the heat mirages rippling through the air obscured the image. In the distance beyond, The Fort Davis Mountains stood forebodingly dark and angry. *Who could blame them*, thought Bishop. *If I were stuck with this view in my backyard, I'd be pissed too.*

Bishop took off his hat and tucked it under his arm, running his hands through his filthy hair. Terri and a pair of dull kitchen scissors kept it short. His wife loved to tease about putting a bowl on his head and making him look like an 80's punk rocker. *I wonder if I'll ever get a real haircut again.* His scalp should have been damp with perspiration, but it was bone dry. *It's the damned air.*

His mind drifted back to the time when he was a child living on a ranch not too far from where he was standing right now. His after-school chores that day were interrupted by a desperate sounding horn in the distance. A small crowd of ranch hands gathered around as a speeding pickup skidded to a halt, quickly enveloped by the pursuing cloud of dust. The ranch's foreman jumped out of the truck as the pack of men approached and solemnly peered into the bed. Bishop knew his place as a boy – especially when something important distracted the men. He was to remain quiet and stay out of the way. As usual, curiosity got the better of him, and he carefully wormed his way around the crowd until he could peek into the back of the truck. He recognized one of his dad's coworkers lying flat in the bed. The man wasn't moving.

A quick, intense discussion ensued, and then just as suddenly as it had appeared, the truck sped away, being chased by the dust. Bishop watched the fast-moving vehicle bounce along the washboard dirt road, growing smaller and smaller as it approached the horizon. He felt a hand on his shoulder and looked up to see his father gazing down at him with a serious look on his face.

"Bishop, do you know what happened to that man?"

Bishop blinked and switched his gaze back to the distant speck, quickly fading from view. "No, sir."

"Son, I've taught you how important it is to drink lots of water when it's hot outside. How the body needs the water whether you're thirsty or not. That man didn't drink enough water, and now he's very sick. He may meet his maker before the day is out…God help him."

Bishop digested his father's words and then looked around. "But dad, it's not hot out today. I'm not even sweating."

Bishop's father sized him up and then motioned for the boy to follow. "Come over to the bunkhouse, son. You're old enough to understand this now. This is an important lesson for you."

Bishop followed his father to the rough wood-planked building that served as quarters for all of the single ranch hands. Since Bishop's mom and dad had split, father and son had been required to move back in with the other non-married men. Bishop didn't mind the new accommodations so much except for the racket at night. He had a recurring nightmare of being attacked by grizzly bears, only to wake up and realize the sound wasn't from a bear at all, merely a chorus of snoring men. The noise ranged from the gentle wheezing of one older cowpoke to several full-fledged, "shake the bunkhouse to its foundations" snores. Falling back asleep with that medley of exhausted men was never easy, regardless of how tightly he wrapped the pillow around his ears. His father was one of the worst offenders, but that was different. No matter what caused young Bishop to waken, no matter how much the dream had shaken him - everything was okay if his father were sleeping soundly in the next bunk.

On that day so many years ago, Bishop followed his father into the kitchen area, or the grub parlor as the men called it. They entered a small room that housed a hand operated pitcher pump and a wood-burning stove. There were shelves along one wall that must have been painted a dozen times over the years. Random layers of color had worn off here and there, leaving an abstract impression of a space that was old and tired. Stacked on each shelf were the dishes, pots, and pans used by the hands. While the main meal of the day, supper, was served in the big house, the men used this area to fix lunch buckets in the morning before heading off to work remote parts of the ranch. Bishop shied away from this place because it meant washing dishes, and that was his least favorite chore. While his father rambled through the cabinets, Bishop's attention was drawn to his favorite place – the tack room.

Even today, isolated and unsure of his own survival there in the desert, thoughts of the tack room brought a painful smile to Bishop's cracked, dry lips. As a small boy, *that room* was off-limits unless he was specifically asked by one of the men to fetch something. He remembered *that* smell, that glorious, intoxicating aroma of rawhide saddles balanced on rails, and bridles lining the walls. The scent was of working leather, sun cured, and sporting a history rife with toil. Some of the saddles were reserved for the 4th of July parades in Alpha, strikingly adorned with highly-polished silver studs and buckles. Those shining emblems were like Christmas lights to Bishop - rare ornaments in an otherwise bleak and dusty world of a working west Texas ranch. The room's real magnet for small boys was in clear view from the doorway. Along the back wall hung the men's pistols and holsters, now mostly used for show. Bishop had intently absorbed the bunkhouse stories of daring Indian raids and brave cowboys barely holding off Comanche warriors. A young fellow with quite the vivid imagination, Bishop recreated battles using a stick rifle and firing pretend bullets at attacking savages crouched behind the barn - after his chores were done, of course. His fantasy was interrupted by his father's pumping of the cast iron handle, and he knew well enough to snap to attention.

His dad removed a sponge from the dishwashing sink and dampened it under the running well water. Saying only, "Feel this," he handed it to Bishop. Doing as he was instructed, the boy watched as his father waved the sponge in the air a few times.

4

His dad waited a bit, and then passed the sponge to Bishop to touch again – it was bone dry!

Bishop had seen some of the ranch hands do card tricks and had even once watched a man dressed in black coat and tails slice his female assistant in half at the 4-H Fair in Alpha. Bishop's voice sounded astonished, "Dad! I didn't know you were a magician."

Bishop's father laughed, tousled the young boy's hair, and replied in a serious tone. "Bishop, I'm going to tell you again, son, you don't have to be hot or sweating for your body to lose water. Today, the air is sucking the water out of everything, including your very lungs as you breathe. On days like this, drink more water regardless if you feel hot, cold, sweaty, dry, or thirsty. Got it?"

"Yes, sir."

That day had been over 30 years ago, and Bishop had never appreciated the lesson more than this afternoon. He knew a man could normally last a few days without water - but not today. The humidity must be below 5%, and the air was draining his body with every breath. *Of all the days to be without water*, he thought. *If I don't find some soon, I won't have to worry about this sore back and dirty rifle.*

In his mind, Bishop determined he would walk a hundred more steps before he rested again. He re-slung the rifle and started counting. As he headed north, he planned to complete the majority of his journey to Fort Bliss at night. Since he was traveling through west Texas, water would be spotty. The few widely known lakes and springs would most likely attract refugees, and after what he had just experienced, he wanted to avoid people. Traveling at night would be cooler, require less water, and help him pass through unnoticed.

He also needed to rest and re-inventory his pack. He had been using a lot of ammo and wasn't sure exactly how much reserve was left. His current predicament would be even more complicated if his supply of lead were as low as his water. He mentally estimated a three-day walk to Fort Bliss if he traveled from dusk to early morning light. Bishop knew he could shorten that distance if he trekked through El Paso, but the risk wasn't worth it. Every scrap of information, rumor, and just plain old common sense screamed, "Avoid El Paso!" The few drifters passing through Meraton whispered wild stories of horrific scenes and terrible circumstances in that west Texas city. Bishop figured there was some exaggeration involved, but his narrow escape from Houston tended to lend some credence to even the most farfetched claims. He judged their tall tales had some foundation in truth.

On the third set of 100 steps, he had to fight down a strong urge to take off his pack and leave it behind. *I can move on ahead, find water, and then come back and get it,* he kept telling himself. It took all of the discipline he could muster to overcome the impulse.

On the fourth iteration, he noticed that the landscape was changing around him. His route was now gradually sloping downhill, and an island of vegetation lay ahead. The small clump of cacti was mostly dead, but it was the first life he'd seen in hours, and it immediately improved his morale.

He hiked a little further, noticing more and more signs of life around him. Even walking was becoming easier, as the ground beneath his boots changed to a flat, packed surface. Random spots of green and dark brown vegetation littered the desert floor, and the rock facade of the surrounding hills seemed to transform into a friendlier color of red. A turkey vulture circled in the sky ahead of him, no doubt having spotted a meal. A dead animal meant something had once been alive, and that meant water somewhere nearby. Bishop was envious of the scavenger's apparently effortless soaring on the thermal waves rising from the desert floor. He tried to imagine what the cool air would feel like rushing by his own head.

Rounding a bend, he saw the first signs of civilization in hours. A fence line suddenly appeared, stretching into the distance. Alongside the barbwire, a pair of worn paths showed clearly in the desert soil. Bishop had a vision of a bored cowpoke driving the fence line in his pickup while looking for downed wire or busted posts. He had performed the same job dozens of times in his youth. Where there was a fence, there were cattle. Where there were cattle, there was water. The fence ran in the general direction Bishop wanted to travel, so he decided to follow it. Experience taught him that the ranch hands would have taken advantage of the flattest terrain when laying the wire and that sounded like good news for his aching knees and tired back.

Bishop managed another mile or so before he came to a dry creek bed lined with smooth, bleached, white limestone. The sun was almost at its zenith, and the day was going to be a scorcher for this time of year. There were occasional clumps of scrub oak along the banks, some of which were actually large enough to provide shade. He considered walking up or down the stream to see if there were any low spots that still held water. He concluded that finding a standing pool was unlikely, and he would be gambling precious energy on a wild goose chase. His head was now pounding – yet another sign of dehydration. He wasn't going to be able to function much longer without something to drink.

6

He moved away from the fence line and followed the creek until he found a large oak, its branches extending over the bank, creating shade over a low spot of sand. Bishop scanned the area and couldn't see a better place to make camp. The relief he felt after taking off his pack, chest rig, and body armor gave him energy. He swung his rifle around to his back, and tightened the sling to secure the weapon. It would take him a second or two to get back in position should the need arise. But he had work to do, and the lack of water was the imminent threat. Bishop dug around in his pack and extracted his entrenching tool and his supply of plastic bags. It was time to start digging for water.

He began burrowing in the dry sand beneath the shady spot. With any luck, he would find enough water below the surface to get a drink. The first 16 inches of sand was so dry it wouldn't even stick to his hands. At two feet below the surface, he noticed barely moist grains sparkling on the blade of his spade. Another half a foot, and the color of the soil changed, indicating it was moist. Three feet down, he hit bedrock and couldn't go any deeper.

Using his hands, Bishop pushed around the damp grit and made a bowl-sized indentation, hoping enough water would seep in from the sand and pool on the bedrock. He knew it wouldn't be much, but even a couple of mouthfuls would work wonders right now.

Rather than sitting around watching the hole, Bishop thought it best to hedge his bet. He began making his hole wider and deeper. When he reached the dampest earth, he started dumping each shovel of tacky soil into a large black trash bag. When he had filled the plastic bag to the point where he worried about lifting it, he twisted the top and struggled up the bank with his load.

Bishop labored under the weight of the moist earth while he searched for a good patch of soft sand that was fully exposed to the sun. He started digging again. In 15 minutes, he excavated a round hole that would be a perfect sized grave for a car's tire. He took another large black bag and lined the entire bottom and sides of the pit, using small stones to hold the edges of the plastic liner in place.

Carefully, he dumped the wet sand onto the plastic liner and spread the damp grains around evenly. Next, he placed his drinking cup directly in the middle of the moist sand, then covered the hole with the now empty bag. Using more stones to act as paperweights, he sealed the cover as tightly as possible using the original contents of the pit. It dawned on him he could add to the moisture content of his new solar still, so he folded back one side of the cover and urinated inside. His dehydrated body didn't make much liquid, but every little bit would help. Bishop re-covered the pit and stood back to look at his field craft. One task remained, and he hurriedly added the final touch. He placed a small pebble in the middle of the cover, directly over the cup inside. The quarter-sized stone was just heavy enough to cause the plastic to sag downward in a concave-shaped roof over the pit without touching the lip of the cup. As the sun heated the black cover, the damp sand would surrender its moisture. The humid air would condense on the inside of the plastic bag. The droplets of pure water would be pulled downward by gravity to the lowest spot, which was right above his cup. Bishop smiled, imagining the small rivulets of water dripping into the vessel. It would take some time to recover a usable amount of water, but it was the best he could do at the moment.

Not far away, he spied a healthy looking cluster of vegetation and retrieved two clear plastic bags from his pack. Picking the leafiest branches, he slid the plastic bag over as much of the green leaves as possible. Next, he placed a good-sized rock in the bag, causing the thin stems to bend, allowing the tip of the bag to rest on the desert floor. He used two of his gear ties to tightly seal the open end of the bag around the base of the stems. His contraption looked like he was trying to protect rose bushes from a late frost, but in reality, Bishop knew that the plant would give up precious moisture in order to cool itself from the hot air inside the bag. The humidity trapped in the plastic should condense and run down the inside to the lowest spot – the rock resting on the ground.

He proceeded back to the streambed, anxious to see if there was any water at the bottom of his pit. Hopefully, among the three sources, he would get enough H2O to continue his journey without harming his body. His heart was pounding, as he slowly looked over the edge of what he hoped was a well and not a dry hole. There was water! Not much – maybe a quarter inch deep and mostly mud, but WATER!

In seconds, the suction hose from the water filter was in the hole, and the discharge end was in his mouth. He pumped once…twice…three times, and a small squirt hit his tongue. Another pump delivered another squirt. It tasted like mud and dirty socks, but Bishop didn't care. He swallowed the foul liquid with gusto. No cold glass of ice tea had ever tasted any better, no frosty brew had ever quenched any more.

There was a moment of panic when the next pump produced dry air. He glanced into the hole and found his efforts had sucked clean a small area around the hose. He moved the tip to another shallow pool and managed four mouthfuls before the hole went dry. He leaned back and relaxed for a bit, the weight of the world lifted from his shoulders.

Bishop vacillated about where to bivouac. While this wouldn't be a great camping spot if a flash flood came roaring down the creek, he decided to chance it. There was shade, good cover - and the bend in the creek limited visibility to any passersby. The small oaks at the edge of the bank were leaning over the streambed due to the last thunderstorm eroding the soil underneath their root system. Bishop climbed up the bank and wedged his way into the cluster of small trunks, the largest of which was about this size of his wrist. Picking the tree with the fullest canopy, he gradually applied pressure until he had bent the top of the tree over the streambed as far as possible. Holding onto the bent trunk with one hand, Bishop reached down and picked up his survival net with the other. It took a bit, but he wove the very top of the oak's small branches into the net and then let it snap back upright. He repeated the process two more times, resulting in his net hanging in the air via three oak branches.

Bishop moved down the stream a bit until he found a rock the size of a basketball. Hefting the weighty stone, he carried it back and set it down next to the suspended net. After gathering two more similarly sized rocks, he slowly pulled the net downward, bending the oaks over the streambed. He strategically placed the rocks to secure the canopy in place. Bishop could safely bend the trees over until there were only a few feet of the net exposed. He quickly used his knife to trim small pieces of foliage, weaving them into the visible portion. After finishing, he stepped back several paces to view his handiwork.

To anyone in the area, his shelter would look like a cluster of scrub oaks, falling into the streambed as the bank eroded away. Unless someone took the time to investigate closely, he would be practically undetectable.

Bishop headed back to his new hut and crawled inside. He excavated the pit until it was long enough to lie in. *It may look like a shallow grave, but it will be nice and cool.* He pulled his rain poncho out of the pack and lined the makeshift bunk. He pushed the spoil piles to the edge of the net, pleased with his cozy foxhole. He could fight from this position, if necessary.

The next task at hand was to clean his weapon. Not having the energy to fully strip it down, Bishop ran a piece of cloth through the barrel and pulled out the bolt, quickly cleaning it and the chamber. He brushed the crusted sand off the outside of the rifle, later applying just the right amount of lubricant to the moving parts. After reassembly, he dry fired several times to verify there wasn't any sand fouling the moving parts. A full magazine was inserted and a round chambered. Bishop then checked his secondary and found the holster had kept the pistol clean. He double-checked everything just to be sure.

Now that the weapons were squared away, it was time to inventory his pack. While he had a pretty good idea of what remained, three long days had passed since it had been packed. He needed a clear mental picture of what there was left to work with.

As Bishop laid the contents of the pack and load vest out on the shady stone of the riverbed, the first thing that became obvious was his low ammo store. He had configured his chest rig to hold four magazines for his rifle before leaving the ranch. Another six had been stored inside his pack. He learned a long time ago not to fill 30 round magazines with 30 cartridges. While rare, failures, or jams did happen. Reducing the spring tension in the box magazine seemed to result in a slight improvement. Experience had taught him that 28 was the right number for his weapon, so he left the ranch with 280 rifle rounds. He expended all but 74. In a full out gunfight, that wasn't very much ammo.

The next task was to check the food situation. The resulting inventory included about a pound of deer jerky, some roasted pine nuts, and one emergency MRE (Meal Ready to Eat) Bishop and Terri had carried with them on the bug out from Houston. *Not exactly 5-star restaurant cuisine,* he mused. While the food situation wasn't critical, he wouldn't be watching his weight on this trip. Bishop's stomach rumbled, reminding him that he hadn't eaten anything in over 24 hours. While he would have loved to chew on a piece of the jerky, he knew that the body used a lot of water to digest food and dulling the hunger would hasten his dehydration. Chow time would have to wait until he had more water.

The remaining items in the pack survived the trip unscathed. He double-checked everything, and then cleaned the small hand pump water purifier, hoping he would need it several times before this trip was over. The spare batteries, mess kit, and other items were all repacked in the proper order along with the empty magazines from his dump pouch. The contents of his medical kit, or blow out bag, had not been necessary so far and remained in good shape. Water and ammo were the top priorities, and he knew both would be difficult to come by.

Bishop pondered setting up some trip wires in case someone wandered by. He determined it wasn't worth the effort due to an uncooperative terrain. The combination of the streambed, flat desert floor, and lack of vegetation made it difficult to hide the wires. Only by pure chance would someone stumble onto his location anyway.

After visually verifying the isolation of his position one last time, Bishop removed his boots and socks and stripped down to his skivvies. He took the garments and rubbed them thoroughly in the dry sand, using a motion similar to someone washing clothes on a washboard. It wasn't the same as using water, but would help a little. After brushing off all of the sand, the clothes were hung in a small spot of sunlight with the hope that the UV rays would kill some of the bacteria causing them to stink. *What the hell, the body armor could use a little airing out as well.*

Bishop set aside one of the few remaining sealed hoohaws, or baby wipes. As he wiped down his body, the evaporating alcohol cooled his skin and made him drowsy. He dry brushed his teeth and then set his watch alarm to wake an hour before sunset. Feeling almost human again, Bishop used his pack to prop up his head and reclined in the pit. The indigenous wildlife didn't seem to notice the gentle snore coming from the streambed a few minutes later.

Chapter 2

Independent Mountain Men

Colonel Marcus looked up from the map spread on the roof of his command Humvee and sighed. His 4th Brigade Combat Team of the 10th Mountain Division was taking up defensive positions outside of Shreveport, Louisiana, and he wasn't happy with the situation at all.

Colonel Marcus was standing in the doorframe of the Humvee, trying to gain just a little more visibility from the extra height. It wasn't helping much. To add to the frustration, he didn't have a proper military map. One of his staff sergeants had pulled this one from the glove box of his civilian car as they were rushing out of Fort Polk. The army didn't issue proper military grade maps of North America to its corps.

Shreveport was the hub of the wheel for several nuclear power plants residing along the Mississippi delta, and it was the 4/10's objective to gain control of the region for the Independents. The decision to pledge his command to the new group had been difficult enough. Now their first mission was causing him to second-guess that commitment.

During the first few months after everything had fallen apart, his brigade had been ordered to perform unthinkable acts by the regular chain of command. While there is no action more demoralizing for a military unit than to enforce martial law on the native populace, this situation had been even worse. Not only was the 4/10 ordered to enforce rule of law, they metamorphosed into the health care provider, fire department, police, and food distribution center for the distressed population.

One night Marcus had been visited by a former commanding general whom he respected. The sales pitch explaining the Independents' purpose had been executed flawlessly. After sleeping on it, Marcus decided he was in. The President of the United States was "off the reservation," and the Independents pledged to restore rule, governing based on the Constitution of the United States. That founding document was what Colonel Marcus and every other U.S. officer swore an oath to protect.

Marcus looked over his shoulder at Sergeant Major Mitchel and shook his head in disgust. "Mitch, this isn't good. I don't know how far back to place our reserve. Is there *any* topography data available?"

Sergeant Major Mitchel shook his head, "I've sent a couple of men into Shreveport to check at the local library, sir. The town's been badly looted, but they're trying to find something – truthfully, I wouldn't count on it, Colonel."

Colonel Marcus looked back at his map and tried to reach a decision. The 4th was spread across a five-kilometer front, halfway between the city of Shreveport and the Texas-Louisiana state line. The northern-most units could see the shores of Lake Cross from their vantage. The brigade had taken defensive positions that spanned Interstate 20 and continued south for another kilometer. The 4/10 was a "light" unit, which meant that their main firepower consisted of thinly armored Stryker fighting vehicles. A "heavy" unit would rely on tanks. The Strykers were one of the latest additions to the U.S. arsenal and had exceeded expectations in Iraq. Faster and quieter than both M1 Abrams main battle tanks and the older Bradley fighting vehicles, the Stryker was an eight-wheeled troop carrier with some very advanced capabilities.

The 4/10 had caught *some* good luck however. When everything had gone to hell, two platoons of the Louisiana National Guard were engaged in exercises at Fort Polk, training with their eight M1A1 tanks. This augmentation was the brigade's ace in the hole, and right now Marcus was trying to figure out where to position this additional combat power.

The Independents had informed him that the 4/10 was about to receive visitors. Just as had occurred thousands of times throughout history, two significant military forces both wanted the same strategic ground at the same time. A collision was inevitable. The Ironhorse brigade of the 1st Cavalry Division was known to be moving east from Dallas and headed right at him. A heavy unit, thick with tanks, the Ironhorse was loyal to the president. Worse yet, Colonel Marcus knew they were highly trained, well led, and very capable. An experienced military man, he recognized that leadership and motivation were often as important as equipment, and the unit heading toward him had plenty of both. If this confrontation turned into a fight, he was outgunned. While his wheeled Strykers were faster, the M1 tanks used by the Ironhorse were about as close to unstoppable as any machine on the modern battlefield. They didn't call the M1 tanks "whispering death" for nothing.

Were it not for the addition of the tank platoons to his order of battle, Colonel Marcus would never consider a fixed line of defense. He would be relegated to a fighting retreat and hope to wear his opponent down. He knew that pure firepower seldom won battles. Maneuver was the key to victory – at least that's what every officer who was outgunned told himself. It would be

14

shortsighted to even consider that his opposing commander didn't know this, and besides, those tanks could move almost as fast as his equipment.

There were a host of other issues plaguing him as well. Both sides were equipped with the latest electronic networking systems. A commander sitting inside of a Stryker could see both friend and foe on a computer screen, and this functionality provided the American Army a huge advantage in recent Middle Eastern conflicts. Marcus's problem was that both sides owned the same technology. To make things worse, no one could be sure that the Ironhorse's computer screens wouldn't show the 4/10's data. The decision had been made to disable the systems. The colonel hoped the Cav would reach the same conclusion.

Air support was another big concern. American doctrine dictated that U.S. troops did not take the field unless air superiority was clearly established. If the United States Air Force were supporting the president, the 4/10 was in trouble. Because of that mandate, his brigade had practically zero anti-air defensive capability. While he had been assured that the USAF was sitting this one out, a good officer never took these things for granted. If fighter-bombers attacked his ground forces, the 4/10 wouldn't last long. Worse yet, if the Cav brought out Longbow Apache attack helicopters, his brigade probably wouldn't even get off a single shot at the approaching force. Normally, he would be counting on his own air capabilities, but their fuel supply had been exhausted while the brigade was occupying Baton Rouge. The Independents promised him a re-supply, but so far, none had arrived. His platoon of flying tank killers was grounded.

While most of the 4/10's commanders were battle-proven and well trained, their CO still had concerns. Over the last 10 years, all U.S. ground commanders had come to depend heavily on either fixed-wing or rotary air support. In the last two wars, his forces had had the capability to stand back and call in either artillery or air support against a well-defended position. If there were going to be a fight today, it would be a fluidic, fast-moving war of maneuver. His troopers were experienced, but with a different type of action. Not since the first Gulf War had the American military fought a force on force battle, and that had been so one-sided it had only lasted a few hours. While most of their equipment and tactics had been originally designed to fight the hordes of Warsaw Pact divisions crossing into West Germany, they had never actually been used against anything close to a technological equal.

Other than the artillery, Marcus figured this to be a confrontation between mobile ground-based forces. While the 4/10 had a platoon of Paladin self-propelled artillery, the

Ironhorse had its own field guns. With modern radar-equipped counterbattery capabilities, the two artillery units would be playing shoot and scoot - a deadly game of chess that would most likely cancel each other out.

A military strategist, the colonel easily recognized the dilemma. An artillery shell flies through the air for several seconds before impact. Since both sides possessed radar units that could detect the incoming round and backtrack to the parent gun, it wasn't unusual for return fire to be on the way before the initial salvo landed. An artillery unit's life must be one of constant movement because remaining stationary meant death. *I can't count on artillery support because they will be playing cat-and-mouse with the Cav's long-range guns,* concluded the colonel.

Marcus scanned the horizon one last time and made his decision. He hopped down from his perch on the Humvee, pulling the map with him. As with all good sergeants, Mitchel read his commander perfectly and stepped forward ready to receive orders. Marcus pointed to the map and said, "Position the reserves here, and tell those Cajun tank jockeys they had better fight those damn machines well, if they want to see the sun set tonight."

Chapter 3

Alpha-Bet Soup

Smokey glanced at the hundred or so men gathered on the front steps of the Alpha courthouse. They were a ragtag group at best, more closely resembling a mob than an organized fighting force. About a quarter of the group consisted of former prisoners Hawk and he freed from the local jail. The rest were mostly starving college students and others who long ago developed an insatiable taste for drugs and booze. Like mercenaries whose allegiance always fell to the highest bidder, many of Smokey's soldiers fought for the contraband that he could provide.

The smell of body odor, gun oil, and fear filled Smokey's nostrils. While they had enough food, water supply was always an issue for his people. Bathing was a luxury available to only a few. He ruled the vast majority of Alpha, Texas with the exception of one small corner of the town. That area was the source of the city's water supply, and it was controlled by Deacon Brown and her congregation at the First Bible Church. Smokey's crew made several attempts to push the holy rollers off of that small corner of Alpha, but the congregation unified, held its position, and eventually fortified the perimeter.

For months, the two groups patrolled, scavenged and skirmished all over Alpha. Smokey lost over 80 men to the Bible thumpers in various ambushes, gunfights, and sniping encounters. Hawk had been his mole inside the church, feeding him critical information. Smokey believed the zealots were losing heart, setting the stage for his men to overwhelm the resistance and seize control of the water supply. This Bishop character had ruined all of his water regulating efforts and more. Not only had Bishop discovered Hawk was a spy, he had "eliminated" several of Smokey's vigilantes, reigniting hope in Deacon Brown's parishioners. Smokey was wise enough to know morale could mean the difference between victory and defeat. Even beyond that, there was the issue of the water.

The Old West had a long and bloody history of fighting over water, or least using the life sustaining liquid as the excuse for a brawl here and there. The Pleasant Valley War, Mason Country War, and the more commonly known Lincoln Country War had all involved water rights to varying degrees, or at least that's what most people thought. In reality, water had very little to do with those historic skirmishes. While the standoff in Alpha did involve water, and Smokey's people truly needed it, there were far more important motivations for this clash.

Deacon Brown's presence denied Smokey absolute power, foiling his every attempt to consolidate his rule of Alpha. Smokey wanted the desirable woman in one of his jail cells, and after having his fun, he planned to crucify her on a cross in the town square. She provided an alternative to his rule, and many had joined her flock. It seemed like every time Smokey tried to establish some service in Alpha, the people who knew how to make things work had already joined this woman and her church.

The latest source of this frustration was an oversized fuel storage tank, owned by the school district and used to feed the large fleet of yellow buses. Smokey needed that gasoline, but didn't have anyone who could figure out how to pump the liquid gold out of the tank. One man finally volunteered to show them where the school's maintenance man lived. A visit to the address revealed the fellow had abandoned his home and taken his family to the church compound. And that was just one example of how Deacon Brown's influence had thwarted Smokey's plans. Practically every step to restore some level of civilization resulted in a dead end, mostly due to a lack of knowledge within Smokey's ranks. Engineers, electricians, and even construction workers had been killed, slipped out of town, or joined the church. Time after time, Smokey's followers automatically blamed Deacon Brown's little band of holdouts for every failure or shortcoming – whether they deserved it or not.

In reality, there were three groups of people remaining in Alpha. In addition to Smokey's army of criminals and Deacon Brown's congregation, there were hundreds of what Smokey's men referred to as "the rats." These were college students and citizens of Alpha who were still trying to survive on their own and not aligned with either side. Smokey realized that as time went on, these people would have to associate with one side or the other. If the church were eliminated as an option, his way would be the only choice.

Smokey's army was divided into two groups. For the past hour, his lieutenants had been gathering the troops and laying out the simple plan he had communicated in the chief's office a short time ago. The first group of about 40 men would function as a decoy, acting as if they were the main assault against the church's fortified perimeter. The second group would envelop, and 10 minutes after the shooting started, hit the church from the west side where Hawk reported the defenses were the weakest. Smokey remembered reading a quote by the American General George Patton, "Hold them by the nose, and kick them in the ass." He planned on doing just as the famous general advised.

Smokey thought about giving a pre-combat speech to the gathered men, but decided against it. The groups scattered around him were not real soldiers, and he didn't like speaking in public anyway. He held up the AK47 rifle, taken from the police station armory, and simply yelled out, "Let's go kick some ass!"

The small town of Alpha, Texas had never witnessed a full-on battle. Populated after the Indian Wars in this part of the world had long been over, the presence of dozens of armed men moving through the deserted streets was something new. The two columns of fighters moved slowly down the sidewalks and unused avenues that were already sprouting weeds here and there. The men avoided large piles of glass from broken storefronts and maneuvered around the rusted, burned out automobiles that littered the streets.

It was only 15 city blocks from the courthouse to the perimeter of the church. As the diversion group approached its jump off point, the leader motioned for the men to spread out and stay behind cover where possible.

Deacon Brown was in her office when the lookout's whistle blew. She scampered down the stairs, grabbing her rifle on the way. She sensed, more than saw, Atlas behind her. Her adopted son was a giant of a man, and it always boosted her confidence knowing he was with her. As she descended the stairs, she found the main sanctuary was already bustling with activity. Men who were not already engaged in sentry duty were scrambling to find weapons, ammunition and kiss family members goodbye. The women who were not assigned to help the fighters herded the children and elderly toward the basement steps. While a stranger might have viewed the scene as absolute chaos, everyone's actions were actually well rehearsed after weeks of what amounted to open warfare.

The First Bible Church's extensive parking lot was ringed with a barrier of automobiles, church buses, and anything else the congregation could throw together to defend the property. All along the makeshift wall, men were running with weapons and bags of ammo. Deacon Brown rushed to the roof of the church's two-story annex building attached to the main sanctuary. A few dozen plastic trash bags had been filled with sand, dirt, and gravel in order to create a command post overlooking most of the defensive positions. Atlas, as usual, stayed beside his mother. In addition to the church's leader and her son, two of the best marksmen in the group took up positions with deer rifles. As suddenly as the mad scramble to man the wall had begun, it was over. All along the line, men with rifles at their shoulders took deep breaths and scanned the area in front of them, wondering if today would be their last. An eerie calm fell over the resistance as they waited for the attack. They wouldn't have to wait long.

~ ~

As Smokey's diversionary group spread out along a one-block area, the men naturally started running from position to position, bent at the waist. Most of them had heard the alarm whistle coming from the defenders to their front and understood there would be no surprise today. As soon as the attackers settled into positions, the leader looked at his watch and nodded. The three men with him all raised their rifles and began sending rounds into the church's defensive positions, signaling the beginning of the attack. A few moments later, dozens of other rifles joined in and began pelting the church's wall with lead.

All along the northern border of the church grounds, bullets slammed into the makeshift barrier. Sparks flew, and metal thumped with the impact. The men assigned to defend this section had seen it all before. They stayed low behind proven bullet stops, only occasionally peering over and around cover.

Many of the attackers were equipped with bolt-action rifles, and their rate of fire was limited. Every sporting goods store, private home, and pawnshop had been looted, with weapons and ammunition being a highly valued prize. Alpha, Texas had been a town of less than 10,000 residents and undergraduates. Hunting was far more popular than any tactical endeavors, so the majority of the weapons found were not military grade by any sense. Still, the number of attackers was significant enough to keep everyone's head down. While the majority of the church's barricade showed signs of battle damage, the skinnies had never been able to concentrate enough firepower to overwhelm the defenses. This stalemate had existed since the congregation had built the wall. Both sides knew it, and one defender was overheard saying, "Don't these guys ever get tired of this silly game?"

The game was about to change.

Smokey and Hawk looked at each other and smiled. The diversion had started right on schedule, and their main attack force was almost in place. Everything was going according to plan so far. As they waited for the main attack column to take position, both men listened to the noise generated by the diversion. Along with the sporadic sound of gunfire, they could hear shouted commands coming from both sides of the fight. Smokey glanced over at Hawk and nodded, indicating it was time. Hawk smiled, mouthed the words, "*See ya later,*" and took off running back toward the courthouse.

Deacon Brown looked up from her binoculars and met Atlas' gaze. She shook her head in puzzlement, as something just didn't seem right about this attack. She had watched over two dozen engagements with the people her men had nicknamed "the skinnies." Normally, when they attacked the church's perimeter, the skinnies tried to keep the defenders' heads down and probe the wall. Today, there didn't seem to be any probing. She waited for five minutes, anticipating a small group to sprint out of hiding and charge the wall, but the attempt to breach never occurred. It seemed like the skinnies were happy to just sit back behind cover and waste ammunition. *This is just odd,* she thought, *I bet we are going to see something new today.*

One of Smokey's ex-cellmates approached and informed him everyone was in position. Smokey nodded and looked at his watch. Hawk should be here any minute. On cue, the attackers heard the sound of a diesel engine, approaching from behind them. Smokey looked around the corner and saw a large garbage truck rolling down the street. The emblem on the door read "City of Alpha – Department of Sanitation," and Smokey thought it prophetic. He was going to take out that garbage behind that wall. Through the front windshield, he could see the outline of several sandbags that had been stacked to provide some protection for the driver. As the truck came to a stop a few blocks away, 12 of their best men started climbing into the empty garbage area where they would be protected by the thick, steel walls. Hawk jumped out of the passenger door and ran to join his leader.

As soon as the men were loaded inside of the truck, the driver revved the big diesel engine, signaling he was ready. Hawk, along with another man, carried glass bottles of gasoline toward the perimeter of the church. Each bottle had a four-inch length of cloth stuffed into the opening. Commonly called a Molotov cocktail, the small mo-gas powered bombs were not overly effective as an antipersonnel device, but they could cause people to avoid or abandon an area. Hawk signaled to the men surrounding his position, and they opened fire on the wall directly in front of him. He pulled a cigarette lighter out of his shirt pocket and ignited the rag protruding from the top of the homemade bomb.

Deacon Brown was proud of the men defending the wall. For the past few minutes, they had hardly fired a shot at the attackers who seemed to be content just harassing them. Ammunition was always in short supply, and she had preached time and again to conserve the precious commodity. She started to turn and comment to one of the hunters when Atlas put his hand on her shoulder and pointed to the west side of the compound.

The four people on the annex roof watched in fascinated horror as two men suddenly appeared close to the wall, carrying smoking glass bottles of what everyone knew was gasoline. It wasn't the bombs that caused them all to hold their breath, as the skinnies had tried to implement this technique before with little effect. What caused a sickening fear in Deacon Brown's stomach was the huge garbage truck barreling at high speed directly at their barricade.

To the leader of the church, everything began to move in slow motion. She watched speechlessly as the two bottles arched through the air, landing just on the other side of the wall. Both bottles shattered on the parking lot surface with an audible whoosh. Flame and black smoke quickly rose into the air. The three men defending that section of the wall naturally ran away from the heat created by the burning liquid spreading across the pavement.

Smokey's tank was less than 100 feet away when the fires started. Deacon Brown started screaming at her troopers, "Shoot the truck! Shoot the truck!" Each man moved his aim, and a few sparks flew from the steel trash bed, quickly followed by holes in the windshield, surrounded by small spider webs of shattered glass. It was too late. A few more shots sparked and pinged off the heavy steel compartment above the cab, but the effect was minimal. The big vehicle slammed into the makeshift fortification at over 20 miles per hour, creating havoc among the defenders.

It had been a Sunday morning so many months ago when disaster struck the peaceful town of Alpha. Electric power had been sporadic for days, and the constant barrage of frightening headlines from the cable news channels left everyone on edge. Worshippers lined the wooden pews in the main sanctuary, and the overflow was barely managed in the balcony area of The First Bible Church. Toes began to tap, and worshippers began to sway to the sounds of "Abide with Me," as the widely acclaimed gospel choir filed from behind the congregation to their designated seating behind the podium. The call to worship had just begun, only to be interrupted by what most of the congregation thought was thunder. When the windows of the big church rattled a few moments later, most folks expected the town was going to receive a rare late-summer storm. No one really knew what happened at the chemical plant just north of the city. The choir had just finished a rousing rendition of "Amazing Grace" when a small boy, frightened of the thunder, was overhead asking his father if the town were on fire. Practically every head in the pews turned to look out the window. What they saw was a huge pillar of smoke reaching skyward over the town's modest skyline. There had been an explosion and now a fire. What no one could have known was that a poison cloud of gas accompanied the disaster, and thousands of their fellow citizens were being killed instantly even as the minister began to read the announcements for the day. The service was in full swing when a woman near the back of the church screamed loudly. Everyone turned to see an injured man, carrying a small child, stumbling toward the altar. The victim's skin was peeling off of his face, and the girl wasn't breathing. Before he died, he managed to gasp a warning that the air was poisoned, and everyone was dead. Those were the first people buried by the church's men, but they were far from the last.

In the beginning, the congregation tried to follow the creed associated with being a Christian organization. As the pastor, Diana's father had initially welcomed anyone who needed aid following the disaster. This generosity was quickly taken advantage of by a desperate population, and the raids started. It became clear that civilized behavior had turned into "every man for himself." During one break-in, the pastor had tried to stop the thieves and had been shot and killed. At that point, Diana had taken over. During the subsequent months, the church members were forced to protect themselves, and thus the wall had been erected.

The parking lot had been full of cars, and their frames became the foundation for the wall. Trees were felled, picnic tables were moved, old pews from the warehouse were stacked, and even the lawnmowers were used to reinforce the fortifications. It had worked. The raids had been stopped cold, and everyone felt more secure sleeping in the modern equivalent of a castle surrounded by a thick barricade. At least it had been secure until this moment.

The family sedans and wooden pallets used on the west side of the grounds were no match for the mass times velocity of the speeding garbage truck. The kinetic energy delivered via the front bumper of the heavy rig pushed the cars aside and cut through the barrier like a hot knife through butter. Were it not for a pile of old bricks directly in the truck's path, the breach would have completely devastated the defenders. As it were, a front wheel of the truck became airborne as it ramped over the brick pile. This not only resulted in a lurching change of speed, but the wheel bounced twice before the truck skidded to a stop. The 12 heavily armed men in the back compartment were violently thrown around inside of their steel box. It took them almost a full minute to untangle themselves, find dropped weapons, and gather their wits enough to start piling out the back. That minute ended up being the difference in the outcome of the battle.

Smokey's group started pouring into the breach created by the truck. At the same time, the diversionary group rose up and began to advance on the wall in earnest. The defenders quickly overcame their initial shock at the violence of the attack and fought back with desperation. For the first time, their wall of security had been overwhelmed, and every single man knew this might be the end of their way of life.

On the annex roof, Deacon Brown directed the hunters to slow down Smokey's men by using their lead to plug the gap in the wall. One retired army officer immediately realized the threat and pulled every other man from his section of the wall to focus on holding the breach. Relentless fire poured into Smokey's men as they attempted to cross into the inner sanctum of the church's grounds. Smokey used the garbage truck as cover while shooting at the defenders with his AK. A constant chorus of bullets pinging off of the metal trash hauler rose above the thunder of gunfire. He noticed men falling all around him, but didn't care. His combatants had achieved the initiative and needed to exploit the situation. He violently waved his men forward, while firing at targets himself. It was working. More and more of the attackers made it past the hole and started spreading out into the parking lot. A larger beachhead meant the defenders had more territory to cover. The breach in the wall was only about 10 feet wide, a small space to acquire targets. Attackers successfully penetrating the interior made the defenders' job increasingly difficult, as anyone shooting at the infiltrators had more and more ground to consider.

Deacon Brown could clearly see they were losing the fight. In another few minutes, her fighters would be completely overrun, and she couldn't think of anything to stop the intruders. She turned around to pick up another magazine for her rifle and noticed Atlas was no longer on the roof with her. She thought it odd that the big man would leave her side. Two rounds hit the sandbag in front of her, drawing her attention back to the fight.

Unknown to Deacon Brown, Atlas understood the dire situation. He rushed to the bottom of the annex stairs, loping down four at a time and pushed open the back door. There, in a small outbuilding, were several old steam radiators, recently rendered obsolete by a more modern heating system. Originally stored in the building to be sold as scrap, the heavy metal units weighed several hundred pounds each. Atlas lifted one of the radiators, turned toward the breach and began running. As he rounded the corner of the building, his image caused the attackers pause. Here was a massive wall of a man, charging directly at them full speed, wielding a large hunk of bronze and steel like it was a simple shield. Atlas had progressed about five big steps, when the first bullet impacted the radiator. He continued his path as more and more of the attackers noticed his advance and directed their fire at him. On the roof, Deacon Brown kept hearing an unusual "ping ping ping" sound coming from below. When Atlas finally came into view, she recognized immediately what he was doing. Shouting at him to stop and come back wouldn't have done any good. There was no way he could have heard her and probably would have ignored the pleas anyway. The only thing she could think to do was kill as many of the attackers as she could. She shouldered her rifle and began firing at the men closest to her son.

The garbage truck was natural cover for Smokey's men, and they had inadvertently bunched up around the wheels and body. Atlas made it to within 15 feet of the truck when he launched the radiator into the air, pushing with both hands, and sending it flying toward a group of five men. The target group stared, mesmerized that something so big and heavy could be tossed so far, and almost didn't move out of the way. One gatecrasher attempting to avoid the flying metal, tripped while scrambling over one of his comrades, and was instantly crushed by the weight of the radiator. Another man was knocked to the pavement, shaking his head as if to get his bearings. And a third was pinned beneath the hunk of metal, his exposed leg bleeding badly. In reality, the man who was killed was the lucky one. Before any of the men gathered their wits, Atlas was among them. The sounds of screaming men and crushing blows could be heard above all else. Three of the attackers were dead or disabled before any of them could react. Smokey started screaming, "Shoot him, goddamnit…Shoot his ass!" Atlas picked up a dropped rifle and began brandishing it as a club. He practically decapitated one attacker before the impact to a second man snapped the stock in half. Finally, a bullet found its mark and struck a massive upper thigh. Atlas didn't even flinch. He rounded the back of the trash hauler and surprised another man before the second bullet struck him in the shoulder. It seemed to have little effect as Atlas roared a blood-curdling battle cry and attacked another group of three men approaching the opening. His presence so confused and shocked the invaders that one thug shot another of his own comrades trying to raise his weapon at the charging colossus. A third bullet struck Atlas in the chest, but it only seemed to enrage him further. He took two massive steps and picked up an overturned picnic table that had once been part of the barrier, holding it like a toy. Several bullets slammed into the wood, showering the big man with splinters and fragments of lead. He lunged several feet forward, using the table to crush three men against the side of a car.

All during the rampage, the attackers' attention was focused on the tornado of destruction in their midst. This gave the church's defenders time to regroup and charge the opening in the wall. Atlas had another man by the neck when Smokey stepped around and began empting the magazine of his AK into the giant's back. It took several hits, but the Goliath finally staggered before landing on top of the lifeless body he still clutched in his hand.

Deacon Brown was leading the charge to repel the breach when her son hit the pavement. She shouldered her rifle and began firing at Smokey, but missed. Someone yelled, "Let's get out of here," and the invaders began to withdraw. The secondary assault quickly petered out when it became clear that the main attack had failed. In less than a minute, Smokey's men were moving away from the compound, scattering between the surrounding buildings, and looking back over their shoulders. The battlefield fell essentially silent, with only the roaring flames of burning cars and the weak moaning of the wounded drifting across the parking lot. Those sounds were quickly joined by the wailing cries of a mother who had just lost her only son.

Chapter 4

And Now Comes the Cav

It was only 322 kilometers from Dallas to Shreveport, Louisiana, across an unchallenging terrain, using Interstate 20 as the primary surface route. For the long column of war machines belonging to the 1st Cav, it might as well have been 1,000 kilometers the way things were going.

For months, the Ironhorse brigade maintained martial law in the Dallas metro area, finally receiving orders worthy of such an elite fighting unit, or at least that's how Major Owens viewed the situation. The past two months had been a living hell for his men and the country as a whole. They had been ordered to leave their home base at Fort Hood and establish rule of law in Dallas. One of three brigades assigned to the city, they had been both mentally and physically unprepared for the duty.

Now, Major Owens was trying to move his brigade to Shreveport and establish control of the area. The president had finally taken action and adopted a plan to kick-start the country's economic engine. The plan, as outlined to the major, seemed both logical and reasonable.

Since being in Dallas, they had guarded limited food stores and distributed daily rations to a starving population. At first, their medics had tried to provide basic, humanitarian aid to the civilians, but their supplies had been sapped in a matter of days. The Ironhorse and supporting units were not equipped to support 1.8 million people who had no resources.

The fact that there was practically zero resupply from Fort Hood or elsewhere didn't help the situation at all. It seemed like everything from bandages to bread to toilet paper was unobtainable. At first, his men had used their tanks and armored personnel carriers to patrol the neighborhoods and establish control. Fuel and spare parts quickly became an issue, and the monstrous machines were soon relegated to fixed position guard duty. Foot patrols were initiated. Tankers don't like patrolling on foot, and while a significant number of the brigade's men were infantry, everyone took turns humping through the sweltering summer streets of Dallas. The tactic managed to conserve fuel and reduce wear and tear on machinery. That wear and tear, however, began showing up on the men. Even then, the vehicles had to be started and run to keep parts lubricated and batteries charged. Conditions deteriorated so badly, it became a coveted reward for his men to spend an hour inside of an air-conditioned M1A2 as it performed its charging cycle.

The fact that Mother Green wasn't prepared for the mission didn't surprise Major Owens. He had deployed to Iraq in the early days and had witnessed what he jokingly referred to as "disciplined chaos." Command from on high wasn't exactly nimble when it came to executing a mission outside of the box. Logistics, command and control, and mission profiles were always the weak links in the chain - each of which made the average trooper's life more difficult.

Major Owens rubbed his chin, clearing his mind of the past in order to focus on the immediate problem. For the first 40 kilometers east of Dallas, Interstate 20 had been a parking lot, completely inundated with abandoned vehicles. In the days immediately following the collapse, people had run out of gas or simply been trapped on both the east and westbound lanes of the well-traversed thoroughfare. Those with fuel had obviously become desperate and tried to bypass the stalled traffic, traveling on the median, embankments, and frontage roads. The major's column ran right into a wall-to-wall used car lot of abandoned vehicles, covering not only the asphalt, but also the grassy shoulders. Desperate motorists had used any space available to advance, causing a gridlock like no other. Discarded vehicles were everywhere four wheels could take them, resulting in no clear path through. His lead elements had to snake their way around, or push the blockage out of the way. That took time – a lot of time.

More than once, he had been astounded as his column passed by makeshift homes constructed from mini-vans, pickup trucks, and sedans. Some crafty people ventured into the nearby woods and carried back bundles of branches to prop against the open doors of their vehicles creating lean-tos and expanding their "living" space. Any forested area in close proximity to the interstate was virtually stripped bare of wood. The few open areas they did encounter were dotted with piles of ashes from campfires.

Practically every semi-trailer was occupied. Many had their content strewn behind the large bay door at the rear as desperate people had searched for food or other usable items inside. Owens marveled at the ingenuity the people displayed in creating shelter. One trailer had steps built from discarded pallets leading up to the back door. A chimney had been cut into the top, and smoke drifted out.

It was the condition of the children that really bothered the major. The young ones were always the worst victims of any war or conflict, and he had grown used to seeing their suffering in combat zones. The hundreds of kids they passed that morning wore filthy rags and gazed at the passing tanks with an empty, trance-like stare. With few exceptions, their stomachs were bloated with the sign of mal-nutrition, and their movements were lethargic, like a slow motion video playback.

The adults were in no better shape physically. More than once, his men used a tank to push a vehicle out of the way, only to discover someone living in it. The occupant was often too weak to move or protest. His men had done what soldiers had always done when moving through a population of displaced, desperate people. They had shared what little rations they had, thrown candy to the children, and tried to help - but it was hopeless and too late. Major Owens quickly lost count of the unburied bodies and bands of turkey vultures they passed.

The next issue had been the intersections and ramps. Every exit with a gas station, country store, or any sign of civilization had attracted the stranded motorists. Some of these pockets of starving people had organized, while others lived in what resembled third world shantytowns. Some of these groups had turned into what his men called "zombies." The effects of malnutrition, lack of heath care, and general anarchy resulted in animalistic behavior unlike anything the soldiers had ever witnessed. Despite the fact that he and his officers constantly reminded the lead elements of the column that these "people" were their fellow Americans, it was demoralizing to see what had become of the general population.

The scout units in front of the main column had encountered everything from masses of beggars to outright hostility. Major Owens was shocked the first time one of his scout Humvees was fired upon by four men with hunting rifles. The fact that one of his men had been injured during the encounter focused everyone's attention on security. The charity of throwing chocolate bars to the children evaporated when they suffered their first casualty. The major had not been issued any orders covering the rules of engagement and was hesitant to order his men to fire upon civilians.

After careful consideration, he instructed his men they could return fire if fired upon. It was the best he could do, and he hoped the desperate people would be frightened of the tanks and leave the unit alone.

His biggest problem right now involved their supply train. Trailing behind the main force was another column of trucks and tankers used to refill his tanks and resupply his troops. One of those trucks had been trying to navigate the downhill slope of an overpass that was hopelessly blocked by a jackknifed 18-wheeler. The supply truck had overturned and rolled down the hill, spilling its contents of MREs and ammunition along the way. According to the lieutenant in charge of the section, hundreds of people literally appeared out of nowhere and began looting the spilled goodies. When the security component and he had dismounted and attempted to corral the vandals, they were fired upon by an unknown number of attackers. This had resulted in his men taking cover without causalities – but all of the supplies were gone. The major's main force not only had to slow down, but also send back reinforcements to keep any more supplies from being pilfered from the now motionless convoy. The loss of those supplies wasn't going to be an easy thing to explain to his commander.

Major Owens scratched the back of his head and continued to listen to the command-net radio. His truck drivers were now trying to right the overturned vehicle and were requesting the only tow vehicle in the entire brigade to come back and help. The first sergeant looked up at his commander, and Owens nodded his approval – *Go ahead and send it back.* Losing a few days' worth of MREs was one thing – losing a truck was another. He ordered the first sergeant to call yet another halt and reached for a protein bar.

It was over an hour before the overturned truck was salvaged, and the column sections reported in that everyone was ready to roll again. Up and down a 14-mile long stretch of I-20, radios cracked with the orders to move out.

Major Owens was actually pleased with the progress over the next 90 minutes and was beginning to relax just a little. The further the brigade moved away from Dallas, the fewer vehicles were on the roadway, impeding their progress. He was just about to say something positive to his driver when the radio sounded in his ear. It was his lead scout, and his heart sank when he heard the words, "Sir, you had better get up here – this is above my pay grade," sounded through his earpiece.

The major ordered his driver and one of the Bradleys from the command company to move out, and they hurried to the front of the convoy. As they approached, Owens noticed an information sign on the highway indicating "Tylerville – Next 5 Exits." As the commander's tank navigated a small rise in the road, he immediately understood why his scout had called him forward.

All four lanes of the interstate were purposely blocked by a well-spaced series of semi-trailers, parked on a bridge. Underneath the span was a wide pool of muddy brown water. It was as if someone had intentionally built a moat and then fortified the bridge with the haulers. The major could see the large man-made pond continued for a considerable distance both north and south of the roadway itself. In addition, an area of several hundred meters had been cleared outward from the moat, enabling the defenders a clear field of fire. Major Owens found his binoculars and studied the bridge. Sure enough, he could make out sentries positioned along the roadblock. He could also see several human skeletons at the base of the structure. Out of the corner of his eye, he saw his lead scout approaching his tank on foot. The commander waved the man onto his tank and waited while the sergeant climbed aboard. Since they were in the field, and potentially visible to a hostile force, the man stifled the impulse to salute.

"Sergeant, what do you make of this?"

The experienced soldier didn't hesitate, "Sir, I don't know if you picked up on the highway signs, but it appears as though we have arrived in Tylerville, Texas. It is also my opinion that the locals are a little more organized than anyone else we've come across and have constructed a moat and barricade to protect their town…sir."

Major Owens appreciated a good dose of sarcasm now and then and decided to add a little himself, "Excellent report, Sergeant – I admire your tremendous grasp of the obvious." After the two professional soldiers exchanged grins, the officer added, "Let's go see what this is all about – we're behind schedule, and I'm going to get an ass chewing from division as is."

After the scout jumped down from the tank, Owens waited until the man made it back to his Bradley, and then the two war machines proceeded toward the fortifications. As they approached the roadblock, Major Owens saw movement, and suddenly a golf cart popped out and headed directly for them. He ordered his driver to stop the tank and the gunner to cover the approaching electric cart. Owens could see two men inside of the cart, one of them appeared to be in uniform. His radio sounded with the observation that dozens of people were now standing on top of the trailers.

Major Owens didn't know what to expect, so he stayed in the turret and waited. The small white transport stopped about 20 meters in front of his tank and two men immediately hopped out. One of them appeared to be a police officer with grey hair and reasonably crisp uniform. Owens surmised him to most likely be the local police chief or county sheriff. The other man was even older, but wore a suit jacket and tie. He donned a fedora hat and smiled broadly, as the two of them walked a few steps closer. Owens again speculated this man was the city manager or mayor. Owens radioed he was dismounting the tank and required the master sergeant to join him – armed.

The rear door of the Bradley lowered, and six fully armed infantrymen exited the back. Owens decided the men did a good job of making it clear there was going to be zero bullshit while at the same time not threatening the two gentlemen who were waiting on him.

Owens and the master sergeant approached the two men, and the older gentleman immediately extended his hand. "General, I am Craig Farley, mayor of Tylerville, Texas." The mayor pointed to his comrade and continued, "This is our Chief of Police, Mike Thompson."

Owens was polite and tried to sound as official as possible. When he introduced himself, he emphasized his rank, but wasn't sure the politician heard him. Handshakes were exchanged, and the honorable Mr. Farley continued, "Major, we are so happy that help is finally here. We had just about given up hope. Our people are hungry, and medical supplies are non-existent. Were it not for the quick action of Chief Thompson, we would have really been in trouble. Thank God the feds have finally stepped in."

The major shifted his weight and looked the man in the eye, "Mayor, I regret to inform you that we are not a relief convoy. We are on our way to Louisiana and need to pass through your town as quickly as possible. I'm sorry, sir, but I can't lend you any assistance at this time."

Both of the men from Tylerville were shocked. The mayor started to stutter something, but the chief found his voice first, "What do you mean, Major? I can assure you and your commander that no one in Louisiana needs help more than we do. Whatever aid you planned on delivering there is just as badly needed here."

The major's response was as firm as he could make it without sounding disrespectful, "Sir, we are not on a relief mission. We have specific orders that I cannot share with you at this time, but I assure you, sir, we do not have the supplies or personnel to render any assistance."

The mayor and chief looked at each other with puzzled, questioning expressions. Owens pressed on, "Gentlemen, I must ask you to allow us passage and as soon as possible. We are already behind schedule, and I am trying to make up time. Please provide an opening for us to pass through."

The mayor's mood quickly turned ugly, "Well this is just a fine how-do-you-do. We've been waiting for weeks on the government to lend us a hand, and now what do we get? We get more work thrown at us with zero payback."

The chief quickly joined in, "Major, we can't just open a door in that roadblock and let you pass through. It's not that simple. After we moved those trailers into place, the fuel was drained from the tractors and used for the hospital's generators. We don't have anything that can open a passage for you unless you have some spare diesel and a way to pump it."

The army officer was short on time, fuel, and patience. He was barely going to make it to the border with the fuel they had onboard. If the resupply convoy didn't catch up to them soon, the Ironhorse was going to be stranded here on I-20 just like all of these other refugees. "Sir, I don't have enough fuel to complete my mission, let alone fill up some of your trucks. We will move a couple of the trailers out of the way and proceed."

The chief had seen that coming and protested, "You can't punch a hole in our wall and just leave us, son. We barely keep out all of *those* people as it is. If we hadn't blown that dam and created this lake, we would be in serious trouble. Without that blockade, we would be overrun in a day."

Major Owens took a deep breath and exhaled. He wanted to remind these two civil servants that "those people" were fellow Americans, but clearly, the situation had deteriorated to the point where no words from a stranger would have any affect. Besides, it would open a debate he didn't have time for. In the calmest voice, he could muster, he replied. "Chief, I'm sorry, but I don't see any alternative. We don't have the time to go around. How about if we close the hole after we pass through? Would that work?"

The two older men looked at each other, and the mayor finally shrugged his shoulders, "I guess so, Major. At least we won't be any worse off. Besides, what we are going to do – fight the U.S. Army?"

It was almost dark by the time the Ironhorse had crossed town and was proceeding toward the state line again. Owens radioed his status to his commanding general back in Dallas and then requested the information on the status of his refueling convoy. The response wasn't what he wanted to hear. Only half of the promised trucks were leaving Dallas – in the morning. Despite that bad news, Owens enjoyed at least some comic relief. Upon informing his commander that the resupply convoy would require a significant security detachment, the three-minute vulgarity-laden rant crackling through his earpiece was a classic example of a professional officer expressing his displeasure.

The major decided he didn't want to completely run out of fuel and turn his fast-moving armor into fixed position pillboxes, so he ordered a halt for the night. He and his men could use a little rest, so when they reached a relatively open area, they circled the wagons and set up camp.

Chapter 5

Strangers in Meraton

Terri folded the sheets into a nice tight crease and began fluffing the pillows. Her thoughts migrated from worrying about Bishop to being thankful for the soft, comfortable bed. She and Bishop had been sleeping on the camper's thin, foam covered bunks for weeks. The old trailer at the ranch provided basic shelter and a good spot to hide, but offered few amenities. *I'd gladly trade this comfy bed for having Bishop back*, she thought. Every time he was away, she felt an undeniable empty spot inside that was almost like being hungry – but not quite the same. When he was doing something dangerous, the hunger became intense. She subconsciously shook her head to clear the negative direction her mind was heading. *He'll come back to me – he always does.* The effort to push down the worry about her soul mate seemed to open another door in her mind. She sat on the end of the bed and realized she was homesick for their home in Houston. They had both worked so hard to get that house. It wasn't anything grandiose or special, just another small home among thousands of similar abodes scattered throughout the suburbs of American cities. Still, they had worked together and managed a home when most other people couldn't. Terri had been a bank teller while Bishop worked as a security specialist at HBR. America had been in the throes of a second Great Depression when the terrorists attacked. The government's reaction had caused further damage to the economy, and it had all been too much. Over a period of a few weeks, everything collapsed.

They had tried to stay put, but supplies were running low, and neighbors were beginning to turn on each other. Looters became bold, and there was no way the surrounding land could support the population. Martial law being declared was the last straw. Bishop had inherited property in west Texas years before and had created a hunting retreat that allowed them both to escape the pressures of city life now and then. When it became clear that they couldn't manage in suburbia any longer, the young couple had bugged out and headed west.

The escape from Houston and ensuing trip through an uncivilized Texas had been another extreme test of their working together. Saving money, managing the budget and the seemingly endless process of acquiring a mortgage paled in comparison to surviving that trip across Texas. They had endured because they were a team, and Terri missed her partner badly.

Her attention turned to her surroundings as she gazed around the beautiful room and wondered how many guests it had pleased over the years. She had always loved travel, and the few meager vacations she and Bishop had been able to afford left special memories that would be cherished forever. She smirked at the irony of staying at the Manor under these circumstances. Before the collapse, such an expensive luxury was beyond their modest budget. She could remember driving through Meraton on the way to their ranch and wondering what it would be like to stay at such a nice place. Now, she wanted very badly to be back at their homestead – with Bishop by her side.

The ranch had supported them for over two months. While desert living had been a struggle, they weren't starving…and had always appreciated the tranquility their hideaway afforded. Both of them needed the time to recover from the bug out trip. Everything had been going reasonably well until Bishop's old boss, the Colonel, had buzzed the ranch in a private plane. The Colonel was on a mission directly ordered by the President of the United States. The plane, low on fuel, had crashed, in the search to find Bishop's ranch. The Colonel had been badly injured, and Meraton was the closest location where Bishop and Terri could get medical help. The arrival of the Colonel had changed their lives. Too injured to complete his mission, the Colonel recruited Bishop to deliver a report to the president. The information in that report might help to avoid a civil war, and Terri had supported Bishop's taking on the responsibility.

Terri ambled toward the end of the bed that dominated the hotel room, lost in thought. She folded her nightclothes and brushed the wrinkles out of the bedspread. A loud knock at the door startled her.

Her first thought was it was David or Samantha, but they had left to spend a few days at the Beltran ranch. As Terri padded toward the handmade, thick plank door, she couldn't help but wonder if the Manor would ever become a desirable destination for traveling families again. Since the fall of society, the small, isolated town of Meraton had used its largest structure as a combination guesthouse, hospital, and defensive fort. Would people ever come here again for pure pleasure and rest?

Terri called out, "Who is it?"

Betty, the proprietor of the Manor, responded in a nervous voice. "Umm…ahhhh…Terri, there are some people here to speak with you."

Something in Betty's tone warned Terri, and she reached for her pistol lying on the bedside table. She held the weapon at her side and slowly opened the door, staying to the side of the opening.

"Good morning, Betty. I have guests? I wasn't expecting anyone."

Betty's voice was strained. "There are two men here who say they know you. They were down at Pete's, asking where you and Bishop are. They are rather insistent."

Terri fought the urge to rush out of the room, the potential of there being news regarding Bishop causing her to abandon caution. She paused and calmed herself, remembering Betty didn't get scare easily. Terri cleared her throat, "Betty, I'm not dressed just yet. Could you ask them to meet me at Pete's in 10 minutes?"

A male voice responded, "Terri, it's Nick."

Terri, still holding her pistol, exploded out of the room and ran immediately to Nick, almost knocking him over with her embrace. The big man caught his balance and spun her around in a spiral of hugging while Terri peppered his cheeks with friendly kisses. Nick finally set her down, and she immediately looked around, spotting Kevin standing shyly against a porch column. Terri, so happy to see the young man, repeated the same scene minus the jumping into Kevin's arms.

Betty cleared her throat, indicating a curiosity as to what was going on. Terri blushed and nodded an apology to her friend. "Betty, this is Nick and Kevin. Bishop and I met them on the trip out here from Houston. They saved our bacon more than once, and we all survived a crazy situation together."

Betty politely squeezed both of the visitors' hands and kindly asked if they planned on staying in town for a while. A confused look on his face, Nick wasn't quite sure how to respond. He had been surprised to learn that Terri was not at the ranch and still had no idea where Bishop was. He finally decided it was best to simply look at Terri with a puzzled expression on his face. Terri smiled and bailed him out, saying, "I'm sure these fellas would appreciate a comfy room after such a long trip."

Betty nodded and pointed to the room two doors down from Terri's. "I'll bring the key in just a bit. Nice to meet the both of you," and turned, strolling back to the front lobby.

Terri waved for Nick and Kevin to follow her and lead them into the pool area. Both men still carried their rifles on their shoulders, until Terri reassured them they could relax and take it easy here at the Manor. Neither wasted much time unslinging their weapons.

Both of them looked at the crystal clear pool, and Kevin gave his father a look that asked, "*Can I jump in?*"

Nick started to shake his head in disapproval when Terri interrupted, "If he wants to go for a swim, it's okay. As a matter of fact, you both might enjoy a quick dip. If you don't have any trunks, I have a pair of Bishop's shorts in my room."

A quick father-son discussion ensued, resulting in Kevin's scurrying out to the truck to get their bags. Terri noted he stopped on the way and picked up his rifle without even thinking about it. *What a world we live in when a 16-year old boy treats his rifle like kids used to treat their cell phones.* Kevin quickly returned with their belongings, and both men used Terri's room to change. In a few minutes, two huge splashes interrupted the tranquil surroundings of the Manor's gardens. If Terri hadn't known better, she would have sworn there were two kids playing in the water.

After a few laps, one semi-serious splash fight, and a minor wrestling match, Nick glided over to the edge and braced his arms on the side of the pool. Terri, sitting in one of the cushy recliners surrounding the pool deck, smiled and questioned, "Feel better?"

Nick rubbed the water from his eyes and responded, "I can't believe I'm swimming in a beautiful pool. This is one thing I thought would never happen again. I think we've finally made it to paradise!"

Terri laughed and bragged, "We have a nice barter market and a fully stocked bar as well. We tried to get you to come with us, but noooooooo. You wanted to stay and help rebuild society. Nobody can say you weren't invited."

Kevin splashed over and joined the conversation, "Miss Terri, you never said anything about a pool. I can't believe how good this feels. If you had told me about the pool, I would've talked dad into coming sooner."

Nick playfully splashed water in his son's face, causing the young man to duck underwater and push off the side. Terri took the opportunity to speak to his father, "So Master Sergeant, what brings you out west, if I may be so nosey? Last I heard, you were going to stay and help all of those poor refugees at the I-10 exit. What happened?"

Nick sighed and looked down. His expression betrayed an intense exasperation tinged with sadness. "We did rebuild as best we could. We even managed to establish trade with a nearby town. After a few months, the people organized their own leaders and even had an election of sorts." The big man's eyes drifted off, and he gently shook his head. "You know me, Terri – I'm a soldier, not a politician. They wanted me to be a policeman, and I just couldn't do that. They were concerned about folks pulling the tags off their mattresses while I was still worried about raiders, looters, and rogue gangs. When there weren't any serious raids or problems the last month or so, I guess I kind of wore out my welcome."

Terri had trouble visualizing what Nick was describing to her. Bishop and she had tried to cross interstate 10 at a remote exit on their trip west. The exit had been taken over by a biker gang on one side and a drug gang on the other. Thousands of cars were stranded on the road, leaving the occupants without basic necessities of gas, water, food, or shelter. The two ruling gangs had systematically taken anything they wanted from the marooned motorists. Bishop and Nick initiated a war between the two sides, resulting in one gang being wiped out and the other taking off before the starving people overwhelmed them. Nick and his son had decided to stay and help those people rebuild.

Terri shook her finger at Nick and playfully scolded him. "You and Bishop seem to have a way about you. Both of you seem to have this bad habit of pissing people off. Bishop is lucky I happen to like the alpha male type – not everyone does."

Nick laughed hard at Terri's remark. "So, speaking of Mister Bishop, where would that old dog have wandered off to? You didn't finally get enough of that cornball humor and do him in, did ya?"

Terri giggled and shook her head. "No, I did not 'do him in,' although his jokes sometimes make me want to smack him a bit." It took Terri about 10 minutes to explain that Bishop was on a mission for his old boss, who had literally just dropped in from the sky. When Terri got to the part about the Independents and the President of the United States, Nick's eyes grew wide with disbelief.

"Terri, you let him go do that by himself? Oh my God, girl! Does he really think he can make it all the way to Fort Bliss *and* convince the president to negotiate with this new group? Wow! I thought I lead an exciting life."

Terri went on to explain that the Colonel, Bishop's old boss and friend of the president, believed there would be civil war between military units loyal to the president and those having sided with the Independents. The Colonel was worried any conflict would go nuclear and perhaps destroy what was left of the country.

Nick took a bit to digest all of this information. He finally looked up and nodded, "I understand now. After thinking about it, I don't blame this Colonel guy. I've never met a better man for the job than Bishop. Still, you have to be worried sick about him. Has there been any word?"

Terri explained what little she knew after the Colonel's grandson had returned with the medical equipment. It wasn't much information, but the last time anyone saw Bishop, he was headed off into the desert north of Alpha. Terri tried to cheer herself up, "You know Bishop - he's like a cat with all those lives. He knows the desert, and I'm sure he'll be just fine."

Deacon Brown realized the survivors of the morning's skirmish were more important at the moment than her grieving over the loss of her son. Promising herself she would take the time to properly mourn his death later, she set about earning her reputation as a strong leader. She moved around the perimeter of the church, calmly issuing commands, reassuring the frightened, and generally taking control of the chaos that followed in the aftermath of the attack. The hardest part was consoling the heartsick family members who had just lost loved ones. Diana knew all of them well, and she counted most as friends. None of these people had signed up to fight a war or do battle. Many were near or at retirement and until recently had planned to finish out their days in the quiet, peaceful life a small western community affords.

Even though the congregation had held its ground, they had taken quite a few casualties. It would take days just to dig enough graves to bury everyone they had lost. Out of the 50 able-bodied men defending the compound, there were now 21 dead or badly wounded. The fight had expended over half of their remaining ammunition, and by the end of the day, their limited medical supplies would be exhausted.

Even though Diana worked tirelessly, trying to recover and regroup, the grim reality of the situation could not be ignored. It became more and more obvious the church followers wouldn't be able to hold out if attacked again. After making sure she had done everything possible in the parking lot, both to console and secure, she retired to her office and sat at her desk pondering the future. The sheer number of sick and wounded made evacuation practically impossible. Even if they did have the gasoline and transportation available to vacate the compound, the group had no place to go. No town or organized group of people would welcome 120 hungry, sick, and injured lodgers.

While she had risen to the immediate challenge of the situation, the physical and emotional stress of the day clouded her mind, making long-term planning difficult, if not impossible.

She had no doubt the "skinnies" would kill most of the congregation if she gave up. The women and children would suffer the most. She briefly entertained thoughts of surrender, but she might as well imitate Moses and lead her flock out into the desert. Thank heavens; *she* had not received instructions from God to lead her people into the wilderness.

A knock on her office door interrupted her train of thought. A young man reported that one of the wounded attackers was talking. It seemed that Bishop had successfully made off with some precious medical equipment, and that had caused the leader of the skinnies to lose his temper and attack. The prisoner indicated the skinnies had marshaled over 100 men and commanded a large cache of ammunition and food stored at the county courthouse.

The mention of Bishop's name caused Deacon Brown to recall a conversation she had had with him before he exited the compound. "Reach out to the people of Meraton," he advised her. Deacon Brown strode to the main assembly area and located one of her key people. "Do we have a vehicle that could make it to Meraton and back? I think I can go there and get help. Is there anything left that can make it?"

The confidant thought about his leader's request for a moment and responded, "Yes ma'am, my truck is in the maintenance shed, and it has enough gas in it to get to Meraton and back. It's nothing fancy ma'am, but it'll get you there."

Deacon Brown thanked the man and headed to her office to pack a bag. While she was gathering her essentials, she informed her lieutenants of her plans. A couple of them were skeptical of her return, but she reassured them that she would indeed come back, hopefully with help of some kind. She planned on leaving for Meraton at first light.

~ ~

Smokey paced back and forth in the chief's office waiting on Hawk's report. When his second in command finally arrived, the look on Hawk's face told the boss what he already knew. Hawk reported the bad news, "We lost 39 men and have another 14 wounded."

Smokey tried to minimize their losses. "We hurt them, too. I know we killed a bunch of them."

Hawk nodded and continued, "Look at the bright side – we have fewer mouths to feed. It will take us a bit to regroup though. Do you want to hit them again tonight?"

Smokey had anticipated that question and surprised his man. "No, let's take a day or so and make sure we put an end to this thing, once and for all. We should've taken more time to teach everyone the plan today. We were too slow, and it cost us. We can't afford to fuck up like that again."

"You got it, boss. It ain't like they're going anywhere."

Bishop's watch alarm beeped in his ear, and he groggily located and pressed the tiny button. He rubbed the sleep from his eyes and gingerly stretched his body. He was stiff and very sore, but the few hours of shuteye had helped. The few mouthfuls of water he had pulled from the sand were all but forgotten; his mouth feeling gritty and parched once again.

After checking the perimeter of his bivouac, he quickly dressed and slung his rifle. He was full of anticipation as he approached the solar still and his bush traps. He decided the still would probably produce the most water, so he checked the bushes first.

Bishop bent down by the first bagged plant and felt the tip of the plastic bag. There was water in there! It wasn't much, perhaps a finger's worth in his cup, but still he would get a drink. The second bush was a bit of a disappointment, as it had produced less of the valuable fluid.

He took a knee beside the still and gently removed the plastic cover. Inside, his cup was about half-full of water. Bishop fought the urge to immediately snatch the cup to his parched lips and down the liquid. He carefully picked up the vessel with both hands and slowly took one sip and then another. The water tasted pure and cool, a more palatable experience than his last drink. He sat the cup back down in the sand and looked at the plastic bag that had been the lid of his still. A few beads of water remained, and he bent over and licked up each and every one.

The next task was to retrieve the water from the bush traps, and that took a bit of work so as not to spill a single, precious drop. After he added their small amounts of liquid into his cup, it was almost three quarters full. It wasn't enough to survive long-term, but hopefully, it would suffice until he could find more.

Bishop sat right where he was and gradually sipped water for almost 15 minutes, savoring every wet droplet. He listened to the few late afternoon desert birds talking to each other in the distance and was fascinated by two small lizards performing some sort of ritual around a pile of nearby rocks. The shadows were beginning to grow longer as the late afternoon sun clung to the western mountains. Bishop wanted to get into his gear and get moving while there was still a little light. It was always easier to break camp without using the night vision or fumbling around in complete darkness.

He folded up the plastic bags and walked back to his shelter. He found the deer jerky and ate a large slice, washing it down with the last few gulps of water. That little bit of food and hydration seemed to recharge his body and mind. He finished packing, double-checked to make sure he wasn't leaving anything behind, and continued his westward journey just as the sun slipped below the horizon.

Terri, Nick, and Kevin spent the rest of the afternoon catching up on the events of the last few months. When their hunger got the best of them, they enjoyed a late supper of homemade burritos at Pete's, and Nick threw back the first "hard" liquor he'd tasted in a long time. Dusk quickly faded into night, as Pete and Nick exchanged stories while Terri and Kevin laughed and inserted a few of their own.

After locking up the Manor's office, Betty stopped by the bar to see how things were going, and decided to hang around and enjoy some tall tales herself. Terri had shared the news of her pregnancy earlier in the afternoon, and Nick had squeezed her tightly at the announcement. However, the revelation prompted a continued barrage of jokes and innuendo, all focusing on the idea of a little Bishop, loose at the ranch. Even Terri had to admit, just the mental image of such a thing made her smile.

"Well, you can't just refer to the bambino as 'Little Bishop' forever," Betty protested. You know, there is even the possibility that you might give birth to a little girl. Terri's mind's eye instantly photoshopped an image of a Shirley Temple singing "The Good Ship Lollipop," except the chubby cherub was wearing Bishop's face, surrounded by ringlets. Terri almost choked on the remaining bite of her burrito.

After regaining her composure, Terri became thoughtful for a moment before responding to Betty's statement. "Well, you know with all that has been going on, we haven't even discussed it yet. I didn't want to know the sex of the child when Doc did the ultrasound, so I guess we need to pick two names. And I suppose there is no time like the present to try out baby names for fit." The conversation quickly focused on what the new addition to the ranch should be called. Everyone exuberantly blurted out ideas, and Terri couldn't keep track of all the suggestions. When she protested, Pete volunteered paper and pencil so the mother-to-be could record all of their suggestions to share with Bishop later.

Pete favored names that had stood the test of time like "James" and "Will." Nick and Kevin suggested "Ranger, Hunter and Colton," for a boy, along with "Terra, Riley, or Taylor," for a girl.

Betty shook her head in disapproval at the testosterone-influenced tags. "Oh my," she declared, "why can't it be something more in keeping with the times? Many people honor a relative by naming their little one after a favorite aunt, uncle, cousin, or grandparent. It might be a nice way to carry on a family name. How about it, Terri? Do you know any of Bishop's relatives' names? What about his parents?"

Terri thought again, "No, not really. He doesn't say much about any family. I guess I'm the same way... especially since Mom passed...." Terri paused, and got a pained expression, betraying her hurt. The memories of watching television that day came rushing back. Everyone immediately realized something was wrong, and silence fell over the otherwise giddy troop. "I'm sorry," she faltered, "let's talk about something else."

Nick decided to plug his earlier observation, while steering the conversation in a slightly new direction. "One thing is for certain. If it's a boy, we don't want him named Bishop. There's only room in Texas for one of those! I propose a toast to absent friends and fast reunions." Nick lifted his glass, as did everyone at the table. "To Bishop," was heard from a chorus of voices, as the glasses of water, bathtub gin, tea and homemade beer clinked together. Nick's toast had done the trick, and the rest of the evening was filled with laughter and good cheer.

Traveling by the light of the moon, the group meandered back to the Manor. Terri's mood became melancholy as she missed her mate. She would give anything if Bishop could have been here to enjoy the laughter shared among good friends. After saying her goodnights, Terri stood in the garden and looked up at the stars. She whispered, "I love you, Bishop – please come home to me soon." A tear wandered down her cheek and was quickly wiped away. Terri took solace in her comfortable bed and was asleep within the hour.

The desert around Bishop was relatively flat, with patches of cactus and scrub, widely spaced. There was a good moon and cloudless sky, so walking at night didn't present much of a problem. More out of habit than necessity, he brought his rifle up and peered through the night vision every so often just to check the terrain ahead.

After he had traveled a few hours, he paused to take a break and scan the horizon. As the green and black world generated by the night vision swept past, a familiar shape caught his attention, and he zeroed in on it immediately. It was a windmill. Thousands of these devices had been used on farms and ranches for over 150 years. One of the first uses of renewable energy, the wind would spin the blades and power a water pump. The pump would fill a trough used by livestock on remote stretches of land. A windmill meant water.

Many ranches also installed these units in the general area of the main house as well, and Bishop approached with caution. Being shot as a burglar or looter wasn't in his plan. In the last 20 years, many of these wind-driven pumps had been replaced with electric models, powered by solar panels. It wasn't a matter of efficiency or capability, but one of cost. The windmill's heavy tower, metal blades, and steel shaft were expensive to purchase when compared to a cheap electrical pump, powered by the sun. It wasn't unusual to see the old mill looming over the newer technology, like a schoolteacher watching her student at the blackboard.

Regardless of what was pumping, the mill's tower was like a beacon to a man needing water. The one Bishop spotted was a remote unit with no buildings or homes in sight. Still, he circled the area quietly, just in case he hadn't been the only one to notice this potential source of life. The ground indicated there were cattle in the area as the earth was chopped up with thousands of hoof prints. The piles of older dung and patches of hair on a nearby fence confirmed his assumption.

Bishop scanned the vicinity carefully with his night vision and judged he was alone at the watering hole. He actually smelled the water before he laid eyes on it. There, shimmering in the moonlight was the most wonderful sight Bishop thought he had ever seen. The large galvanized tub was brim full of wet, cool, life-sustaining water. He wasted no time in removing his pack and retrieving his filter. Even though he was sure the water was fine, now wasn't the time to risk diarrhea or worse.

It took him a few minutes to strip off his load vest and water bladder. He submerged one end of the water purifier's hose into the tub and positioned the outlet into his cup. After about 20 pumps, the cup was full, and he guzzled it all in a few seconds. He then proceeded to fill his camelback to the brim. Bishop paused, having a crazy thought. On a whim, he pulled his flashlight off the vest and turned it to the red filter. He shined the light into the watering tub and saw it was completely clear with the exception of a few dead bugs on the surface. He thought for a moment and figured, *Why the hell not*? Another two minutes later and Bishop was equipment-free. Still wearing his clothes, he stepped over the edge of the trough and slowly submerged himself in the cool water. While not quite up to par with the pool at the Manor, the feeling was still incredible. He hand-scrubbed every part of his clothing and skin within reach, including a vigorous scalp massage.

After the bath, he leaned back against the side of the tub and relaxed. As he gazed skyward, he couldn't help but admire the view. The effects of light pollution had always made the stars less visible in Houston than out here in the west. Bishop wondered if the decline of man and the demise of electric lights had changed that. The night sky was so thick with distant suns there were sections that seemed more white than black.

Feeling just a tad guilty about his mini-spa treatment, Bishop exited the water and picked up his rifle to scan the area. Nothing had changed. He smirked and began wringing out his socks and shirt. Before long, he was ready to head off into the night, renewed in spirit. Bishop paused and looked back at the windmill, noticing how the moonlight silhouetted it against the evening sky. It was an image he would remember the rest of his life.

Chapter 6

The Warlords of Wal-Mart

The moon continued to set as Bishop made his way northwest. The terrain was starting to flatten out with only the occasional ridge or line of small hills hindering his progress. The landscape was well illuminated by what remained of the lunar glow and a bright star field. Still, Bishop was a creature of routine, and he used the night vision more often than necessary to scout. This tactic involved a full three hundred and sixty degree scan as he didn't want anyone to angle into his path or catch him unaware from behind. While the chances of blundering into any human being were low, there were some big predators nearby. The cats in this part of the world were not overly large, rarely topping 200 pounds. That was little consolation, as Bishop knew they were 10 times as strong as a man, pound for pound. As a teenager, hunting in the mountains, he had watched in awe as a large lioness climbed a steep cliff with a whitetail deer in her mouth. The deer must have weighed almost as much as the cat, and her seemingly effortless scaling was an impressive demonstration of power and grace. Running into one of the big felines could ruin your day.

The apparently lifeless desert was actually inhabited by many dangerous animals. He remembered getting lucky when encountering a rather large dog some months before – an episode he didn't want to repeat. A pack of ravenous canines would be a serious issue if they surprised him.

Bishop crested a low rise and kept close to a tall cactus to avoid silhouetting himself. He took a knee and cradled the stock of the rifle against his shoulder to see what the valley below had to offer. His scan revealed something he hadn't seen in the last few days – the perfectly straight line of a major roadway. Bishop was surprised by the sight, but quickly realized he shouldn't be. He had made good time and had traveled in relatively straight lines. After verifying there was nothing else of interest nearby, he detached the night vision from his rifle and pulled out a map from the zipper compartment of his load vest.

Bishop spread out the map on a sizeable, smooth stone and flipped on the night vision's infrared illuminator. After focusing the eyepiece, he could read the map almost as well as he could in broad daylight.

The roadway in front of him must be I-10, and the thought of crossing that highway made him shiver. Terri and he had encountered the worst of mankind trying to cross this interstate on their bug out from Houston. The mere thought of doing so again made his stomach tighten up and the back of his knees become cold and clammy.

Using the compass built into his watch, he picked the tallest peak in the distance and eventually triangulated a close estimate of where he was. According to the map, he was just less than 80 miles east of El Paso, and there wasn't a significant town anywhere nearby. That, at least, was positive news.

A rumbling in his stomach indicated it was time to take a break and put on the feedbag. The desert night had cooled significantly, and he wanted to be as fresh and alert as possible before crossing the interstate below. After folding and storing the map, he reattached and focused the night vision on his rifle and scouted the area again. This time he was not only looking for trouble, but a place to hole up and take a short break. Slightly behind him, he spied a dense clump of vegetation close to an exposed formation of sandstone. The rock looked like it had pierced the desert floor from below, standing about 10 feet high, and pointing toward the southwest. It wasn't perfect, but would have to do.

After finding a flat, barren patch of sand that was reasonably well hidden, Bishop stood silent, listening to the sounds of the desert in conjunction with the regularity of his own breathing. He sighed with relief as he removed his pack and was tempted to do the same with his rifle. Caution overcame that brief moment of temptation, but he did sling the weapon around to his back. At least the weight would be on a different part of his shoulder for a bit. It took a few minutes to gather a nice pile of the sandstone and create a small, circular, knee-high wall. Bishop wanted to cook something, but didn't want the flame visible, especially given his elevation as compared to the surrounding countryside. The rock pit would hide the flame.

Inside of his pack was a German infantry stove. The small metallic device was about the size of a deck of cards and when unfolded, made a handy little cooktop. Normally, these units were operated with chemical pellets that burned for several minutes when ignited. Bishop wanted to conserve his fuel and decided to build a small fire from the dead kindling of a nearby scrub oak. The longer the fire was burning, the greater the odds someone would smell or see it, so after collecting his small bundle of firewood, he set about making sure everything he wanted to heat was ready before igniting the flame.

While he was preparing his food, Bishop thought about the small, metal stove. Hundreds of thousands of them had been distributed to the German Army throughout the years. He imagined a small group of infantry, fighting on the icy Russian steeps, huddled around while fixing a quick meal. Bishop despised the German leadership of the World War II era, confident that hell was a little more crowded with the souls of those evil men. He also recognized that the average German soldier was just another guy, handed a rifle and ordered to go fight. Bishop grunted when he thought about the German army from that period in history. The military man in him had to respect what they had accomplished. Despite the horrific actions of their leaders, their soldiers had been some of the most tenacious and resilient in history. Bishop knew his situation was nothing compared to what those men had endured during the retreat across Russia in late 1944 and 1945 - temperatures so cold their rifles became frozen and couldn't be coaxed to fire. Bishop remembered seeing pictures of German soldiers stuffing their uniforms with newspaper to provide some insulation from the arctic air. It had gotten so bad, heavy motor oil was freezing in the engine blocks, disabling machines. Bishop shuddered, thinking about the suffering on both sides of that conflict. His situation was actually not so bad when compared to what those men had endured. He reached down and pensively examined the diminutive stove, wondering how many times one of its kind had provided just a little comfort to some poor soul thousands of miles away from home and missing his family. When you peeled away all the political layers, it didn't matter what language the soldier spoke or what flag he saluted. The Roman Legionnaire was no different from the British Grenadier or the Sioux Warrior. The sacrifice, misery, and anguish were always the same. Why did they do it? They had a purpose…a plan…a goal…a cause. There was some end game in their future - some exit strategy that allowed those men to carry on. Bishop inhaled deeply and deliberately, forcing himself to refocus on the here and now. "*This is an important part of the message to the president*," he thought. "*I have to drive this point home. The people need that exit strategy. They need to believe there is a way out.*"

He unfastened a side compartment and extracted several small zip-top plastic bags. In one were a few handfuls of green spiked needles, collected from a pinion pine. These, when boiled in water, would make a harsh tasting tea that was rich in vitamin C. Since sugar wasn't available, Terri had discovered that a small bit of ground up wild onion would make the concoction palatable. The desert onions tasted like sweet lemons. The pinion had also provided pine nuts, which he had roasted and stored in salt some time ago. These seeds were slightly smaller than a peanut, with the same consistency. The salt made them taste almost like pretzels. His largest bag was full of deer jerky, and he picked a good-sized piece to enjoy with his meal.

A few hours earlier, Bishop had hiked past a patch of amaranth and took the time to extract some. The leaves tasted a little like spinach and could be eaten raw. While some oil and vinegar would have made them tastier, the solo greens would have to do tonight.

After everything was set out, he gathered a small bundle of twigs and dried bark, about the size of his fist. He set the fuel into the rock pit and used one of his disposable lighters to start a small fire. After the sticks were burning, he positioned the steel camping mug onto the unfolded cooktop and began to heat a cup of water, containing a mixture of pine needles with a pinch of wild onion. Bishop scanned the area around his temporary camp again, thinking about how just one pack of sugar would really help his tea. No matter, he needed the break and the nutrients. It didn't take long for the water to begin bubbling, so a quick adjustment to the camp stove allowed a simmer. Boiling the tea would remove a lot of the vitamins.

It took 20 minutes for him to prepare his meal and far less time to feel the surge of energy flowing through his body. The synergistic combination of fire, food, and drink helped his outlook as well, and by the time Bishop had covered the small pile of smoldering ashes with neighboring sand, he was ready to approach the dreaded roadway below.

Stalking to within one hundred meters, he found a small undulation that provided good cover and an excellent view of the interstate. He went prone and began to study what lie ahead. A first, he thought something was wrong with his night vision. From this angle, both east and westbound lanes were visible for a mile in each direction. He had expected the roadway to be packed with abandoned cars, trucks and buses, similar to the scene he had witnessed a hundred miles outside of Houston, but there were absolutely no vehicles whatsoever.

The more he thought about it, the more it all made sense. The population density in this part of Texas wasn't even close to the Houston, Austin, San Antonio area. People out here regularly kept their vehicles topped off, even during normal times, because of the distances between filling stations. When everything had gone to hell, the existing gas stations had probably not been overwhelmed as quickly as in the larger cities. It wasn't uncommon for ranches and other businesses to have their own fuel tanks as well. Bishop remembered the large silver tank on the other side of the main house where the hands filled their pickup trucks before heading out to remote parts of the property.

It was with great relief that he casually ascended the embankment and stood on the eastbound lane of the interstate, looking both ways. Nothing but empty pavement could be seen in either direction. Walking on the smooth surface would allow for a faster pace, and Bishop spun around, heading west.

The first sign of civilization Bishop encountered wasn't a car or truck, but a motorcycle. A country lane crossed I-10 via an overpass and there, sitting in the night shadow of the bridge, was a late year touring bike propped on its kickstand. The gas cap had been unscrewed and was hanging on the side of the tank via its tether. Bishop thought it was ironic that the mode of transportation likely to get the best mileage was the first one he encountered. It wouldn't be the last.

He had been walking along the interstate for about 12 miles and could easily determine his exact location by coordinating the mile markers and his map. The motorcycle was soon followed by a family sedan, parked on the shoulder of the roadway. Bishop approached cautiously, but there was no one around. The four-door family car had Arizona plates and a shattered driver's side window. A large stone, no doubt picked up from the nearby desert floor, had been used to break into the vehicle. Bishop paused to take a pull of water and wondered about the occupants of the car. He couldn't help his thoughts as they drifted toward melancholy scenarios. Had these people been on vacation? Traveling to see a new grandson? A college student on their way home?

He walked around the back of the car and noticed the truck lid was unhinged and pulled it open. Inside there was a box containing a quart of motor oil, a tire repair kit, and an air pressure gauge. He smirked at his sexist attitude after his mind declared the car owner to be a male. He continued around to the passenger side and opened the door. The glove compartment had been searched, but Bishop found the insurance papers on the floorboard. The car was owned by a Mr. Harland W. Jones of Phoenix, Arizona. The discovery caused him to smile at his detective skills. He returned the paper to its original location and gently shut the door.

So, Mr. Jones, you probably stopped outside El Paso to get gas, but there wasn't any or perhaps the line was too long. You decided you had enough in the tank to make it to the next exit and continued on your way. Maybe that decision was repeated once too often, and you ran dry.

Bishop tried to envision the dilemma experienced by a stranded Mr. Jones. He looked both directions and decided the man would have chosen to start walking east. *Maybe some nice person stopped and gave him a ride. Perhaps his bones litter the highway a few miles from here. There is no way to know, so stop thinking about it, and concentrate on getting to Fort Bliss and delivering these letters.*

As he progressed westward, the number of abandoned cars and trucks gradually increased. Again, this made sense to him because he was getting closer to El Paso and its large population. After clearing a small rise, Bishop paused and studied the roadway ahead. The topography was becoming hilly, and his visibility was limited to the next valley. Below him, there were dozens of vehicles in both lanes, and he could tell that at least one of them had burned. He estimated he was now about 65 miles east of El Paso and would soon be approaching a series of small towns along the interstate. It was time to leave the comfortable path provided by the manmade road and branch off to the north.

Bishop moved about a quarter mile off the interstate and found what appeared to be a relatively flat route. The map indicated that I-10 also followed this general direction, and if he encountered terrain he couldn't climb safely at night, he could always backtrack and take his chances on the freeway pavement.

Thirty minutes after leaving the roadway, Bishop looked through the night vision and studied the increasingly problematic topography. The jagged rocks and thick parcels of spiny bushes somehow looked less menacing in the green and black world of the monocle. It was an illusion of tranquility. Turning an ankle here would be easy. The thorn and cactus were nature's own barbed wire and could shred skin and clothing like razor blades. This was a harsh environment, and everything that lived here defended itself well. There were clear pathways that would have been easily maneuverable in the daylight, but the moon had set an hour ago, and the darkness was showing off. Traveling at night might help avoid some problems, but progress through this area was sluggish. He plotted out 20 steps, lowered the rifle and began walking, keeping a small map of surrounding rocks in his head. He was about halfway through the segment when he heard the noise of an internal combustion engine. Immediately he squatted down and scanned his surroundings, but didn't see anything unusual. Where there was an engine, there were people. The sound was barely audible and quickly drifted away on cool, desert air.

As he continued on his route, the noise faded in and out several times, gradually becoming more consistent. After about a quarter mile, he realized the sound's source was directly in front of him. His progress around another small rise revealed a glowing sky just beyond the next line of hills. There were electric lights ahead, and judging from the illumination of the sky, there were a lot of them. Someone was running generators to power those lights.

Bishop nimbly crossed the small ribbon of valley floor in front of him, before carefully working his way up a hill toward the light. He had no idea what lay on the other side, so he took his time, stalking from boulder to outcropping to cactus bed. When he neared the top, his progress became a slow crawl, as he didn't want to silhouette himself cresting the hill. Keeping his back bent low, he began to step forward when he felt a tug on his ankle, quickly followed by a brilliant crimson light engulfing the area. Diving prone, adrenalin flooded his system, and his head snapped back and forth trying to figure out what just happened. It took a few seconds to realize he had just engaged a tripwire that was connected to some sort of flare. The entire area was illuminated by a pulsing redness, and he could hear the spitting fizzle of phosphorous burning close by. Someone had set up an early warning device on this ridgeline, and that same someone was probably wondering who or what had just set it off.

Bishop remained motionless and unsure of what to do for a few minutes. His mind was moving a thousand miles an hour, trying to figure out his next move. Whoever was in charge of the electric lights just over the ridge in front of him wanted to know if someone were approaching that position. The device looked to be a common roadside flare like the police used to warn traffic around an accident. Rigging such a flare to a tripwire would have required some skill. The position of the wire further indicated someone who knew what they were doing. *Was there a sniper scanning the area for trespassers? Was a bullet going to slam into his body any second now? Was a team on the way to search the area, or was everyone's attention simply drawn to the flare?*

The sound of voices floating over the hill answered his questions – a team was on the way. The random beams of flashlights cresting the hill soon validated that fact. Bishop slowly backed away from the crest and retreated back down his original path. He made it to the bottom of the hill and turned to his right, scanning through the night vision looking for some place to hide. The light from the flickering flare wasn't as pronounced this far down the hill, and he needed the night vision to find a narrow gap between two formations of rock. Bishop squeezed his body between the rough stone surfaces, drew his pistol, and waited. If they found him here, there wasn't room to use the rifle.

He had managed three or four deep breaths before the voices became clear. There were at least three men checking on the tripped booby trap – maybe more. Bishop was perplexed by the casual approach to the area as the men were using flashlights and talking at normal volumes. Those actions didn't match the professionalism and field craft used to set the wire.

The words, "It was probably just another fucking deer," followed by, "Who knew we had the clumsiest rabbits in west Texas around here?" solved the puzzle. Bishop exhaled and relaxed. The men had evidently investigated so many false alarms they no longer took the flares seriously. His reprieve was short lived however as one of the voices announced in a serious tone, "Hey! Is that a boot print over here?"

Footprints? Oh shit, did I leave footprints? Bishop held his breath and waited to hear the answer from above, but everything had gotten very quiet. That wasn't good news at all. The reaction team had gone silent, which meant they thought someone was within earshot. *Not good – not good at all.*

The sound of crunching soil nearby told Bishop the area was now being searched and without flashlights. Bishop's thumb was on the pistol's safety, his figure holding off the trigger. Without thinking, he tried to squeeze a little further back into the rocks.

After 10 minutes, a whispered voice broke the silence. The men were surprisingly close by. "I ain't no fucking Indian tracker, but that sure as shit looked like an indentation from a boot up there. What do you think?"

The response almost made Bishop laugh out loud. In a very good impression of John Wayne, someone responded, "Well, pilgrim, I reckon we needed to check it out. Ya never know when them redskins might be get'n ready ta bushwhack us."

A third, more authoritative voice found no humor in the situation at all. "Would you two ass-clowns shut your pusses and finish the damn sweep?"

"There ain't nothing out here, Sarge. I haven't seen any other sign – it was probably another deer. Besides, I just cut the hell out of myself on one of those damn thorn bushes. Let's reset the wire and head back. My shift is about up, and I'm beat."

Evidently, the men turned around because the voices became muffled, and Bishop couldn't make out any more of the conversation. He remained hidden in the crevice for what seemed like hours, finally exiting his hiding spot when his leg started cramping. Bishop slowly moved across the valley floor until he found a good place to hole up for the day. An ancient stream had eroded a glass smooth indentation a few feet into the side of a shallow canyon. The overhang would keep the sun off of him and provide good cover. He pulled some dead bundles of scrub and blocked the view of anyone casually patrolling the area. It was a huge relief to get out of his gear and boots. He sat up the solar battery charger and switched to fresh night vision cells. After a quick field cleaning of his rifle and pistol, Bishop scarfed down a cold meal, took a long drink, and made a pillow out of his pack. He took his survival net and folded it into the shape of a bed. It wasn't very thick, but it provided some cushion. The cool sensation of the rocks underneath him was a welcome relief after hours of sweating in a cocoon of body armor and chest rig.

He entered REM before the sun broke over the mountains to the east.

Chapter 7

Shades of Brown

Pete woke before first light, as usual. The modest apartment, located in the back of the bar, had been one of the building's biggest selling points when he first arrived in Meraton a few years back. Recently divorced, he didn't want or need a lot of living space to keep clean and relished the thought of a simpler life. The only belongings he had brought with him from back east had fit in the back seat and trunk of his Nissan Altima.

Pete shifted his legs over the edge of the single bed and stretched his arms high over his head. As was his habit, he congratulated himself on making it through another day. He rubbed the sleep from his eyes, while his mind was already running through a mental checklist of the day's priorities. There was a fresh batch of rye aging in the still, and soon he'd need to barter with old man Johnson for another load of firewood. While the bar's glasses had been washed and neatly stacked after closing last night, his personal dishes still needed attention. He wondered if Betty had finished his laundry and smiled at how she didn't want anyone knowing she enjoyed a little nip now and then. *Being a bartender is a lot like being a priest,* he thought, *sometimes people confide their deepest secrets, and you can't violate the trust.* Betty did Pete's laundry every week in exchange for a covert canteen of his bathtub gin.

His eyes still closed, Pete reached his hand over the nightstand, locating the partially used book of matches resting there. A luxury for most folks now, he purchased two cartons of them in celebration of the grand opening of his new establishment. Each brightly colored box displayed the words "Pete's Place," inscribed in a fancy script generally associated with old West saloons and matched his street front signage. He still had several boxes left, and they were no longer used as giveaways to loyal customers. The little packages of cardboard, phosphorus and gelatin were simply too valuable now. He carefully scratched one stick across the emery board on the back of the cover and ignited the small flame. A few moments later, a votive candle resting on a saucer illuminated the dark bedroom.

After pulling on a pair of well-worn jeans, Pete padded barefoot into the tiny bathroom, carrying the candle with his hand cupped in front of the flame. He brushed his teeth using a bucket of water brought in fresh the night before. A couple of handfuls of the cool liquid quickly smoothed what remained of his hair. Pete headed to the kitchen and readied his wood-burning stove for making breakfast. There were two five-gallon buckets nearby, one containing dry kindling and the other cured splits of pine. The stove had originally been a metal box constructed to store mail while it was being transported across the country. Evidently, Pete's Place had once housed the Meraton Post Office, because he had found three of the old containers when he bought the building. Roberto, down at the gas station, cut and welded the heavy, steel box, converting it to a perfect kitchen sized heat source. That little job had cost him six beers, and he never regretted the investment.

Pete grabbed a bit of kindling and tore off a small scrap of paper, which he ignited in the candle's flame. In a few minutes, a small smoldering fire provided a warm glow in the kitchen. Pete opened the makeshift chimney and watched as the smoke was drawn outside. He felt a sense of pride at having accomplished his morning routine while using only one match. He thought it probably would be a while before any salesman visited Meraton and tried to sell him more.

Coffee was the next order of the day. While that first cup of hot brew was one thing he looked forward to the most, lately it had been a little depressing as well. His supply of coffee was running low. His storeroom normally held about twenty pounds back-stocked for the bar and fortunately just received a shipment on his last regular order. There hadn't been any more deliveries, and he was down to the last, precious canister. That was a problem he would have to solve later, after his brain was functioning at full speed.

He grabbed a small iron skillet in one hand while he dipped a finger into a cup of bacon grease sitting on the back of the stove. A year ago, he wouldn't have gone anywhere near the cholesterol-laden stuff. Now, cooking seemed to depend on lard, and he happily smeared the surface of the pan with the slippery substance. A brown chicken egg quickly followed the grease into the pan, and was soon popping and sizzling above the open flame. Pete rubbed his eyes again, adjusting the coffee water and frying pan so each got its fair share of heat. He liked his egg *with* his coffee.

He sat down at the small dinette and waited on his breakfast to cook. Glancing over at the sink, he was reminded of the forgotten supper dishes, and stood up quickly to wash and dry the few items there. Glancing at the now steaming coffee water, Pete strode out back and refilled the kitchen bucket from a five-gallon cooler resting on the back porch. He paused when a hoot owl sounded off to the north. He waited a bit to see if it had attracted a mate's return call, but heard no response. *Don't sweat it none, pal*, he thought, *I'm in the same boat, and we're both probably better off.*

Returning to his egg, Pete flipped it over and waited a few moments until it was perfectly golden on the edges and still soft in the middle. Wrapped in a kitchen towel and sitting on the counter was a small loaf of bread, recently baked by one of the local women. Her husband had a taste for moonshine, and Pete liked her bread. The barter had been one of the easy ones. Pete sliced off a hunk of the crumbly loaf and poured his coffee into a well-used porcelain cup. He returned to the dinette and tasted the first mouthful of his hot, fresh meal. The hoot owl had reminded him of his ex-wife and despite how the woman had treated him, he couldn't help but wonder for a moment how she had managed after the collapse. His attention shifted as he lifted his coffee cup and glanced at the faded emblem on the side. The golden badge of a Police Detective, City of Philadelphia adorned the old mug. Pete remembered the celebration when his promotion had been posted. The coffee cup was one of many gifts of congratulation that had followed the event. As far as he knew, this memento was the only reminder he had left from that happy day. The real shindig had been when he was promoted to a district captain. Pete smiled at the memory while thinking, "*Now that was a serious party.*"

It was all behind him now. The marriage, career, retirement to the Jersey shore, and fishing with the pensioned cops who flocked to the area in droves – it had all vanished into thin air. Pete looked down at his egg and sliced off another bite. *Now, Pete*, he thought, *you're probably better off than any of those people back in Philly – you have eggs and bread.*

Leaning back in his chair, he thought about those last few months on the force for the thousandth time. He had been a rising star, making captain by age 32. In five short years, rumors started spreading that his name was under consideration for commissioner. Pete hadn't believed the rumors at the time, but one of his rivals had. Pete had always been an honest cop. He had never taken a bribe or performed a favor for anyone. There had been times where he had circumvented the system or manipulated a few rules in order to achieve justice – but never to benefit his family or himself.

One morning while driving into the station, he noticed a black car pull out and begin following him. The Philly police were really putting the pressure on several drug gangs operating in the city at that time, and Pete stayed more vigilant than normal during those operations. The same black automobile reappeared on his trip home, again following a few car-lengths behind him. Calling the station for backup, Pete drove around for a little bit until he spotted the two patrol cars approaching the suspicious sedan from behind. Pete stopped right in the middle of the road and got out of his car with weapon drawn. To Pete's surprise, the sedan contained two Justice Department investigators. Pete's name had been mentioned in the wrong circles by the wrong people, and the feds had placed him under surveillance.

Pete took another sip of coffee; his gaze lost in the space of the diminutive kitchen's yellowed walls. Two days later, he was arrested on federal corruption charges, and his life unraveled almost immediately.

When the headlines hit the newsstands the next day, he had already been released and warned by the federal judge not to leave town. Over the next few months, Pete was suspended without pay, his wife moved back home with her parents, and every single one of his friends seemed to abandon him.

It took almost a year to clear his name, and during that time things looked pretty dicey more than once. For twelve and a half awful months, men he had served with since the academy avoided him. Phone calls and emails weren't answered or returned. The favorite watering hole, frequented by dozens of cops from his district, was suddenly empty, a replacement having been chosen without his knowledge.

When he did run into a co-worker, the response was frequently polite to his face but vague in commitment. "Let's get together and have lunch Monday," was often answered with, "I'd love to have lunch sometime Pete, but can't Monday. I'll get back to you once my schedule clears up." They never got back.

The worst of it all was his wife of twenty plus years. Despite his repeated assurances that he was completely innocent, she couldn't handle the social poison created by the incident. Halfway through the ordeal, she left him withering in the storm by himself. Their divorce was finalized three months later.

Pete absent-mindedly swallowed another fork's worth of egg. Despite all of this happening over three years ago, he couldn't help but relive the past now and then. There was some good news – it had been four days since he had thought about it last. The gaps between these little, bumpy trips down memory lane were growing longer over time, and he concluded that meant he was healing or whatever the politically correct psycho-babble was for the healing of his spirit.

A couple more bites of egg and bread finished off breakfast, and he moved the dirty dishes to the sink. He decided to wait and wash them later. After he finished getting dressed, Pete unlocked the heavy metal door that separated his apartment from the bar. The sun would be up in a few minutes, and the early, gray light was already making Main Street visible out the front windows of the bar.

As Pete set about readying for another day of business, he thought about how apologetic the mayor and commissioner had been when the feds finally dropped the charges. A rival officer had joined forces with one of the city's most powerful drug lords and proceeded to set up a very sophisticated frame job involving bank accounts, digitally altered photographs, and fake email addresses. It had taken months to sort it out. The mayor had immediately ordered Pete returned to active duty with full pay and benefits, but it wasn't enough. Those who had turned their backs on him were now embarrassed, and Pete couldn't bring himself to trust them anymore. A police captain doesn't function in a vacuum. He needs his officers, staff, advisors, and even street snitches working with him to be effective. Pete's network was destroyed by false accusations and could never be rebuilt. Besides, he didn't have the motivation or the heart to work with those people anymore. His lawyer approached the mayor and made his wishes absolutely clear; the city needed to cough up an early retirement and modest compensation, after which Pete would disappear. The mayor agreed.

Pete had always wanted to see the great American West. He had spent all of his life in Philly, never venturing further than the Appalachian Mountains. He took part of his compensation and purchased a modest, late model sedan and packed it with a few personal items. With the tank filled and a stack of AAA roadmaps resting in the passenger seat, the former police captain began driving and only looked back now and again.

It had taken a little over a year to burn off his wanderlust. One by one, he successfully crossed off all of the household name national parks from his list. He toured California via the Pacific Coast Highway and spent considerable time in the northwest. He was walking out of a New Mexico truck stop after filling his tank and empting his bladder when something caught his eye. There, just inside the door, was a wire stand full of glossy, tri-fold tourist brochures. He was heading to Texas, and while he had seen hundreds of these advertising displays over the last year, this was the first one containing information about destinations in the Lone Star State. He browsed the dozens of choices and picked one touting Big Bend National Park and a small town he never heard of called Meraton. He casually flipped to the inside of the fold out, proudly featuring pictures of the Manor's gardens. Their striking beauty and seeming tranquility made up his mind. After a quick cell phone call to verify reservations, Pete started driving toward his future.

He had fallen in love with the dusty, little town immediately. The sheer beauty of the Manor was only part of the lure. The fact that he was becoming a little road weary, no doubt played a role as well. But what really sucked Pete in was the apparent lack of concern about his past. No one asked where he was from or commented on his out-of-state license plates. Everyone was polite and friendly – always offering suggestions about finding the best place to eat. No one ever even asked him where he was from or what he was doing in Meraton.

He was sitting in the Manor's gardens one evening when a long forgotten conversation with his grandfather suddenly popped into his head. A retired foot cop, Pete's granddad lived in a modest south Philly bungalow surrounded by black and white pictures of policemen sporting their handlebar mustaches and nightsticks. Pete had just noticed his first facial hair, when the old man had broached the topic of Pete's future. A child of the '60s – Pete was immersed in a time when challenging authority was as common as free love and communes. A slightly rebellious adolescent, he remarked that he wasn't sure he wanted to follow in the family tradition of becoming a policeman. Not one for long soliloquies, the old man pondered the teen's response before observing, "There are only two things where we Irish excel – being a cop or running a bar. Make up your mind soon, young man."

Meraton was the kind of town where you could throw a rock from end to end. And as he sat in the restaurant that night, Pete admitted he was tired of driving. This isolated part of Texas seemed just perfect for him, and the town didn't even have a bar. A month later, he signed the papers at the Big West Title Company's office in Alpha. The real estate agent handed Pete the keys to the small, unoccupied building on Main Street and a new business was born.

Despite cigarettes no longer being manufactured or sold, the faint smell of stale tobacco smoke hung in the air. Pete went to the oversized windows looking out onto Main and began to crank them open, hoping for a slight breeze. The sun had climbed completely over the horizon, and it promised to be another cloudless day. He was almost finished opening the window when two gunshots rang out. "*Shit,*" he thought, "*what now?*"

Pete rushed behind the bar and retrieved the MP5 sub-machine gun he had bartered from Terri. He slammed a magazine into the short weapon, while heading out the front door. There were already a few people up and about, and his first instinct was to check on Betty down at the Manor. He always worried about her being down there all alone. Betty was on the

64

front steps of the hotel and looked more annoyed than scared. He noted she was holding a shotgun at her side. He hurried her way, half-mounted the first concrete step leading to the Manor's front door and asked, "Any idea where those shots came from?"

"Well, not exactly. I was out here beating the rugs when I heard a sound that seemed to come from that direction." She pointed toward the south, and Pete decided to walk that way to see what was happening.

It's probably something innocent. Somebody probably found a coyote by the hen house this morning and was scaring it off, he thought. Pete hadn't walked two blocks when he was joined by two other men from the town. They were curious about the shooting as well and both were members of the town's volunteer posse. The trio soon met a crowd of people standing around and gesturing toward a nearby home. The center of attention was old man Parker's place.

Pete knew Mr. Parker as a customer at the bar. The old timer basically kept to himself, sharing the occasional story of his son and grandson who had both been star football players at Alpha State University. Mr. Benedict Jefferson Parker had lived in Meraton for as long as anyone could remember and was mainly known to be a reclusive, quiet man. Pete seemed to recall someone saying Parker was a retired railroad worker, but couldn't be sure.

The assembly gathered in the middle of the street was a mixture of both men and women. Several of the bystanders had apparently been rousted out of bed by the disturbance, as they were still dressed in nightclothes and pajamas. One of the women turned to see the town's volunteer lawmen approaching. She took a step toward Pete and raised her voice. "That man is crazy, Pete. He's gonna git somebody killed. He scared the shit out of my kids this morning. Somebody's gotta do something about him."

Another man turned and added his frustration. "I let my dogs out this morning like usual. That old fool Parker shot at my animals, and they weren't even on his place. It's a damn good thing his ass is half-blind, and he missed. There's an accounting for a man shooting another man's dogs."

Several members of the crowd nodded their agreement. Another man stepped forward, "You know, last week I met him out here on the street. He was nice as could be. Two hours later, I caught him aiming that shotgun of his at my kids! I yelled, and he stopped. But I'm sure as shit he was gonna shoot at my kids, Pete. We've got to do something about that freaked out old fool."

Pete looked at the two men with him and then back at the crowd. "All right, all right. I'll go up and talk to him. Ya'all can go back to your business. I'm sure everyone has better things to do than stand out here in the street and wait to be shot at."

Some of the townsfolk nodded and left, but quite a few stayed, waiting to hear the outcome. Pete took a deep breath and moved the sub-machine gun to his back as he strode toward the Parker residence.

Pete hesitated at the mailbox, taking mental note of his surroundings. The single story home was in obvious disrepair. The yard consisted of about one-half acre of dirt, peppered with weeds, surrounded by a waist high chain link fence. About the only noticeable green growth was along the fence line, where knee high nettles and dandelions flourished. The driveway had managed to sprout its share of unwelcome vegetation as well. Two dusty vehicles with flat tires sat in front of the garage door. Paint was peeling from several different spots on the house and garage. Two frayed rope ends hung from the single, large elm tree in the front yard, strong evidence that a swing had once hung on the sturdy limb.

There wasn't any movement in or around the house as far as Pete could see. He decided to announce himself. "Mr. Parker! Mr. Parker! It's Pete from the bar. Anybody home?"

His greeting must have been heard, because Pete could see movement inside of the house. A shadow appeared behind the screened front door, and Parker's voice answered back. "Pete, damnit, I told ya I would pay my bar bill as soon as my social security check comes in the mail. You just wasted your time coming out here this morning. I'm tapped."

Pete would have normally laughed at the response, but Parker didn't have a bar tab, and there hadn't been any mail in months. *Maybe Ben Parker had misunderstood or didn't hear well*, he thought.

"Ben, I need to talk to you. I'm coming up."

Pete hesitated for a moment, waiting for the old man's protest, but none came. Pete kept his eyes on the front door and began walking up the sidewalk. When he reached the front stoop, he again waited for a moment. "Ben, where are ya? I need to talk to you."

"Come on in Pete. It's been a while since I had company. Now I know I have some chocolate chip cookies around here somewhere. They're just the packaged kind, but they'll hit the spot," came the response from beyond the darkened doorway.

Pete climbed the two brick steps and onto the porch. He really didn't want to go inside, but also didn't want to be rude. He glanced over his shoulder and saw several of the town's residents still gathered a few blocks away. *If Parker sees them down there gawking, it's not going to help,*" he thought.

Pete brought his weapon around to the front, but kept the barrel pointed downward. He flicked off the safety and reached for the screen door.

The first thing he noticed about the home was the smell. It reminded him of the odor of the nursing home where his own Aunt Edna stayed before she passed. This place was ripe with whatever caused that particular aroma. Pete repressed the urge to storm the place and raise all the windows simply to invite in the fresh air. He poked around the living room and was surprised to see stacks and stacks of newspapers and magazines. The floor was littered with old, yellowed copies of The Alpha Tribune as well as an ample assortment of magazines covering everything from fly-fishing to gardening. Some of the stacks reached almost to the ceiling. Pete had seen this sort of thing before. His years of experience and training as a cop sent his senses on full alert – Ben was not mentally stable.

Pete didn't know what the real medical term was for this condition. The average person referred to it as "being a pack rat." Hoarding by itself was not a sure sign of danger – hoarding and losing touch with the real world and using a firearm was cause for concern.

About then, Ben appeared from the kitchen and caught Pete staring at the mess in the living room. Pete braced for the worst, but Mr. Parker merely shrugged his shoulders and said, "I've been meaning to go through and clean out some of that stuff. Never seems to be enough time. Come on in, Pete. There's room to sit in the kitchen."

Pete didn't want to go into the kitchen, but again his training kicked in. It was always best not to insult or agitate someone who was unstable. Calm, regular tones should be used, and the best way to handle a person on edge is humor. "Keep them laughing," had been the advice of one instructor, "Humor doesn't stop at the boundary of sanity or self-control."

Pete couldn't think of anything funny to say at the moment, but did comment on the stacks of paper. "Any of that you don't want Ben, just let me know. I could use the kindling and would be glad to take it off your hands."

Pete passed through the threshold into the kitchen. This room looked similar to the living room; its countertops piled high with all manner of literature and sprinkled with piles of old mail. He followed the slight path that wound between the stacks of newspapers to the small galley. Pete was surprised to find that the sink was perfectly clean, probably more so than his own at the moment. The second wonder was the dining table where Ben stood, pointing to a chair for his guest. The table was one of the most beautiful he had ever seen. Ornately carved, with detailed inlays on the surface, Pete couldn't help but stare. Ben noticed his gaze, and inquired, "Do you like my table, Pete? I made it for my wife years ago. She passed away in '98…or was it '99? Anyway, I worked on it in the shop for weeks. I used 13 different types of wood in all."

There was a small family room off the kitchen, and Pete could see various carvings and other handmade pieces scattered around the room. "Was that what you did, Ben – make furniture?"

The older man shook his head, "Oh my heavens, no. It was a hobby. I worked for the Union Pacific Railroad for 31 years before I retired."

Pete didn't take the indicated chair, but glanced back at the kitchen. Something else had caught his eye. There, beside the faucet, sat three prescription medicine bottles. The caps were off and they all appeared to be empty. "Ben, have you been to see the doc? We have a pretty good one in town now, ya know."

The question seemed to aggravate Mr. Parker. Pete noticed the older fellow came up on the balls of his feet and rocked back and forth a few times before he answered. "Hell no, I ain't been to see no sawbones. I feel fine. I've been out of my pills for a bit, but I'm doing okay. I've been waiting for that damn mailman to deliver my social security and pension checks. I'm so broke, they shut down my telephone and electric. There's no way I can come up with enough money to call my grandson to drive me into Alpha and get those prescriptions filled."

Pete walked over and picked up one of the bottles, and caught himself before he whistled out loud. While he couldn't pronounce the name on the bottle, he knew enough to recognize it was a psych drug. The other two bottles were labeled with similar medications, and the dosages seemed quite large.

Over the next 15 minutes, Pete sat and talked with Mr. Parker. The conversation revealed enough information for Pete to realize what was going on. Ben Parker had lost his only son and wife in the same car accident. A drunk driver had killed his family as they were returning from visiting relatives back east. The experience had caused something to snap inside. Pete had been on maintenance doses of some pretty strong antidepressants ever since.

There was no way to know if Ben Parker were a time bomb or would live out the rest of his life as a slightly eccentric, benign fellow. While the gentleman sitting across from him was both rational and entertaining at the moment, all of that could change in a heartbeat.

Pete needed to get back to the bar. He looked Mr. Parker in the eye and said, "Ben, I heard some shooting going on down here this morning. I've been told it was you. Do me a favor, my friend, and leave that shotgun right where it is by the front door. If someone comes onto your land, then you have every right to defend yourself. But if you shoot one of these neighborhood kids by accident, their families will hang you from that tree out front, and nothing will stop them."

"I was just scaring off some dogs, Pete. I'm afraid they are after my laying hens. Until I get that check in the mail, their eggs are the only food I have, and I can't afford to lose one of them."

Pete nodded his understanding. "I didn't think a good man like you would do something stupid, Ben. But you are concerning your neighbors – tone it down it bit, would you, sir?"

Ben agreed. On his way out the door, Pete spied Parker's supply of shotgun shells. An open box sat on a small table next to the front door. He suddenly had an idea, and when his host wasn't looking, he reached down and picked up a loose shell and dropped it in his pocket. The idea was a little crazy, but it might defuse a bad situation.

A few minutes later, he strode out of the Parker house and up the street toward the still gathered neighbors. Pete announced, "I talked to him, and he agreed to leave everyone alone if they didn't come onto his place. I have to warn you folks, he is very old, and I think a little dementia has set in. I would give him a wide berth if I were you."

The man who had accused Mr. Parker of aiming at his kids stepped forward, clearly upset. "And what are we supposed to do, Pete? Wait until he shoots one of our children or our wives?"

Pete snapped back, "What do you want to do? Lynch him? We don't have a jail, mental health system or even a doctor who can help him. Should I just go back and shoot him? Is that what you all want?"

The man didn't back down, "Well, if I see him even looking at my kids, I'm going to put his ass six feet under."

Pete took a step toward the man and poked him in the chest with his finger. "You shoot someone around here that doesn't deserve it, and you'll answer to me." Pete then looked around the crowd and made sure everyone understood the dilemma. "Society has gone to hell, people. I have no idea how folks used to handle these situations, but right now, I don't have any answer to this. Protect your families, but don't….I repeat DON'T go over the line." Pete spread his arms wide and turned in a slow circular motion, addressing no one and everyone, "If you harm that man without cause, you're no better than he is."

Pete left without another word and headed back toward Main. He knew deep down inside the situation was a powder keg, but didn't have a solution. He could only hope everyone kept their cool.

It had been so long since she had driven any sort of car, the sensation felt a little odd at first. It wasn't long before the feeling of motion and the freedom of the open road returned, and she actually managed a smile for the first time in days.

Deacon Diana Brown was experiencing her joy ride in an older pickup truck while driving down the smooth, deserted Texas highway. She had left her besieged compound in Alpha only fifteen minutes before. Her first few moments of freedom were complicated by the need for careful navigation around the debris littering her thoroughfare, but nothing was in front of her now except the wide, open road.

It had been years since she had driven to Meraton. Her career in the Navy had kept her on the ocean and far away from the deserts of Texas. After her return, there just hadn't been time. She had visited the famous gardens at the Manor many times before, and she had envisioned a quiet, peaceful getaway with Atlas some Saturday. Now, her son was dead, and this visit was anything but a relaxing day trip.

As she drove along, Diana tried to visualize how the meeting would take place. The stranger called Bishop had proven to be both honest and capable. Diana tried to recall every little tidbit of information learned during their brief time together. In the lunchroom, Bishop had told her that he was married, and his wife was with child. She had also heard him mention something about "the market" to David, the younger man who accompanied him. That was really about all she knew.

She continued to mull over the last statement he had made before leaving the church grounds – "Reach out to the people of Meraton." His eyes had been so serious and full of good intent. She, at the time, couldn't imagine any scenario that would require her to contact the neighboring town. Now, all that had changed.

As the desert miles passed by, the wind blowing into the open window felt liberating. It had been months since she had been away from the church's compound, and the open spaces and bright sunshine felt good despite the lack of air conditioning in the old truck. Diana didn't even notice, as she hadn't felt cooled air since the collapse. Her mind was occupied, rehearsing the speech she planned for Bishop. He understood their dilemma, and she was, after all, simply following his advice. The retired navy captain sighed and decided to be honest with herself. She wasn't normally the one asking for help – she was the one who provided assistance, and she simply wasn't comfortable asking anyone for anything.

She was so focused on how to word the conversation with Bishop that she failed to notice another vehicle had caught up to her. Its engine noise suddenly flooded the cabin as the farm truck passed her on the otherwise empty roadway. The old man driving the truck waved as he went around, and she noticed two tethered goats in the back.

Diana was struck by that simple image. She realized there were still people in this world who were going about "normal" tasks. While she didn't know where the rancher was heading with his livestock, he clearly had some agenda for loading his animals on that truck. *Why else use precious gasoline?* Whatever his destination or reason for travel, she smiled at the thought of people doing routine, productive things. Over the next few miles, Deacon Brown reminisced about what life without the constant fear of death, kidnapping, or murder had been like, and longed for that kind of secure existence again. Most assuredly, she would sleep better at night without wondering if she had just ordered some father to his death on a patrol. What would it be like to savor a meal without first wondering if the perimeter were well prepared?

It had been so long since she had experienced such a mundane lifestyle; she had forgotten what it was like. A roadside sign ahead announced "Meraton 5 Miles" just as it dawned on her that was what Bishop had been trying to tell her. Bishop was letting her know there was another world out there. He was trying to get her and her people out of the little fortified cubbyhole they had been trapped in so long. They needed to see it was worth fighting for. They needed hope for the future.

Diana's first impression of Meraton was as much about what she didn't see as what she did. There were no burned out or discarded vehicles blocking the roads, and the storefronts appeared to be intact. The place was alive with activity. A section of the main street through town was loosely blocked off, apparently more for space definition than for barricading. People with tables as well as several cars and trucks decorated with handwritten signs were inside the square.

Diana was intrigued by the simple market. Here was a group of folks peacefully exchanging goods and services rather than high velocity lead. She eased the pickup to the side of the road and cut the motor. This was as good a place as any to begin her search. In truth, the lure of the bazaar was almost hypnotic, and she longed for a closer look. As she exited the vehicle, Diana was immediately faced with her first dilemma of the day. Should she take the rifle along? Just how civilized a community was this, anyway? She looked to see what the locals were doing, but her parking spot was not close enough to make out many details. In the end, she decided that since she hadn't been outside without a weapon for months, this might be a nice change. It would feel wonderful to walk around without carrying a firearm, so she shoved the rifle onto the floorboard of the truck, locked the door, and proceeded to walk downtown.

It took her only a few minutes to reach the first booth of the Meraton market. Diana was completely absorbed as she slowly meandered through the assortment of goods, animals, and services being offered. She had no idea anything like this still existed and believed this venue would have been popular even before the collapse. She passed tables offering homemade bread, sewing supplies, and old books. One of the most popular booths featured a teenage boy on one side of a table, taking in shoes that needed repair. Silently beside him sat an older gent, his deft fingers busy reworking a piece of leather with remarkable precision, clearly an accomplished cobbler. At first, Diana was a bit confused over the retailer's exchange system, but watching the bartering between two women over a batch of noodles being traded for a bag of freshly sheared wool cleared it up.

Deacon Brown was so amazed by the activities going on around her; she had no idea of the attention she was garnering. A stunningly beautiful woman caused heads to turn even in these times, and Diana was no exception. The sheer joy she was feeling after months of thinking the world ended at the church's barricade caused her to violate the first rule of survival – be aware of your surroundings.

The two big men watching the gorgeous stranger stroll through the outdoor bazaar were probably experiencing a sensation of happiness, not unlike the growing mood of exhilaration overtaking Diana. A visit to Pete's bar, combined with a broad sampling of the available thirst quenchers, no doubt added to their euphoria. Anyone who noticed the two men would have probably described them as young ranch hands, perhaps even cowpokes. It wasn't out of the ordinary for some of the local spreads to provide transport for the hired help into Meraton now and then. Ranch hands needed a break, too. It also wasn't unheard of for these men to visit Pete's. If there had been any younger ladies in the market that day, they would have probably considered both men reasonably good-looking and polite.

Diana turned away from a table offering an extensive collection of canning jars and lids and inadvertently stepped into the chest of one of the cowboys. The tall young man tipped his hat and uttered a "Pardon me, ma'am," but made no effort to move out of the way. He remained right where he was and smiled down at the attractive woman who was 20 years his senior.

Diana had been an officer in the United States Navy and immediately understood the man's leer. The expression on his face combined with the strong smell of alcohol on his breath spelled "immature male hormone surge," and she mumbled, "No problem, junior," and tried to move out of the way.

Her well-executed side step and pivot resulted in her staring directly into the chest of another large male, who immediately tipped his hat and said, "Good morning, pretty lady. Would you care to join my friend and me down at Pete's for a drink?"

Diana smiled and responded immediately, "No, thank you, young man. I'm here on business." The two men looked at each other, and one of them let out what was an unmistakable growl – an obvious attempt to imitate a cougar. Despite her rejection, both men moved closer and hemmed her in. This wasn't Deacon Brown's first rodeo with drunken, horny men. It was, however, the first encounter she had experienced where her rank didn't automatically give her an advantage. Unaware that the two oversized, testosterone generators could care less about her service in the United States military, she automatically responded as she always had in such situations.

"Stand down immediately - both of you," she ordered in her best voice of authority. "I'm here on business, and I have a son who is..." The thought of Atlas made her voice drift off, and the two men mistook her action as one of indecision. One of the cowpokes took her roughly by the arm and proceeded to guide the now frightened woman away. His friend put his arm around her shoulders, and she was immediately pinned between the two very robust ranch hands. After being half carried and half dragged around the corner of a building, Diana regained her composure, and her training kicked in. She raised her left foot and kicked hard against a knee. A twisting motion and a hard elbow to the other's ribs resulted in her being freed, but only for a moment.

Mr. SoreKnee spoke first, barking, "Now just a damn minute, lady." His buddy quickly added, "Sooooo, we like to play

73

a little ruff, eh? Nooo problem, pretty lady. I've busted fillies a lot wilder than you."

Diana took a step backwards, but her back was against a wall. The two smiling cowboys took a step forward with raised hands when a clear, loud female voice sounded from behind them, "You boys ain't causing trouble, are ya?"

The two men hesitated and then turned quickly to see who had been so rude as to interrupt their courtship. Between the two hulks, Diana spotted a petite woman standing with her arms folded and a broad smirk on her face. One of the big fellas smiled and looked at his partner saying, "Well, looky here bud; now there's one for each of us." His body moved to step forward when his friend's hand shot out and pressed against his chest, "Whooooah there, buddy. You don't know who that is - do ya?"

A look of utter puzzlement answered the question. The wiser of the two took off his hat and bowed his head slightly, "Good Morning Miss Terri, what can we do for ya, ma'am?" Before Terri could even respond, the other cowboy looked at his friend with huge eyes and mouthed the words, "Bishop's Terri?" That question was answered with a nervous nod and within seconds, both of the large men were standing with hats in hand and heads bowed.

Most of the exchange went unseen by Diana, but she caught enough of it to realize these two drunken bigmouths were actually frightened of the small woman.

Terri's hands moved to her hips, and she began to scold the two men, "Do I need to have Pete cut you boys off? We can't have two nice, young men such as yourselves causing trouble in the market. Now why don't y'all go on down to the Manor, and tell Betty I sent you. Tell her you both need a cup of coffee – strong and black."

Diana watched, fascinated as both men humbly nodded their heads without even the slightest protest. When they started to step away, Terri's left hand went to the shoulder of the biggest one, sending a clear message that she wasn't done yet. As fast as Diana had ever seen, the woman's right hand produced an automatic pistol and for a brief moment, she thought someone was about to get shot.

Terri didn't point the weapon at either man, but waved it in front of their frightened faces. "What is wrong with you two? Where are your manners? You scared the hell out of that lady standing behind you, and neither of you has issued an apology. I'm beginning to think you two aren't such nice fellas after all." The pistol stopped moving, and the woman's voice became low and serious, "Maybe you two haven't heard, but I don't like rude men."

Both men quickly turned and mumbled apologies to an astonished Deacon Brown. She nodded at each, noticing that their faces now carried the expression of teenagers who had been caught and were being punished. Gone was any sign of lust or determination.

After watching the two scolded men shuffle off with heads hung low, Terri tucked her pistol in her belt and stepped forward, offering her hand. "Are you okay?" she asked the other woman. After a brief introduction, Terri suggested Diana accompany her to Pete's for a cup of coffee.

Diana, still stunned by what she had just witnessed, ignored the offer. "I've not seen anything like what you just did since I was in the Navy. I don't mean to be nosey or anything, but how did you..."

Terri shook her head and interrupted the question. "Oh, that. My husband has quite the reputation around here. Most of the people in town know he is a little protective of the baby and me." Terri patted her tummy and smiled at the stranger. "You still look a little shaken, and I don't blame you. Let's get you that cup of coffee."

Terri's suggestion of her husband's notoriety, coupled with the mention of her pregnancy, prompted Deacon Brown to put two and two together. She asked, "Would your husband happen to be named Bishop by any chance?"

Terri's smile disappeared immediately. She looked Diana up and down with a sneer on her lips and her right hand darted behind her back where the pistol was stashed. Her voice snarled, "And how would you know Bishop?"

For the second time in the last few minutes, Diana was taken aback by the action of someone in this town. *Was everyone here crazy?* The small woman in front of her looked ready to launch a full frontal assault, and there was zero fear in her eyes. Deacon Brown did her best to remain calm and responded, "I met him a few days ago in Alpha. He and a young man named David stayed at our church. He was on a mission to procure some medical equipment, and when we met, he mentioned that his wife was pregnant. As I recall, he also mentioned you were a very good shot. I thought he might have been exaggerating until just a minute ago."

Terri relaxed and a look of calm returned to her face. "I'm sorry. These are such troubling times, and I never know what's going to happen next. Bishop has made more than his share of enemies, and a girl can't be too careful these days. I'm always concerned one of his old adversaries might come looking for me. I haven't heard from Bishop in days, and would love to hear all about Alpha. Then maybe you can tell me what brings you to Meraton."

The two women made their way to Pete's without further incident and pushed open the thick wooden door. Pete, as usual, was behind the bar, talking to a customer, and looked up to greet his newest guests. "Terri! Well hey there, pretty lady." When Diana walked in behind her, Pete's expression showed clear curiosity. "Well, hello to you as well, ma'am. Welcome to Pete's Place."

Terri pointed to an isolated table toward the back of the saloon, telling Pete he would have her eternal gratitude if he could serve up two cups of his famous coffee. Pete nodded, "Coming right up. I've got a fresh pot brewing."

Over the next twenty minutes, the two girls exchanged stories and drank coffee. Diana immediately took a liking to Terri and vice versa. Diana choked back hot tears as she confided in Terri how Atlas sacrificed himself and that she had come to ask Bishop's help in countering another attack. The poignant moment was interrupted when the barroom's door flew open, and the sound of laughter filled the room. Loud, proud, and bold, Nick and Kevin strode into Pete's, obviously in good spirits and enjoying the day. Nick let his eyes adjust to the darker room for a moment and spied Terri, sitting in the corner. As he strode toward her table, Diana came into view, and he paused for a moment before approaching. Terri thought it was funny how such big, strong capable men could be so influenced by a pretty woman. She had seen the same kind of response time after time in the business world but still found the reaction interesting. Nick strode over and gave Terri a kiss on the cheek, and then looked longingly at Deacon Brown. Terri intentionally waited, knowing Nick was eager for an introduction. After she had played with the big man for a moment, she finally crooned, "Oh now, where are my manners," and proceeded with the social amenities.

Kevin soon joined the group, carrying two glasses of tea. When Nick introduced the teenager as his son, Diana's reaction was surprising as she was polite, but instantly distant, and somewhat melancholy. Her demeanor changed so markedly, Nick tried to quietly lean across to Kevin and see if the boy had a foul odor about him or something. Kevin, preoccupied with the activity in the market beyond the picture window, seemed not to notice the invasion of his personal space. Terri, as perceptive as ever, saw the move and had to smile. After regaining a serious face, she moved toward her friend and said in a quiet voice, "Nick, Diana just lost her son yesterday."

Nick immediately felt a sense of gratitude that Kevin didn't somehow offend the striking lady sitting across the table.

But he struggled with the best way to respond to the information Terri shared, wanting to express his regrets and not really knowing what to say, having just met Diana. A parent himself, he could not imagine the heartbreak that accompanies surviving your own child. After a brief pause, during which he considered his options, proper condolences won out. "I'm sorry to hear about your son, Miss Brown. These are such difficult times. Please accept my best wishes and prayers." As Nick spoke, Terri reached out to Diana, patting her arm gently, as if to coax her out of her trancelike state.

Nick had no more uttered his last sentence when the reason for Kevin's distraction became perfectly clear. Another teenager was outside the bar, browsing the market. Kevin, who had been straining to get a better view through the front window at Pete's Place, leaned toward Nick and winked before saying, "Hey, Dad. I think I need to go check on those new socks at the marketplace. Whattaya think?"

Nick grinned and waved the youth away. After Kevin left, Nick smiled at his two tablemates and conferred, "He saw a pretty girl about his age walking around a bit ago. I think he wants to see if she's still around. God, it's good to see him acting like a 16-year old boy, rather than a solider."

Nick's comment brought Deacon Brown back to reality and the purpose of her visit. She sipped from her mug, preparing her thoughts. "I was just explaining to Terri how I came to Meraton to talk to Bishop and ask for his help. After the attack yesterday, we are in desperate straits, and I'm not sure what to do."

For the next hour, Terri and Nick listened to and absorbed Diana's story. With the majority of the townspeople shopping at the market, bar business was a little slow, so Pete pulled up a chair and joined in the conversation. Nick listened intently without comment until Diana got to the part about Bishop's raid for the medical equipment. He grunted as Diana described the ambush Bishop had busted up and the role David had played.

When Diana finished recounting the story, Nick shook his head and chimed in. "I can't believe Bishop would do something like that – he's such a shy, reserved man." Nick's sarcastic remark made everyone grin.

Pete, with the learned ear of a bartender, picked up on Nick's humorous comment and followed his lead. "Now, now…it's not fair to pick on Bishop when he's not here to defend himself. We all know the young man means well. It's not as if he goes *looking* for trouble or anything."

The humor was contagious, and Terri couldn't help herself. "Diana, I told you my husband had a reputation for bringing out the worst in people. I guess I was preaching to the choir, huh?" It took everyone a second to catch Terri's double entendre, before invoking another round of chuckles.

The door opened about then, and Betty stuck her head inside. Saying, "Oh good, there you are," she continued inside and ambled toward the table. "I have two sobered up young Beltron boys outside. They realized they behaved badly and wanted to express their regrets. They are, however, a little concerned that Terri is going to shoot them on sight. I was asked to come in first and make sure you had 'settled down.'"

Nick immediately looked at Terri and smirked, "Talk about the pot calling the kettle black." Terri, feigning insult at Nick's remark immediately reached back, as if going for her pistol. In her best western drawl, she retorted, "Why you old polecat...take it back right now, or I'll fill my hand with iron!" Everyone except Betty started laughing out loud.

Terri recovered first and smiled at her. "Betty, I'm not going to shoot anybody. Tell them it's safe to come in."

The two young men from the Beltron ranch approached the table shyly. Diana accepted their apology and to everyone's surprise, asked them if they wanted to have a seat and another cup of coffee. After a quick glance at each other, they each pulled up a chair.

Diana continued, "We are down to less than 30 men and our ammunition is almost gone. I know we hurt them badly, but we won't withstand another attack. Before Bishop left our church, he told me I should reach out to the people of Meraton...and...well....here I am."

The two Beltron hands had to be "read in" on the events at Alpha, answering their many questions about the situation in the neighboring community. When they were finally up to speed, the older one commented, "I bet those are the same people who raided our ranch. They have rustled cattle, shot some of our men, and taken weapons. Old man Beltron sure would like to get his hands on those vermin."

Pete shook his head and stared out the window. "A lot of people think of me as the mayor around here, and I just don't believe we can raise a lot of support from the townsfolk. We are barely holding on as it is, keeping order in our own town. I wish it wasn't that way, but that's the truth of the matter."

Terri looked at Pete and nodded understandingly. "I hear what you're saying, Pete. We both know that view is short sighted, but you're right. If Diana's people lose, it won't be long before those crooks will be looking for new territory to plunder, and Meraton is the closest town. Still, most of the folks around here probably won't see it that way."

Diana was disappointed, but understood. She stared out the window for a bit and then said, "I had better be getting back. It will be dark soon, and they will probably hit us again in the morning."

Nick cut her off. "Now hold on just a minute. I have some knowledge in these matters, and I don't think you should give up just yet." The older Beltron hand agreed, adding, "Ma'am, I think you can count on Mr. Beltron lending you some help. I can't speak for him, but I bet if I were to relay your situation, he would do what he could."

Pete rubbed his chin, "While the whole town wouldn't support such an effort, I can think of five or six men who had relatives in Alpha or who have lost family members when those crooks raided us."

Nick thought for a moment and seemed to make up his mind. "Kevin and I are in. I think you two gents should head back to the ranch and see how much help Mr. Beltron is willing to offer."

The momentum was building to help the people of Alpha. At least it was until Terri spoke up. "Well count me in, too. I'm bored around here, and besides, that was the last place anyone saw my husband. I imagine he'll come back through there on the way home."

Nick and Pete both blurted out, "Whooooah there," at the same time. The two men looked at each other, and Nick went first, "Terri, I don't think it's a good idea for you to go."

Pete quickly nodded his head in agreement. "He's right Terri. Besides, if something were to happen to you, I don't want to be the one explaining to Bishop why we let his pregnant wife charge off into a battle."

Terri waved them both off, replying in her best southern belle tone. "Now, it's mighty sweet of you two strong, brave men to be all chivalrous and think of my protection. But you fine gentlemen are forgetting one very important fact. Even if Bishop were here, do you think he could stop me if I wanted to go?"

Pete and Nick didn't like it one bit, but there was little they could do. The two ranch hands hurried out, rushing back to the ranch to inform their boss of the situation. Pete left Terri in charge of the bar and headed off to spread the word while Nick left in search of his son.

Chapter 8

Executive Worries

The President of the United States paced back and forth with a steady cadence. While his body moved in a relatively straight line, his bobbing head betrayed an indecisiveness regarding which direction to focus first. To his right was a large LED display, not dissimilar from the thousands installed in high-end media rooms around the country – only this screen wasn't featuring movies or sporting events. Today, the light emitting diodes were tasked with indicating the latest tactical information graphically across a map of the United States.

The other contender for the president's concentration was the commanding conference table stationed dead center of the room. Unlike its high tech competition, its imposing granite surface was littered with stacks of old-fashioned paper reports and documents. Loosely sorted into some unfamiliar order, the coal black lettering overlaying stark white paper was an extreme contrast to the brightly colored hues of the wall display.

At the moment, the Commander in Chief really didn't want to look at either, but couldn't help but try to attend to both. He was losing control, and that fact weighed heavily on a man whose resume included being the single, most powerful individual on the planet. Men who achieve such lofty positions don't like the fall – having no understanding as to the cause often accelerates the descent.

There were two uniformed men in the room with the chief executive. Both had been present during the emergency escape from a White House that was being overrun with thousands of angry citizens. Like the chief executive, the man seated at the table was no stranger to extraordinary authority and responsibility. General Wilson had been the Chairman of the Joint Chiefs of Staff for almost two years. He now found himself as not only the highest-ranking military officer in the land, but also as the president's closest advisor. Many of the executive branch's cabinet had been killed that fateful day. Many more were classified as "whereabouts unknown." The few who had managed to flee Washington were no longer trusted by their boss. Fueled by a string of bad decisions resulting in horrendous consequences, paranoia ran deep in the troubled administration.

The third man in the room stood quietly by the door. Agent Powell took his duties as head of the Secret Service's protection detail seriously and seemed always to be at the president's side. While General Wilson waited on the leader of the free world to digest the latest bad news, he secretly wondered if the stoic bodyguard ever slept.

A continuing decline in the number of territories that would execute the president's orders was the root cause of his pacing. Some military units simply didn't respond anymore. Others replied with terse messages ranging from repeating bogus requests for clarification to outright insubordination. The communications infrastructure of the United States was in complete turmoil. Citizens normally received their news via television, radio or the printed word. All of these media required electrical power to both send and receive. Electricity had become a luxury that currently only 5% of the population enjoyed.

While operating at a fraction of pre-collapse levels, the military fared better than the private sector. Wherever they were available, high-tech satellite systems, originally appropriated for the foreign war on terrorism, were distributed to field commands. Some domestic bases and forts used civilian communication networks and were just as susceptible to the failure of those structures as were town councils and other local authorities. The cold war era Emergency Broadcasting System was a shell of its former self, a direct result of budget cuts enacted as the threat of nuclear war faded from the government's priorities. Regulated to weather alerts, most EBS locations had suffered a decline in maintenance and upkeep. Within a few days of being activated, the vast majority of EBS transmitters failed. Even those stations that were broadcasting didn't have many listeners. About 99% of the nation's radio receivers required either batteries or electricity to run, and both were in short supply.

Despite a seemingly hopeless situation, there was a plan, and the president believed it to be a good one. Operation Heartland could be summed up as a strategy to take control of the nation's heartland, focusing all available resources to jump-start society there, and use the Mississippi River Delta as a springboard to recover the rest of the nation. The area 150 miles on each side of the Mississippi River had all of the key ingredients: nuclear plants to generate power, the river for a transportation artery, and the nation's breadbasket to feed the people.

While the plan appeared to be the best course of action, the president hesitated to implement the actions necessary for its execution. Some critical regions of the heartland had been on their own for months since everything had gone to hell. Other areas had been under control of the military for some period, but those units were disintegrating for various reasons. There was also the issue of pulling troops from areas that were barely hanging on as it was. Initially, the military had occupied the 40 largest American cities and declared martial law. Now, almost 30% of those commands either refused to follow orders or didn't respond at all.

When the president ordered the Pentagon to find out what was happening to the military, the resulting report appeared incomplete and confused. Many national guardsmen were said to be going AWOL due to the desperate situation of their families. Other sources indicated the morale of regular troops was so low that it was a credit to the officers that more units hadn't ceased to function. It was a single paragraph buried deep inside of the report that was the most troubling. Rumors had been circulating of another authority taking control of some units. One source had described the coexisting command structure as "an alternative government." This supposed government even had a name – "The Independents."

Power, especially in time of crisis, wasn't something men like the president shared. His every instinct was to take control and move the country forward. To his way of thinking, he needed every pair of boots marching in step toward the same goal. He expected his leadership to go unchallenged and his authority to be supreme. There was no way the nation would recover without a strong, purpose-minded hand at the helm, and the American people had elected him to be that hand. No other confirmation was necessary.

POTUS cleared his throat and began. "General, I'm not satisfied with this report. You have to admit it isn't up to your people's normal standards. I realize I pressured you, but the information it contains is sketchy at best."

General Wilson rubbed his chin, using the delay to carefully choose his words. "Mr. President, the resources available to me are severely limited. My orders were clear and precise – don't include rumor, innuendo or anything else that can't be backed up with facts. As I told you before, sir, I believe there is another group or organization that is filling the vacuum of control this situation has fostered. I believe that organization is growing daily. I just can't prove it at this time."

The president nodded his head in acceptance of the general's words. He paused for a moment and then changed the subject. "General, can you show me the progress of Operation Heartland?"

"Yes, sir. Coming up on the display now."

The large map changed to show an enlarged view of the Mississippi River delta with Chicago bordering on the north and New Orleans on the south. An area approximately 150 miles on each side of the river was depicted with dashed red lines. Certain key assets, such as nuclear power reactors, were circled in white. Two of these milestones were blinking white and blue, indicating that the military or other government agency had taken control as planned.

The map also showed several dark blue arrows at various locations. All of these indicators were pointing inward toward the great river. These were military ground units on their way toward objectives inside of the heartland. At the lower section of the map, along interstate I-20, one blue arrow was approaching the outlined border for Operation Heartland. The arrow was labeled 1st Cav DIV and seemed to be resting on the Texas border with Louisiana.

The president nodded his approval. "General, I feel like we are finally taking a step forward here. Our next step is to use the military's Psych Ops capabilities to communicate with the people. Are the leaflets being printed?"

General Wilson replied that indeed, millions of leaflets were being printed and would be dropped from aircraft over the major population centers in the heartland. He was right in the middle of explaining the process to the president when a polite knock sounded on the door.

The executive secretary entered the room and announced, "Sir, it's time to board Air Force One for the flight to Fort Bliss."

Chapter 9

Divide by 10th

First Sergeant Fitzpatrick rubbed his side and cursed his driver for the third time in the last hour. After blowing off some steam, he decided it was wrong to blame the young corporal. The kid was only pointing the Stryker where he ordered and wasn't at fault for the jarring ride. Still, it seemed like the kid ran over every possible bump and lump this part of northern Louisiana had to offer. As far as his side was concerned, banging into the turret was just part of the job. With the high-tech surveillance systems installed in the carrier, he could have ridden down below and had basically the same view, but he liked sticking out of the turret and using his own eyes and ears. The pain from his sore ribs distracted him for a moment, and a low branch from a nearby elm scraped his cheek. *That was the one good thing about Iraq*, he thought, *no trees, and the desert was smooth.*

Fitz, as the crew called him, double-checked that the radio was set to intercom so only the crew of his Stryker could hear his words. "This looks good right here, corporal. Nudge her up against the berm, and we're good."

"Rodger that Top."

When the eight wheels of the large armored vehicle finally rolled to a stop, everyone inside was relieved. Fitz pushed a button, and the large aluminum ramp at the rear opened, providing a means for the 10 members of the 1st Scout platoon to exit. The sound of their boots thumping down the ramp was reassuring to Fitz, as the team dismounted without delay. That was the way it was supposed to be done. He placed both hands on the butterfly trigger of the large .50 caliber machine gun mounted beside him and made ready to cover his men as they spread out to form a perimeter. The precaution proved unnecessary. He switched his radio to the battalion frequency and calmly stated "3-1 in position and deploying."

As the troopers moved away from the armored transport, each two-man team knew its role and hurried to locate concealed positions. Ten minutes later, radio traffic indicated that all five teams had found good spots, forming a roughly 180-degree arch to the front and sides of the Stryker. Fritz again checked his frequency and updated battalion with a short, "3-1 deployed...3-1 deployed."

Fitz raised his binoculars and scanned the area. His was one of eight squads that had been ordered to move forward of the main force and provide early warning of any approaching threat. When his LT had conducted the briefing yesterday, Fitz had been surprised when his commanding officer had indicated that they should be looking for an American unit approaching along the I-20 corridor. Everyone had been further taken aback when they were informed that the approaching aggressor would be the 1st Cav, and the rules of engagement were to return fire if fired upon. That shocker was quickly followed up with, "Use any force necessary to protect the men, assets, and *territory* of the 10th Mountain Division." That word "territory" was disconcerting.

Fitz lowered his glass and shook his head, thinking about the briefing. After four years with this outfit, it was the only time he could remember the gathered NCOs repeatedly asking for confirmation of an order. Everyone knew that the brigade commander had pledged the unit's loyalty to this new government called the Independents. It had been clearly communicated that the Colonel believed this new outfit more closely aligned with the purpose and intent of their oaths. Everyone had been given the choice to continue with the brigade or leave Fort Polk without dishonor. Everyone had stayed.

What practically no one had realized was that there were other American military units still loyal to the old chain of command. They hadn't been lied to or mislead, it was just no one had thought to ask. With what he and his men had witnessed since everything fell apart, who would have thought any government agency, military unit, or even the local dogcatcher would have the wherewithal to do anything but try and hold the country together? It just didn't make sense.

Before leaving Polk, the mission had been to secure this remote section of northern Louisiana, so the Independents could kick-start the heartland of the country. It was the first orders they had received that were proactive, and the plan sounded reasonable and well thought out. After arriving in Shreveport, word had come down that the Independents weren't the only ones who thought this was a good plan. The president's men and the old regime had evidently decided to execute the same basic operation.

To Fitz and most of the other troopers of the 4/10, this hadn't immediately translated into the potential for conflict. Wouldn't both sides work toward the same goal? Wasn't the wellbeing of the population more important than who controlled the government?

The sergeant glanced down at the blue armband and adjusted the recent addition to his uniform. His men had the same color Velcro patches on their helmets and load gear, his Stryker had panels of blue cloth in strategic locations. Fort Polk was a training base as well as the home of the 4/10. These "blue force – red force" patches had been used during exercises and war games to differentiate between friend and foe. Every trooper and vehicle in the brigade now was adorned with the blue emblems.

Fitz returned to his primary job – scouting his sector. His team would have set up observation posts at least 200 meters from their Stryker. Their job was to report any sort of movement or activity, not to fight. Nevertheless, they were reasonably well armed, with one of the teams carrying a Javelin missile launcher and one carrying a .50 caliber machine gun. He even had some anti-air capabilities, as they had been issued a single Stinger ground to air missile. He had one sniper, and the rest were lightly armed infantry. The Stryker he was riding was equipped with another heavy machine gun as well as a TOW missile launcher. Should trouble come their way, the 1-3 was as ready as any light unit could be.

If the Cav was really on its way, Fitz's primary concern was that 120mm gun mounted on their Abrams tanks. With a range greater than three kilometers, the weapon had enough power to shred his lightly armored troop carrier to bits. It wasn't so much the actual gun that concerned him, but the targeting and sensor systems inside the big tank. The M1A2 could fight at night, through dense fog or even in a hurricane if need be. He knew from training that the crew would be using their infrared thermal sights, and some of the new systems even had automatic target detection. Fitz was sure the tank's computer would think his Stryker was the perfect target.

Back at Polk, the 1st Sergeant had achieved quite the reputation for his creative methods of defeating thermal gun sights during the numerous exercises at the base. He had pulled every trick in the book to make sure his platoon came out on top in order to claim the most leave. Fitz had developed quite a taste for Cajun cooking, finding it a welcome alternative to the typical fare of his rural New Jersey upbringing. He was savvy to the fact that the tank gunners were trained to look for hot spots and straight edges. Military vehicles had both, and enemy troops emitted a lot of heat as well. While others had tried brush piles to distort the lines, ravines for off the grid hideouts, and even emergency foil blankets that wrapped the vehicle and obscured the heat, Fitz had gone in the opposite direction and cooled the skin of his Stryker. A soldier in constant search of his edge, he had once diverted the irrigation system of a farm bordering the exercise area to accomplish this objective. The watering truck from the base's extensive softball complex had been tapped to guarantee his success on another occasion. The combination of breaking up the outline of the big-wheeled troop carrier and lowering the temperature of its skin had done the trick.

Fitz didn't have any water at the moment, but he had identified a unique place to hide. The 4/10's scouts had been moving through fields of some untended crop, heading for the highest ground in the area, when he spotted the perfect setup. Like many farms in the region, this one had a scrapheap towards the rear of the property. There were two rusted hulks of 1950's era tractors, a 2.5-ton farm truck without tires, and stacks of miscellaneous equipment discarded from the farm's operation. Weeds grew rampantly around the old implements and junked machinery. There was even a large hardwood tree growing in the center of the junkyard, providing some shade and limited camouflage from above. Once the engine of the Stryker had cooled, there would be no reason why its skin would be any different color than the surrounding cast-offs when viewed through a thermal sight. The piles of rusted metal and old vehicles would break up the outline of his fighting machine, and that suited him just fine. As he looked around at the scattered junk, he noticed the door of the old truck had been painted with white letters. The once proud and now faded signage read, "Scott's Farm and Dairy."

Well, farmer Scott, he thought, *you sure picked the perfect place to throw away your junk.*

~ ~

Major Owens had been waiting to see the sign along the edge of I-20 for what had seemed like days. "Welcome to Louisiana" seemed like such an anti-climactic greeting after the monumental effort required by his team to travel this short distance.

As his tank rolled into what the sign claimed was a "Sportsman's Paradise," he felt a short, but welcome sense of relief. There was little between him and his objective of Shreveport but rural farm country, and hopefully, open road. It had taken the resupply trucks almost four hours to reach him this morning, and then another two hours to refuel his vehicles. Topped off with full tanks and with enough in reserve to easily make it to their area of operations, the major had eliminated at least one of the hundreds of worries associated with this command.

His relief was short lived, however, as the now dreaded static of his radio sounded in his earpiece.

"Major, you need to get up here, sir. We are at Louisiana mile marker 3. There is a Colonel Marcus up here who wishes to speak with you."

What the hell is going on, was the first thought that shot through the major's mind. The words, "*Who the hell is Colonel Marcus*," almost left his lips, but he only responded with a weary sounding, "On my way."

As the major's tank pulled out of line and began passing the lead vehicles of the convoy, he was tempted to radio back to HQ in Dallas and ask if he had missed a transmission or other orders. The captain in charge of the refueling convoy hadn't mentioned anything, and after his status report, there had been no communications. His radio was working just fine – at least on his command frequencies.

It took him only about eight minutes to travel the three miles and meet up with his lead scout. There, parked in the eastbound lane of I-20, was a Bradley, nose to nose with a Stryker. The Stryker had a white flag pinned atop of one of its tall antenna. Standing on the ground, next to the two fighting machines was a group of soldiers, one of them a tall, thin man who Owens immediately identified as a senior officer.

The major dismounted from his tank and approached the group of men. The insignias immediately confirmed his observation that the taller man was the colonel, and he walked directly up and smartly saluted the senior officer.

The salute was returned, and then the colonel stuck out his hand. "Major, my name is Colonel Marcus, commander of the 4th Brigade Combat Team, 10th Mountain Division."

Owens responded with, "Sir, Major Owens, commanding Ironhorse Brigade, 1st Cavalry Division. How can I help you, Colonel?"

The colonel looked around at the small group of gathered men and then back at the major. "Walk with me please, Major." As the two officers casually wandered a distance sufficiently out of earshot, the colonel began:

"Major, I don't know how much you know about what is going on in the country right now, so I'll start from the beginning. A new government has formed. This is in addition to the old one still trying to maintain control. I'll be blunt, Major. I'm with the new government, and you, evidently, are still with the old."

The look of confusion on the major's face made his response redundant. "Sir, I'm not quite sure I understand. A new government? An old government? My orders from General Lynch are simple…to secure the region around Shreveport, sir."

Colonel Marcus smiled and folded his arms across his chest. His voice was steady, "So I understand, Major. I have orders to secure the same region. It seems both sides decided this little stretch of real estate is critical. I'll come right out with it – we both can't be here. My orders are to deny you this area." The colonel paused for a few moments and then continued, "And I will follow my orders."

Major Owens was an officer in the United States Army and in command of one of the most potent fighting forces on the planet. He had never even conceived of being denied anything and was beginning to dislike this colonel's attitude. His contempt bled through as he looked around and pointed back at the colonel's Stryker, saying, "No offense, sir, but I hope you brought a little more than *that* with you."

The colonel smiled again, and a careful observer would have noticed his eyes became just a touch friendlier. He liked this young officer and appreciated his aggressiveness. The colonel also understood this was a method to buy time in order to digest what had to be a shocking bit of news. "Major, I have sufficient force to hold this area. I won't go into any more detail than that. I know General Lynch. We served together in the 101st some years ago. I suggest you radio and apprise him of the situation. I'll be happy to wait right here, but before you go, I want to make it perfectly clear. I will fight to hold this area. I will fight anyone who tries to take it from me. Think about that for a minute before you talk to the good general. Think about what that means."

The colonel's last words were like a slap in the face to Major Owens. While he had been standing straight with his shoulders squared, those words caused him to become even more rigid. Without thinking or proper military protocol, the words "civil war" escaped from his mouth.

The major spun on his heels and started walking back to his tank when the colonel's voice called out, "Major, one more thing – you and the Cav would be welcome to join us if you are willing to swear allegiance to the Independents. I would be honored to sit and brief you on that option if you are willing. I didn't make my decision without good reason, and neither did my men."

The major paused at the colonel's last statement, but continued back to his tank without comment. In truth, he didn't want to chance the senior officer seeing the fear and bewilderment he was feeling. He ignored the small group of men standing around the two large green battle machines and strode with purpose directly to his tank. As he started to gracefully climb aboard, he yelled out, "Ironhorse - Mount up!"

As he shimmied his way into the turret, he looked up to see the colonel standing beside his Stryker and started to salute out of habit. He paused, unsure if he still had to do so, or even wanted to do so. The colonel made up his mind for him as the senior officer threw a crisp right hand and held it. The major returned the salute, and then both men proceeded to issue orders to the men under their commands.

Major Owens keyed his radio and ordered his driver to return to their lead units a few miles behind them. As the tank began to spin around, he noticed a full infantry squad rise up from the surrounding forest and hustle back toward the colonel's Stryker. *The man had deployed security for the meeting. He is clearly serious.*

Ten minutes later, Major Owens reached for the volume knob on his radio just a wee bit too late as General Lynch's voiced boomed in his ear, "HE SAID WHAT? ARE YOU FUCKING WITH ME, MAJOR?" Owens didn't immediately respond, and in a few seconds, his CO continued, "What a damn mess. Give me your coordinates. I'll be on a bird in five minutes. I want to talk to Colonel Marcus personally. He is clearly out of his fucking mind."

Private First Class Raymond Pilowski was scared. The 4/10 was his first unit after finishing Advanced Individual Training (AIT), and he had received orders to report to Fort Polk only two days before the collapse had begun. His squad leader was suffering badly from a stomach virus and was making what seemed like the 20th trip into the bushes due to cramps.

The squad was deployed in a forward position less than a kilometer away from the location the first powwow had occurred. They had received a very specific briefing before moving to this position, and that "pep talk" had made it absolutely clear that they should all expect to die today. If that hadn't been bad enough, less than 20 minutes ago, an M1A2 tank had pulled up to a position not more than 300 meters in front of them. The tank wasn't one of the 4/10s'. Private Pilowski knew the capabilities of that beast, and he envisioned himself while carrying his M4 carbine as a modern day David facing Goliath.

Before this last mad dash to relieve himself, the sergeant had looked around and pointed at Pilowski, motioning him to man the shoulder-fired Stinger anti-aircraft missile he was holding. Private Pilowski had never held a real Stinger. He had received 20 minutes of training on the weapon during AIT, but that was an inactive mockup, not the real thing. He hoped the sergeant wouldn't take too long.

The distant sound of a helicopter's blades, chopping through the air, filled Pilowski's ears and diverted his attention back toward the tank in front of him. About the only thing that frightened the private more than the tank was an attack helicopter. If the Abrams tank was an infantryman's bad dream, the Apache gunship was his blood-curdling nightmare.

Major Owens wanted to meet his commander away from the main column of troops. This entire situation was unprecedented, and he really didn't know what to expect. After his conversation with General Lynch ended, he had ordered his driver to proceed a kilometer north of I-20 to the spot his map indicated to be a small regional airport. The major figured the small facility would provide plenty of room for the general's bird to land, and the two men could meet in relative privacy there.

Owens was leery, knowing that a potential hostile force was close by. When his tank approached the cluster of hangars and buildings, he ordered a halt in a wooded area, bordering the facility. They would wait here until the general arrived. Owens had no clue that he was parked so close to one of the 4/10's forward observation posts, and that his tank was causing Private Pilowski such concern. The command net radio sounded in his ear, informing him that the general's Blackhawk was five minutes out.

The major waited a few minutes, and then ordered the accompanying Humvee to move onto the tarmac and pop smoke. The sound of the Blackhawk could now be heard over the tank's idling turbine motor. Before it came into view, "popping white smoke," was announced over the radio, and Owens watched the small canister arch away from the Humvee and bounce across the pavement. This was standard procedure as it lessened any chance for misidentification and also gave the pilot some indication of the wind speed and direction in the landing zone. Almost immediately, an artificial cloud of billowing white began covering the area, a few wisps rising skyward. A short time later, a single helicopter appeared over the tree line, heading directly toward the airport.

Private Pilowski's angle allowed him to see the approaching "enemy helicopter," long before any of the soldiers meeting the aircraft. His vantage point blocked both the Humvee and the upwardly rising smoke from view. To the worried young solider, it looked like the damned thing was pointed right at him. When the craft flared its nose upwards during its landing approach, the inexperienced private thought the pilot was aiming for him, and that made his heart stop. Some of the smoke grenade's cloud was caught in the hovering bird's updraft appearing as small whiffs of white smoke directly underneath the skids. That convinced the now breathless private that rockets had been fired – at him.

Private Pilowski's training, all be it short, was effective. His fingers disengaged the safety from the Stinger's main body, squeezed the trigger to stage one, and watched the display until it read "locked." He pulled the trigger further back and heard the sizzle as the rocket's motor ignited. What he didn't hear was his squad leader screaming at the top of his lungs to "STOP!"

The Stinger's small, two-pound warhead exited the launcher tube, propelled by a 70mm rocket motor. The missile had traveled only a short distance from the launcher when Pilowski's squad leader tackled him, knocking both the young soldier and the now spent launcher to the ground a second too late. True to its specifications, the Stinger was a "fire and forget weapon," and the entire squad watched in horror as the missile wobbled just a little and then accelerated quickly toward the landing helicopter.

Movement to his right caught Major Owens' eye, and he snapped his head around just as the Stinger reached a speed that made it invisible to the naked eye. The first thought that went through his mind was, *"That looked like a missile plume."* Just as the thought registered, the general's helicopter erupted in a brilliant white ball of light. The spinning rotors were moving at almost full speed as the fuselage turned into a boiling cloud of red and orange fire and veered sharply right. What remained of the craft slammed into the ground, spreading even more flame and destruction.

The major stared without comment for almost a full two seconds before uttering a weak, almost undetectable, "Holy shit." By the time the helicopter's momentum had bled off, there was nothing left but a smoldering trail of burning scrap, scattered for almost two hundred meters across the concrete. It was inconceivable that anyone could have survived the wreck.

Fitz was in the turret watching the helicopter's approach and was initially confused when the Stinger launched from near his position. His first instinct had been to fire up his engine and move to render assistance to the crashed copter, but he quickly changed his mind once he saw the huge yellowish ball of flame rise over the treetops. *Nobody walked away from that*, he thought. The sergeant did maintain the presence of mind to switch his radio to the command net and report both the missile launch and a single downed Blackhawk.

The resulting fireball drew the attention of several people, and radios sprang to life up and down both lines. It took the officers almost a full minute to calm everyone down. In that time, Major Owens went from surprise to shock to outright boiling anger. His gunner was now scanning the area where he thought he had seen a missile plume and sure enough, there were human heat signatures all over the place. *So that's how it's going to be, Colonel? So that's how your 'Independents' are going to fight?*

It suddenly dawned on Owens that whoever had just fired a missile at the general's bird might have anti-tank missiles as well. They might be locking onto him at this very moment. He screamed an order for his driver to move and for his gunner to load HEAT, or a high explosive shell, into the tank's main gun. As the enormous machine lurched forward, it accelerated more like a sports car than a 135,000-pound instrument of destruction. In a few moments, Owens heard the status word of "Up," from his gunner, and he ordered him to fire into the middle of the soldiers he knew had just killed his commanding general.

The M1 tank's smooth, bore cannon let loose with its deadly ordnance, generating a sound so loud it could crush unprotected ear bones from several hundred feet away. A ball of fire some 30 feet in diameter spread out in front of the tank, announcing the shot to anyone looking from afar. The air pressure generated by the passing shell's wake parted and sliced the damp earth beneath it, throwing up a cloud of mud and spray for almost 100 feet, and leaving a furrow plowed through the soft earth.

The accuracy of the German-designed gun was legendary, as were the skills of the crews who controlled them. Hundreds of Iraqi armored vehicles had fallen prey to the smooth bore cannon during the First Gulf War, many at distances that were almost unbelievable. Abrams simply didn't miss, and the first tank shot of the Second American Civil War was no exception. The round exploded right next to Private Pilowski's position, sending white-hot shrapnel ripping through the air in all directions. The army of the Independents experienced its first two casualties from that shell. Private Pilowski was KIA, as was his squad leader.

Major Owens was issuing commands as fast as he could think. His first action was to order additional units to his location as his tank rolled for cover behind a hangar. The second set of commands was to get the Cav transformed from a convoy into a battle formation. Within minutes, the long, single file line of armor was realigning itself into a three-pronged pitchfork, aimed directly at the 4/10. The closest platoon to the airport reacted immediately and began rolling hard to reinforce the brigade commander's position. Four Abrams, accompanied by six other vehicles, were moving at top speed from their location less than a kilometer away. Weapon systems were being booted, and breaches charged on both sides. The flash of flame in the sky rendered the warnings and orders issued over the radios redundant.

Fitz saw the explosion right where one of his recon teams was positioned, instantly understanding the relationship between the Stinger launch and the return fire. He quickly switched the TOW missile launcher to active mode and unnecessarily ordered everyone to full alert. The attacking tank was nowhere to be seen, and the only evidence of what had just occurred was the pillar of black smoke still billowing off of the downed Blackhawk.

Everything had been quiet for almost two minutes when Fitz's radio crackled with the news from his scout teams. They heard engine noises, including the unmistakable whine of several Abrams tanks. The sounds were moving toward their position and doing so at high speed.

Fitz's Stryker was equipped with the TOW-2 missile system, but not all of the units in the 4/10 were the same. Some were equipped with cannons and targeting systems, similar to that mounted on the Abrams tanks they faced. While the Strykers didn't have the protective armor of the big tanks, they could still deliver a punch. Fitz switched frequencies, reported the new contacts, and then began asking for help.

Major Owens was relieved when his second platoon reached his area and would soon be joined by the rest of the Ironhorse's command platoon. He decided to make the airport his command post. He watched with pride as the 2nd platoon's vehicles executed a perfect maneuver and took up defensive positions bordering the airfield. The back door of each Bradley lowered, and infantry began hustling out the troop carriers to clear the surrounding area of any threats. One of these squads moved directly toward Fitz's recon teams, and only a few minutes later small arms fire erupted to the east.

Fitz could see the thermal signatures of several vehicles clearly now and was trying to remain calm on the radio as he reported his observations. It was a difficult task. From his perspective, the entire 1st Cavalry Division was marshaling just a kilometer away, and he was urgently begging for either permission to withdraw or reinforcements to hold his position. He had just received word to expect two other units from his platoon to be moving on his position when the distant popping noises of M4 rifles reached his ear and reports of "Contact! Contact! Contact!" filled the airwaves on both sides. When a crew-served .50 caliber machine gun opened up, it became clear to everyone that the battle was joined.

It was about then that Fitz could make out two targets; one was clearly a tank moving to support the enemy's infantry. His fingers were shaking as he pushed the appropriate button and flipped the right switches to fully arm the TOW launcher. He muttered "God forgive me," as the first missile hissed and soared from the launcher. It was quickly followed by a second launch, and both warheads tracked perfectly to their targets.

The sound of the first Bradley being struck by Fitz's missile echoed across the rural Louisiana landscape. The missile hit the lightly protected vehicle at a slightly downward angle, and the cone shaped charge pierced the armor with a stream of molten metal moving at over 10,000 feet per second. Designed to kill heavily armored Soviet era tanks, the thin skin of the Bradley didn't stand a chance. Fortunately, the infantry had already dismounted from the carrier, but the crew was killed instantly. While it appeared as a single explosion, in reality there were two separate events – the missile striking the vehicle and the secondary blast caused by all the ammo and fuel igniting from the 4,000-degree heat. Pieces of the dead machine weighing several hundred pounds were thrown into the air like confetti and had just begun the descent back to earth when the second missile struck a nearby Abrams tank.

The M1A2 tank was better suited to handle the TOW's wrath. Its armor was not only thicker, but of a superior design. The missile's warhead struck just behind the turret above the engine compartment. The explosion generated a jet of liquefied metal that destroyed the tank's power plant and rendered the turret inoperable. The tank's commander was killed instantly, but the rest of the crew survived with only busted eardrums and some severe burns.

The commander of the remaining Bradley witnessed his two sister units destroyed in a matter of seconds, and had a general idea of where the missiles had been fired. He motored his 25mm cannon around and sprayed rounds into the area where he thought the attackers were hiding. At the same time, he fired several smoke grenades from the four-barrel launcher and screamed at his gunner to find a target for the TOW missiles. He eventually ordered the driver to withdraw from what he thought was the kill zone of an ambush, and prayed the smoke would help cover his movement.

Major Owens had been looking directly at the tank when it was struck. He was stunned for a moment at how quickly the fight was escalating, but shook it off, and ordered additional units to join him. He surmised that he had somehow bumbled into the primary force opposing him and was going to make them pay for the cowardly ambush of both his CO and his men.

Colonel Marcus listened to the avalanche of reports being broadcast over the command net. While several observation posts reported sporadic movements, it was clear that the serious action was concentrated at one point along his front. Marcus heard confused reports of a helo being shot down and was yet unaware that the U.S. Army had just lost its first general officer in combat since WWII. He had no way of knowing the impact of that act, nor did he realize that his counterpart witnessed the event. What he did know is that a force-on-force skirmish was taking place, and he still believed a large-scale battle could still be avoided if he could send a strong message to the young major he had just met. The message must convey that the Cav was up against a capable foe that had no reservation about fighting. He hoped calmer heads would prevail, and the act might get the higher ups on both sides talking.

Marcus decided to reposition some of his forces and focus them on the hotspot. He looked up from his map and then stabbed his finger onto the paper while looking around at his gathered staff. "Right there gentlemen...right there is where this is all going to go down. Let's send the Cav a message. I want our combat power concentrated in this section. Anything not absolutely necessary to cover our flanks should be busting ass to this position immediately. Any questions?"

The huddled group of officers and NCOs all peered at the spot marked by the colonel's finger. Notes were scribbled and radio commands began flowing to the field. No one had any questions.

In the history of warfare, it's not uncommon for a specific location to become the center of a battle. Often, there is a logical reason why some feature of the terrain or its tactical value results in men dying by the thousands over a relatively small, otherwise insignificant, piece of ground. During WWII, the small town of Bastogne was such a place, with its intersection of roadways being of importance to both sides. During the battle of Gettysburg, a strategic rise called Cemetery Ridge was another such example, where thousands of men died while fighting over a 40-foot high track of elevated ground.

Other instances have puzzled historians, unable to explain why a certain aspect of some location caused it to become a fulcrum of death and destruction. Hill 875 during the Vietnam War is one such occurrence, with Hitler's fixation on Stalingrad during WWII being another. The history of conflict is rife with examples of commanders' illogical, relentless pursuit of some piece of real estate that held little or no long-term strategic value. Perhaps some of those instances were the result of quantum physics or random chaotic circumstance. Maybe others were due to some sort of weird, armor-sized type of molecular cohesion. Regardless of the cause, on this day in 2015 the area around Scott's Farm and Dairy, eventually known simply as Scott's Farm, would achieve such infamy. If the history of battles were ever to be documented again, the clash at Shreveport would become known as the Battle of Scott's Hill.

Fitz's radio informed him that two friendly Strykers were approaching his rear, and he provided their commanders instructions on where they were needed. One of the new units was a MGS, or mobile gun system variant. This unusual-looking machine had a slightly smaller version of a tank turret sitting on top of the eight-wheeled chassis. The MGS used the same basic aiming technologies as the Abrams tank and was the newest member of the Stryker family. While the MGS could shoot with any tank within a certain range, it was still equipped with the same thin armor as the other Stryker models.

Just as those fresh units were taking up positions, four of the Independents' tanks were arriving as well. Colonel Marcus had won the battle-within-a-battle, managing to reinforce his position first. It was a critical turning point in the engagement.

~ ~

Major Owens was trying desperately to gather his forces in order to apply one of the cardinal rules of American military doctrine – strike at the enemy with overwhelming force. The problem was that his assets had started the fight while spread in a column formation, and it was taking them far too long to regroup for an attack. He was trying to marshal his forces in a field just south of the airport where the wreckage of the general's helicopter still burned.

While the Ironhorse's armor may have withdrawn from the first clash, two of her scout snipers had remained in hidden positions where they could see Scott's Hill. When one of the snipers reported he saw tanks approaching, Owens' skin turned cold, and his mind raced with unanswered questions. *Tanks? The 10th didn't have tanks. Whose tanks were those?*

Reports were now coming in from both of the snipers; the 10th was reinforcing the area directly east of his position, and the major's confidence waned ever so slightly. Suddenly, he wondered if his counterpart was gathering *his* assets faster than the Ironhorse could get on line. Perhaps *the Cav* was about to be hit with overwhelming force?

The major made up his mind to strike with the limited assets currently available to him, rather than wait for the rest of the brigade to form up. He issued the orders, and immediately 9 tanks and 14 Bradleys pulled out in formation, heading for the enemy.

Fitz held the high ground and saw the approaching tanks first. The Cav had learned its lesson from the first skirmish and was letting its heavy armor lead the charge. Fitz heard commands being issued by several friendly units to load SABOT, meaning they were loading anti-tank rounds into their guns. Before Fitz could activate his TOW launcher, the Independent's cannons cut lose with their deadly fire. A hail of TOW missile plumes followed close behind, their warheads seeking 1st Cavalry armor.

Fitz watched as one shot hit the lead tank dead center, but just a little low. The round blew the tread from its guides, and the tank momentarily swerved sharply to the left, and then lurched to a halt. The chassis still rocked from the sudden stop, when a TOW missile struck, causing the disabled tank to disappear in an enormous flash and explosion.

Along a half-kilometer line, the two titans clashed. While the 4/10 was outgunned and outnumbered, they held a superior position. Fitz's selection of the junkyard was both a tactical and strategic advantage. Many of the piles of metallic junk were burning, and that caused problems for the Cav's thermal sights. The slight elevation and cover provided by the piles of scrap iron gave the defenders just enough edge to equal the odds.

The Cav's attack was vicious and well executed. The lead tanks were manned by the most accurate gun crews, and their initial salvos destroyed several vehicles. The air was filled with the screaming sounds of high velocity projectiles, roaring missile motors, and the cries of dying men. It wasn't just a battle of armored machines. All throughout the area, dismounted infantry joined the fray. A few of the Independent's men were equipped with the latest portable missile system, the Javelin. The two man crews carrying these affective weapons would hide until an enemy tank came to within range and then quickly rise and fire. More than one of the Cav's battle machines died this way. Squad sized elements of infantry skirmished all along the line, maneuvering like pieces on a chess board and dying by the score in the process.

The Cav kept coming like waves of steel crashing against an iron beach. Fitz was waiting on his TOW launcher to be reloaded when his Stryker was hit. The SABOT round from an approaching tank destroyed his vehicle and killed one of the crew. Fitz was thrown 30 feet away by the blast, taking shrapnel in the leg and suffering a deep gash to the head. Two crewmen from a nearby unit dragged him to cover, where a medic was performing battlefield miracles in the midst of the mayhem. Fitz was triaged and deemed salvageable. He demanded the medic move on to men in worse shape. After wrapping his scalp enough times to keep the flow of blood out of his eyes, he limped to an open area and began directing arriving reinforcements to key positions. When a nearby Stryker's commander was shot out of the turret, Fitz climbed aboard and took command. He was an adrenaline charged warrior, motivated by anger and purpose. Gone was any sense of self-preservation or belief in any ideology. Fitz fought with desperate determination to hold his ground.

The reasons why men join in battle vary. A few do so for country and honor, while a small fraction risk it all because they consider it their job. The vast majority fight because of the brotherhood shared with fellow soldiers. When men see friends and comrades fall to the enemy, a powerful reaction often takes place. Rather than mourn or lose control to disabling emotions, they enter a state of mind where revenge, rage, and sense of purpose override any concerns of survival. For some, combat provides a catalyst to clarity they have never experienced before. Deep questions posed by every human are answered with amazing precision. Why am I on this earth? What is the purpose of my life? Can I make a difference? It all becomes clear in combat. Mental clutter is melted away and realization of core values emerges. Many times observers will note that a soldier performed with a "cool professionalism," or with "extreme courage" under fire. More often than not, the soldier is experiencing a single-minded transparency of purpose, and his brain is functioning at unprecedented levels. Most will never experience anything close to that state for the rest of their lives. Few can describe it, and none will ever forget it.

All around Scott's Hill, thousands of men were simultaneously experiencing that mental state. The United States Army was the most powerful in history. The high level of training, combined with state of the art equipment, enabled a level of violence here before unseen in warfare. The devastation experienced by both sides was well beyond anything in the long history of conflict. Despite the indescribable havoc and destruction, more and more men and material were thrown into the battle. As additional units arrived, they charged into what had essentially become a meat grinder, chewing up equipment and flesh. None of them hesitated or baulked. As men and machines moved forward into the fight, they passed the wounded being taken from the conflict. Many passed friends, or what some even considered family, being carried back from the inferno of destruction roaring just beyond. Witnessing their brothers in arms injured or dead only made them more determined.

Both commanders realized the battle taking place at the farm was depleting their units at an unsustainable pace. Both attempted every possible maneuver available to them. Left hooks, right hooks, feints, envelopment, and blocking were employed to various degrees when allowed by the fog of war. Most attempts were countered by equal application of maneuver or offset by circumstance. In the end, it all boiled down to a desperate fight for Scott's Hill.

The Cav actually pushed the 10th from the dairy on the third attempt. The unrelenting weight of the Ironhorse's superior firepower and armor had taken its toll on the 10th. Most approaches to the junkyard were now impassable, littered by burning hulks of armor and felled trees. Bark and wood was no match for modern weapons. Mature trunks were snapped off or splintered, and the woods around Scott's Hill looked as if a tornado had torn through the countryside. An infantry squad spotted an approach that was clear enough for the big armored machines to maneuver, and a squad of four tanks charged at the weakened defenders on the hill.

There were only three functional Strykers left in the junkyard. When one of these exploded from an incoming round, Fitz couldn't see any alternative but to order a retreat, and told his driver to get the hell out of there. As the defenders gave ground, Major Owens felt a small sense of relief that his forces were finally moving forward. He would hold the high ground in just a few minutes.

Fitz retreated behind a small mound 400 meters away from Scott's Hill. He was waiting on orders when the last two tanks belonging to the 10th pulled up to his position. They were quickly joined by another Stryker with a fully loaded TOW launcher. After a few moments of radio confusion, it was clear Fitz was senior and in command. Colonel Marcus's voice sounded through Fitz's ear – take that hill back at all costs. After a quick agreement on formation, Fitz's retreat turned into a counter-attack.

Major Owens was approaching Scott's Hill after his platoon reported they had finally taken the junkyard. He wanted to regroup any forces he had left and decided the small rise would be the best rally point. As his tank was approaching, explosions began erupting all around him. The enemy was counterattacking.

Fitz's patchwork of armor charged at the hilltop with guns blazing and missiles launching. A couple of thrown-together infantry platoons engaged from the south and immediately ran into a group of the Cav's troopers trying to rally with the tanks. The men of the Cav couldn't determine the strength of the counteroffensive, and confusion ensured. Major Owens' tanks began withdrawing from the hilltop they had just occupied and paid so dearly for.

Something snapped in the major's mind. They had sacrificed so much to take this damned hill, and he wasn't going to just give it back. He started screaming commands on the net, demanding his troopers hold that ground. He ordered his driver to tear ass up there and "get this fucking tank into the fight."

Owens' gunner spotted a Stryker moving at an intersecting angle. The turret of the major's tank spun toward the target, and the computer's aiming program kicked in, efficiently pointing the deadly gun at Fitz's charging Stryker.

Fitz saw another fucking tank approaching the junkyard. He armed and locked on with a TOW, hitting the launch button just before the target's main gun belched with a cloud of fire and smoke.

Both vehicles were destroyed, killing all aboard. The Cav lost Major Owens, and his death caused confusion. With their commander dead, the two remaining tanks belonging to the Cav began backing down the hill. The loss of Fitz didn't immediately impact the counterattack by the 10th. Momentum was on their side, and when the shooting stopped, one Abrams and one Stryker made it to the junkyard. The 4th Brigade Combat Team, 10th Mountain Division, held Scott's Hill.

Suddenly, as if a switch had been pulled, everyone stopped shooting. The air was still polluted with an assortment of foreign sounds - the roaring flames of burning vehicles… the suffering of wounded men…. But this was practically silence, when compared to the orchestra of death booming only a short time before.

While the men of the 10th still held the junkyard, in reality, the Cav had the better day. Colonel Marcus' Independents suffered 80% losses - the 4-10 was no longer a combat effective unit. The Cav ended the battle with 40% losses, including their commanding officer and a significant number of his junior. Both sides ended the fight thinking they had suffered the worst of it.

A kind of unofficial truce ensued on the battlefield surrounding Scott's Hill. Teams of medics searched for injured survivors from both sides, often in plain sight of each other. The carnage was so prolific that neither side had the energy or motivation to start shooting at the other. The counting of causalities and the tending to the wounded became the mission, and that would continue for hours.

Both the Independents and the Loyalists believed they had lost. Both of their radio networks were filled with desperate requests for reinforcements. In New Orleans and Beaumont, the Independents had organized several brigades. Orders went out for these sizable forces to immediately proceed to Shreveport and relieve the 4/10.

The Cav was about to receive help as well. Thousands of men and hundreds of armored vehicles had been on the move before the beginning of the battle. Most were on their way to one city or another as part of the president's Operation Heartland plan. When news of the battle reached the Commander in Chief, many of these units were diverted to Shreveport with orders to bust ass, and save what was left of the Ironhorse.

For five hundred miles in every direction, units from both sides were converging on Scott's Hill, now commonly referred to as, "Scott's Hell."

Many Christians believe the battle of Armageddon is to occur on the Plains of Megiddo in the Middle East. Those who understood what was materializing in rural Louisiana wondered if Biblical scholars, interpreting Revelations, had gotten the location wrong.

Chapter 10

Unintended Consequences

Senator Moreland sat with head down, elbows braced on his knees, and face in his hands. The basement of his West Virginia mountain retreat more closely resembled a war room than the 1950's pool hall it had been decorated to mimic. Two general officers, both formally members of the Joint Chiefs of Staff, had joined the normal administrative staff running the Independents' daily affairs. Both of the senior officers had brought along several staff members. All of them proudly wore uniforms of the United States armed forces.

The satellite phones being used by their organization could transfer data as well as voice. Both modes were delivering bad news. All around the basement, laptop computers clicked and flashed as various staff members updated reports, issued orders, and checked on progress. It had been difficult enough for the small group of staffers to handle running their part of the country before conflict. Now that a war was on, it was complete bedlam.

As the number of dead and wounded from the Mississippi Delta region increased, it became clear to everyone that a civil war had truly begun. The battle at Shreveport was the worst, but skirmishes had occurred all up and down the great river that day. In a few hours, the Independents had lost over 6,000 men, many dead and many more critically wounded. Enemy causalities were estimated to be nearly as high.

The senator lifted his head and stared off into space, speaking to no one in particular. "How did this happen? How did this escalate so quickly?"

One of the nearby generals shook his head in disgust. "Senator, it was inevitable. The frustration level of the average soldier on both sides is very high. We have thousands of armed men moving about the country in the same general area. Anyone who thought they wouldn't fire on each other because they were 'fellow Americans' never studied the civil war."

The honorable gentleman nodded his head in understanding. He had expected some minor skirmishes, but not pitched battles. He stood and rotated his neck in small circles trying to work some of the stress out of his muscles. Movement in the center of the room drew his attention, and he strode toward the pool table. There, a large map of the central United States had been spread out over the green felt surface. Someone had procured a few bags of green and white plastic toy soldiers and tanks. These were being moved around on the map to indicate the positions of military units. The senator had heard the officers refer to his pool table as the "sand table." Each plastic toy had been fitted with a toothpick and a small piece of white tape. The unit's designation had been written in neat text on the tape.

Even to someone without military training, it was clear that lines were being drawn. Both sides had recovered from the initial clash and were repositioning to fight again. The senator knew he couldn't stop now, as they were committed. He turned away from the depiction of the looming conflict and shuffled to the stairs leading upward to the main level of the house. As he left the basement, his mind raced with everything he knew about the president and his advisors. Every meeting, political event, speech and even the man's personal preferences was analyzed for the nth time, trying to guess the opponent's next move. Senator Moreland knew he couldn't contribute much to the military side of the equation. His expertise was the political aspect of the situation, and he was desperately trying to predict how the president would react to recent events.

He was met at the top of the stairs by his long trusted aide and friend. "Wayne, I'm afraid our worst fears have been realized in northern Louisiana. A battle has been fought, and thousands of young men are dead."

Wayne looked at the senator long enough to judge how his friend was handling the news. After assuring himself the senator was okay, he looked down and said, "God rest their souls. God be with their loved ones."

The two men walked silently to the mansion's parlor. The room was actually small for a home of this size, and rarely were guests allowed to enter. It had become the senator's private retreat since the fall of the government, and his home becoming a substitute capital.

Wayne immediately knew where his boss was headed and accelerated the last few steps to get the door. After his boss entered, he quickly closed it behind him and threw the lock. Without hesitation, Wayne crossed to a small serving cart and quickly poured two glasses of brandy.

The head of the Independents nodded his gratitude and sipped the warming liquid. Wayne lifted the small glass to his lips, sampled the contents, and then exhaled a sigh of refreshment. "Sir, you knew this was a possibility. I know that doesn't help much right now, but we all knew. Tell me, where do we stand?"

Senator Moreland didn't answer immediately. He took another sip from his glass and stared at the rows of leather-bound books lining one wall of the room. He had always enjoyed their smell more than the contents. Many of his colleagues on Capitol Hill were surprised to find out that he preferred an e-reader electron table to the traditional bound volumes. "Just because I'm old doesn't mean I'm old-fashioned," he had told them.

After a short pause, he returned Wayne's gaze and answered the question. "We still hold the ground around Shreveport, but I don't know for how long. Only twenty percent of the military has joined us, and we seem badly outnumbered."

Wayne nodded his understanding. While the number of officers and men joining the Independents had been gradually increasing since they had started recruiting from the military, the overall percentage was still small. It took time to convince men to do something as drastic as switch allegiances, especially during troubled times. This topic had been thoroughly discussed by the leadership during the past few weeks. The consensus had been that the intelligence gathered from their network of spies would offset their overall lack of numbers. The Independents knew what the president and his staff were doing before most of his military commanders did. Almost every remaining government organization had people inside who were loyal to the Independents. Radio operators, clerks, managers and even the heads of some agencies had pledged their allegiance some time ago, and provided a constant flow of information. Every military commander knew that information was a very powerful weapon.

Senator Moreland looked at his old friend and trusted advisor with a scowl on his face. "I never thought this would escalate so quickly. I miscalculated their response. We can't make the same mistake again. The president is on his way to Fort Bliss, and I have to wonder if there isn't more to that trip than an effort to boost morale."

Wayne pondered the senator's thought for a bit. "Our sources are not that close to their inner-circle, sir. There's no way to know that. You're not considering that other option, are you?"

Wayne was referring to a proposal that had been floated soon after the president's trip had been verified. The Independents had a significant number of men stationed at Fort Bliss. Originally assigned to slowly recruit new converts, they were to otherwise conduct themselves as normal and remain quietly embedded in the ranks. One of the military commanders had suggested that the men stationed at Fort Bliss could all but insure the Independents' success if they were to "chop off the head of the snake," or in other words, assassinate the President of the United States.

Senator Moreland and some senior members of the Independents had rejected the plan outright. Moreland's primary justification was an innate dislike of subterfuge. The senator believed the movement tainted its legitimacy by even considering such activities. To his surprise, several of the senior members disagreed with him. Their position in the debate focused on saving lives and rebuilding the country as soon as possible. If an end to the American people's suffering could be accelerated by skullduggery, so be it.

By the end of the meeting, Moreland had to admit the point was valid. A vote was taken, and the coup attempt lost – but just barely.

Moreland looked at Wayne and retorted, "My vote isn't the final say of this organization, my old friend. Our direction is determined by majority ballot. I must tell you though, we are going to have another meeting tonight, and after the battle in Louisiana, I'm afraid that plan will be revisited and approved."

"Senator, you are too humble. Your voice carries a lot of weight with the council. If you argue against assassination, it won't happen."

Moreland nodded his understanding of Wayne's point. After smiling at his aide, the senator finished his brandy and stared at the empty glass in his hand. "I'm not sure I want to argue against that plan, Wayne. I'm not so sure at all."

~ ~

Colonel Marcus was running on pure adrenaline. He had moved his field command to the outskirts of Shreveport in order to be close to the makeshift field hospital. The facility had been hastily set up in a middle school gymnasium. Even after 15 years of warfare in the Middle East, the colonel was shocked at the carnage. He remembered being briefed before the First Gulf War on the anticipated causalities. He had been a young shave-tail lieutenant then and had sat wide-eyed when shown slides detailing the tons of medical equipment being stationed behind the Saudi/Iraq border. That war followed a very different track, and those medical supplies had, for the most part, been shipped home. He would give anything for even a small portion of that cache now.

Marcus was visiting the wounded troops from both sides. The gym was lined with row after row of cots filled with burned, wounded, or dying men. Poles with bags of fluid and dangling tube stood like sentries next to dozens of cots. Large plastic bags, overflowing with bloody bandages, scraps of uniforms and medical wrappers were scattered throughout the area. Men and women moved hastily back and forth carrying blankets, syringes, medications, and all too often – body bags. Several nearby classrooms were now makeshift morgues, and they were almost full. Medical personnel, chaplains, and enlisted men hurried from one man to another, trying to do the best possible humanitarian work. Marcus was thankful when two civilian doctors from Shreveport had heard the battle and shown up to help.

He had already given blood twice and had organized shifts so the 4/10's remaining men could get a little down time and donate too. The school's cafeteria had been converted into an operating room. As he walked past, he noticed groups of exhausted doctors and nurses standing in small groups or sitting with head in hands. Many of the operating room personnel wore sky blue masks over their faces, but Marcus could tell from the body language they were wearing thin. Outside the operating room, scores of litters lined both sides of the long hallway – men being triaged and waiting for their turn in surgery. Two nurses moved from man to man, and Marcus watched as they covered one soldier's face with a sheet. *Another one that didn't make it to surgery.*

As he walked outside, several of his junior officers huddled in a small group waiting on him. He appreciated the show of respect they had afforded by not interrupting his visit to the hospital. Even now, they held their ground and waited for their commander to approach. The 4/10 had been shredded as a unit. Most military experts agreed that any single organization should be considered "combat ineffective" after 30% losses. The 4/10 had suffered 70% killed or wounded. The percentage of vehicles destroyed or unserviceable was even greater. Still, the 4/10 had held against a superior force. That fact gave the colonel little consolation at this point. He had watched his command be torn apart in less than three hours, and holding the field at the end of the battle didn't seem to mean that much right now.

Regardless, he considered himself a professional soldier and would carry on. The Independents had been marshaling a significant number of assets in New Orleans over the last few months. Originally comprised of small units that had joined the cause one or two at a time, the officers there had been working hard to organize and integrate these elements into a large, effective fighting force. According to the reports given to the colonel, the interstate between Shreveport and New Orleans was filled with military vehicles heading north to join what was left of the 10th Mountain's brigade.

The first convoy of reinforcements had arrived a few hours ago, and every few minutes it seemed like another line of tanks, trucks, or personal carriers pulled up. School busses by the hundreds drove in, each discharging about 50 combat troops and their gear. The ruling council of the Independents had decided to leave Marcus in charge. That vote of confidence wasn't important to him right now. His immediate priority was to integrate the newly arriving assets and position them as best he could. It was no secret that the other side was regrouping and being reinforced as well.

As he walked away from the medical facility, his officers gathered around him and politely took turns delivering the latest status reports and asking for orders. Marcus made his decisions quickly and without hesitation. By the time he reached his command post, all but of few of his officers had received their orders and peeled off from the group to execute them.

The colonel was handed yet another cup of coffee by someone, and without even thinking, held it up to his lips. He strode purposefully over to a makeshift table, constructed from two sawhorses and a piece of plywood. Spread out on the surface was a large map of the immediate area. After carefully glancing at the position of the newly arriving units, he couldn't help himself and let out a long whistle.

Laid out before him was a force almost three times the size of the 4/10. He now had over 30 M1 tanks on the line and more arriving every hour. There were at least 100 additional armored vehicles in the area and over 10,000 infantry. That number was expected to double by morning.

Marcus shook his head and looked around at the countryside and thought, *Why here?* If the Cav were receiving even half of the assets he was, the next clash would result in tens of thousands dead. At some level, it didn't make any sense to the colonel. If this fight was taking place near Washington D.C. or a major city, then it might seem justified. There was nothing of critical strategic value here except the approach to a few nuclear power plants and a big muddy river some miles away. Still, he was a professional and in command. He took another sip of his coffee and turned to find an aide. He wanted to check on the pre-positioning of ammunition.

Chapter 11

Feint Accompoli

Bishop awoke about an hour before sunset. He was both concerned and curious about the noise, lights and booby-trap encountered the night before. After making a quick breakfast, he organized his gear and cleaned up his bivouac. Just as the ambient light was fading in the west, he began to climb up the ridge that had been the scene of the previous night's encounter. He wanted to scout the area in the natural light as much as possible and be in a secure position as darkness closed in.

After carefully following the same path as the night before, Bishop found the new trip line. He was tempted to peek over the ridge more than once, but decided it was too risky, and resisted his curious nature until the light completely faded. It would be a while before the moon rose, and that helped his cause even more.

He was about to move toward the ridge when the sound of an internal combustion engine floated across the rocks, and electric lights began producing an eerie glow over the surrounding area. Whatever was on the other side of that ridge was now in business, and Bishop moved carefully to see what all the fuss was about.

After eventually finding a good vantage to peep over the crest, he froze for several seconds, taking in the sights below. There was an immense building that would have covered several football fields spread across the desert floor. The entire length of one side consisted of massive, elevated doors - the kind used to unload semi-tractor trailers. Several of the bays were occupied by trailers, still backed up to the warehouse, no doubt to have cargo loaded or unloaded.

To the rear of the giant structure was a paved parking area capable of holding at least 50 semi-trucks. Twenty or more of the big rigs sat there now.

Surrounding the building and parking area was a 10-foot high fence with serious-looking strands of razor wire, angled outward along the top. The lights Bishop had been seeing were mounted on high posts in the enclosure every so often, as well as at each corner of the building. The entire grounds of the structure were very well lit, as was several hundred yards of the surrounding desert.

Bishop's gaze finally made its way to the parking lot in the front of the complex, and what he saw there was really out of place. There were at least 50 vehicles parked around what appeared to be the main entrance. Well over half of them were police cars. Bishop used his magnified optic to scan the different cruisers and saw the emblems of at least five different law enforcement agencies, a few associated with the state of Texas, and a few others from nearby towns. There was even a SWAT van parked near the back of the lot.

While he was trying to figure it all out, movement caught his eye, and he adjusted his rifle for a view of the roof of the giant structure. There, concealed behind sandbagged emplacements at each corner, were two-man teams with long rifles and some serious-looking scopes. These over watch positions were well hidden by the back glow of the bright spotlights mounted on the building just below them.

Before he even finished looking at those locations, more movement directed his attention to two men exiting a side door. These two fellows were wearing motorcycle helmets and mounted a pair of all-terrain vehicles parked nearby. After a couple of quick kicks to the starter, a mobile patrol headed toward the west. Both men had AR15 rifles strapped to their backs.

As Bishop's eyes followed the riders, his scope scanned past a large sign that had escaped notice until now. He immediately recognized the familiar branding on the sign, solving a large piece of the puzzle before him. The words confirmed his conclusion, reading "Wal-Mart Regional Distribution Center."

Bishop slowly lowered his rifle and moved a few feet back down the ridge. He needed time to digest it all. He pulled out a small notebook and began drawing diagrams of what he had just seen. The exercise helped him commit detail to memory and to work through what it all meant. His neurons were firing in all directions, in an attempt to wrap his head around the unbelievable scale of the treasure trove of food, medicine, fuel, water, and other miscellaneous necessities located on just the other side of the ridge. As he sat drawing, he began doing a mental, virtual tour of his last visit to the big department store before the collapse. It had aisle after aisle of groceries and almost as many freezers. A large distribution center like the one below would have enough stock to supply several of those individual stores.

Bishop remembered walking by entire sections of clothing, furniture, and electronics. When his mind wandered to the pharmacy section, he subconsciously scratched his head, thinking about the rows and rows of shampoo that had been stocked. *I bet they have my brand of toothpaste*, he thought.

As he recalled, the sporting goods section had been just a few aisles over, and the thought of those large glass cases of ammunition made him smile. At the time, he had smirked at the quality and prices. He wouldn't now.

There had to be enough goods in that building to keep an entire town the size of Meraton supplied for months. Just one of those semi-trailers carried tons of food that would enable hundreds of people to gorge themselves for days.

The complex was a natural fortress. No doubt, the designers and architects had chosen the location to service as many stores as possible. Bishop envisioned a map in some corporate office with pins depicting all of the stores in the region and this tract of secluded desert being right in the middle. Since it was so remote, security must have been a priority when the site was being designed. In addition to the fence, Bishop guessed the doors and structure were built with would-be burglars in mind. There was probably a sophisticated video system and perhaps even remote sensors built into the surrounding grounds or fence. During the last few years of the Second Great Depression, so much wealth concentrated into a single location would have been a target for thieves.

So what were all the cops doing there? Had some wise, quick-reacting county manager decided to seize the building in order to provide care for the citizens? Had some government agency taken control in order to distribute the goods to the people?

While the thought was a positive one, Bishop didn't think that was the case. If a government agency were truly in charge, the sentries would have the manpower and support to hold the building without early warning systems. Why the booby traps and trip wires then? If a local agency or officials had commandeered the compound, that might explain the situation – but why had they sent a team when Bishop tripped the flare? Why hadn't they identified themselves right away when they were looking for him?

The police cars explained why one man had called the other "Sarge" the previous night. They weren't military – it was a police sergeant. Why the heavily armed mobile patrol?

Bishop quickly realized he wasn't going to get any answers by sitting around daydreaming. He needed more information before he took his next step, and that meant observation. That also required being careful, as the SWAT truck indicated some high-tech sniper and surveillance capabilities might be searching for trespassers.

Sheriff Watts strolled through the hallway leading from the offices at the front of the building to the main storage facilities. His men had named their new home "Wallyworld," and that was good enough for him. He glanced at the pictures hanging from the walls, their perfectly even spacing agreeing with his general philosophy of an orderly existence. A dedicated officer of the law for most of his adult life, he had won the last three county elections unopposed. He was an honest man who performed the duties of his office with a fair hand and positive attitude. He had never taken a bribe or anything else that he hadn't earned – at least not until the events of the last few months.

When everything had started falling apart, things had changed. The deputies' paychecks bounced, leaving their children hungry and their families stressed. The mechanics who worked on his patrol cars refused to perform repairs, and the civilian staff that supported the jail started calling in sick. The lawman couldn't blame them – no matter how much folks believed in the importance of their jobs, they just couldn't afford to work without pay.

But that was just the beginning of his change of heart. Watching good, solid, law-abiding citizens he had known for years start fistfights at the local bank when it ran short of cash, degraded the sheriff's outlook on life. Having those same upstanding members of the community turn on his men when they attempted to calm the situation made things worse. He had personally served eviction papers on at least two dozen families in the last few months. Many of these people were friends he had known since elementary school. For three years, one of the families sat beside his in the reserved section of the Cougars' stadium, as they both cheered their sons to a state championship. He could have handled all of that in stride, but for one key event that pushed him to the other side of the law.

The sheriff's only son had joined the department a few short months before. An athletic, good-natured kid with sandy, blonde hair and a clear complexion, Deputy Watts was sort of a local celebrity, having been the star of the local high school football team. Unlike so many of the popular athletes of the day, Tony Watts Jr. didn't let his popularity go to his head. He was always polite to everyone around town and was never known to leverage his father's powerful position. He worked his way through college flipping burgers on the weekends and working construction in the summers. Having just graduated magna cum laude last June with a degree in Criminal Justice, Tony Jr. hoped to follow in his father's footsteps.

The Wal-Mart Distribution Center had been a welcome addition to the area when it had been erected four years ago. At least it had been welcomed by everyone but Sheriff Watts. Since its grand opening, the huge complex had been nothing but trouble for his force and him. The additional truck traffic had led to a host of issues. In addition, the center had been the site of several burglary attempts and random vandalism. While the issues caused by the facility would hardly be noticed in many areas, Sheriff Watts presided over a very quiet county. Still, the jobs that were created were welcomed in the mostly ranching community, and most viewed the new warehouse as a positive. When the economy had taken a dive, the incidents at the distribution center increased markedly, and it seemed like dispatch was always sending a car to check on one thing or another. A few days after most of the county lost power, Sheriff Watts received a call that the alarm system at the big warehouse had been tripped - yet again. The closest deputy had been his son, who had responded to the call immediately. When nothing had been heard from Deputy Watts for over an hour, the dispatcher became concerned.

Sheriff Watts arrived to find his son's patrol car sitting in the parking lot with the engine still running and the sound of the dispatcher's repeated calls coming over the radio. Using his flashlight, he found what had evidently piqued his son's interest. A side emergency exit showed signs of being pried open.

He picked up the microphone and asked for more help as his instinct told him something was very wrong. Sheriff Watts drew his weapon and entered the dark warehouse. He found his son, lying on the cold concrete floor, with a bullet wound in his side and another in one leg. The lightweight body armor issued by the department had taken the blunt of the chest wound, but the bullet had still penetrated his boy's body.

The sheriff ran outside to escape the radio interference of the huge structure and called desperately for an ambulance. He grabbed the first aid kit from the trunk of his patrol car and rushed back to render aid to his only child. He still wasn't sure how long he waited, but at some point in time, it dawned on him that he should be hearing the sirens of approaching help. Eventually, two other patrol cars from his department arrived, and a Texas Highway Patrol car responded as well. Still, no EMTs arrived.

When Sheriff Watts radioed his dispatcher to find out what the hell was going on, he was informed that the first ambulance ran out of gas, and that the other two had left the county hours before, responding to riots that had broken out in El Paso.

Throwing down the radio receiver, the sheriff rushed back inside. He hoisted his son on his shoulder and carried him to the cruiser. After arranging the injured man in the back seat, he drove to the local hospital. His son was pronounced dead a few hours later.

Everything had been a blur after that. Losing his child in such a way tore at the very soul of the lawman. After grieving with his wife for hours in the hospital chapel, he couldn't help himself and returned to the scene of his son's murder. On the way there, the peace officer hardly noticed the number of cars pulled to the side along I-10. He hadn't listened to a news broadcast for days and initially had no concept of what was going on. His wife found out where he was and drove to meet her husband at the distribution center, where the couple sat and mourned for hours. It became clear the next day that everything had fallen apart.

The sheriff's wife, expecting relatives to arrive for the funeral, stopped to pick up a few things on the way home from making arrangements. When she returned from the local grocery store empty-handed and frazzled, her report of bare shelves and panicked people was the final straw. What little news that did drift in, mostly television reports when the electricity was still working, made it clear to him what was happening.

Normally, in times of dire circumstances, the good sheriff's first thoughts would be of protecting the public and serving society. Not anymore. Now his priority was protecting his men and their families. A plan formed in his head while driving to the office the next morning. He quickly picked up the radio and made a call on several different frequencies – Sheriff Watts was seizing the Wal-Mart Distribution Center and any officer who wanted to take shelter there was welcome. Immediate family would be accommodated as well. He turned back, gathered up his wife, and set off to the warehouse. They had never returned to their home.

At first, Sheriff Watts wasn't sure anyone had heard his call. It took a few hours, but one after one, both his men and officers from other agencies showed up at the gate with their families. When a neighboring county's SWAT team had arrived in their fully equipped truck, the total number of lawmen was over 40. Counting all of their family members, the community of Wallyworld numbered well over 110.

For the first few days, the policemen, deputies and other lawmen had organized themselves and learned as much as possible about the facility, its contents, and especially how to operate the building's extensive generator system. There were over 30 huge walk-in freezers stuffed to the gills with food. The designers of the building realized that one significant power outage could ruin hundreds of thousands of dollars' worth of stock and had equipped the center with a state of the art uninterruptable power supply. Buried in the ground at the rear of the building were two, 5,000-gallon diesel storage tanks. These tanks were not only used to fuel the massive fleet of trucks that served the warehouse, but also as a source for the two, huge diesel generators wired into the building. In addition, there had been dozens of trucks loaded with additional supplies, docked at the various stations waiting to be emptied. Many of these tractors had tanks full of additional diesel fuel.

On the third day of occupation, one of the officers ran up to Sheriff Watts and informed him a group of people were at the front gates, asking for food and water. The people claimed to be stranded motorists from the nearby interstate. A quick meeting of the senior lawmen resulted in the people being given some water and sent on their way. The next day, the exact same group returned, this time with several additional people. Again, they were given water and sent away. On the third day, over 50 desperate people were at the gate. Sheriff Watts realized where their charity was headed, and told the men guarding the gate to send everyone away. This resulted in a heated argument, and things came close to getting out of control. Eventually, the beggars shuffled off, mumbling about the greedy cops. That night, several men with rifles attempted to storm the property, resulting in two officers and five attackers being killed.

It was that incident that transformed Wallyworld from being a refuge to a defended camp. Over the next few weeks, several attempts had been made to dislodge the cops. One very creative group of men even approached under a white flag and offered to barter for goods. It had been a trap, and gunfire had broken out resulting in more death. The residents of Wallyworld brought women and children with them, and like most families, they needed to get fresh air. Playground equipment and even a blow-up swimming pool had been scavenged from the shelves and assembled at the back of the building. A few days later, a sniper from a nearby ridgeline fired several shots at family members enjoying the makeshift playground. That incident had really upped the ante on security, and the men set about stringing trip wires and enhancing the general security. These preparations had included posting clearly printed signs along the building's drive that said, "No barter. No food. No water. Trespassers will be shot. White flags will be ignored."

Some of the officers eventually realized that civilization wasn't going to return anytime soon and set about preparing for the long-term occupation of the site. A flat patch of land on the west side of the parking lot had been converted to a vegetable garden using the seeds from the lawn and garden department. Rabbits were trapped from the surrounding area and placed in pens for breeding. One group of officers mounted an excursion into a nearby state park and looted every solar panel they could find. The panels had been installed to provide more security in the remote areas of the grounds. They were combined with batteries from the automotive department, and reusable power now took a small, but growing burden off the diesel generators. Everyone knew the diesel fuel would eventually run out, and the solar cells would then be the sole source of electrical power for Wallyworld.

Even the process of rationing food resulted in some creative planning. Originally, the freezers had been stocked by category of goods, with one freezer being full of beef while another contained chicken. The new residents of the center had rearranged the contents so as to consume the perishable items, freezer by freezer. As soon as one was empty, it was taken off-line to conserve fuel. The empty units were converted into special rooms to be used by the community. One empty freezer was now a break room used by the sentries as they changed shifts. Another became the movie theatre and a third was now a makeshift schoolroom for the younger children. Even the textbooks for the school had come from the storage shelves.

Using the floodlights at night had been the subject of hot debate. Some of the officers believed the lights made the property a big target for anyone in the area. Others believed an assertive posture was best. Over time, the number of "visitors" challenging the center dwindled, and for the last two weeks, the only disturbances had been the local deer and other wildlife.

Bishop decided he needed a different angle to observe the complex below and set about trying to find a better perch. Twenty minutes later, he leaned back against a large rock, disgusted by the entire situation. The building and surrounding grounds were right in the middle of where he needed to go. To the south was I-10, complete with thousands of abandoned cars and trucks. While he couldn't be 100% sure, there was little doubt in his mind that the guys occupying the distribution center would have that entire area wired and perhaps patrolled. Given his recent experience on the interstate, the thought of trying to weave his way along that stretch of road made him shiver.

To the north of the building was a seemingly endless expanse of wide-open desert. For as far as he could see, there was nothing but flat, featureless sand. The ridgeline he was atop became very steep less than 1,000 yards north of the center, and even if he decided to detour in that direction, he wasn't sure he could descend those cliff-like walls. He wanted desperately to bypass that area and be on his way toward Bliss, but the geography wasn't cooperating. Even if he did head north and found a way to get down from the ridge, he would still have to cross a wide expanse of absolutely open terrain. The people at the complex had fast moving ATVs and most likely night vision – he would be exposed and outgunned with no possible egress.

Bishop had no quarrel with the people below. He wanted to deliver the letters, have a quick chat with the President of the United States, and get back home to his wife. That thought made him laugh. "Hi honey, I'm home. How did my day go? Oh, I had a great chat with the President of the United States and took a tour Fort Bliss. I'm tired though, what's for supper?" Bishop shook his head – his kids would never believe this one.

He needed some diversion to draw the sentries' attention away from that open stretch of desert to the north. That was the right direction and the right terrain for traveling. If he could keep the lookouts busy for just 10 minutes, he could scurry across, and be out of their visual range, and on his way. How to do that was a problem.

After detaching the night vision from his rifle, Bishop refocused the eyepiece and flipped through the notes he had been taking while scouting the complex. There was a trash heap on the very southwest corner of the property, and he pondered starting a fire to distract the occupants. There was no way he could even get close to the mound of cardboard boxes, trash bags and other discarded rubbish. He couldn't think of a reliable way to remotely ignite it from a safe distance.

Another train of thought was to simply approach the complex with a white flag and pass on by. He had seriously been thinking this was the right course of action until he had read the posted signs. The evidence of several human skeletons made Bishop believe the guys at the compound weren't bluffing.

He spent a few minutes thinking about firing a couple of wild shots at the building and circling around the response team. That course of action was dead-ended for several reasons, not the least of which was he couldn't maneuver quickly in this landscape. He didn't believe the gentlemen down there were so stupid as to send all their manpower galloping up the hill to find the shooter, and even if they did, Bishop wouldn't be able to get around them fast enough. Those snipers on the roof weren't going anywhere, and they were lord of everything within 1,000 yards of the complex – maybe more.

It was those snipers that bothered him the most. The ATVs would be easy enough to avoid with any but the worst of luck, but those guys on the rooftop were well placed and well equipped for their job. Bishop had seen them holding a variety of objects up to their eyes and scanning the surrounding countryside. While he had never worked with police snipers, he was sure they were equipped similarly to their military brethren, and that translated into night vision, laser range finders, extremely long-range rifles and perhaps even infrared sighting systems. While he couldn't make out the specific weapons, there was a good chance they had at least one or two capable of hitting targets over a mile away.

Bishop looked down at his M4 and shook his head. His favorite weapon seemed small and anemic compared to what he believed the men below could access. The lack of ammo made the situation seem even more dismal. He needed some way to divert those snipers – some method of using their technology against them. Chewing on a piece of jerky and pulling cool water from his drinking tube, Bishop started to form an idea. The concept of using an enemy's strength against itself was an age-old art of battle, and his mind was running with a plan.

Thirty minutes later, Bishop slowly approached the upwardly sloping embankment leading to I-10. He had backtracked a little over a mile to the east where the congestion of abandoned vehicles began. After verifying that no one was around, he quickly found what he was looking for and trotted to the side of a semi-truck sitting in the westbound lane. Clearly, the driver had run out of gas and simply walked away from his rig. Both of the fuel caps had been removed, and the glass on the driver's side door had been broken out, probably by someone checking the cabin for food and water.

Bishop pulled his flashlight off of his chest rig and switched to the red filter. He cautiously climbed up the side of the tall vehicle and peered inside. Papers and other personal effects littered the cabin floor and seats. The scene reminded Bishop of the old movies where the spy came home to find his apartment had been ransacked by someone combing through his personal effects, looking for hidden flash drives storing covert government plans. The searchers in this case had been looking for food and water, not national secrets or hidden safes. Bishop shined his light on the sun visor above the steering wheel and sure enough, there was what he was looking for.

The red glow of the flashlight revealed a state of the art fuzzbuster, complete with the lettering "Dual Mode – Laser and Radar." Used by motorists to avoid speeding tickets, Bishop had ridden with a friend who had equipped his sports car with a similar device. Following the little unit's power cord, Bishop verified it was indeed connected to the big rig's 12-volt battery. He found the power button and was only a little disappointed to discover the truck's batteries were dead. That might be a problem. A quick scan of the interior revealed nothing more of interest. Bishop sat in the driver's seat and pulled the door shut. After positioning himself carefully, he kicked the side mirror hard once and then again, until large sections of the coated glass fell to the pavement below. Bishop climbed down with the "borrowed" electronic whiz in his dump pouch, and gathered up the larger pieces of mirror.

He stood on the pavement of the big highway and looked both directions. It dawned on him that there might be a big hole in his plan. He needed 12-volt power to pull off his scheme, but as he looked up and down the road, he saw that every single vehicle had at least one of its doors open. It was obvious that people had driven until they had run out of gas. Before setting out on foot, most had probably locked their cars either out of habit or with the optimistic thought of returning with a can of fuel at some point. As the situation had deteriorated, hungry or thirsty people had probably taken to breaking into the discarded cars looking for food. Maybe some had been vandalized looking for valuables.

Regardless of the motive, open doors and trunk lids meant dome lights, and those lights left on for extended periods of time resulted in drained batteries. He was just about to give up on his plan when he walked past a motorcycle leaning against its kickstand. The bike didn't have dome lights, but that presented another problem. The bike used a 6-volt power system, half of the typical automobile. Bishop scanned the road in both directions as far as his optics would allow and didn't see another bike. He could wire two 6-volt batteries together and obtain his goal, but there wasn't a second scooter to plunder. What he did see was a small fishing boat still sitting on its trailer a few hundred yards away. In less than 15 minutes, Bishop was hefting the starting battery out of the bass boat and moving off into the cool, desert night.

As he approached his previous position overlooking the distribution center, Bishop kept thinking about turning the enemy's strength to his advantage. He needed to convince the

121

force in the compound below that they were under attack by a significant threat. The key to his plot was to draw everyone's attention to the ridge, so he could sneak past them in the open desert to the north. Since the trip wires had been set off by chance roaming deer and other wildlife, Bishop envisioned a low state of alert when the devices were engaged. The flares had cried wolf one too many times for anyone below to get excited. While it would have been simple enough to set some sort of time delay and trip one of the devices, Bishop didn't think that would be enough. He had to have everyone's attention pointed away from his route.

Another issue was the reliability of any hastily constructed or complex device. He had enough experience in the field to know that purpose designed and built equipment often failed, let alone something put together with bailing twine and paper clips. He had to implement redundancy in case something went haywire. Bishop solved this problem by using the existing trip wires and their attached flares. While scouting the facility, he had located three of the clever devices and disabled them. He had a lot of respect for whoever had built the nifty, little booby traps. Each flare had a 9-volt battery attached. The leads from the battery were connected to a piece of steel wool. When the wire was pulled, a connection was made with the battery, and the steel wool ignited. The burning metal would then ignite the magnesium flare.

Bishop couldn't improve the devices, so he decided to leave them just as they were. What he did do was rig the three flares together. After burning for 10 to 15 seconds, the first flare would burn through the trip wire for the next device. In less than a minute, all three of the bright red warning devices should be causing concern to the men below. It was a simple matter to connect a time delay to the first flare. Bishop removed his roll of duct tape from his pack and tore off a three-foot long strip. One of the hundreds of uses for this sort of tape was making a torch. Duct tape burned very slowly and was fairly consistent. Bishop rolled his adhoc fuse into a tight line and left it ready to light, as the last step before moving off.

The snipers most likely had laser range finders, and Bishop knew it was critical to keep those guys occupied. Failure to do so would probably result in a rather large piece of high-velocity lead slamming into his body. To avoid this unpleasant outcome, Bishop rigged the truck's radar detector where the beams from the lasers below would pass by the device. The little black case contained LED-warning lights to alert the speeding motorists when a police radar or laser unit was nearby. Bishop hoped it would issue a similar warning regarding the snipers' equipment. Moving carefully, he strategically placed the broken pieces of mirror where they would catch the flashing white lights from the detector. With any luck, the mirrors would make the blinking lights look like muzzle flashes to the people below. He stood back and walked through it in his mind. The flares would cause the snipers to scan the ridge. The mirrors would reflect the flares' light and would look unusual to the snipers below. They would scan the area with their range finders, setting off the detector. The detector's white lights would reflect in the mirrors, and hopefully look like muzzle flashes to the men below. Bishop rubbed his chin, concerned the whole plan reminded him of a Rube Goldberg cartoon mousetrap, but couldn't come up with anything better.

Worried about his laser contraption, he decided redundancy was in order. His solution was to tape a few of his precious, remaining cartridges to each flare. Being careful not to trigger the device and blow off one of his fingers, he slowly wrapped each round so that its primer was positioned against the tube of the flare. As the heat from the flare reached the primer, the round should explode, causing a lot of noise and not much else. Hopefully, to the people below, it would sound like a gunshot.

It took almost three hours to rig everything up. After one quick check that he was ready, Bishop pulled a disposable lighter from his chest rig and ignited the long strand of duct tape and trotted away to the north.

He stayed close to the top of the ridge careful not to expose his movements to anyone watching from below. He traveled to a wash that was about 1,000 yards north of the complex and checked his watch. He carefully climbed down the steep slope of the rocks, working his way to the desert floor below. Bishop found a good place to hide at the bottom and remained out of sight. He waited until the burning duct tape finally made its way to the first flare's trip wire. With an auditable pop and fizzle, the ridge south of Bishop was suddenly aglow in pulsating red light. He risked peeking his rifle around the corner of the rock he was hiding behind, and watched with anticipation the activity at the complex. He was a little disappointed when the night vision revealed very little activity on the rooftop of the structure.

Almost a minute later, the first flare burned through the second trip wire, and its magnesium ignited, contributing to the illumination of the ridgeline. Bishop smiled when the reaction to the second flare was considerable. He could see hurried activity and men moving in the shadows of the building. The third flare caused absolute bedlam.

Right on cue, the first flare burned down to the cartridge Bishop had taped to the tube. The sound of a rifle round being discharged was louder than Bishop had anticipated, and he actually jumped just a little as the noise echoed off the rocks. That discharge was soon followed by a second, and now Bishop could hear shouts coming from the complex.

It's now or never. Bishop sprinted from his hiding spot and headed out into the open desert. He was wagering his life that the men guarding the distribution center were completely focused on the obvious attack coming from the other direction. He didn't even breathe for the first twenty steps. After he had traveled a hundred yards or so, he started to replenish his oxygen and slow his pace. That was when he heard the first shot come from the roof of the warehouse.

His instinct was to dive for cover and roll. There wasn't anything to hide behind, so he hoped the movement would cause a long distance shot to miss. When he finally stopped moving, he looked back at the building, trying to determine if he could arch a shot that far. The distance was way, way out of range for his rifle, but he might be able to keep their heads down for a minute or two. A flash of light on the ridge distracted him, and it took a moment to realize his radar trap was working. From his position, he watched, fascinated, as small white twinkles of light flashed on the ridge. It actually looked like the muzzle flash from a rifle, and the snipers on the rooftop were returning fire.

Bishop scrambled up and began jogging west and away from the complex, happy his plan had worked and wanting to get out of range as soon as possible. He ran hard for three minutes, and then slowed to scan the area in front of him with his night vision. As he was bringing the weapon to his shoulder, the squawk of a radio made him freeze.

There, less than 50 yards to his south, was one of the ATVs. The driver was standing in the seat, concentrating on the warehouse with binoculars, and hadn't seen Bishop. The target was simply too good to pass up, and Bishop kept watching the preoccupied rider as he slowly circled up behind the man. When he was within 30 steps, he detected the noise of the engine idling. At 10 steps, he broke out into a full run and put his shoulder into the man's knees. The tackle would have made any high school football coach proud.

By the time the startled, confused policeman had regained his composure, he was looking into the barrel of Bishop's rifle. Bishop started to ask the cop for his license, registration, and proof of insurance, but thought better of it. Instead, he growled, "Friend, I'll cut you in half, if you even look at me funny. Work with me here, and you'll be home with your

124

wife and kids in less than an hour. Try and be a fucking hero, and they'll find your body in two pieces tomorrow morning. Your call." Bishop accented his threat by clicking off the safety of his rifle.

The frightened man nodded rapidly and finally managed to mumbled, "Okay."

Five minutes later, Bishop was riding on the ATV carrying the former owner's shoes, pistol, four full magazines, and a couple bottles of water. The wind felt wonderful against his face, and he couldn't help but let out a long-winded "Wooooooohoooooo" as he sped off into the desert night.

Chapter 12

Welcome to El Paso

Combined, the cities of El Paso, Texas and Ciudad Juarez, Mexico have a population larger than Philadelphia or Phoenix. Were it not for the Rio Grande River splitting the two metropolitan municipalities with an international border, the area would be the fifth largest city in America. Almost two thirds of the population resides on the Mexican side of the border, however, leaving El Paso as the 19th largest in the United States, slightly ahead of Memphis, Tennessee.

Most Americans visualize El Paso as a dusty cow town, often mentioned and seldom shown in Hollywood's depictions of the Old West. The city doesn't even get respect in the state of Texas, given it falls short of Houston, Dallas, San Antonio, Austin, and Fort Worth in population.

El Paso is in fact a culturally rich and diverse city with a history as colorful as any, and older than most. The first recorded Thanksgiving Holiday celebrated in El Paso was over 20 years before the pilgrims threw their bash at Plymouth Plantation. The land around the modern downtown has been home to civilized cultures for thousands of years.

None of that mattered to Bishop as he sat on the ATV and chewed his third "power bar" of the morning. He had been like a kid on Christmas day when he found the stash of food in the off-road vehicle's small storage compartment. Despite his best intentions of saving some of the goodies for Terri, he was quickly eating his way through the treasure.

His mood was elevated further by the fact that he was overlooking his destination. Spread out across the valley below was Fort Bliss with its million plus acres of land. To the south, he could see the outline of downtown El Paso's skyscrapers. To the north was nothing but open desert, fading away to mountains in the distance. Bishop knew White Sands missile range was connected to the base in that general direction. From his elevated perch, he realized he was probably looking at New Mexico and Texas from the same vista.

He swung a leg over the ATV's gas tank, while shoving the last of the chocolate flavored treat into his pie hole. A passing pang of guilt pulled him down for a moment, as he thought about how much Terri would have enjoyed sharing it with him. He consoled himself with the excuse that before everything went to hell, the nutritional snack wouldn't have tasted all that good.

While the print on the foil wrapper advertised the product as having a "rich chocolate flavor," Bishop remembered most of these products had tasted like raw oats coated in cardboard. Today, however, nothing could be further from the truth. His palate had been deprived of anything sweet for months, and even the hint of chocolate caused him to gobble down the first two bars in a few bites.

After sucking the last few morsels from his fingertips, Bishop pulled his gloves on and began to scout the base below. He could easily make out the area around Biggs Field, and its long landing strip that serviced the fort. Huge hangars dwarfed the other structures in the area. It took him a few minutes of searching, but he eventually saw what he was looking for. The towering white tail fin of a large commercial jet was visible between two of the hangars. While his four times magnification couldn't make out many details, Bishop was reasonably sure the aircraft was Air Force One. Looking further south toward the border, Bishop could see the hazy outlines of the main base's buildings, including a taller structure that he remembered was a hospital.

Bishop sat on the fender of the ATV and tried to recall everything he knew of Fort Bliss. He remembered a large expansion of the base being ordered a few years ago, as the 1st Armored Division was being brought home after 40 years of being stationed in Germany. Bliss was the perfect place for tanks to roll all over the desert and shoot their massive guns. Although he didn't know who, someone had once said Bliss was the largest fort in the United States in terms of square miles available for gun ranges. *I bet it's a hell of a lot of fun busting ass all over the desert in a tank and shooting that gun. I wonder if I could tank-jack an Abrams?*

Recalling all of this didn't help him make the critical decision where to enter the property. On one hand, he considered just driving up to the main gate and announcing himself. He was here on legitimate business and had nothing to hide. The problem with that course of action was that it necessitated a drive through a heavily populated portion of El Paso. The main entrance to the facility bordered on the north side of the city, and according to everything he had heard, El Paso wasn't a place where one casually strolled around these days.

Had he simply wanted to meet with the base commander or other higher ups, he would have driven the ATV onto the property until he found a road and followed the signs to the HQ building. The problem with that strategy was the President of the United States was most likely staying at the base, and that meant security would be tight – very tight. A lone stranger with a rifle strapped to his back would probably invoke a "shoot now and ask questions later," response.

Bishop had no way of knowing how Bliss and those assigned to the base had weathered the storm of collapse. The 1st Armored Division would have at least four brigades. According to what the Colonel had detailed, the army sent brigade-sized forces into the major cities when martial law had been declared. It was a strong probability that the 1st had been taxed with the same orders. Bliss was a major training center as well, so there was no telling how many forces were here on temporary duty assignments when the economy collapsed and sent society reeling. Regardless, base commanders would have retained enough force to secure their facility. It was their job, and besides, their families were typically living with them on base.

Bishop dug around in the ATV's storage compartment and eyed the last two nutrition bars. One was chocolate, and the other featured cranberries and raisins. He had to save one of them for Terri, no ifs-ands-or-buts about it. He was already in enough domestic trouble as it was, but couldn't help wondering if his wife liked cranberries or raisins. He chuckled to himself as his mind raced with wild tales of savage mountain lions, raiding his camp and eating the chocolate bars. *No*, he thought, *I'll tell her I had to use them to bribe a rogue lynch mob in order to save my neck.* On and on his mind raced, creating ever-greater fabrications and excuses to explain to his wife why she only received one treat, and it wasn't chocolate. *Maybe I'll say the president saw them in my pack and wanted them.* Bishop rested his hand on the grip of his pistol, and the feel of the weapon reminded him of Terri's skill with a handgun. *I'll leave the chocolate one damn it…just my luck to marry a girl who can shoot.*

The thought of being straight up with Terri led to the more immediate decision. Bishop sat back in the driver's seat and kick-started the motor. He would chance traveling through a portion of El Paso and approach the front gate like a regular visitor. It just seemed the proper thing to do.

~ ~

One thing that bothered Bishop about riding the ATV was the engine noise. Not only did the mechanical beast's rumblings let everyone within a half mile know where he was, it also blocked his senses as well. Riding the machine across open desert was worth the risk. As he approached the suburbs around El Paso, he felt an ever-growing need to be stealthy.

A cluster of car-sized boulders provided an excellent place to stash his ride. While the weight of his pack was an unwelcome addition to his shoulders, being able to hear while moving was worth it. After one last check that his kit was in order, Bishop sat out on foot toward the first housing development he knew was over the next rise. It was broad daylight, and he considered waiting until nightfall, but decided this little adventure was taking too long, and he wanted to see Terri again – chocolate or no chocolate.

Bishop went prone as he approached the crest of the rise and looked down at the houses below through his optic. There was a cluster of nine middleclass homes on two cross streets. The neighborhood was laid out like thousands of others nestled on the outskirts of American cities from California to the Carolinas. This specific development was designed with a southwestern, stucco flair in mind. Bishop liked the design and surmised the primary occupants would most likely be married soldiers stationed at the base.

As he scouted the subdivision, he noticed that some houses had large mounds of trash bags stacked by the curb, while others didn't. He shook his head at the oversight by the occupants. It was a clear sign that someone was home, and the occupants either had cleaned out the garage, or at minimum, were eating. While a lack of trash wasn't a guarantee of an empty house, a large pile of bags did stand out. Unless the owner was crafty and stacked his bags on the neighbor's lawn, trash was a sure sign of food. The observation also made Bishop wonder about the mindset of the people down there. Did they still believe trash pickup was going to resume at some point in time? How big did they intend on letting the heaps get before going to plan B?

The other, more important point was that the homes were separated and surrounded by privacy fences. This was a good thing, as it would allow Bishop to move with more cover. Privacy was a two-way street.

Bishop was just about to head down into the neighborhood when movement caught his eye. The small cluster of homes was accessed from a larger street a few hundred yards away. Bishop could see a few people walking along that street, one person carrying a large bundle on his head. What really drew his attention was the Humvee sitting right in the middle of the intersection. While details were difficult to make out at this range, he could tell that there were soldiers at the crossroads. It looked like a checkpoint, and that actually made a lot of sense. If he were in charge of base security, establishing control points on the major roadways leading to the base would be a good tactic.

This revelation gave Bishop a moment of pause. It would be risky enough approaching the base's main gate. An armed man passing by these checkpoints was sure to garner unwelcome inquiries. While he had no way of knowing the situation below, it wouldn't be a surprise if now the all-powerful military granted considerable leeway to the men stationed at these outposts. In some parts of the world where Bishop had worked, soldiers such as these even preyed on the civilians. Bishop didn't believe the U.S. military would resort to that – but he didn't want to find out the hard way. He needed another plan. After observing the foot traffic around the checkpoint, he finally came up with an idea.

After carefully picking his route, Bishop slowly made his way down the hillside, moving from cover to cover, approaching the civilization below. The first thing he noticed was the smell. Rotting garbage, human waste and dead flesh hovered over the valley like a cloud. The foul air was so unpleasant, Bishop considered changing his plan. He took cover in a concrete drainage ditch and removed his pack. Digging around inside, he pulled out the pine needles used for tea, and ground up a pinch under his rifle butt. He took the oil and rubbed it on the skin under his nose, hoping the smell of pine would override the horrific odors assaulting his senses and distracting him from his initiative.

When everything was repacked, Bishop moved out and approached the back fence of the closest house. He had picked this specific structure because it didn't have much of a trash heap, and appeared to have already been looted. There were miscellanies spread all over the yard, and the front door appeared to be open. As he carefully peered over the fence, he noticed the backyard showed no signs of either looters or life. Like many homes in this part of the world, the yard was mainly sand and rock. Grass required expensive watering, and many homeowners had chosen to go 'native' with their landscaping. A small child's plastic wading pool and a rusted metal swing set were the only indicators that the residence had ever been occupied.

Bishop waited for almost 20 minutes to see if anyone were really home and just doing a good job of hiding in plain sight. After he was sure his approach had gone undetected, he pulled his fighting knife and picked up a baseball-sized rock. He used the crude tools to pry three boards loose from the fence and entered the toddler's playground.

Relieved that no one shot at him or otherwise sounded any alarm, Bishop cautiously approached the back of the home. The door was ajar and lead to a laundry room where an undisturbed washer and dryer sat looking like they were ready for the next load. Bishop paused and decided to announce himself in case someone was hiding with a shotgun inside. "Hello…hello inside…I mean you no harm. If anyone is home, just let me know, and I'll leave. I don't want any trouble." After broadcasting his presence, he felt a little silly. If an elderly couple were hiding inside, they would be smart not to answer. *How would they know I wasn't just trying to draw them out?*

Bishop looked around the corner into the kitchen and relaxed. All the cabinet doors stood ajar, and the non-editable contents were strewn all over the floor. Every drawer was either hanging from the rails or had been removed, searched and flung across the room. The side-by-side refrigerator stood with both doors wide open. Someone had ransacked the kitchen, looking for food. Bishop had to walk carefully because the floor was littered with broken glass, silverware, papers and other content once neatly stored. He made it to the fridge and absent-mindedly, reached up and closed the doors. There, held in place with magnets, were two items that caught his attention. The first was a picture of a young couple. The man was dressed in an army uniform, sitting with his arm around a pretty young woman in her early 20s. On their laps sat two children, both under the age of ten.

The second item was a handwritten note. Bishop pulled it from under the cartoon character magnet and read the neat handwriting:

My Dearest James,

The children and I are leaving for my sister's house in Prescott. The power has been out for seven days, and we haven't had water for five. The grocery store had a riot and was burned out. People are going nuts Jimmy, and I'm scared. The kids and I hear guns being shot, and some sound like they are close by. There are strange men driving around the neighborhood, and Mr. Young's house was broken into last night.

Little Jimmy only has enough insulin for a couple more days. There are no phones, and it took all day just to drive to three different drug stores. All of them were boarded up or looted. I tried the base, and they wouldn't let me in without you. I took my ID and papers and tried to get in the base as a dependent. There were hundreds of people at the gate, and I got shoved to the ground. I lost my papers Jimmy; I think someone took them out of my hand. I begged them for some food and insulin, but the guards just ignored me. I'm so frightened and don't know what

*else to do but leave. We tried to stay Jimmy...we tried really hard
to wait for you to get back from overseas. A lot of the neighbors
are leaving, too.*

*I'll be at sis's place, waiting on you. I love you so much,
and the kids miss you. Please hurry, my love.*

Love,

Linda

Bishop looked up from the note and stared out the
window for a little bit. He wondered how many million times this
same story had been repeated all around the world. He knew
what it was like to have to abandon a home. The sickening
feeling that went through his gut as Terri and he drove away
would be something he would never forget. To leave one's life
behind while knowing deep down inside that returning was
unlikely was an indescribable sorrow.

His mind then drifted to the husband and what the
reaction would be if James ever read the note. The country he
was serving had abandoned his family. The people he had
committed to protect had turned their backs on his wife and kids.
Bishop grunted out loud and put his hand on the rifle slung
across his chest. *I know what my reaction would be.*

Bishop carefully placed the note back on the door in
exactly the same place as he had found it. He looked around the
kitchen again, this time in a new light. This had been a happy
home, full of laughing children. He could imagine the smell of
baking cookies and happy squeals when ice cream was being
dipped into bowls. Bishop sighed and had to clear his mind of the
melancholy trap it was falling into. *I'm sure she made it to her
sister's house*, he thought, *I hope Jimmy joined them there.*

The living room was trashed, but not as thoroughly. The
looters had been digging for food. Bishop went into the master
bedroom, avoiding even a glance inside of the children's rooms.
He was already in a foul mood and didn't want to go there.

Jimmy was a little larger guy than Bishop, and that was
a good thing. Pushing back a tinge of guilt, he fingered through
the soldier's clothing, hung neatly on one side of the closet. After
a few minutes, he found what he was looking for and consoled
himself. *What I'm doing may help everyone. I'm not taking these
things for myself, but to help end this madness.*

Bishop found a bundle of clothing as well as a suitcase
with wheels and extending handle. He took his loot outside and
poured just a little water on the ground, quickly stirring the soil
into a muddy concoction. He dirtied the pants, overcoat, and
suitcase as much as possible. He then gathered papers from the
kitchen and even found a small stain of grease on the garage

floor. Rubbing the clothing in the oily substance added to the affect.

The next step was to remove his chest rig and rifle. This part disturbed Bishop greatly. He was going to be without easy access to his primary weapon, and that was uncomfortable. Still, it had to be done. After packing his gear into the suitcase, he donned the now filthy clothing and looked in the mirror to see the results. The final touch was to bundle a spare shirt and several pieces of paper to the handle of the pull-along suitcase. He unlaced one of his boots and cut the fingers out of a pair of gardening gloves he found in the garage.

Anyone watching the house would have seen just another homeless vagabond walking across the front yard and onto the street. Even the careful observer would notice a hunched over man whose ill-fitting clothes hung on his frame. Streaked with dirt and grime, the shuffling gait of the stranger projected an image of a lost soul. The pull-along suitcase being dragged along was torn and ripped, with a hobo's collection of newspaper and other items tied to the handle. The wandering man wasn't a threat. He kept his head down, and his eyes never looked out more than a few steps ahead of him. Anyone approaching would have heard him humming an out of tune rendition of "When the Saints Come Marching In." But, there was no need to approach the stranger. He clearly had nothing of value and seemed intent on just passing through.

Bishop came to the first intersection manned by army troopers after traveling three blocks. The soldiers were bored, sitting on the hood of their Humvee and laughing about something. Bishop kept his gaze downward and his pace slow, the weight of his pistol against his hip providing little comfort. If the soldiers noticed him, they made no comment. He relaxed somewhat after he had made it more than a block past the checkpoint without being challenged.

Bishop passed by two more intersections manned by army troops before he could see the front gate of Fort Bliss ahead. He limped off the main street and found shelter in an abandoned doughnut store.

Corporal Peterson looked at his watch again. Two more hours of guard duty, and then he would have an entire day off. He remembered when having leave meant a trip to El Paso to chase girls, but that was no longer possible. Still, a day off was better than sitting at the front gate and watching nothing. He looked up at the avenue approaching his position and wondered how things really were out in the world. They were certainly bad enough here on the base, and with a VIP visiting, things had gotten worse. Scuttlebutt had it that the President of these United States was going to be at Bliss for quite a while, and that meant extra duty and more restrictions. Still, the fact that the president was traveling around the country had to mean something positive – didn't it? Peterson was shocked when his CO posted the duty roster, and he had the day off. As far as he could tell, he was the only one, and that had resulted in some serious ribbing as well as several attempts to bribe a trade in shifts. No one had anything worth a shit for bartering, so he kept the free time.

The corporal looked down at the M249 SAW (Squad Automatic Weapon) resting on the sandbags in front of him. *Thank God the machine gun hadn't been required for several weeks.* When the White House had been stormed, orders had been received for three of the 1st's brigades to move out. He had heard two of them were headed to Phoenix and one to Tuscan – but that was just rumor. The 4th brigade wasn't ready to move as it was in the middle of a seriously needed refit, and half of its vehicles were non-functional. That had ended up being lucky because those troopers had been needed right here at home.

Almost overnight, El Paso had turned into a nightmare rivaling those old post-Apocalypse movies. There had been dozens of stories describing atrocities and sub-human behavior. Who knew what was true and what was bullshit? What Peterson did know was that lots of *very* angry and *very* hungry people saw the soldiers from Bliss moving their families onto the base, and that seemed to set off a chain reaction. Those same increasingly desperate folks tried to enter the base, and it had taken hundreds of soldiers to stop them.

Peterson had been at his barracks when the first protest outside the main entrance started getting out of hand. An unknown MP had rushed through the building screaming for every available man to report to the front gate, with weapon, as soon as possible. The crowd of about 1,000 people hadn't even flinched while facing the line of a hundred or so soldiers with their carbines. It had taken two Abrams tanks rolling up to disperse the mob.

Over the next week or so, larger and larger crowds could be seen milling around the entrance to the base. Peterson remembered some asshole had a bullhorn. The guy seemed to be intent on inciting the throng. When the wind was just right, the guards at the front gate could make out the words. "Why should the army get all the food when we paid for it? Why should the military get to sit back in comfort while we, the people, are starving? Why don't they use their guns on the predators roaming our streets and killing our families instead of us? There must be thousands of tons of food on that base and a huge hospital as well. The military has to share. Our children are starving, and our elderly are dying. We have to demand justice! We demand what is ours!"

For a few days, it was all talk. The corporal wasn't sure if it was the eleventh or the twelfth day when two police cars approached the gate. Inside was the head of the city council of El Paso and a ranking police officer. The other car was driven by two heavily armed SWAT officers. The two civilians asked to speak to the base commander and were passed through the gate.

Corporals aren't privy to high-level meetings such as the one that took place that day. What eventually filters down to the lower ranks is a mixture of fact, rumor, and speculation. All over Fort Bliss, gossip spread that the city of El Paso was in a war with gangs of civilians and drug cartel soldiers from Juarez, and the city police were losing. The word was that the city officials had come to ask for help with the invasion from the south.

Peterson was at the gate when the guests left. The look on their faces said it all – no help would be forthcoming from Bliss. The reaction among the troops was mixed. Some people thought Mother Green should mount up and go kick some ass. America was what everyone had taken an oath to defend. Others agreed with the decision, reasoning that "The army can't help everyone all at once." It was three days later when two separate events occurred.

The first involved a firefight between several city police officers and a bunch of heavily armed men in black SUVs. The police were losing and retreating back toward the guardhouse of the base. No one knew if it was intentional or merely coincidence that the fight ended up at the front of Bliss.

Several members of the 1st Armored Division looked on as the cops fought like cornered animals. The vicious gun battle raged for several minutes as more and more soldiers came to the front gate to watch the fight. The cops had no chance. Whoever the attackers were, they had the advantage in numbers and weapons. Two of the police cars were even destroyed by RPG rockets. The last few remaining police officers retreated back to the guardhouse and begged for help or sanctuary.

By that time, one of the brigade commanders, a full colonel, arrived at the gate and took command. He was on the radio pleading for permission to help the police officers. The reply was always the same – any action is authorized to protect and secure Fort Bliss. No other action is authorized.

Two police officers were dragging a wounded comrade back toward the colonel's position while a fourth was covering their retreat. It was at that point that one of the attackers rose up and threw a hand grenade. Everything got a little confused after that. One story had it that the shrapnel from the grenade hit a private from A-Company. Someone else claimed that a piece of hot steel flew right over the colonel's head. Whatever the motivation, the reaction was swift and overwhelming. Within seconds of the blast, orders were being screamed up and down the line – HIT THOSE MOTHERFUCKERS, AND HIT THEM HARD!

It was one thing to take on 11 lightly armed law enforcement officers. It was another to fight an armored brigade of the United States Army. The two M1A2 Abrams tanks were the first to open fire with their heavy M2 and coaxial machine guns. They were quickly joined by over a hundred M4 and M16 rifles creating a firestorm of lead. The hostile SUVs were instantly shredded to scrap metal, with one of them exploding and burning. There was no cover for the attackers that could withstand the blistering fire leveled in their direction. It was over in less than fifteen seconds with zero survivors. Unfortunately, all of the police officers died that day as well.

That evening, just as the bodies were being bagged for cremation, the second event occurred. The normal gathering of protestors was joined by a large crowd of onlookers gawking at the results of the "battle." As usual, agitators began working everyone into a frenzy. Before long, the soldiers at the gate started seeing the occasional rock or glass bottle being thrown their way. Just before dusk, someone shot at the post. The shot was low and slammed into the concrete roadway well short of any sentries, but the message was clear – this was turning into a riot.

Fortunately, the colonel was still present, supervising the cleanup. It only took a single, short .50 caliber burst, intentionally fired high, to make the approaching crowd break and run. Even though no one was hurt, the message was clear to both sides – the army is not your friend and will shoot at you. The soldiers understood that the population they had sworn to protect hated them. Neither side was pleased with the outcome.

It was a few days later that someone in high command finally grasped the situation at hand. Suddenly, orders were issued for several thousand troops to form up. The 1st Armored Division was going to establish law and order in El Paso.

Peterson remembered watching column after column of vehicles full of troopers move out into the city. It took less than three days to establish rule of law. Those invading from the south were pushed back or killed. While tens of thousands were starving and thousands more were already dead, El Paso was firmly back in American control – for whatever that was worth. The army couldn't feed, house or treat the population, but order had been established.

Ever since that time, the front gate had been peaceful. Occasionally, civilians came to the guards, begging for food or medicine. Now and then, someone would walk up to report a problem. For the most part, the base was on a quiet state of alert.

Corporal Peterson was bent over, re-lacing his boot, when he heard a nearby sentry's voice. "Corporal, we have a visitor." Peterson finished his re-tie, and then looked up to see a single man approaching on foot. The guy was armed, but his rifle was on his back and the barrel pointed down. He carried a small white cloth in one hand and a sheet of paper in the other.

Peterson let the man approach to within 50 feet and yelled, "Halt! State your business at Fort Bliss." The stranger yelled back, "I have a letter for the base commander. I am here under orders of the President of the United States and have urgent information for his eyes only."

Peterson heard the private whisper "*Bullshit*" under his breath, and had to admit this guy's answer didn't make any sense. Still, a decision like this was above his pay grade. He yelled back, "Stand where you are and wait – don't move, sir."

Peterson turned to the radio and eventually was connected to the duty watch captain. The man seemed annoyed that he was being bothered, but informed the corporal to take no action until he got to the gate. It was almost five minutes later when a Humvee pulled up, discharging the captain and brisk, square-shouldered sergeant.

The Captain immediately walked to the sandbags surrounding the gate to sum up the stranger. He motioned a quick "*beats the hell out of me*" gesture to the sergeant, and then returned his attention to the man standing patiently on the roadway.

"State your business."

The man paused for just a moment and then calmly replied. "Captain, I have traveled through 200 miles of hell to get here. I'm tired, sore, and low on food, water, and patience. I was ordered to report here and brief the President of the United States. I have a letter of introduction to the base commander. I suggest you read it, and let the general know I'm here."

Something about the man's tone rubbed the Captain the wrong way. Still, he didn't want his ass in a sling. "Please place your weapon on the ground, walk forward 10 steps, and go to both knees with your hands behind your head."

"Fuck you."

The Captain wasn't pleased with Bishop's answer. "Look hotshot, I don't know who you are, or why you're here. I wasn't told to expect anyone, so as far as I'm concerned, you are nothing but a target. Now do as I ask, or be on your way."

The harsh response drew a sharp look from the sergeant, but the officer ignored it. He started to say something when the stranger answered the challenge.

"No, you look captain, we can stand here all day and play 'who's got the biggest swinging dick,' but I'm not in the mood. Why don't you send someone out and retrieve the letter. If it's bullshit, then shoot me or whatever. If it's not, I promise not to tell the general that your fucking IQ is less than your boot size."

Bishop's remark generated a couple of muffled chuckles among the men, and the captain threw a harsh look in their general direction. He started to respond when the sergeant interrupted. "Sir, what would it hurt to take a look? He doesn't look like the typical troublemaker we see here at the gate."

"Fine, Sergeant. If you want to see the man's paperwork, feel free to go get it. I'm telling you this is some sort of con."

"You're probably right sir, but it will only take a minute." And with that, the NCO climbed over the sandbag and strode toward Bishop.

After Bishop handed over the letter, the sergeant stood and quickly read the first page of handwriting. When he finished the note, he flipped to the second page and quickly checked the document. He concluded by looking Bishop in the eye, and then nodded. He did a nimble about face and double-timed back to the gate, holding the papers in his hand. Without saying a word, he walked up to the captain and handed over the documents. The first page read:

Dear General Westfield,

The man carrying this letter has information critical to the President of the United States. He is delivering this under executive order 15-23442, issued directly to me personally. I, in execution of my duties, have suffered severe injury and am incapacitated. This man is my surrogate.

The information being delivered should be considered G15CS-Eyes-Only.

The letter was signed by a colonel. Attached to the note was an official looking order, complete with the president's signature and the official seal of the White House. Everything appeared to be in order and official. The captain looked up from the papers and squinted at Bishop through narrow eyes. After a moment, he looked back at the sergeant and asked, "What do you think I should do with this, Sergeant?"

"I would inform the base commander, sir. The order should be easy enough to verify. In the meantime, I would ask that gentleman to unload and safe his weapon, and then offer him some shade and a drink of water."

The officer considered the recommendation for a moment and nodded. "Go ahead, but keep a close watch on him. I still think this is some sort of game. I'll call the CO."

Bishop was sitting on a sandbag wall with his weapon unloaded and drinking a cup of water, when a second Humvee joined the first. This time, it was a full bird colonel that jumped out and walked directly toward the captain. Again, after a quick review of the paperwork, another radio transmission was made. The two officers stood, ignoring Bishop.

Five minutes later, a civilian SUV screeched to a halt, and this time two men in suits hopped out. They joined the two army officers and began yet another review of Bishop's papers. The older one eventually walked over to Bishop and offered his hand. "Agent Powell, United States Secret Service."

Bishop shook the man's hand, expecting bravado via a crushing grip. There was none of that, just a firm, businesslike handshake. Agent Powell looked at Bishop with a trained eye and inquired, "So, how's the Colonel doing?"

Bishop was a little surprised by the question. "He wasn't in good shape when I last saw him. I don't know if he's still alive or not. I've been traveling for three days, trying to get here and deliver his report."

Agent Powell thought about Bishop's remark for a second. "Did the Colonel's wife make it out of Houston with him?"

Bishop smirked at the weak attempt to verify his story. "Agent Powell, the Colonel's wife died over eight years ago from colon cancer. As far as I know, he didn't dig up her body and bring it with him. Now, sir, while I appreciate your diligence, I would like to deliver my report and be on my way. I have a pregnant wife who is alone at the moment, and in case you haven't noticed, the world isn't such a safe place these days."

Agent Powell smiled at Bishop. "Sorry, you just never know. I can't let you meet the president while you are armed. You'll have to check in all of your weapons and gear, and we'll have to search you before the meeting. I might be able to arrange a hot shower beforehand though."

Bishop smiled at the agent's offer, "How hot?"

Both men laughed, and then Powell motioned for Bishop to follow him to their SUV. The president's bodyguard stopped at the back of the vehicle and opened the rear hatch. "You can store your gear in here."

Bishop paused and then shrugged his shoulders. "I suppose if I had your job, I'd be paranoid too. No problem." After unloading all of his kit, Bishop sat in the backseat and was driven to a building with a sign on the well-manicured lawn indicating they had arrived at the "Visiting Officers' Quarters."

After the SUV was parked, Bishop walked to the back and stood waiting. Agent Powell commented, "I'll have someone bring your gear inside for you. Let's get you some food and a shower. I have some influence around here and might even be able to drum up some of our famous White House coffee – it's considered the best in the world by many."

Bishop's face brightened, "Coffee? Oh my god … I haven't had a good cup of joe in …." Agent Powell patted Bishop on the back, and the three men started walking to the entrance. Bishop stopped and turned back toward the SUV. "I need to get the Colonel's report out of my pack. He asked me to deliver it to the president personally."

Closely supervised by both agents, Bishop retrieved the packet of papers. After they verified the package contained nothing more dangerous than a paper cut, the party again proceeded to the building.

Bishop and the agents walked through a small, featureless lobby and then down a long hallway painted in government standard, light green. The mystery agent opened the door marked #11, and all three men entered. Bishop found himself standing in what amounted to a very small hotel room. As he looked around, Agent Powell returned to the hallway and could be heard talking on his radio. Bishop took the opportunity to size up his other escort. The agent was about 6'2" and probably tipped the scales at around 240. God had forgotten his neck while issuing the gentleman shoulders that were almost twice as wide as his mid-section. The dark suit and sunglasses did little to disguise the fact that the fellow was obviously in very good shape. *No doubt an ex-football player,* thought Bishop, *probably a linebacker for a Division I school.* Bishop couldn't help himself and said, "I bet you've never been accused of talking anyone's ear off." The comment met with zero reaction, and after an uncomfortable moment, Bishop decided to busy himself by inventorying the shampoo and soap in the bathroom. There was even shaving crème and a disposable razor. Deciding he had nothing to lose, Bishop looked back at the stone-faced bodyguard and said, "Don't worry, I'm not the type of guy to steal towels, and the shampoo isn't my brand." As expected, he received no reaction. *I've always heard building all those muscles makes your dick shrink* Bishop smirked to himself.

About then Agent Powell returned and informed Bishop that it would be awhile before the president could see him. It was suggested Bishop "freshen up," while he waited. Eyeing the shampoo and razor, Bishop agreed.

The two agents left the room, and Bishop had no doubt one of them remained in the hallway. He turned on the shower and undressed while the water warmed. Standing under the hot spray, the world suddenly became a better place. While he and Terri had their solar shower at the camper, being able to control the temperature with the simple twist of a knob was an extravagance he hadn't experienced in months. He embraced the shampoo to the extreme, lathering and rinsing his entire body no less than three times.

When he had soaked to the point where the skin on his fingers was wrinkled, Bishop turned off the water and grabbed a fresh, clean smelling towel. While the linen would have been insulting at a five star establishment, to Bishop it was as if he was drying his skin with soft clouds of luxury. The shave bordered on orgasmic.

Wrapping the towel around his waist, he exited the foggy bathroom to find his clothes were missing. A tray of food accompanied by a large pot of steaming coffee was sitting in their place on the bed along with a note that read, "You clothes will be returned to you shortly - Powell." Next to the food was a robe, which Bishop used to replace the damp towel.

His lunch consisted of sandwiches and a cup of clam chowder that obviously had never seen the inside of a can. Bishop consumed every last crumb with the gusto of a man who hadn't eaten anything but what he had killed or gathered in some time. It was the coffee, however, that was just shy of a miracle.

To the select few who had ever experienced it, the White House's coffee was known all around the world as unquestionably the finest anywhere. Grown in the Kona rainforest and shipped fresh from Hawaii, only a small percentage of the beans were chosen for the nation's first family. While everyday citizens could purchase a similar mix, the absolute best was saved for the Commander in Chief. Bishop had never tasted anything so smooth and delicious in his life.

~ ~

Drinking the excellent brew reminded Bishop of something a co-worker had once said. "Drinking a good cup of java is like making love to a beautiful woman. It starts off hot and sharp. The middle is smooth, warm, and rhythmical. The end leaves a glow of satiation." Bishop smiled at the memory and had to agree with the man.

He was on his third cup when a quiet knock disturbed the experience. Before he could even move his legs off the bed, the door opened, and a small Asian man entered, carrying Bishop's freshly laundered clothes. His boots had even been cleaned. Bishop started to ask if they had applied the proper amount of starch, but before he could speak the man left, closing the door behind him.

Five minutes later, Bishop stood, admiring his new image in the mirror. Another knock, followed by an immediate entrance of Agents Powell and What's-his-name, signaled it was time to meet the most powerful man in the world. Bishop was surprised that he actually felt a twitter of nerves in his stomach.

The three men crossed the base's parade grounds and up the steps of the clearly marked headquarters building. As they approached, Bishop noticed the outline of two snipers on the building's roof. There was another agent at the front door, and the military police, by sheer number, indicated a strong, secure presence all around the general vicinity. Bishop started to make a snide remark about feeling like a rock star with an entourage, but thought better of it. *Mr. Microdick wouldn't think it was funny anyway.*

Agent Jabber-Mouth stood and held open the beautiful doors, which were trimmed in thick brass and polished to a mirror-like luster. The ornate entrance reminded Bishop that he wasn't out in the field anymore, and the thought occurred to him that he should probably clean up his act.

The escorts guided them to a door marked as the Commanding General's Conference Room A. Mr. No-neck knocked precisely three times, and then his hands immediately returned to his sides. *Now I know the secret knock*, thought Bishop. A moment later the door opened, and Bishop was ushered inside.

The carpeting on the other side of the threshold was the first thing he noticed. His boots seemed to sink deeply into the plush flooring, and the effect almost caused him to lose his balance. The dim room contained a conference table about the size of a tennis court and several flat panel displays were mounted flush into the walls. *I wonder if they have any popcorn*, thought Bishop. Sitting at the far end was a single man. The light from the various wall displays was enough to make out his outline, and Bishop recognized that it was the President of the United States.

Slowly, the Commander in Chief stood and walked around the table toward Bishop. When he was a few steps away, he held out his hand, and for the first time, Bishop could clearly see his face. Bishop almost betrayed his shock at how "old" the nation's leader had become. While it had only been a few months since he had last seen this man on television, the change was drastic. His hair was almost completely silver, and his facial features betrayed exhaustion. The eyes were sunken deeply behind his taunt cheekbones, and his skin looked stretched and veiny. Normally, the tall, thin politician stood ramrod straight with squared shoulders for the television cameras. Today, he was slightly bent at the waist, and his shoulders slumped as if he was carrying a heavy pack.

Bishop managed his reaction and shook the president's hand. The leader's grip was weak, and his hands were cold. After the handshake, the older gentleman gestured toward a chair, and said, "Please, please have a seat." Bishop waited until the president had returned to his chair, before sitting down himself. *At least the man will know I wasn't born in a barn*, he thought. After settling in, the man looked at Bishop and said, "I understand you have some information for me from the Colonel."

Bishop nodded and handed across the papers he had been carrying. The president cleared his throat before pulling out a pair of eyeglasses. The specs were another revelation, but not surprising after he thought about it for a minute. The statesman pushed the glasses further up his nose, and then looked up at the ceiling. To his right, several buttons were installed in the surface of the table. After a few moments of indecision, the chief executive looked at Agent Powell with a helpless expression on his face. The bodyguard immediately moved to his boss's side and hit a button that turned on a small, directed overhead light toward the president's seating area.

For almost 30 minutes, Bishop sat in silence as the politician read the reports. Ever curious, he studied the displays around the room. The Colonel had described his mission as involving the mid-section of the country – specifically the Mississippi Delta. It was clear from the various computer graphics that something important was going on around Shreveport, Louisiana. The largest monitor, mounted at the end of the room, was constantly being refreshed. Bishop suddenly realized something had gone terribly wrong. At one corner of the huge map a counter was ticking. The label read "KIA," or killed in action. The number was in the thousands.

The chief executive looked up from his reading noticed where Bishop's attention was focused. He made sound and showed no expression. Bishop waited for the man to say something, but after blinking a few times, his head lowered, and the older man returned to his reading.

The president flipped to the last page and came to the final paragraph. It read:

Mr. President, since you are reading this, I believe it is a safe assumption that it was delivered by a very rare breed of young man. My advice, sir, is that you embrace his counsel. He has no agenda except that of the common citizen. He is, however, anything but common. I have seen him repeatedly wade through the deepest, most vile cesspools of evil that men have to offer, and yet still give freely of himself to others. My old friend, you would be wise to keep him close and use his ear.

The leader of the free world looked up at Bishop. He was a master at the game of international politics and knew how to deadpan his expression. Bishop didn't want to be rude and stare, but he also didn't want to appear uninterested. After a few minutes of scrutiny, the older man finally spoke. "The Colonel speaks highly of you, son. That is quite a compliment, given the source. Unfortunately, his report comes too late. We are painfully aware of the Independents. They caught us flatfooted in Louisiana, but now the genie is out of the bottle and won't be easily corralled."

Bishop nodded and replied, "Sir, I'm sorry it took me so long to get here. It's not easy to travel these days."

The president waved off the apology. "Don't worry about it young man. I wouldn't have reacted, nor done anything differently, even if I had known the details in this report a week ago. I wouldn't have believed it possible then, and quite frankly I'm still struggling to believe it now."

Bishop's brows knotted, his speech slow and deliberate, "Believe what, sir?"

"I can't believe my fellow countrymen would stoop to such traitorous acts. I can't believe so many military officers would violate their oaths. I can't believe so many of the people support these…these…Benedict Arnolds."

Bishop didn't know what to say. He found it easy to believe people had flocked to an alternative. The population had been suffering for years during the depression. The government wasn't functional and had completely lost any perspective of its purpose. He decided what the man across from him needed was a big dose of reality. "Mr. President, I lived in Houston with my wife. When everything went to hell, we tried to stay in our home, but there wasn't enough food. We took off on a desperate

145

journey across Texas. During this trip, I saw people eating bugs to survive. We witnessed dogs being butchered for meat. I saw entire forests completely destroyed just so people could build fires. A kind, wonderful man died in my arms because he couldn't get prescription medications. I watched women exchanging their bodies for food. I *can* understand why so many decide to go with the Independents – they are different and have a message. Why wouldn't people at least hear them out? Why would you expect any reaction other than, 'What do we have to lose?'"

Bishop's words didn't have any visual effect, but his instincts told him they had hit a nerve. The chief executive finally pushed back his chair and slowly stood. He walked around the table and pointed at the KIA number in the corner. "It's too late you know. It's already started. There were battles yesterday, and thousands are dead. Right now, both sides are licking their wounds and regrouping, but blood has been spilled - a lot of blood."

Bishop wanted to see the man's eyes, so he joined his host at the map. When a glance acknowledged his presence, he spoke. "Sir, it's too late for what?"

The older man's reaction startled Bishop. The president took a deep breath and exploded in anger. "They are traitors! Subversive conspirators, hiding in the shadows! Turncoats! They weren't elected by the people! No one in authority appointed them! *They*, whoever *they* are, crawl through the sewers and stink of the very worst humans can offer. I will hang each and every one of the backstabbing scum. I owe it to the good people who abide by the rule of law. I swore an oath to do so."

Bishop recovered quickly from the outburst and remained silent, waiting on the man to continue. After assuring himself no more was to follow, Bishop spoke in a calm, metered monotone. "Sir, you don't know what it's like out there. The good people of this land are living one rung above being animals and barely hanging on to that. No one gives a shit about elections, transfer of power, or who should be in charge."

The president's head snapped in Bishop's direction, and he spoke with passion. "We've done everything we can do. I've sent in the military, we have sent in food and what medical supplies we have. Every effort has been made to restore electricity and other basic services. I don't think anyone else could do more. What do people expect? What more can we possibly do?"

Bishop shook his head in disgust and responded harshly. "I'm not qualified to debate the role of government with you, sir. I'm by no means an expert. What I do know is what men are made of on the inside. Your actions took away people's freedom. The military killed initiative when it moved into the cities. That's why we left Houston rather than trying to stay and help rebuild. The only thing a lot of us had left was our freedom. The federal government didn't come in to help – they rolled in and took control. The message was clear – we are in charge, even though we don't have the ways or means to fix the problem. It was unrealistic to believe Americans would exchange their freedom for a life of depending on a government that couldn't deliver before the problem, let alone even the basics after it had all fallen apart. I didn't hear or see one single piece of advice from the army."

Bishop's statements changed the Commander- in- Chief's attitude. His response was more scholarly than political. "What were we supposed to do? Let the people who couldn't care for themselves starve? Let the wolves run rampant among the sheep? You are a big, strong young man and can no doubt fend for yourself. What about the people who can't? One reason why the government exists is to help those in need. Your point-of-view is too narrow and ego-centric to be practical."

Bishop wasn't going to debate social sciences with anyone. "Sir, why didn't the military use its resources to educate the people? Why didn't someone round up farmers and have them show folks how to grow a garden? The local governments would know best how to care for those needing a hand. The federal government has no choice but to implement a one size fits all solution." Bishop pointed to a map on the opposite wall where the growing territory controlled by the Independents was depicted. "They are doing something right. While you and I sit here and rehash old debates about centralized versus local authority, those so-called sewer rats are winning. I suggest you work with them, instead of fighting them."

The statesman started to respond, but Bishop interrupted him. "Sir, I can take you to a town nearby here that will prove what I'm saying. Since the collapse, it has become self-reliant. There is an economy, security, government and most importantly – free people improving their lives daily. Rather than you and I pretending we are the framers and arguing the extent of federal powers, why don't you go have a look and see for yourself?"

The president started to respond when there was a sharp rap on the door, and General Wilson entered the room. "Sir, our forces are in place around Shreveport. I need your confirmation to commence the operation."

Bishop looked at the exhausted man standing next to him. Clearly, the burdens of his office had taken their toll, but he hoped his message had gotten through. The Commander in

Chief's response made it clear Bishop's message had fallen on deaf ears. "General, I need to review the final stages of the order, and then you'll have my approval to proceed." Before Bishop could say anything, the president continued, "Oh, and general, please get this young man anything he needs, and let him be on his way back to his family." The president's expression made it clear that their meeting was concluded. He stuck out his hand and said, "God help us all, son.... God help us all."

Bishop was perceptive enough to know when a conversation was over. He started to protest, but shrugged his shoulders, and shook the man's hand. After he followed the general from the room, Bishop was escorted to a staging area where all of his gear was laid out on a large table. General Wilson tasked a nearby major with securing anything Bishop needed before escorting him off the base. Bishop asked to refill his water and inquired if any spare ammunition might be available. He asked for a few gallons of gas to refill his hidden ATV, and at the last minute, decided to fill his pack with as many MREs as he could carry. *I wonder if they would loan me a tank? That would be cool. Or, I know...I know...a helicopter! Could they give me a lift home in an Apache gunship? That would impress the hell out of everyone in Meraton.*

While the major left to retrieve Bishop's wish list, Agent Powell entered the room and offered his hand. Bishop and Powell made small talk for a few minutes until the major returned with two enlisted men in tow. Each had an armful of MREs, ammunition and water bottles. The major was carrying a five-gallon plastic gas can. Powell exited the space, as did everyone else, leaving Bishop alone to finish his packing.

When he was organizing his kit, Bishop felt a sense of failure. The Colonel had trusted him to deliver the message and to try and convince the man to work with the Independents, not fight them. Of course, the Colonel had no way of knowing that a war had already started. No, he wasn't going to feel bad at all. He had done his best and didn't think anyone could have convinced the man to back away. The POTUS clearly felt betrayed and was spoiling for a fight.

While Bishop was filling his camelback from the bottled water, his kept replaying the meeting in his head. The more he thought about it, the angrier he became. *That guy is all worried about everyone in the country kissing his high and mighty ass than helping the folks. He is so wrapped up in destroying the other side, he's not even thinking about the suffering going on out there. I should go back and try again. Surely, that Secret Service dude understands what's at stake; maybe he can get me a second time at bat.*

He was just about finished, when he thought to ask permission to see a doctor. He was curious if there might be anything he could carry back with him to help Terri's pregnancy, like vitamins or something. It was also a great excuse to delay leaving the base and perhaps get a second meeting with the president.

Bishop started to open the door and stopped cold. He heard the unmistakable sound of weapons being charged – a lot of weapons. As quietly as possible, he twisted the doorknob and cracked it open ever so slightly. There were several, heavily armed men lined up along the hallway wall, and someone was issuing orders. "There are only two Secret Service agents with the president right now. There are four more that will react within seconds. We need to get in there, kill the president, and get this over. I just saw the orders to attack at Shreveport, and this needs to be stopped right here and now. Remember – we are doing this for the people. We are doing this for the Independents."

Bishop could see the man issuing the orders was dressed like a Secret Service agent. The few men in his field of view wore a mixture of military and civilian clothing. He closed the door and leaned back against the wall taking a few deep breaths. *How fucking primitive are we? How stupid is this all going to get?* Bishop was torn between just walking out and letting the cards fall where they may, or taking action and trying to warn someone. He decided there was little he could do, and perhaps these assassins were right. Perhaps their actions would shorten the whole ordeal. He walked back to the table, lifted his pack onto his back and had started to sling his weapon, when the lights went out. Before he could even turn on the NVD, the door to his conference room burst open, and two men came charging through with weapons at the ready.

Bishop was lucky. He was slightly behind the doorway, picking up the can of gas, when the intruders entered. It took them a second or so to acquire him in the darkness, and that instant gave Bishop time to raise his weapon, while ducking low behind the table. The two men opened fire, and the shots went high, the muzzle flashes blinding everyone in the small room. Bishop, more from memory than aim, raised and fired back with four rounds, and then moved hard to his right. He felt bullets tearing through the air past his head, and again fired four more quick rounds. There was no return fire. Turning on his night vision, he moved cautiously around the edge of the table until he could see the two men lying on the floor. He recognized one of them as the captain who hadn't wanted him to enter the base. The man was still breathing and looked at Bishop with hatred in his eyes. Bishop kicked away the wounded officer's weapon, closed the door, and then bent over. "Why dude? What the fuck do you have against me?"

The dying man took several deep, raspy breaths and responded. "You are with *them*. You are against the Independents. I was ordered to take out any messenger who came here to see the president."

Bishop didn't like being shot at any more than anyone else did. He could justify a dozen different motivations for trying to kill someone, but politics wasn't one of them. As he thought about what the captain had said, he began to get angry. The people were going to suffer the most from this out-of-control power struggle. Just like any civil war, it was the innocent civilians who bore the blunt of the agony. As the initial shock of the whole situation began to wear off, Bishop felt a sense of helplessness. What could he do? He was one man, and this drama was being played out on a national stage.

As the young captain took his last breath, a thought occurred to Bishop. When he was a teenager, he and his father had often played the mental game of "what ifs," in world history. What if Hitler hadn't been so fixated on Stalingrad? What if someone had stopped John Wilkes Booth? As a boy, Bishop had always fantasized about being able to go back in time and watch history unfold. What did General Washington really say to the troops before crossing the Delaware? What was the look on his face? What was the tone of his voice? Did he take a sip of brandy from a flask before addressing his army?

Bishop's boyhood daydreaming always led to his wondering what he would have done if he were at that point in history. Would he have stopped Oswald from pulling the trigger on Kennedy? What would the world have been like if Bishop had been there?

It suddenly dawned on him that he was there – right here, right now. Should he try and stop the assassination? What was the better course for the world? Should he interfere with destiny? The sound of gunfire in the distance snapped him back to reality. As he slammed a magazine into his rifle, Bishop had one last philosophical moment. In all of the mental exercises with his father, a single thread of history prevailed – a leader or key person had died, causing pain and suffering for millions. Bishop knew he wasn't smart enough to determine the outcome of the president being killed. What he did know was he was sick and tired of watching people die, and it all had to stop somewhere. Maybe there was something he could do. Maybe one guy could make a difference.

Bishop cautiously opened the door and saw the hall was empty and very dim, lit only by the battery- powered emergency lights. The hit squad had no doubt killed the electricity to gain an advantage. Bishop raised his rifle and peered through the night vision in both directions before hustling down the hallway toward the gunfire in the distance.

He came to a point where the hall intersected with a main corridor of the building. The conference room where he had last seen the nation's leader was to the left, and so was the sound of the gunfight. The tempo of the battle was increasing, and Bishop guessed it would all be over soon.

After pie-ing the intersection, Bishop moved quickly down the main hall toward the conference room. He was careful to not stay to close to the walls, because he knew bullets sometimes hugged flat surfaces. He came to another corner and stopped, realizing he was very close to the ongoing fight.

Bishop thought about pie-ing this corner, but the wall behind him was full of bronze plaques and awards. He realized anyone waiting around the corner would have an advantage if they saw his reflection. He checked the building's construction, flicked off his safety, and fired three rounds about waist high into the plaster at the corner. These walls wouldn't stop his bullets, and if anyone was hiding around that corner, he probably had just taken them out of the fight. Sure enough, a body slumped over, falling out into the main walkway.

Bishop sprang around the corner and encountered a spectacle unlike anything he had ever seen. Somewhere off in the distance, battery-powered emergency lights provided just enough illumination to outline vague, dark shapes. A rolling cloud of smoke obscured the strobe of muzzle flashes, and the roar of so many weapons in such an enclosed space sounded like thunder. It was like Bishop had stepped into the very soul of hell's own thunderstorm.

The first man he came across was on a knee, spraying the conference room door with automatic fire. Bishop didn't hesitate and plugged the assassin from behind. His shots attracted the attention of others, and random rounds began to come his way. He was committed, and charged headlong into the fray. It all became a blur at that point. The doorway leading to the president had been hastily barricaded with chairs and a small table. Two Secret Service agents were barely holding off the assault. The attackers were advancing when Bishop's arrival changed the odds. The element of surprise was on his side as he tore into the midst of the gathered assassins, delivering pandemonium.

The fog of muzzle flashes, smoke, and debris littering the air didn't slow Bishop down. He could simply fire at any shape or outline he saw. The other side had to make sure they weren't shooting one of their own, which was working against them. The shooters on both sides were wearing body armor, and that proved to be a two-edged sword. The small space, combined with a large number of men equipped with high capacity weapons, meant everyone just kept pulling the trigger until the target went down. The resulting blizzard of lead eventually found a soft spot and did its work. Before the hit squad managed to pull back in the opposite direction, Bishop took out four of them and leaned against the doorway, panting for breath. He yelled into the conference room, "Hey inside! This is Bishop, and I've bought you some time. I suggest you get the president out of that coffin before these guys come back."

Before anyone could answer, the wall beside Bishop's head exploded with the impact of lead. Plaster and bits of wood stung his face, sending Bishop diving for cover. Unrelenting fire snapped through the air all around him, forcing Bishop to dig and squirm underneath two dead men lying on the floor. He managed to get his rifle up and began firing blindly as fast as he could pull the trigger. The attackers had evidently regrouped quickly and were pushing to regain their position. Unfortunately for them, the hallway wasn't that wide, and Bishop kept walking his rounds from one wall to the other, spraying fire into anything that entered the narrow space. The weight of the bodies Bishop was using as a shield limited his aim to knee high, but those bullets found legs. The first two men leading the charge fell not 15 feet from Bishop's face. Another man crashed to the floor in the next volley, narrowing the already-constricted fatal funnel by adding to the casualties lying everywhere. Despite the barricade of their dead comrades, they kept coming.

Bishop's rifle locked back empty, and he realized there was no way to reload - he was prone and covered in a blanket of inert flesh and heavy Kevlar. His hands were slick with other men's blood, and there was no way he could reach a magazine before they would kill him. Adrenaline does a lot of things to a man about to die. On this day, it gave Bishop physical strength. The surge of fear and certain death pulsated through his sinew and allowed him to rise up on all fours, lifting the two dead men still draped over his back and shoulders. He managed to crawl backward across the ice-slick floor while the body armor-equipped corpses took round after round of incoming fire.

Bishop could feel the thump and tug of bullets slamming into his shield, and it motivated him even more. Despite the floor being coated with urine, blood, sweat and dozens of spent cartridges, he made it to the corner and out of the line of fire. He shook off the dead men and regained his feet, while digging for a fresh magazine. His plan had been to buy enough time for the president's guards to get their boss out of that deathtrap conference room. It hadn't worked too well.

That fucking hallway is hell itself, and I'm not going back. One visit was enough for me – that was bullshit, he thought. Bishop's hands were shaking, and his skin was covered with drying sweat and blood. His shirt, pants and boots were covered with small flecks of flesh and who knew what else. A few seconds went by, and Bishop began to recover a bit, when another salvo of shots erupted. He knew the assassins were back, reengaging at the barricaded doorway. The cries of men and the roar of battle filled the halls for several seconds. Bishop was having trouble, commanding his legs to move back toward that meat grinder. *What the fuck am I doing here*, he kept thinking, *I've got no dog in this fight.*

He was standing there, gulping air and trying to muster enough courage to go back in, when suddenly, it all stopped. Bishop, thinking the assailants had finally overwhelmed the defending agents, moved back to the corner. No one shot at him. Taking a deep breath, he forced himself forward and began stepping around the causalities that were strewn everywhere. Small rivers of blood flowed, and the air was thick with cordite smoke and the stench of urine, feces and copper. Bishop quietly looked into the conference room and saw two men standing at the far end. One was the president with his hands in the air, and the other man held a pistol at arm's length. Bishop raised his rifle and shot the man with the pistol.

There were still sounds of gunfire in the distance, and Bishop could hear commands being screamed from several different directions. He turned to the president and yelled, "Come on sir, we *have* to get out of here. Everyone in the hall is dead or dying, and we have to move now!"

The older man seemed in shock at the entire episode and wouldn't move. Bishop grabbed his arm and commandeered him toward the door. The stunned executive followed without protest, as if in a trance. After kicking some of the blockage out of the way, Bishop cleared the hallway, and began guiding the president through the gruesome maze. They made it to the first corner when Bishop heard sporadic gunfire and the sound of boots running in their direction. More to avoid the converging men than any knowledge of the building's layout, Bishop pulled the president with him in the opposite direction, and the two wound their way toward the back of the building.

A minute later, Bishop quietly pressed the fire escape bar on a heavy steel door and poked his head outside. They had navigated to a small loading dock area, serviced by an alleyway that ran along the rear of the building. The alley was empty. The president was recovering from the shock of it all and becoming more lucent. Bishop pointed to the building on the opposite side of the lane and said, "Give me just a second to see if it's clear." Bishop bounded across the alley and up three concrete steps, landing a well-timed kick against a wooden door. The door exploded inward, and Bishop encountered what appeared to be an empty office of some kind. The inner door to the room was locked, and the layer of dust covering the floor made it appear as if no one had occupied the space in years.

Bishop waved for the chief executive to join him and covered the path as the slower man crossed. Both of them leaned against the wall, catching their breath, as the sound of voices, gunshots and racing engines grew louder in the distance. "We can't stay here, sir. The first problem is not knowing who is on your side and who is trying to kill you. The bigger problem is that I might be mistaken for either side if we try and find some help. No offense sir, but I don't work for the Secret Service, and I'm not taking a bullet for you."

The president nodded. "No offense taken."

Bishop wanted to see what was through the door leading to the interior of the building, but before he could look, something motorized came roaring down the alleyway they had just crossed. The vehicle sounded as though it stopped right outside their door, and Bishop raised his rifle preparing for a breach. Despite his previous declaration, he placed himself between the doorway and the president. The two men could hear voices outside, and when it became apparent that no one was going to kick in the door and shoot at them, Bishop took a chance and peeked at the alley. There was a military police Humvee parked outside, complete with flashing lights on the roof and the MP logo on the door. Bishop could see a single soldier standing in close proximity. The army cop was scanning both ends of the alley. After closing the door, Bishop leaned back and pondered what to do. He had to get clear of this base and bring his guest along. He really couldn't think of any other option, since it was impossible to tell who was friend and who was foe. From the sound of the gunfire around the base, other people were having the same problem of identification.

Bishop pulled a bundle of para-cord out of his pack and cut off about a four-foot length. He cracked the door open again and observed the young soldier pacing back and forth outside. The Humvee was still there, motor idling. When the patrolling private had his back turned, Bishop opened the door a little wider to get a better look up and down the alley. There wasn't anyone else around. He scanned the rooftops, remembering the men positioned up there, but couldn't see anyone.

He drew his pistol and when the sentry was in the right position, Bishop quietly passed through the door and approached the unsuspecting MP. The cold barrel against the man's skull, right behind the ear, had the desired reaction. Bishop said, "Don't give me any trouble, and you'll be fine. Turn around and walk back with me."

After the frightened man had been securely tied with para-cord and relieved of his helmet and weapons, Bishop again verified no one was in the alley. The two men quickly exited their hiding spot and jumped in the running vehicle. Bishop looked over at his passenger and said, "Fasten your seatbelt please, sir – you can never be too careful these days, and I don't want a ticket." The president didn't get the joke and just stared for a brief moment. Bishop put their new ride in gear and sped off down the alley, telling the stunned statesman to put on the helmet, duck low and keep out of sight.

Bishop didn't head for the front gate, but guided the Humvee to the north and away from the primary complex of buildings. Thirty minutes later, they were going cross-country over rough desert terrain and officially crossed the base's boundary shortly after that.

Bishop looked over at his traveling partner and asked if he should officially change the designation of their ride to Humvee One. The president rolled his eyes, seemingly finding no humor in the remark. Finally, the passenger spoke, "Where are you taking me?"

"Well, sir," Bishop started, "I'm not sure. First of all, I will take you anywhere you want to go. I'm not kidnapping you. Is there someplace you'd like to go?"

The Commander in Chief thought about the question for a moment and then replied, "No, no I can't think of anywhere safe. On the other hand, I do have a country to run."

Bishop, without thinking, added, "At least half a country anyway," and then immediately regretted the remark. Trying to recover, he quickly added, "I don't know of anywhere safe either. If we have enough gas, I can get us back to some friends, but I would hardly call that safe. Maybe we'll think of something along the way."

As they drove through the desert, Bishop couldn't help but keep an eye skyward. He was worried about helicopters being used to search for them. He looked over at his passenger and said, "Mr. President, please keep a lookout for aircraft of any kind. The people back at the base will find the MP I restrained and realize we are mobile. If I were them, I would spin up a helicopter and search for us from the air."

There was no way of knowing how deeply the Independents had penetrated the units at Fort Bliss, or how well organized they were. Someone looking for them from the air could be from either side. He decided that there was one sure way to tell – the Independents would automatically fire without question, while the Loyalists would seek to rescue the man beside him. Bishop was rooting for the Loyalists.

As they drove through the barren terrain, the discussion centered on how long it would be before both sides would start searching. Bishop was gambling it would take quite a while for things to get sorted out back at the base. Bliss was an enormous facility with hundreds of buildings capable of hiding the Humvee. They would have to search there first. One side couldn't be sure the other didn't already have the president. The Loyalists would assume he had been kidnapped, rather than murdered. The Independents might believe their target had been stashed away for safekeeping, an attempt to bait them out into the open. The bottom line was that every minute that passed gave them distance, and that improved their odds.

After an hour of bumping, jolting travel, Bishop saw a good place to take a break. The Humvee wasn't known for its smooth ride and would never be favorably compared to a luxury-touring sedan. The lack of suspension was aggravated by Bishop's aggressively driving a little faster than normal to maximize their head start.

He parked under a large outcropping of rock that had separated and slid off a cliff face thousands of years ago. From the air, it would be difficult to spot their transportation since it was painted in desert camouflage and actually blended in quite well with their environment. Both men climbed out of the oversized jeep and began stretching stiff legs and sore joints. After a quick scan of their surroundings, Bishop decided to inventory the contents of Humvee One's rear storage area. He was surprised to find quite the arsenal and cache of supplies. There were two M4 carbines, a can of 5.56 ammo, and a pump shotgun. There was a full carton of MREs and two cases of bottled water. A large, well-stocked medical kit rounded out the contents. In the backseat, Bishop found a freshly laundered set of fatigues and spare pair of boots. He held up the clothing and looked over at the politician standing nearby. "Mr. President, I'm not a fashion expert, but I think you would be more comfortable if these duds fit you. We may have to set out on foot, and you definitely don't look dressed for cross country hiking."

The pants were a little too short and the boots half a size too big, but the Commander in Chief looked reasonably comfortable, dressed in the garb of a sergeant in the United

States Army. In reality, Bishop thought the man looked timeworn and weary. Bishop decided to press his luck, pulling out one of the M4 rifles. "Mr. President, have you ever fired one of these?"

Before long, the Prez was working the action of the carbine like a recruit in boot camp. Bishop wished he could video the scene, as the guy who could launch hundreds of nuclear warheads struggled to remember where the controls were on the most basic weapon in the inventory. He had to admit though, the man wasn't stupid and caught on quickly. After a few minutes of basic instruction, Bishop believed the president could fire the rifle if he had to. *Wish we had a little time on the range, Mr. President,* Bishop mused.

There was a five-gallon can of diesel in a welded bracket on the back of the Humvee. Bishop tapped on the can and was surprised to find it full. He wasted no time in draining the fuel into the primary tank. The gauge on the dash didn't seem to be working, and he had no idea how much fuel was aboard, but knowing at least five gallons was available, provided some peace of mind.

After both men decided they weren't hungry, Bishop pulled the Humvee from under the outcropping and continued heading southeast across the barren landscape.

General Westfield and Special Agent Powell sat and listened as two different officers reported there was no sign of the leader of the free world or the visitor. The soldiers aligned with the Independents, as well as the two rogue Secret Service agents, had been killed in the ensuing firefight. But the skirmish had continued for some time because loyal units had mistakenly engaged each other in the confusion. The young MP had been discovered and was immediately debriefed, along with his sergeant. There was no sign of the missing Humvee.

Powell looked at the base commander and shook his head in disgust. "General, we obviously have to find the president if he's still alive. General Wilson is dead, and the vice president didn't make it out of Washington. The House and Senate are disturbingly vacant. There is no one to secede. There's no Supreme Court Justice to swear someone in. As of right now general, I guess you are the acting President of the United States.

General Westfield's head snapped up, and he stared hard at Agent Powell. "I don't think so. I'm only a major general in the United States Army, sir. I'm not even in the top 100 to succeed the parking attendant at the White House, let alone run the country. I've never ridden on Air Force One, kissed anybody's ass, or accepted a dubious campaign contribution. Clearly, I'm not qualified and wouldn't want the job even if it were constitutionally sound. I'll pass."

Agent Powell had to admit he had zero authority to appoint anybody. He was also happy to hear General Westfield wasn't a power-grabbing maniac. He had listened and heard enough to know that a very large battle was looming in Louisiana and didn't believe the boss had approved the final orders yet. They had to find the president if he was still alive.

Yet another knock on the general's door sounded. A scared shitless lieutenant nervously reported that two Blackhawk helicopters were making ready to search the area. The Secret Service was to have two men on board each aircraft. Agent Powell intended to be one of them.

The Humvee's front wheels dipped hard into a rut that wasn't visible until the very last second. Both passenger-one and Bishop were jolted forward and then slammed back into their seats as the heavy vehicle cleared the depression. The leader of the free world looked at Bishop and frowned. "Are you trying to hit every bump, sir, or are you simply blind?"

Bishop thought he was innocent of any bad driving and decided to defend himself. "This ain't no Mercedes limo, sir, and this sure as shit ain't Pennsylvania Avenue." Right about then the left front wheel found a basketball-sized rock and proceeded to climb it. Both men were shoved right and then when the wheel cleared the obstacle, they were thrown left. The process was repeated when the rear tire performed the same trick. The chief executive had had enough. "I certainly hope you shoot better than you drive, sir. I should demand you return me to Bliss immediately so the assassin's bullet can put a quick end to it, rather than be slowly bludgeoned to death out here. Have you ever driven a car before....SIR?"

Bishop loved it! Here he was, rubbing elbows with the Commander in Chief, and the guy was actually busting his balls. Not only that, he was pretty good. Rolling up his intellectual sleeves and preparing for battle, Bishop returned the salvo. "Sir, at least I drive my own car and hold my own rifle. Not everyone can afford hired help for the menial tasks. When, if I may ask, was the last time you planted the executive gluteus maximus behind the steering wheel of a car?"

The president laughed and then became thoughtful. "You know Bishop, that's a good question. I can't remember the last time I drove anywhere. I remember a bright red Ford Mustang convertible my father bought me for my 21st birthday. Oh how I loved to drive that car up and down those abandoned New Mexico highways. That was fun."

The Humvee began crossing a rock field that made both men's teeth rattle. It seemed the surface was trying to slam their bodies in all four directions at once. The president sounded off, "That's it! I've had enough! I demand you pull this rolling torture chamber over, and let someone with more experience and competence drive."

Bishop snorted, and then began looking around. After playing it just the right amount of time, he looked at the president and said, "I'd be happy to sir, except I don't see anyone that meets the requirement." The politician rolled his eyes at the remark and both of them laughed. After another jolting desert landmark compressed both men's spines into the thinly cushioned, military issue seats, Bishop slowed down and decided to take a break.

The president mistook Bishop's actions to signal a change in drivers. He laughed again and said, "Oh, I was just joking, Bishop. While I would surely enjoy the novelty of driving, I couldn't do any better than you are, son."

Bishop thought about the remark and sighed. Despite his better instincts, he made up a little white lie. "Mr. President, I would actually prefer if you took the wheel for a while. I've been up for more than 24 hours straight."

For the first time since Bishop had been in the man's presence, the chief executive's face actually brightened up for a moment. The reaction was short lived; however, and he began shaking his head no. "I don't know that I could, son. It's been so long."

Bishop waved his arm at the empty horizon, "Sir, it's not like you're going to run over anyone or have an accident. It there was ever anyplace to re-learn how to drive, it's out here."

"Well, you certainly have a point there."

Bishop stopped in the open desert. There wasn't any place to hide, but he didn't intend to be here long. The two men were stretching their legs and backs when movement caught Bishop's eye. He quietly said, "Sir, please get your rifle...but do slow slowly."

The older man looked startled and started to ask what was wrong, but Bishop put his finger up to his lips and made the

"*Shhhhhh*" noise. The president then followed Bishop's arm as it pointed in the distance, and he strained to see what had Bishop's attention. Finally, movement caught his eye as well, and he spotted a hefty Texas jackrabbit about 200 feet away. The animal had moved ever so slightly, but was now sitting on its hind legs with long pointed ears searching the area for predators.

The man looked back at Bishop with a puzzled look on his face. Bishop mouthed the word, *"Dinner."*

The president braced the M4 on the open door of the Humvee, as Bishop watched him try and recall how to fire the weapon. Both men were happy when the trigger was pulled, and the weapon's report went echoing across the desert. *I sure hope no one hears that*, thought Bishop. The rabbit, however, didn't move. The president steadied his aim while muttering, "Missed...damn it," and soon the weapon bucked again. This time, the dust directly to the left of the target splashed into the air, and the animal scampered off.

With great disappointment, the hunter started to lower his rifle, but Bishop motioned for him to wait. Sure enough, the rabbit bounded about 20 times and then stopped. After another few seconds, both men watched it rise on its back legs and look around. Bishop whispered, "They aren't too bright. Take your time, and try to hit him in the head. There will be more meat left that way."

The third shot was good, and the animal fell immediately. "I got him!" Bishop thought about the excitement in the president's voice and wondered if the man had ever been hunting before. He decided he would ask later, if there were time. The president started to walk across the open space to his prey, but Bishop insisted they drive in case the sound of the shots drew unwanted attention.

Chapter 13

Meraton Rescue

Meraton's main street was filled with more excitement than even the oldest residents could remember. Two pickups full of armed men from the Beltron ranch had arrived. They rolled into town, truck beds brimming with men holding onto ten-gallon hats with one hand and rifles with the other. While waiting for everything to be arranged, Pete's was experiencing a boom in business.

David had returned with the Beltron crew. He reported to Terri that Samantha had lost the argument over who was going to Alpha and who was staying behind to help Mr. Beltron run the ranch. Mr. Beltron had asked David's sister to stay, and that request had won her over. Sarah didn't want anything to do with returning to her alma mater, and had happily stayed behind too. David hurried off to see his grandfather and say goodbye.

Pete had managed to gather up five men who either had family in Alpha or had lost relatives in the raids from the neighboring town and wanted to settle a grudge. Reluctant family members hovered around the soon to be departing warriors, trying to either lend support or talk them out of the endeavor.

Terri, Nick, and Kevin were in the gardens of the Manor getting their gear and kit together. A friendly debate had been in progress as to whether or not to stop by the ranch on the way. Terri knew Bishop had cases of ammunition in the bat cave, as well as several rifles. Nick, despite wanting to utilize Bishop's additional firepower in the upcoming fight, didn't think they should take the time, or chance pissing Bishop off. It was finally decided that they would "run what they brung," and head directly to Alpha.

Betty was trying to organize a last minute, hurried food drive of sorts for both the Meraton men and the needy members of Diana's church. Given the lack of notice and communications, she was doing surprisingly well. The lobby of the Manor was the central gathering depot, and twice she had to shoo off Beltron ranch hands from eating all of the gathered supplies.

Diana, true to her military training, had assumed a command position. She was standing in the bed of one of the Beltron trucks, attempting to organize the chaos. Using a borrowed pad of paper from Pete, she was taking note of the number of men, weapons, and supplies being gathered. As Nick and Terri exited the gardens, Diana hopped down from the bed and approached with a scowl on her face. "What's wrong?" asked Terri.

"I don't want to appear ungrateful, but I'm worried about this. Some of these ranch hands have less than 20 rounds for their rifles. Three of them are in Pete's trying to bolster their courage with hard liquor even as we speak. One man from Meraton has never fired his shotgun before. I don't think they realize this isn't a cowboy movie fight at the O.K. corral. They are going into a war zone and are unprepared."

Nick tried to reassure her, "Diana, I understand your concern, but you can't tell me your church members were ready for World War III when it all went to hell."

Diana interrupted the big man, "And a lot of them died."

Nick paused for a moment and then tried to reassure her, "Those ranch hands look mighty tough to me, and like any group of men entering battle, they will perform based on what's inside of them. You can't control that, Diana. Every single one of them volunteered to be here. They know what could happen."

Diana looked around at the swarm of activity and then back at Nick. "I know...I know. I guess I'm a little burned out on sending people to their death. I should just chill and be happy we are getting some help."

Twenty minutes later, the Meraton militia rolled out of town in three pickup trucks. The gathered townsfolk stood along both sides of Main Street, waving their goodbyes and yelling out "good luck," "love you," and "hurry home." Many of the observers stayed right where they were, watching the small convoy head west until the trucks were only small specks on the horizon.

Pete reached in his pocket and pulled out the shotgun shell he had borrowed from old man Parker. He hung a "Back in 30 minutes," sign on the bar door and walked down one of the side streets paralleling Main. A few turns and blocks later, he came to a smallish blue-gray shingled sided home with two goats tethered in the yard. He didn't even bother with the front door, but walked around to the shed in the rear. "Josh, it's Pete; you home?"

Josh's head showed around the corner of the building. "Hey, Pete. What brings you out this way?"

Pete sauntered up and shook hands. Josh was in his mid-60s, tall and thin with a scratchy, gray beard and hair. Pete had always thought Josh both looked and acted like the patriarchal Clampet from the old television show *The Beverly Hillbillies*. Several people in Meraton thought the same thing, and the man's nickname around town was "Jed."

Josh was a widower and one hell of a nice guy. Once a week or so he would show up at Pete's Place and have a single shot. A few stories would be exchanged along with a joke or two, and then he would tip his hat and say his goodbyes. Josh had also volunteered for the town posse, serving whenever asked.

The older gent was a retired oilfield worker from Midland, Texas. Pete asked him one time why he had moved to Meraton. Josh had just smiled and said that Midland was getting too crowded for his taste. By accident, Pete had found out that Josh reloaded his own ammunition. One night while sweeping the floor of the bar, Pete found a wallet. The driver's license inside told him it belonged to Josh, and after closing, Pete had set off to return it to its owner.

Pete had knocked on the front door a few times with no response. He chanced around to the side of the home and saw a light burning in the back shed. Naturally, Josh was thankful Pete had returned his billfold. After a few jokes about how empty it was, the tall man offered Pete a tour of his workshop. That's where Pete saw a lot of interesting equipment, some of it for reloading.

Pete handed Josh the shell and explained the situation with Mr. Parker. "I don't know what we can do Josh, but I'm not going to sleep well at night, worrying about him shooting one of those kids."

Josh nodded, "There's a whole herd of youngin's running around down at that end of town. I think that Gomez family has six or seven just by themselves. Don't the Hutchinson's have another one on the way, too?"

Pete nodded, "Yes, I saw her at the market the other day. She's due in March, I think. That will be their third, if I remember right."

Josh looked at the shotgun shell Pete had handed him. His weathered fingers toyed with the plastic case for a bit, and then in a "eureka!" moment, his fist snapped closed around the brass head. "I've got an idea, Pete."

After motioning for Pete to follow him into the shed, Josh went directly to a workbench and plucked a handheld tool from a drawer. He held the shell in his hand and worked on the folded plastic opening at the top. In no time, he turned the shell on its side and dozens of small round lead pellets poured out onto the bench. Pete watched, fascinated, pretty sure he knew where this was going. The pellets were called "shot," and flew out of the end of the barrel into the target. They were what did the damage.

Josh went outside and looked around the yard for a bit, finally settling on a bare piece of ground not far from the driveway. He reached down and scooped up a small handful of sand and carried it back to the bench. After painstakingly removing any rocks larger than a pinhead, he refilled the shell with the powder-like sand before moving to a different section of the workbench. He placed the shell into a press- like device and pulled down on the handle.

After retrieving the shell from the press, Josh held it up to the light and admired his handiwork. He handed it over to Pete and said, "This wouldn't harm a baby sparrow outside of 20 feet. It will go boom and make a lot of smoke and noise, but anyone more than 20 feet away is as safe as if they were in their mother's arms."

Pete took the shell and looked it over. He couldn't tell any difference from the original, except it felt a little lighter. He didn't think old man Parker would notice. "Okay Josh, I like the idea. Now we have to think up a way to replace his box of shells with these non-lethal ones."

"If he has a full box, it would take me about 30 minutes to pull the swap. Can you get me those shells for that long?"

Pete thought about it for a minute and nodded. He propped his leg on the bench, settling in to tell Josh his plan.

~ ~

A short time later, Pete was seen walking toward the Parker house for the second time that day. He paused at the mailbox again and shouted, "Ben. Ben, you still home?"

As before, movement could be seen inside. "Pete? Did you forget something?"

Pete opened the gate and took a few steps toward the house. He stopped about mid-way and said, "Ben, meeting with you this morning got me to thinking. I double-checked your old bar tab, and I overcharged you. I owe you a drink or two, my friend. I was in the area and wanted to let you know. I run a square business and don't want to cheat anybody."

Ben took a second to reply. "Well thank you, Pete. I appreciate an honest businessman. We could use more of that in this country. What time does the bar open?"

"I'm heading back there now. If you want, I'll wait, and we can walk together."

Ben nodded vigorously, happy to have someone to talk to and free drinks to boot. "I'll be right there."

As the two men strode toward Pete's place, they passed by a man leaning against a streetlight, reading a book. Josh lowered the old novel and smiled as he watched the duo entered the bar. Josh immediately headed in the opposite direction.

A short time later, Josh returned to Ben's house and laid the modified shells right where they had originally rested on the table. He opened the double-barrel's breech and replaced the two rounds that had been inside. As he closed the weapon and sat it next to the doorframe, he thought, "We did a good thing today, as long as he doesn't have any spare ammo around." Josh quietly left the house and sauntered home.

Agent Powell watched as an army private mopped the floor outside of the conference room. The lights had been turned up, and several men were busy cleaning up the last remnants of the firefight. Normally, the Secret Service would have immediately called in the FBI to process the crime scene, but the El Paso field office had ceased to function months ago. He had considered calling in experts from Washington, but every available government official in the capital was trying to rebuild the White House, Capital Building and other official offices that had been ransacked during the riots. The few FBI agents who did report for work were busy running down a long list of missing government officials, including the majority of the House and Senate. The military had established order two days after the White House had been overrun, and in reality the riot had pretty much burned itself out before the tanks had rolled into town.

While the Pentagon's location had prevented it from being damaged, the number of soldiers and civilian staffers showing up to work had been next to zero. The riots had made several nearby streets impassable, and most people took the D.C. police's orders to "stay in your homes" seriously. Agent Powell normally stood behind the boss during status meetings and knew the number of people reporting for duty and work had been trickling higher since the outburst of violence, but still a vast majority of the federal agencies were non-functional. A big part of the problem was the fact that practically every interstate and surface road within 50 miles of a major city was a parking lot of abandoned vehicles. Even if employees wanted to show up for work, there was no way they could drive to the office.

Powell remembered the president being upset after reading one such report at Fort Knox. The man had taken it personally and believed it some sort of measurement of loyalty, directed at him personally. Powell had been listening to that meeting from his normal post at the door. That misinterpretation had been one of the first signs the commander had shown of cracking under stress. The service was trained to watch and observe for such reactions, but there had been few other incidents, and no action had been required. Powell was unsure, given the collapse of the government, what he would have done about it anyway.

The senior agent actually liked this president. Given his 31 years of guarding various heads of state, he had seen it all. While this man wasn't the brightest person to occupy the oval office, he wasn't the dumbest either. Truth be told, he was relatively honest and seemed to be truly motivated to do a good job for the country. His analysis ended immediately at that point. It wasn't the service's job to decide if any president were effective, a clown, or a genius. Their training and policies were very strict, and Agent Powell believed that narrow view was appropriate, given the job of protecting the chief executive at all costs. An agent was more likely to throw his body into the line of fire for a man he admired, than a man he despised. The agency realized this, and thus structured their training to avoid the personal evaluation of any specific president's job performance from entering the equation.

Now, the man he had sworn to protect was missing. Agent Powell had lead the counterattack against the assassins only to find a pile of bodies, and none of them belonged to the boss. At first, everyone assumed that the Independents had captured the president, but within 15 minutes the bound MP was found, and the facts became clear.

They didn't even know the stranger's real or full name. He had shown up at the guardhouse with valid papers and an attitude. Powell didn't believe the messenger was involved in the assassination attempt. One of the Independents was found wounded and lying on the floor of the hallway. The man was dying and in a lot of pain. The morphine injection not only eased his suffering, but also loosened his tongue, and he claimed that the stranger was to be executed as well. The two dead bodies found in the room where the stranger had last been seen, added credibility to that information.

So this single man had shot his way through a death squad, rescued or taken the president, and escaped a major military base unseen. Agent Powell grunted and shook his head. The guy had been a smart ass according to all reports. He clearly had a large pair and some skills to back them up. Powell didn't believe the president was dead. If the stranger had wanted to kill the boss, he could have done so a dozen times before leaving the base. If the guy's story was to be believed, he had traveled across the desert to deliver the Colonel's report, so he had some level of loyalty to the chief.

They had his fingerprints on the documents delivered to the president. They also had the serial numbers from his weapons and night vision. In normal times, Agent Powell would have known every single detail about the guy within 15 minutes. These were not normal times. The usual fingerprint identification systems were down. The Bureau of Alcohol, Tobacco and Firearms had burned to the ground in Washington, so tracing the serial numbers from the weapons was next to impossible. It was all maddening to the agent – all of his normal tools were unavailable…and just when he needed them most.

Still, he didn't think the guy wanted to hurt the boss. *He probably will show up at the gate with the president soon*, thought Powell. *I wouldn't be surprised if he walked through that door with the chief in tow any minute now.*

Powell couldn't count on some guy he didn't know. That wasn't part of the job. They were going to be searching from the air with the two Blackhawks soon, but he didn't hold out much hope for that being a success. Whoever this stranger was, he was smart enough to hide from an aerial search, and it was a mighty big desert out there.

Suddenly, the senior agent remembered the president's jacket. That was it! The GPS locator sewn into the collar should still function. The service had never used the system as no one had ever lost track of the chief executive. Powell rushed out of the room and down the hall to General Westfield's office. Rudely barging through the base commander's door, he blurted out, "General, can you get me in contact with the Air Force's Space Command up at Peterson?"

The general brushed aside his annoyance at being interrupted and replied, "I'm not sure. Those Air Force boys have had their heads buried in the sand since this all went down. They claim to barely be holding their own bases and protecting those precious flying machines of theirs. I'll have communications see if they can raise them on the sat system. I'm here to tell you though; they aren't going to give us any aircraft. They keep fussing and making excuses about having no spare parts or fuel or flying blind without weather reports."

Powell shook his head, "The air assets I want are already up there, general. Let's hope they answer."

Smokey pointed to the large map of Alpha, spread out on the courthouse's marble floor. The map had been found in the Visitor's Bureau lobby and moved to its current location. Gathered around the detailed representation of the small town were several of the head criminal's lieutenants.

"We were too slow to enter the gap created by the garbage truck," he began. "The holy rollers had too much time to react, and that's what cost us." Smokey looked around at everyone's eyes, making sure his words were being taken seriously. "This evening, when we punch through their wall, we have to pour in like crazy. Once inside, don't allow your men to bunch up or stop to close to the entrance. Spread out, and keep moving everyone forward."

Again, his gaze was met with nods of understanding.

Smokey knew they had hurt the defenders badly. Had it not been for the last second heroics of that giant Russian, they would have overrun the church, and he would be having his fun with that Deacon Brown woman about now. He chuckled at the thought, *"If she lasts that long."*

It had taken his men some time to recover as well. Despite his better instincts, Smokey had discovered that even the most hardcore of men would fight better if they believed medical attention was available to the wounded. In the first few skirmishes with the church, he had ordered the wounded left in the field to die. The reaction from his followers had proven this to be a mistake. Smokey 'adjusted' his thinking on the subject, and since then the wounded had been treated as humanely as possible. Some had healed and gone on to fight another day. Now, the majority of his lieutenants boasted of gunshot wounds, showing off the scars to the men with less experience.

While they had killed several of their foes, they had suffered as well. A head count revealed 28 fewer men than had started the attack. It was the worst single day death toll so far, but Smokey knew he had to press his advantage and do so quickly.

Over the next 20 minutes, Smokey made every man repeat the plan back to him. He wanted to verify each of his group leaders knew his role and where everyone else was going to be. He had watched too many attacks peter out because of confusion or lack of communication. He wanted to get this over with while he still had enough manpower to control the town.

One thing that puzzled him was the report of a single truck sneaking out of the church compound early this morning. The observer couldn't tell who was driving, but the vehicle sped southeast toward Meraton. Smokey's people had raided the tiny town a few times, but had returned with little loot. At least the ranch a few miles north had cattle and other livestock to steal and butcher. After he had mopped up that little chapel and secured their water supply, he would focus his attentions on that ranch next, and then the little town if it suited him. For right now, he had to motivate his men to fight even harder and take apart those people at the church.

~ ~

Colonel Marcus slowly bent over and began unlacing his boots. He hadn't slept in 48 hours, and he was feeling the pain in his lower back. His aide set up a cot next to the receptionist's work area, outside of the principal's office. He could close the door and have some privacy. A pair of windows had been opened, letting in the light breeze from the southwest. As he slowly pulled off a boot, the odor from his socks drifted up and caused a grimace. A shower would be the first thing on his agenda when he woke up. The second boot didn't produce any rosier results. He started to smell his armpits, but decided he'd had enough torture for one day. He managed to stand for a moment and took a knee next to the folding cot. Bracing his elbows on the edge, he lowered his head and whispered a prayer:

Father in heaven, forgive me my transgressions against others this day. Forgive me if I have not done your will. My father please be with the families of the men who perished on the field of battle today. Please welcome every single soldier's soul into your kingdom as those men and women have already suffered through hell. Please God, give those who command us here on earth the wisdom to stop this madness. Show them the way, Lord. Amen

The colonel laid back on the stiff cotton surface. All of the pillows were being used for the wounded, but he didn't care. It was a relief to stretch out and remove the pressure from his lower vertebra.

Marcus stared up at the block panel ceiling, the grids reminding him of the maps he had been working with all day. The reinforcements arriving from all over the region had to be logged, briefed, and assigned sectors of operation. The flow of units reporting to his command had finally slowed to a trickle a few hours ago, and his officers had insisted he catch a few Zzzzzzs. The fact that he couldn't remember the command frequencies probably worried his juniors.

The colonel sighed and rubbed his eyes. He had done everything possible to get his command ready. After the last battle, he doubted it would be enough. He wondered if every commander felt the same hollowness in his gut after watching the destruction of an entire brigade. His beloved 4/10 was gone, the faces of his men still flashing before his eyes.

When the Independents had informed him that he was still in command, his initial thought had been to protest. Hadn't he done enough? Now that he was winding down, he realized their decision had been a blessing. The work had kept his mind from the previous day's slaughter.

Visions of exploding tanks, screaming men and flames kept cycling through his head. Ordering two Strykers full of infantry directly into an ambush... watching the burning men trying to crawl across the ground through his binoculars.... Talking with a young lieutenant on the radio to be suddenly interrupted by screams and chaos as his tank was hit.... Marcus wondered if the memories would ever fade.

It wasn't just his men. Perhaps that's why it seemed so bad. He had watched *Americans* on the other side suffer just as badly. Marcus wondered if recalling the enemy's destruction would normally offset the pain he felt at his own losses – if they hadn't been his countrymen.

There had been two different points in the battle where Marcus had thought to order his command company into the fray. As he looked back, he had wanted so badly to join his men on the field, but a last second maneuver or event had canceled the need. His desire to engage hadn't been about bravery or honor. The colonel had long ago established he possessed plenty of both. The assortment of ribbons on his dress uniform were impressive, even for a command level officer. No, it wasn't to prove anything to anyone – it was for his brothers in arms. Marcus had wanted to join the fight because his men were dying and needed his help. That situation peeled back the layers of responsibility, command and common sense like a sharp knife removed the skin of an apple. Men he had sacrificed, suffered, and served with were being killing by the hundreds, but he had pushed down an almost uncontrollable urge to join in their struggle.

In the end, it hadn't been necessary. Marcus wondered what he would be feeling now if he had "found work," on the battlefield that day. Would he not have this empty feeling inside? Would he actually feel worse?

"Come on old man, this isn't your first rodeo. You've seen your share of death before," he whispered aloud to himself. No, he decided, not like yesterday – nothing like that. Not since D-Day had an army suffered so many casualties in such a short amount of time. Even the Israeli routes of their Arab neighbors had seen less death stretched over a longer period of time.

A man doesn't reach the rank of colonel in the United States Army without possessing an abundant amount of self-control and discipline. Marcus pulled deep from inside and corralled his emotions. He *had* to rest, and sleep wouldn't come if he kept on this current mental path. He found the best way to push past events out of his mind was to concentrate on the future. He focused his thoughts on the upcoming engagement.

The Independents had now marshaled over 50,000 men and 300 armored vehicles in the immediate area around Shreveport. That was almost 10 times the number that participated in the Battle of Scott's Hill. What was even more troubling was the fact that intelligence believed they were still outnumbered. Not since WWII had such a force on force battle been joined, and the capabilities of the modern war machines far outperformed their counterparts of 65 years ago.

Marcus had been waiting on the other side to tear into his forces for several hours, but no attack had been launched. There had been a lot of speculation about why the other side had held its lines, but no one really knew. Were they still gathering assets, hoping for overwhelming force? Was there some logistics problem putting their attack on hold? Rumors ran rampant all up and down the line, but facts were few and far between. One whispered story had it that the Loyalists were just going to nuke the Independents and "get it over with." Marcus had to admit, if he were commanding the other side, that option might be tempting.

Just over an hour ago, he had received yet another call on his sati-cell. The man who had been issuing his orders since he joined the rebel group informed him that he shouldn't expect any attack for some time. Furthermore, the Independents were not to initiate any offensive actions. That last part of the message was clarified in an unusual way – "No, I repeat zero offensive actions or tactics. The enemy is not to be provoked, probed, or baited. If they move against you, Colonel, then unleash the dogs of war, but do nothing until then, or until you receive further orders. Is that clear?"

"What an odd little war," thought Marcus. He went back to thinking about his reserve forces and their deployment using the grids on the school's ceiling. He didn't notice when the square panels began to blur. In a few minutes, anyone walking past the principal's office would have heard a gentle snoring coming from inside.

Chapter 14

Alpha Males

Bishop was riding shotgun as the chauffeur-in-chief drove the Humvee across the rugged desert terrain. They had carefully crossed over a road some time ago, and both men had been tempted to use the paved surface, but decided against it.

After a platitude of jokes focused on the rough ride and each other's driving abilities, both men had become quiet the last few miles. Bishop estimated they were about 20 miles north of Alpha, and he was trying to determine the best way to approach the church's compound.

An extra hard jolt snapped him back to the situation at hand, and he decided they needed another break. "Mr. President, how about we cook that rabbit? I recall the vegetation gets pretty sparse ahead, and these hills will block most of the cook fire's smoke. This may be the last chance we get to eat something hot for a while. Besides, I don't think I have any more fillings for you to jar loose."

The older man next to him started to voice a comeback, but decided he didn't want to waste the energy. He simply nodded his head and asked, "Where should we stop?"

Bishop pointed to a flat area underneath a steep hillside not far away. In another few minutes, both men were stretching aching backs and stiff legs. Bishop hobbled to the back of the Humvee and pulled out the dead rabbit. He gave his fellow traveler the option of gathering firewood or skinning the kill. The president decided to hunt for wood, so Bishop pulled his knife and quickly cleaned the hare.

In another 15 minutes, a rather effective, field-expedited rotisserie was cooking the fresh meat over a roaring fire of scrub oak and mesquite. Bishop decided he wanted to scout around a little bit before they began dinner, so he strapped on his rifle and moved a few hundred yards in every direction but up the hill. Nothing of interest was found.

After he returned, Bishop wanted to clean his rifle while he waited on the hare to cook. He opened a small pouch on his load vest and reached in to pull out a cleaning rod, patches, and small bottle of CLP. He thought something felt different and soon realized the pouch had taken a bullet during the last firefight. His cleaning rod had evidently taken the worst of it because the brass rod was completely sheered. The small bottle of CLP was empty, having taken part of the bullet as well. Bishop perched on the bumper, leaned back and sighed. They weren't making cleaning kits anymore, and he had only one left back at the ranch. Running down to his favorite gun store for another bottle of cleaning fluid wasn't exactly an option either.

Bishop thought about just letting the rifle go. He had fired less than 60 rounds, and his rifle should function fine without a scrub at 10 times that number of shots. Most guys wouldn't have bothered, but Bishop wasn't most guys. The weapon slung across his chest had saved his life more times than he could count. He was operating in a dusty, desert environment; and besides, he didn't know when he would have the chance to clean it again. *Admit it Bishop*, he thought, *you can justify it all you want, but the truth is you're just anal about a clean gun.*

After checking on dinner, he went to the driver's side of the Humvee and popped the hood. He found the stick to check the engine's oil and pulled it from the tube. He rubbed a small pinch between his forefinger and thumb and found the engine's oil was reasonably clean.

He then bent over and unlaced one of his boots. Once he had the long lace clear, he tied a very small knot at one end and proceeded to use the dipstick enough times to get his shoelace nice and oily. He broke down the M4, and then ran the unknotted end of the lace down the barrel. When that end appeared at the breech, he pinched it, pulling the knotted end through. After repeating this process a few times, he untied the knot on the dirty, oily end and retied a similar knot on the clean, dry end. One pass through the barrel removed the oil residue.

Bishop used the engine oil to clean and lubricate his bolt as well. After he reassembled his weapon and boot, he worked the action several times to spread the lubrication around, and felt better. About then, the cook-in-chief announced the rabbit looked done.

The fresh rabbit was accompanied by the best portions of two MREs, and the men devoured what turned out to be a pretty good meal - at least by Bishop's standards. While they were eating, Bishop explained to the president where they were headed, and gave him some background of what to expect.

The politician took it all in without comment as he chewed on his meal. When Bishop got to the part about the ghoulish and the skinnies, the president interrupted him. "What happened to the local law enforcement? How did those men escape their incarceration? "

"I'm not sure, sir. I would guess a lot of the police officers didn't report to work. Perhaps they had to protect their own families or homes. I'm sure others were killed in the poison gas cloud."

The chief executive digested Bishop's explanation for a moment and then responded. "Well, that's the problem all over the country, isn't it? We wouldn't be having near as many issues if more people had honored their oaths and not been so self-centered."

Bishop didn't agree with the man's position, but decided not to press the point just yet. If, after seeing Alpha, he still had the same point of view, then Bishop would consider him a fool. Any words Bishop could use right now would pale in comparison to what the leader of the country was about to see.

There was something else hanging in the air, and Bishop decided to broach the subject. "Sir, I hope you aren't counting on me for some sort of game plan here. Short of keeping you alive, I don't have any long-term solution for getting you back to friendly forces."

The fire crackled and hissed softly, while the president thought about Bishop's statement. Without moving his gaze from the flames, he rested his chin in his hand and absent-mindedly stirred the embers with a long stick. "I still can't believe all of this has happened. That soldier had a gun in my face just a few hours ago. I thought he was going to blow my head off. I'm not so sure I want to go back. Even if I do, I'll be looking over my shoulder until all of this is over – maybe forever."

"Sir, I believe you'll be safe at the church in Alpha. If they have transportation there, I'll take you to my ranch or Meraton. But I think that's only a short-term solution. We need to come up with some way to hook you back up with the people who are loyal to your office so you can fix this mess."

The president nodded his understanding, but offered no response. He stirred the coals around, his expression troubled. Bishop waited a bit and then added, "I suppose once I have you stashed somewhere safe, I could go back to Bliss. I don't think either side would shoot me on sight. They would want to torture your location out of me before putting a bullet in my head."

The Commander-in-Chief grimaced at the thought, but couldn't disagree. Bishop was hoping for the man to say something like, "You've sacrificed enough," or "Noooo, they wouldn't do that."

When he received no such reprieve, Bishop inhaled and continued. "My problem is I don't know how to separate who's on which side. I could be handing you over to the assassins and never know it until it was too late. The way I look at it, we've had a lot of fun out here driving around shock absorber hell. My spinal column and hip joints will never be the same. I'd hate to let all that sacrifice go to waste."

So often a campfire is therapeutic, warming the soul. The combination of Bishop's humor and the smoldering wood seemed to snap the older man out of his melancholy state. The chief executive looked up from his trance and smiled at Bishop, "Oh, don't worry. I'll put you in for a medal when I get back. I'll even write up a nice little ceremonial speech."

The president stood at attention, and in an official voice spoke to the surrounding desert, gesturing to command its attention. "Today my fellow Americans, we gather here to honor a man who has paid a dear price for his country. The man on whom I bestow this honor was wounded in the execution of his duties while serving the United States of America. He experienced indescribable pain and suffering in his lower extremities due to a case of cathedral-sized hemorrhoids, and for this sacrifice I hereby award him the Distinguished Sphincter Medal."

Bishop busted out laughing, and soon both men were holding their ribs. The comic-in-chief seemed to relax a little after his theatrical display, and then became serious. "Bishop, I don't have an answer right now. I wouldn't blame you if you dropped me off right here and drove away. If you can buy me a little time to get my wits back, I'm sure we'll come up with something. Besides, I'm getting a lot of thinking done. It's refreshing to be outside of that bubble I've been living in."

Bishop decided to get a little payback. "You sure you don't mind if I leave you here, sir?"

Again, both men laughed.

The president decided to change the subject and scanned the horizon in all directions. "I'm surprised they haven't come looking for me yet. Do you think there were that many traitors at the base?"

Bishop shrugged his shoulders, "Maybe, but there is no way of telling. I know that is one helluva big base, and they would have to search all of it before looking elsewhere. I'm sure they'll come looking for you, sir."

They finished their meal and cleared the campsite. Energized from their desert cuisine, coupled with the break from the road, both men's attitudes seemed to brighten. Bishop even noticed the older man had more purpose in his gait, as he strode to their vehicle. The president paused after opening the door and looked all around. Bishop watched as he got in the Humvee. *The man almost seems disappointed they haven't sent the entire U.S. Army looking for him.*

The pool table in the basement of Senator Moreland's West Virginia home was the center of attention. Both the military and civilian managers were gathered around, examining the status of Operation Delta. A one-star general had just finished briefing the movement's brain trust and stood waiting for questions. There were none.

Senator Moreland broke the silence, addressing no one in particular. "What is the president doing? Why wait now? Is he stalling for a reason? Some sort of trap?"

A senior admiral, recently a member of the Joint Chiefs of Staff, responded. "Sir, from a military perspective there is no reason for them to delay. As a matter of fact, there is every reason for them to proceed with offensive operations against us."

Another man spoke up, "Senator, perhaps our operation at Fort Bliss is the cause. We still aren't one hundred percent sure we failed. Nearly losing his life may have incapacitated the president."

Senator Moreland digested that last suggestion. *More death and skullduggery*, he thought, *I regret agreeing with that move*. The justification that killing the opposing leadership would save thousands of lives had probably been used to justify who knew how many assignation attempts. *I wonder if I would feel differently if we had succeeded.*

The honorable gentleman from West Virginia was through with the low road. There was a line, and in desperation, he had crossed it. It wasn't so much the attempted coup that concerned him, but the other recent briefing he had received.

The Independents now controlled a dozen small nuclear weapons and the capability to deliver them. His military advisors had briefed him that these devices could be used for both tactical and political advantage. A potential target list had even been compiled.

Moreland had practically become unglued at the suggestion. The use of such weapons against an enemy nation was horrific enough, let alone deploying them on the soil of the United States of America. He had dismissed the concept immediately and left the briefing. The officers in the room were a little surprised by his reaction, but noted he had not ordered the weapons returned or disabled.

Humvee One drove for another hour before Bishop pulled over and stopped. He knew the ammunition in the back would be welcomed at the compound, but he didn't want to carry the extra weight through a hostile Alpha. Bishop decided to stash their ride in one of the airport hangars and proceeded to drive into the same structure where David had found the functional plane a few days before.

The shot-up trucks were still sitting on the airport grounds, but the bodies had been removed. Bishop got a funny feeling in his gut as he approached Bones for a closer look. The bullet-riddled dune buggy was still sitting where he and David left it just a few days ago. He could tell someone had rummaged through the interior, and the battery was gone from the engine compartment. Bishop noticed lots of empty brass, scattered on the floor from the firefight David and he survived against the pursuing ghoulish, and that made him smile.

The president exited the Humvee and advanced to inspect one of the abandoned ghoulish relics. As Bishop joined him, the statesman met his gaze, saying, "Looks like somebody shot the hell out of this truck. I see bloodstains all over the place. Why would someone do that?"

Bishop replied, "I have no idea, sir. We have another few miles to hike, and I suggest we get going."

"After you, my good fellow."

Bishop paused, "Oh, sir, I almost forgot. It's going to get cool as soon as the sun goes down. Do you need your jacket from the Humvee?"

A strange look crossed over the president's face. "My Jack….my jacket…Oh, my god! My jacket! I forgot all about it. There is some sort of transmitter in there. They told me about it a long time ago. Some type of GPS type transmitter. I was told to always keep it on because it's bulletproof, and they can find me with that jacket on."

Bishop immediately scanned the sky all around, half-expecting fighter jets, attack helicopters, or even stealth bombers to be vectoring in on his head. After verifying no threat was in sight, he launched into one of his prolonged sessions of foul language. He was so mad he started splitting words in order to insert profanities. Finally, after the harangue began to falter, he looked at the stunned chief executive and simply uttered, "Let's get the fuck out of here…SIR!" The president had to hurry to catch up.

Chapter 15

The Bad Tailor

General Westfield held out the phone to Agent Powell and mouthed the words, "It's for you."

"This is Agent Powell, United States Department of Treasury, Secret Service, whom am I speaking to?"

A thin, weak voice on the other end of the call nervously stammered, "Th...th...this is Airman Moore." Agent Powell looked at the general sitting behind his desk and rolled his eyes. After covering the phone with his hand, he said, "Is this kid, what? Twelve years old?"

"It's the fucking Air Force...what do you expect?"

Agent Powell went back to the phone. "Airman Moore, do you have access to the president's GPS locator, designated POTUS 1.6?"

"I do, sir, but I need authorization to provide those coordinates."

The stress bled through in Agent Powell's response, "And who the hell can authorize *that,* Airman Moore?"

"Sir, General Wilson or any of the joint chiefs have authority. I can also accept the authority of the Secretary of Homeland Security, the Director of the FBI, or the Vice President of the United States...sir."

Agent Powell took a deep breath to calm down. The volcano of anger that was about to erupt wasn't going to do him any good with a scared shitless young man several hundred miles away. Calmly, he asked, "Airman, who is the base commander at Peterson?"

"Sir, that would be General Coleman."

"And is General Coleman available, young man?"

"Sir, I wouldn't know, but I can transfer you to his office, if you wish."

Agent Powell's voice changed to the most sickeningly, sweet tone he could muster, "Please, if you will, Airman. I wish to speak to the base commander."

After a few moments, Airman Moore announced that the general's aide was on the line. An older voice said, "General Coleman's office, Major Hollingsworth speaking."

"Major, this is Senor Agent Powell, United States Treasury Department, Secret Service division. I am in charge of the president's security detail and need access to his GPS locator unit designated POTUS 1.6."

There was silence on the other end of the line for several moments. Powell started to relax just a little bit, thinking he was finally getting somewhere.

The USAF Major responded, "Ummm…sure you do, buddy. We give out the president's location to just any old Tom, Dick, or Harry that calls in. I suppose you'll want the launch codes as well. Richards, is that you? If this is another one of your goddamn pranks, I'll have you busted down to recruit, you sick bastard. This ain't funny."

It took all of Agent Powell's restraint to keep from exploding. He could feel the veins were popping out on his forehead, and the blood rushing through his ears sounded like a freight train. After several deep breaths and a super human effort at self-control, the agent's calm voice answered. "No, Major, this is not a joke. The president is at Fort Bliss, and there has been a coup attempt. We believe he is still alive, perhaps in hiding. Now, how do I go about getting access to his location?"

Again, there was a long period of silence on the other end. When he finally answered, at least the major's tone was serious. "Sir, my apologies if this is legit. You have to admit – this is a very unusual request. Just to make sure I understand, you claim to be in charge of the president's security detail, and you have lost the president? Do I have that right?"

The major started to reiterate the persons with access to the system, but Powell interrupted him. "Major, the vice president is dead. He was killed in the Washington riots. General Wilson is dead as well – he died in the attempted coup. I don't have any idea how to contact any of the JCS or the Secretaries. There has to be another way, Major; and time is critical."

"Hold on," was the response.

Powell looked up to see General Westfield smirking at him with an "*I told you so*" grin. Ignoring the inter-service rivalry, the agent asked, "Do you know this General Coleman?"

"Negative."

The phone clicked twice in Powell's ear, and another voice came online. "This is General Coleman. Sir, I cannot provide access to that system without some verification of who you are. That system has a security requirement as high as it gets."

Something clicked in Powell's mind, something that the major had said. Powell turned to the general and asked if he could summon the football to the office. The general's eyebrows arched, and he mouthed the words "*Good idea*."

The "football" was slang for the nuclear missile launch system, or more accurately, the device used to communicate with the National Command Authority. Since the world-destroying weapons could only be launched by the president, the briefcase-like device followed the man wherever he went. The football was carried around, secured to an officer of O-4 rank or higher. The current man assigned to the duty happened to be an Air Force officer. Powell thought he might get lucky, and the two men might know each other. In a few minutes, one of the general's aides knocked on the door, and Air Force Lt. Colonel Prichard was shown in.

Powell wasted no time, "Colonel, do you happen to know General Coleman, the base commander at Peterson?"

The puzzled officer thought for a moment and then answered, "Yes sir, I do."

Powell handed the colonel the phone and said, "The good general is on the line. Would you please verify for him who I am, where we are, and what the situation is?"

The man took the phone and spoke, "General Coleman? This is Mark Prichard. How's Carol and the kids?...Great!...Have you fixed that hook yet?...Oh, yes, sir, last time I spoke with her, Mindy was doing well, thank you for asking, sir."

Agent Powell looked at General Westfield and whispered, "You've got to be kidding me." General Westfield responded with his usual "It's the fucking Air Force – what do you expect?"

After the pleasantries had been exchanged, the colonel got down to business. "General, the man you were just speaking with is the head of the president's security detail. I can personally vouch for that. In addition sir, there was an attempt on the president's life just a short time ago."

Within 10 minutes, Agent Powell had the GPS coordinates for the president's jacket. He and General Westfield looked on a large wall map mounted on the wall. "Alpha, Texas," said the general. "Never been there. I'm sure it's lovely this time of year."

Powell was ready for action, "It looks like they are at the airport. Get those birds wound up, general. I want the best men you have with me."

After a quick call, the tarmac at Biggs field was bustling with activity. Four Blackhawk copters were winding up their massive blades while 20 of the base's best infantry prepared their kit. In addition to the heavily armed infantry, the base's best field medics were going along – just in case. The United States Army was going on a rescue mission.

Terri wanted a mulligan. As she sat in the cab of the lead pickup heading toward Alpha, she stared out the window, wishing she could start the last few days over. The sparse, arid landscape didn't offer much of a distraction for her racing mind as they approached the troubled town. She wasn't frightened, no, more so the opposite – she was eager. When she admitted that she was actually a little excited by what was ahead, the realization caused her to grunt out loud. Nick was driving and looked across at his passenger, "You doing okay over there, Terri?"

She smiled at him and replied, "Oh, I'm fine Nick. I was just sitting here thinking about Bishop, and how he always seems to end up in the middle of something dangerous. You don't know how many times I've wondered why he allows himself to get drawn into these things. Now, I think I know."

Nick pondered her statement for a bit, "Okay. You're going to have to explain that to me. I've had my share of risky endeavors, but mostly I was following orders. Lately, it's been to protect my family more than anything else. How Bishop lets himself get involved in all this shit beats the hell out of me."

Terri's voice became academic, "I don't think there's any one single reason. Just sitting here, what I'm feeling is a combination of purpose and good old-fashioned maternal nesting. I feel this strong urge to contribute, to right a wrong…make things better." Terri's gaze drifted off into the distance for a while, and then she looked at Nick. "Part of what I'm feeling is a strong urge to get all of this cleaned up before the baby comes. I know I'm not far enough along to actually be nesting, but my child's future is always on my mind. Meraton is a miracle in a bottle. Wouldn't it be better for my child if we had two such places close by? At what point does everyone start thinking of the greater good and not just simply individual survival? I feel a strong need to be one of the leaders of that effort. I want to pioneer the building of things, not be involved in destroying them."

The depth of Terri's inner perspective took Nick aback. This wasn't the type of conversation he was accustomed to having when facing a fight. The Special Forces types he worked with wouldn't be caught dead having a conversation like this before heading into trouble. After he replayed Terri's words a few times, he had to admit her feelings weren't far from his own. He just didn't want to talk about it.

"When Kevin and I decided to pack up and go find you guys, we both envisioned a camper out in the middle of Bumfuck, Egypt. We pictured you two hiding out in a damp cave, eating lizard casserole – or worse. Our biggest concern with coming out here was boredom. We were hoping you guys had a deck of cards or a worn out Monopoly game or something to pass the time. I confess that Meraton surprised me, too. After what we've been living through, I would've bet Bishop's ranch that no such community existed. But despite that wonderful surprise, why not hunker down and keep to yourselves until things get back to normal? I mean really, who needs all the excitement?"

Terri saw right though his cover. She decided Nick was a lot like Bishop, in that he believed exposing any feelings about conflict might make him appear weak or hesitant. She pressed, "Oh, come on now, Nick. How many times have I heard you say you were worried about Kevin's future? Just today, you were thrilled when he wanted to go talk to some girl in the marketplace. Isn't that the same thing I'm talking about? Isn't that worth some risk?"

Nick stretched and shifted position behind the wheel. He was trying to buy time to think of a response. Terri interpreted his movement as a squirm and decided to playfully pounce on the man sitting next to her. "I mean you've got to admit, it's not just Kevin's future we're talking about. It's everyone's. Let's take you, for example. You think Diana is an attractive woman - right?

Nick started to protest Terri's observation, but she cut him off, "Don't you think it would be easier to get her attention if she wasn't fighting a war?"

Nick wasted no time in formulating what he thought was a safe response. "Oh, come on now Terri, you can't think that Ms. Brown would have any interest at all in a broken down old war dog like me."

The corners of Terri's mouth rose only slightly as she tried to disguise her grin. She immediately knew that Nick was fishing to find out if Diana had said anything about him. Terri decided a little good-natured teasing wouldn't hurt. She, probably a little too quickly, fired back her response, "Why Nick, you wouldn't want me to break a confidence between girls, would you?"

Nick was beginning to get the feeling that he was mentally outgunned, so he decided to go for broke. "Yes, I would expect you to break a confidence if it meant keeping a dear, old friend from being embarrassed."

Terri was pleased with herself. Nick had taken the bait. "Embarrassed? Did I just hear the big bad Green Beret say 'embarrassed'? I thought all of you hard-core warrior types expected the girls to fall all over you. Don't tell me that a big, strapping man like you is nervous over a little old preacher's daughter?"

Nick, using all of his warrior's instincts, finally saw a way out of Terri's verbal ambush. "Jesus, Terri, no wonder Bishop runs off on all these adventures. They must be a vacation after bantering with you!"

~ ~

Bishop guided the leader of the free world from the airport grounds and headed toward Alpha. He elected to avoid the road leading to town, as it would be logical for the ghoulish to keep an eye on all common approaches. His intention was to use the same basic route through the berg as David and he had followed a few days before. This meant circumventing around the eastern edge, a detour that would add a mile or so to their journey. As the first structures came into view on the horizon, Bishop went on alert, and their progress slowed. That was fine with the president, as the older man didn't exactly consider himself an avid backpacker, especially when carrying his newfound companion – an M4 rifle.

It was during their approach to Alpha that it dawned on Bishop just how many things he took for granted. The president was obviously an intelligent individual with an advanced education, yet struggled with basic military and security jargon that seemed second nature to Bishop. This became evident when Bishop turned and said, "Sir, I'm going to scout that outbuilding ahead. Please stay here and watch our six. When I have verified it's clear, I want you to vector into my position from 4 o'clock."

The commander of the most powerful military in the world simply stared back at him with a blank look. After a moment, he shook his head and in an annoyed tone, said, "In English, please."

Bishop, realizing his error, tried again. "My apologies, sir. Let me try again. I'm going to move ahead of you and scout that building up there. I want you to stay here and watch behind us. When I have verified the building is clear, I will signal you. At that time, I want you to come up to where I am, but I want you to approach me from an angle like this." When Bishop held up his arm to indicate the direction he wanted the president to take, his action was met with a grunt and another blank expression.

"Why wouldn't we go check it out together? Why do you want me to approach from a different direction? How can I stay here and watch behind us and still see your signal? What will the signal be?"

Bishop held up his hand to stop the questions. It was his turn to be annoyed and with terse voice instructed, "Just stay put, sir. I'll come back and get you." Before the president could protest, Bishop was running toward the structure.

By the time Bishop returned to retrieve his companion, the younger man had cooled off. *He's just trying not to make a mistake and is overthinking everything – don't be mad at him.* The president wasn't accustomed to being treated like a novice and protested, "I know you don't think highly of my experience in the field, but if you would take a moment to explain things, I assure you I'll catch on quickly. Why, for example, do you not want me to use the exact same route as you lead with?"

Bishop took a deep breath and explained, "Sir, if a sniper is watching this area, he would see me run up to that building. He would be trained to watch for the next guy to follow me. I might be out of sight before he could zero in and get off a shot, but he would be ready and waiting on the next guy - you."

By the time the duo had progressed to the outskirts of town, the president was actually beginning to catch on to how Bishop wanted to move from point to point. Since they would now be traveling through an urban area, Bishop hated to do it, but had to change their pattern. "Sir, now that we will be moving through all of these buildings, I want you to stay closer to me. I want you to go exactly where I go, and stay about 10 steps behind me at all times. If I stop at a corner or intersection, then come up directly behind me, but other than that, stay about 10 steps back. I'm the front of the accordion, you are the rear."

The prez looked puzzled, "Why do you want me to follow in your footsteps here, but not out in the open? Wouldn't the same logic apply?"

Bishop looked at the man and smiled, "In here sir, it won't matter – the distances are too short to make any difference." Bishop pushed off, and after a bit, the pair reached the football stadium where Bishop had found the medical equipment on his last visit. Bishop pointed out the ghostly marching band formation spread across the football field. The band had been practicing when the gas cloud had exterminated them all. Their bodies and instruments had fallen in straight rows and columns. Now, the grass had grown high, partially obscuring the remains. To the chief executive, it made the scene appear even more melancholy. Bishop then proceeded with a somewhat eerie tour of the Alpha State campus – sans students or other signs of life.

While they were exploring the ruins of what had once been a picturesque small town university, Bishop had to stop several times and shepherd his traveling companion. The politician seemed entranced by his surroundings and couldn't help but pause and stare.

On one such occasion, Bishop crossed a street between the hulls of two abandoned cars. When he reached the other side, he expected his companion to soon join him. After an inordinate amount of time, Bishop looked back to see nothing but the empty street. *What now*, thought Bishop, as he hustled back, searching for the other man. Bishop found the President of the United States on one knee, staring spellbound into the front glass of a photography studio. The window display contained a joyful collage of wedding pictures, family portraits, student activity photos, and even some pets. The overwhelmed president looked up at Bishop with a dark expression, "They're probably all dead; aren't they, Bishop?"

Bishop only nodded, not being able to think of anything to say. He gave the older man a few moments and finally said, "Sir, we need to get going." The man looked up and signaled he was ready, and the two crossed the street together.

Bishop worked his way to the ice cream shop where Sarah Beth had been living when he rescued her. When it was explained how the airtight freezer had saved her life from the poison gas, the president could only manage a grunted, "Amazing."

Bishop decided to hold up and rest in the ice cream shop. They had been moving very quickly, and he could tell the older man was beginning to tire. Before long, they would be traveling through the most dangerous section of Alpha, and he wanted both of them as fresh as possible.

Bishop sat two chairs upright in the trashed dining area. The floor was still sticky, where gallons of ice cream had melted and drained out of the display freezers. A trail of ants appeared to be working on cleaning up the mess. The president sat, mesmerized by the back room where Sarah Beth had lived for several weeks. "I can't believe that girl you told me about survived in here all that time. She is a hero by some measure, I'm sure."

"She climbed the trees in a nearby park and scavenged bird eggs to survive. When I met her, she was about to be gang raped by several men, but I helped her avoid that situation."

The president detected a flash of violence behind Bishop's eyes. "I've no doubt those men won't be a threat to any more young women." Bishop looked off into the distance and then back at the man beside him. "No sir, they will not."

"Bishop, if you don't want to talk about it, I'm okay with that. I am curious though, why do you think those men resorted to such evil behavior?"

Bishop scratched his chin and thought for a bit before his pensive reply, "Well sir, there are no doubt several contributing factors. A lot of people were on prescription medications for mental issues like depression. The economy had stressed a lot of people, and I remember hearing newscasts reporting more and more Americans being dependent on those drugs. If I recall correctly, the newscaster said six percent of the country took these medications? When the shit hit the fan, they could no longer go to the community drug store for a refill. I've never taken drugs, sir, but I can't imagine their sudden withdrawal was easy. The combination of that dependence and the added stress of the world falling apart all around them, probably pushed many folks over the edge."

The man beside Bishop looked at his hands and then around the room again. He cleared his throat and replied, "I know I could use a drink."

Bishop smiled, the remark bringing him back to the statesman's original question. "Yes sir, I imagine all of this is quite a shock. Speaking of drinking, have you considered the people who had an addiction problem with alcohol? Suddenly, there's no more neighborhood liquor store. Most people probably handled it reasonably well, but I'll bet there were plenty of others who didn't. I've seen people who got out of hand when they overindulged, but they normally pale in comparison to someone with a problem who can't get a fix."

The president nodded his understanding. "The drug addicts would probably not handle things very well either. I'm sure their supplies dried up quickly. Anyone with any sort of daily habit would probably get mean real quick."

Bishop agreed, "Oh, no doubt about it. But you know, I think the worst of a man comes out when he watches his loved ones die. I don't know how I'd react if something happened to my wife. I can see myself sinking so low I wouldn't care who I hurt or what I did. I might become something worse than the ghoulish."

"I'm receiving such an education, Bishop. I had no idea it was like this out here. Do you think it's the same all over?"

Bishop adjusted the rifle lying across his lap and then looked down. "Before we left Houston, a neighbor approached me with a portfolio of his investments. He had two children at a university some 90 miles away. He offered me all of his money to go bring back his teenagers. Now, this was before it became clear how bad is was. At that time, we all thought things would recover quickly. And this was a considerable sum of money...but I couldn't go. It was simply impossible." Bishop paused for a moment, reliving that memory. "Can you imagine how a man might react if he had to watch his children starve before his very eyes? What if your daughter needed some medicine to stay alive, and you had to watch her die? There are lots of things that can turn men into animals, sir. You and I could probably speculate here all week and still not account for them all."

The president grew quiet for a while, drawing a picture of what Bishop was saying in his mind. It must have been a bad depiction, because he suddenly shook his head as if to clear the image. "And yet, you tell me a young girl survived right here in this very room. She didn't take the easy way out, and she maintained her stability."

Bishop nodded, "I've found mindset is a large portion of what it takes to survive. It's amazing what people can endure if they have hope." After a contemplating pause, he continued, "That's what I was trying to say back at Bliss, sir. The way the government reacted, destroyed hope; and that only lowered everyone's ability to deal with the problems."

The president seemed puzzled by Bishop's statement. "I don't see how establishing order does anything, but improve a bad situation."

Bishop sighed, trying to find the right words. "Loss of freedom destroys hope. A man with fewer options has less hope of solving his problems. Rule of law is one thing – removing initiative is another. When the army announced martial law in Houston, it broke my spirit. There was nothing said about a solution, or a plan to rebuild or optimism for the future. There was zero hope in the message."

The president raised his head, his tone becoming defensive. "In Iraq, we learned the hard way that security was job one. Without security, nothing moved forward. People wouldn't open their shops, repairs were never implemented, and society ceased to function. They stayed at home, hiding and scared to come out and move the country forward. We had to establish security, Bishop – we believed nothing would improve without it."

Bishop didn't hesitate, "I agree with you sir, but from my perspective, we didn't learn the entire lesson. Our well-intended attempt to secure Iraq was implemented without local involvement. It was only after the tribal leaders were brought into the process did things start to change. From my perspective, the Independents have acted a lot like the insurgents did in Iraq. They are receiving support from a population that sees no hope – no alternative."

The older man leaned back in his plastic ice cream parlor chair and rubbed his chin. Bishop couldn't tell if the man was pissed off, bored or simply thinking things through. He finally asked Bishop what he would have done.

Bishop wasn't ready for that question and took his time. He stared at the wall, thinking that the pink and yellow balloons were a far too lighthearted décor for this conversation. *We should be in a wood paneled conference room with high back leather chairs and ashtrays full of partially smoked cigars*, he thought.

"Sir, I would have assigned army units and resources to the local politicians and leaders. Rather than roll into a city with tanks, I would have used the fuel to run local generators. I would have implemented similar actions to what Roosevelt did with the WPA. Could busses full of men recruited from the city centers have harvested crops somewhere? Could volunteers have been organized to distribute seeds and teach everyone how to produce their own vegetables? Could the Navy have docked the carriers and other nuclear powered vessels and used their reactors to provide electricity for some of the coastal cities? I'm not smart enough to know what would've worked and what wouldn't. To be blunt, I don't think it would have mattered if most of what the government tried to do eventually failed. What I do know is that taking away everyone's freedom was a mistake. The door was opened to the Independents, and now they aren't going to go away."

The man across from Bishop smiled knowingly. "The Colonel was right about you. I should've known that old bastard wouldn't send just any old Joe Nobody in his stead."

Chapter 16

The Storm Before the Calm

The caravan from Meraton arrived at the church compound without incident. The remaining defenders seemed relieved that help had finally arrived and were especially happy to see their leader had returned. Deacon Brown immediately introduced Nick and let everyone at the compound know he was in charge of defensive matters. After making sure her wishes were known, she busied herself with checking on the wounded and other priorities.

Nick's Special Forces' training and experience immediately showed through. Being a Green Beret, his primary role in the military was to take irregulars, or untrained people, and convert them into an effective fighting force. He had performed these duties all over the world, and the defenders of the First Bible Church of Alpha, Texas were a perfect match for his experience. After gathering the "middle management" of men designated to protect the grounds, the first thing that drew Nick's attention was the fact that the church had never conducted any offensive tactics. As the history of the conflict was explained to him, he noted that the word "defense" was taken far too literally by the congregation. Throughout the entire three-month affair, the men gathered around him had basically let the other side attack, attack, and attack again. Never had the church's men attempted anything along the lines of a pre-emptive strike against their foes. Not once had they ever tried an ambush or counterattack. Initially, the congregation viewed such tactics as anti-Christian. Evidently, the old saying, "The best defense is a strong offense," was assumed to apply only to football. The foe had been allowed to call the shots, and Nick was about to change all of that. The famous words of General Patton echoed in his head, "Fixed fortifications are a monument to the stupidity of man."

His first step was to divide the force into two groups. The less mobile men were assigned to perimeter defense, and he significantly altered where each man was positioned. A second, more agile group was formed with the stated purpose of conducting offensive operations.

Nick then took the group assigned to the wall and sub-divided them into two sections. He left a core group of men stationed along the walls, but he also culled out what he termed a "quick reaction force." This group was to lie back and wait during any attack. When it became apparent where the primary threat was focused, they were to rush in and reinforce that area.

Nick struggled with where to assign his own son. Kevin had proven himself in combat, and Nick trusted the boy's judgment and capabilities more than he did anyone else at the compound. On the other hand, there was a higher level of risk here than anything they had encountered before. The father inside of him conflicted with the warrior. In the end, the father won out, and Nick was assigned as Deacon Brown's new bodyguard. Nick made it absolutely clear that any heroics wouldn't be tolerated. The boy begrudgingly agreed.

Terri was another dilemma. Nick had fought beside her as well and knew she was as good, if not better, than most men. Months ago, when the rovers had attacked Nick's hideout, Terri had battled like a wildcat and saved Kevin from certain death. She was also the pregnant wife of the only friend Nick had left. Terri was a different situation than Kevin. She was an adult and responsible for her own actions. Nick started to leave the decision up to her, but then realized he hadn't done so with any of the church's other members. Why should Terri be given special consideration? Terri was assigned to the quick reaction force, and put in charge.

Despite a hurried evaluation and reorganization, Nick was concerned. Ammunition was low, as was morale. The perimeter consisted of far too much real estate for the number of men available to hold it and was way too porous for a proper fixed defense. After positioning the men on the wall where he thought best, Nick went to work on the mobile team. He gave them a quick, twenty-minute briefing on what he had in mind and made sure that everyone in the small group understood the tactics and terms.

Deacon Brown ventured out of the main building and watched Nick for a while. The man's confidence was reassuring, and he seemed to understand he was commanding civilians, not soldiers. She marveled at how he explained things in quick, simple terms, and then made sure everyone understood. Diana thought Nick should have been a college professor. He seemed to boil down complex subjects to simple, understandable terms and showed patience when the student didn't understand. The thought of the big warrior standing at the lectern with chalk dust on his hands made her giggle.

Nick heard Diana's reaction and mistook it. After finishing his task, he marched over with a questioning look on his face, "Did I do something you thought was funny?"

Diana read him immediately, and blurted out, "Oh...no...no...no.... That wasn't why I laughed. I was admiring how patient you were with the congregation and had a vision of you teaching college. It was so ridiculous…I had to laugh at myself. Don't worry; you're doing great."

Nick smiled and relaxed. "I surely do hope we can end this conflict soon. I look forward to a time where people are building things, not tearing them down."

Diana nodded her agreement, "I've wanted that for so long. In a way, I'd kind of given up hope. Lately, it takes everything I have to just make it through one day at a time. There's been little thought about tomorrow."

Nick reached out and put his hand on Diana's shoulder. She didn't recoil from the gesture, nor did she seem to embrace it. In a warm voice, Nick said, "I understand taking things one day at a time. I've been there. You have and are doing a great job with these people. We are going to fix this. I'm in it with you all the way, if you want me here."

Diana looked into his eyes and said, "Thank you. You don't know how good it is to hear that. I really am glad you are here."

Nick knew it wasn't the time to get into personal relationships. There was business to attend to, and he decided to pull back just a little. "Don't be so quick to judge. I seem to have this tendency to wear out my welcome. We'll see how the day goes and like you said, 'One day at a time.'"

Diana nodded her agreement, "You're right. These are good Christian people for the most part. Other than the loss of life on both sides, I worry the most about what all of this conflict is doing to their souls. None of them signed up to be soldiers. Even if we survive, I wonder about the quality of their lives afterwards. Nothing we can do about that now, I guess."

The statement about Christian people reminded Nick of a thought that had been rolling around in his head. "Diana is there any statue, cross or other religious symbol here at the church that is large enough to draw attention, but light enough we can carry?"

"I don't know what you mean?"

Nick thought for a moment and then expounded, "Something like a big shiny cross or a statue of some sort. Something that we could sit out, and people would notice it. If it were something that looked valuable, that would be even better."

Diana still didn't quite comprehend what Nick was wanting, but turned and motioned him to follow her. The pair walked through the main floor, then down into the basement. Diana picked up a candle on the way and when they entered the darker part of the building, she lit the wick. They eventually entered a storeroom and she explained, "When we built the new structure, we stored a lot of things down here. My dad couldn't seem to part with this stuff. You can use anything down here that meets your needs."

Nick took the taper and investigated the large room, checking its contents. There were desks, chairs, artificial plants and an assortment of other items. In the corner, he saw a brightly painted statue of the Virgin Mary. He handed Diana the candle and moved a few items so he could access the porcelain decoration. He picked up the figure and hefted its weight. After satisfying himself it was portable, he moved the piece to an open area and examined it closely with the light.

The statue was about four feet high and brightly painted. Mary was standing with her arms spread wide as if to welcome everyone. She had been adorned with a blue robe and white headdress. Surrounding her head was a shiny golden crown that actually glittered in the candlelight. The inside was hollow and one arm had been broken off and reattached at some point. There was a bronze placard indicating it had been donated to the First Bible Church by the VFW Ladies Auxiliary of Alpha. One hand was missing.

"I remember this," said Diana, "my father was very upset when it was broken during the move. I think he kept it down here hoping to have it repaired one day."

"Do you mind if we use it? Odds are it won't survive."

Diana didn't hesitate, "If it'll help save one person's life, you are welcome to it. It's just a *thing*, and I've realized these past weeks that *things* aren't really that important anymore."

Nick didn't want the statue to save lives. As a matter of fact, his intent was quite the opposite, but he decided to keep that to himself. He handed Diana the taper and gently hoisted the statue onto his shoulder.

Within three hours of arrival, ten stealthy men and one virgin snuck out of the church's perimeter. Nick was leading the group.

~ ~

The four Blackhawk helicopters performed a textbook simultaneous landing at the Alpha Airport. Before the skids touched the ground, the airmobile infantry hit the ground, moving rapidly to establish a perimeter. Within a few seconds, the well-trained troopers were fanning out in all directions, a search and rescue mission to secure the President of the United States.

The small regional airport could boast only a few buildings, and it didn't take long to discover the abandoned Humvee Bishop had "borrowed" from Fort Bliss. Even less time transpired before a sergeant came rushing back to Agent Powell with the president's jacket. "There's no sign of them, sir. I believe they parked in that terminal and proceeded on foot or obtained another vehicle."

Powell held the jacket in his hands and glanced at the waiting soldier. "Thank you, Sergeant. Please let me know as soon as you have finished searching the remaining facilities."

The sergeant replied with a crisp, "Yes, sir," and spun quickly to return to his unit. The man took a single step, paused, and then pivoted back around to face the Secret Service man. "Sir, there is one other thing. I believe one of the president's party may be injured. There is a small amount of blood in the back of the Humvee."

Powell's head snapped up, and he demanded, "Show me."

Both men sprinted to the hangar where several soldiers were examining every plane, nook, and cranny of the building. Powell was led to the back of the Humvee, where a few small drops of a dark, red substance were pointed out. Dipping his finger into one of the beads, Powell smelled the suspicious liquid, rubbed his fingers together, and stared at the results. "It sure looks and smells like blood, sergeant. But there's not much here. Tell your CO I want someone flown in from Bliss immediately to take a sample of this. We need to find out if it belongs to the president or someone else."

Powell walked back to the cluster of idling copters and scanned the terrain. There were four possibilities: The first was the fugitive and president had left by aircraft. "Unlikely," thought Powell. The second was they left via another motorized vehicle, commandeered from the airport grounds. The third was the missing pair had met someone here and left with them. Again, Powell thought that was low on the probability list. The last, and what Powell's gut told him was the most likely scenario, had the stranger and president leaving the airport on foot.

He reached that conclusion via simple deduction. The shot-up vehicles littering the airport grounds had been looted of their batteries, and the gas caps of every single tank were open or missing. Some locals were scavenging the area, and any motorized transport left behind by Bishop risked being discovered and stripped. Powell didn't think the man would take that risk. The same logic applied to the aircraft. Every single gas cap was removed, indicating someone had siphoned all the fuel. If Bishop did have a plane waiting here, he risked coming back and finding empty fuel tanks. Meeting someone for a ride would have required pre-planning or communication. There was no way Bishop could have planned for the coup attempt or stealing a Humvee. Powell had searched the man's personal items, and there had been no radio. *No*, the agent thought, *He and the boss headed off on foot.*

Powell instinctively ducked under a Blackhawk's spinning blades and yelled at the pilot, "If you were to leave here on foot, where would you go? Is there anything of interest around here other than the town?"

The pilot looked at his GPS navigation display and a chart clipped to the dash. The helmet and mirrored aviator's sunglasses made the man appear more machine than human. After scanning both sources, the pilot responded, "No sir, there is nothing but open desert every direction for miles, and frankly, sir, it's pretty desolate-looking terrain. I'd head for town, sir."

Powell nodded his thanks and walked away from the noisy engine. In a few minutes, the sergeant, accompanied by his lieutenant, came trotting back up. This time the officer reported, "All clear, sir." Powell nodded and decided on a plan. He turned to the nearest Blackhawk and climbed aboard. He approached the cockpit and told the pilot his idea. "I want two of these birds to search the surrounding desert. Stay away from the town. If they are headed there and see you, the will go to cover and we'll never find them. I want the other two choppers to stay here, ready to retrieve the president at a moment's notice. I'm going to take these soldiers and head into Alpha. If the air patrol finds them, radio us. After you conduct the search, return here and wait to come get us."

The pilot nodded and immediately began relaying the agent's wishes over the radio. Two of the big helicopters powered up as Powell returned to the waiting soldiers. Again, the agent relayed his strategy, and within minutes the scouts were double-timing away toward Alpha.

After getting everyone settled in the former t-shirt shop, Nick carefully moved to the roof of the building. He had calculated that the enemy would attack before dark, and that left them only a few hours to move into place. If the ghoulish were going to hit the church today, it had to be soon.

The small, two-story brick building provided a good position to observe the enemy's approach. While he was almost certain they would attack the breach created by the garbage truck, there was no way to be absolutely positive about which route they would opt for entry. He wanted to hit them as they were staging for the attack. That's when they would be the most vulnerable, and his small number of men could cause the maximum amount of disruption.

Nick had warned his troopers that they would probably be cut off and might not make it back to the church. They had brought extra water and food for just that scenario. He had chosen the old building for the thickness of its walls and the location. If the other side got too clever, his men might be completely out of position, but he didn't think that would be the case.

As he lifted the heavy wooden trap door a few inches to peer outside, the first thing he looked for was any nearby structure that offered a higher vantage than his own. There was only one building some five or six blocks away that was taller and would provide a clear view of his position. It was in the opposite direction of the church, so he doubted the skinnies would have an observer there.

Keeping low, he pushed himself out onto the flat, pitch covered roof and slow-crawled to a nearby air conditioner hood. The shiny metal box looked like millions of others that adorned commercial buildings all over the world and would provide him limited cover. The anticipated sniper's bullet didn't slam into his body, so Nick proceeded to scoot to the raised edge of the roofline and peeked over. While he couldn't see the courthouse building proper from his vantage point, he did have a clear view of several intersections in both directions. Unless the foe took a very out-of-the-way route to attack the compound, they should pass through his field of view.

Whereas Bishop had angled toward the campus after leaving the airport, the soldiers headed straight for downtown Alpha. Two scouts lead the way, keeping about 200 meters in front of the main body of troops. Powell noticed their progress slowed as they drew closer to the outskirts of town.

The fringes of Alpha consisted of a few scattered homes with detached garages and small outbuildings here and there. As they progressed, the surroundings gradually changed to neighborhood streets serving homes adorned with gingerbread and sidewalks lined with shade trees. This section of Alpha had once been a modest neighborhood of middle class family homes.

The first thing the army infantrymen noticed was the lack of noise. It was unsettling to approach what was clearly a place where people should be, and hear absolutely nothing but the occasional bird song or buzz of a passing insect. Absent was the hum of power lines, exhaust of internal combustion engines, televisions, radios, and children playing outside. There was nothing but a few quiet sounds of nature, highlighted by the light rustling of leaves tossed about in the calm breeze.

Powell noted that every yard was littered with trash and debris. Clothing, pots and pans, paper bags and all sorts of household items were scattered randomly in front of each home. Shrubs hadn't been trimmed, and small limbs lay where they had fallen, polluting once pristine lawns. Grass hadn't been mowed, and knee high weeds were growing from sidewalk cracks and along curbs. As the column slowed, he began to notice every door had a splintered frame or broken glass. This area had been ransacked and looted. In the middle of the second block, they encountered the first burned out residence. The brick chimney stood blackened and charred, surrounded by the low outline of its block foundation. A few wall studs were still erect, looking more like burnt matchsticks than the strong timber once tasked with supporting the roof. Mounds of charred grey ash and lumpy clusters of cold cinders filled the foundation to the brim. Powell thought the phrase "burned to the ground," described the place perfectly. No fire department had responded to fight this blaze.

Agent Powell was impressed at how quickly the soldiers accompanying him moved and he relaxed somewhat, as it became clear he was working with experts. No doubt many of these men had seen combat in the cities of Iraq and were experienced in urban operations. Despite the hundreds of hours of instruction received by Secret Service personnel, Powell was a little out of his element here. He could probably outperform any of these men with a pistol or short-barreled weapon, but they were obviously more adept at moving through a populated area. Without any order being issued, the patrol immediately broke into two columns when they reached the first city street. At first, the soldiers methodically entered and searched the scattered buildings on both sides of the roadway. As the column progressed, it became clear that the area was uninhabited. The men at the front began to ignore the structures unless something unusual caught their eye. Still, caution ruled their progress. Rifles snapped around the corners at intersections, vehicles parked along the street were approached slowly, and weapons were carried at the ready. Eyes scanned second-story windows over and over again, searching for any signs of movement or occupation.

The point man of the column suddenly raised his fist into the air, and the soldiers on both sides of the street instantly moved for cover, their weapons pointing outward, looking for work. After a few moments, the lieutenant was called to the head of the column, and Powell went with him to see what was going on. As they approached, the corporal pointed down at a small pile of spent rifle cartridges scattered around the street. The man then continued pointing here and there, drawing attention to several similar groups of brass. Dark red lines stained the sidewalk, looking very much like old, faded blood trails. The lieutenant turned and motioned for three men to move forward and set up a perimeter. When they were in place, he turned to the Secret Service agent and said, "There was a firefight here. Look at that house. See the bullet damage? Somebody had a pretty serious shootout."

Powell stood and began surveying the area. He noticed at least three different calibers of brass, lying around the street, and there must have been at least 200 spent cartridges. The agent drew his pistol and opened a small gate leading to the front yard of the home. As he approached the porch, the story of what happened here became clear. The front door had been boarded up with several cross members of 2x4 lumber. That door and every window facing the street were peppered with dozens of small bullet holes. One window in particular appeared to have been the focal point of the attack. As Powell waded through the knee-high weeds in the yard, he could see the window frame had been severely eaten away by incoming lead. The agent stopped and ducked his head around the glassless opening, making sure no one was home. When his action didn't draw any response, he gradually advanced to peek inside.

The wall directly behind the window was completely destroyed. Shredded sections of drywall, strips of wallpaper, and splinted wood gave evidence to the volume of incoming fire. Pink insulation had been blown all over the room. Someone had tipped over a large metal filing cabinet under the windowsill to use as cover. A heavy, wooden desk appeared to have hastily joined it as additional reinforcement. Lying behind the makeshift bullet stop was the remains of the defender. Scattered yellowish-white bones were still partially covered by a plaid shirt and overalls. The carpet was stained with a faded red pool that time and the elements had faded to a distressed pink color. The floor was littered with colorful shotgun shell casings and dozens of pistol rounds. The skull had a large bullet hole in one side.

Powell turned and returned to the waiting lieutenant, shaking his head. "There's no one left here, LT. That poor bastard put up one hell of a fight though. He died defending his home, and from what I can tell, he didn't go down easy."

The young officer agreed, "Yes, sir – I count four blood trails. The amount of brass lying around here tells me this went on for a while." Both men stood and stared at the scene for a few moments before Powell whispered, "We need to get going."

Without comment, the officer waved his command forward. Powell stood in the street and watched as the soldiers passed by. He smiled as one private stopped and came to attention in front of the house. Staring directly at the window, the soldier threw a crisp salute, held it for precisely three seconds, and then snapped his hand back to his side before trotting off to catch up.

Smokey stood on the top courthouse step, his hands behind his back with his chin jutting out. Anyone observing him might have sarcastically compared his posture to Napoleon marshaling his forces before a campaign. While none of the hundred or so men gathered around the square would have had the guts to say that out loud, it would have been difficult not to make the association.

Smokey was suffering from two conditions that were absolutely dangerous to any leader. First, he was out of patience and wanted results, regardless of how realistic the situation was. The second problem with the man's mental state was paranoia. Smokey was convinced that hundreds of people were flocking to his archrival in Alpha, Deacon Brown. His conviction was centered on the observation that his men were encountering less and less "unaligned" people in the town. No matter how hard his men tried to explain, there was no convincing Smokey that there simply weren't that many people left in the city, and the ones that were not in the church complex had become very adept at hiding.

Smokey's state of mind wasn't uncommon for megalomaniacs. Practically every dictatorial leader from Alexander the Great to Adolf Hitler had suffered from similar conditions at one point in time. Fortunately, Smokey's scale of influence was limited to a few dozen hardened criminals controlling part of a small western town, but the man had aspirations.

As he stood there motionless, Smokey was in fact daydreaming about attacking the Beltron ranch and then annexing that little town down the road as part of his domain. His mind raced with terms like consolidation, power base, and loyalty. He had already mentally achieved victory in the upcoming battle and was off on futuristic conquests to expand his realm. Hawk approached his boss, having no idea he was interrupting the creation of an empire. "Hey chief, the men are about ready. Anything you want to add or say?"

Smokey flashed just a touch of annoyance at the interruption. "No, I've nothing to add. They all know that failure is not an option this time. Let's get moving."

The word was quickly passed to the waiting lieutenants who started forming the men up. In a few minutes, over 100 armed men were moving in two columns toward Deacon Brown's church. One group of attackers was led by Smokey, the other by Hawk.

~ ~

Nick's attention was immediately drawn to movement several blocks away. A line of men was moving down the street, and he brought up his rifle to get a better view through the optic. The man heading the column could be easily identified by his perfectly bald scalp and scruffy goatee. Nick could also tell his arms were heavily tattooed. His ensemble included a dirty, white wife-beater sleeveless shirt, brown leather belt, and blue jeans. Some sort of work boots rounded out his attire. The leader carried an AR15 rifle on a traditional shoulder sling, and Nick counted five magazines, shoved in various spots on the man's belt. There was no canteen or other visible sign of hydration, no blow out bag. When the man turned to examine his column's progress, Nick noticed a long-blade, hunting knife in a sheath on his hip.

Nick observed the next three men in line and found the level of their equipment lacking even more so than the leader. Clearly, no thought had been given to a prolonged fight. There wasn't a single bottle of water or medical kit in sight. He was also surprised at the casual way that the column moved through the city streets. Apparently these guys had operated with such impunity for so long they didn't even consider that someone might actually attack them. Nick's eyes changed to those of the predator. He would make them pay for their over-confidence.

After watching the approaching enemy to verify their route, Nick hurried back into the store and briefed the small group of men gathered there. He quickly barked instructions, and everyone scrambled to get into position. He made it absolutely clear – no one was to fire until he initiated the ambush. Nick picked up the statue of Mary and carried it down the street, strategically staging the figurine in front of the shop. He had picked the perfect spot upon their arrival. There was an intersection that was absolutely clear of any vehicles just down from the storefront. Unknown circumstances had seen to it that no one was driving in this area when the gas cloud had killed thousands. The rare open area could be seen from all four directions, and Nick placed the statue directly in the middle of the crossing. The smiling woman looked odd sitting there, her brightly painted clothing and crown in sharp contrast to the black pavement surrounding her. After one last glance around, he hurried back to the t-shirt store. He couldn't help but notice the sign on the front of the building, which read, "Mary's Embroidery and Silkscreen."

Nick glanced around at the men in the storefront one last time. Like any commander of men about to do battle, he had a long wish list. He wished he had the time to train them on this, that or the other. He wished he could have found a slightly more protected position. The list could go on and on and Nick stopped the mental process almost immediately. The time for organization and instruction was over; the outcome would soon be determined. There was never enough time to prepare for a fight.

The men waiting in the t-shirt shop watched as the first few of their enemy passed by. Several of the Christian soldiers looked up at Nick with questioning expressions, but the big Green Beret paid them no attention. He only risked a slight head movement to the right in order to verify the progress of the column.

Chapter 17

Meet Me in Alpha

Hawk saw the statue first and stopped walking immediately. He had passed down this street several times and knew it hadn't been there before. This thoroughfare was his favorite approach to the church because there was less clutter to walk around and less chance his men would be distracted or get out of line.

His first reaction to the statue was one of caution. He carefully glanced all around but didn't see anything out of place. What he didn't notice was the long column of curious men behind him had started to bunch up right in front of Nick's position, and that had been the intent all along.

Everyone in the store heard Nick's safety click off, and several of them jumped when his rifle began shooting at the gathering men on the street. It took a few seconds, but eventually, 10 rifles began slamming rounds into the surprised skinnies.

Hawk's initial reaction when the shooting started was to duck behind a nearby car. He knew almost instantly that his column had walked into an ambush, but he couldn't think clearly enough to react appropriately. He glanced back and saw that at least 12 of his men were lying on the street, motionless. The rate of fire coming from the storefront across the street was almost constant and appeared to be working its way back along the line. Hawk raised his weapon and started firing at the dark windows without acquiring any specific target. That proved to be a mistake as his action drew attention to his hiding place, and rifle rounds began impacting all around him. He ducked around the corner building, being chased all along by thumping lead, tearing into the concrete structure. When he had safely made it to cover, he leaned against the wall, breathing deeply in and out. He had to think of something and do so quickly. He scanned the immediate area and identified two of his men standing nearby with frightened expressions on their faces. He pointed to the closest man and ordered him to inform Smokey's group that they had been ambushed. He forgot to tell the man to ask for help.

There is no small unit tactic more devastating than an ambush. In addition to the extreme loss of life inflicted on the victims, the effects of the action include confusion and demoralization. Nick gave his men almost a minute of firing into the enemy column and then stopped the attack. Anyone caught in their kill zone was either dead, injured or behind cover by then. Any additional shooting would only waste precious ammunition. As suddenly as it had started, the shooting stopped, and the men from the church hustled out the back door of the t-shirt shop. It was time to go.

Smokey was four blocks away and moving his line of men on a parallel route with Hawk. When the shooting started, his first thought was that Hawk had started his attack too early. When the sound of gunfire ceased, he was puzzled and stopped his column. Like Hawk's formation, halting their forward progress caused his men to bunch up and gather together.

Nick wasn't sure how the ambushed men would react and wanted to swing a wide arch around them on the way back to the church. He and his men were moving rapidly down a street and rounded a corner, running right into Smokey's column. Nick overcame the surprise first and opened fire on the 20 or so men in the middle of the block. His men followed his lead a second later, and by the time they had broken contact and moved on, another bunch of men were dead or dying on the ground.

Nick hadn't considered a second group of skinnies and didn't want to be caught out in the open with such a small force. While his men had gotten the better of the second encounter, breaking off the fight caused them to flee in the wrong direction.

Agent Powell was five blocks away to the north of the ambush site. When the shooting had begun, the army troopers around him had all reacted immediately and sought cover. In a few moments, it became clear that there were no incoming rounds, and everyone waited for the Secret Service man to determine a course of action. Powell's goal was to find the president, and so far, they hadn't encountered a single living soul. After a quick conference with the lieutenant and top sergeant, orders were issued to move cautiously in the direction of the gunfire. Where there was shooting, there were people pulling the trigger. The short duration of the fight led Powell to visualize another incident like the home they had just passed. In reality, he didn't care about the who or the why of the gunfire. He wanted to interrogate someone to see if his boss had been spotted.

Bishop and the president were just exiting the ice cream shop, when the gunfire erupted some nine blocks away. Like everyone else, he initially ducked back into the doorway, but quickly realized the fighting was some distance off. Bishop's decision how to react was probably the most difficult of anyone's. His first thought was that the church was under attack. He wanted to go and help the congregation, but felt stewardship of the man traveling with him. The last thing he wanted was to bumble into a full-fledged battle with a man whose experience with a weapon consisted of shooting a single rabbit. When the second round of shooting began, it was clear to Bishop that the fighting had moved closer to his location. This posed a real dilemma, as he was not in a good defensive position and had little chance of surviving an encounter with a superior force. The fact that the president wasn't very nimble didn't help things one single bit. In the end, Bishop decided to move off at an angle away from the last sounds of battle, but still in the general direction of the church. Along the route, he hoped to find some place better to hide and defend. The Commander in Chief was clearly concerned about the sounds of fighting so close by and simply nodded when Bishop explained his plan.

The duo had moved a few blocks when Bishop turned to find his partner missing yet again. "Jesus Henry Wilson Montgomery Christ," he mumbled, "where has he wandered off to now?" Backtracking quickly, he found the president, mesmerized by the wall of a building. There on the whitewashed plywood were hundreds of pictures and notes. Some were stapled while others had been glued or taped. Bishop looked around to make sure they were alone, before reading one of the messages:

Looking for Carrie Perkins, Junior at Alpha State. 5'4", blond hair, green eyes. If you see her, please let her know her father is in Alpha, and I'm sleeping in my car at Woodridge and Elm…God bless and thank you.

Bishop hadn't seen anything like the display since the news coverage of 9-11. Evidently, some survivors of the gas cloud had been looking for family members. Carrie's father must have driven to Alpha from somewhere. He hoped the man had found his daughter.

The chief executive was clearly touched by the collection on the wall. He didn't seem to be able to pull himself away. Bishop waited until he was about to jump out of his boots, and finally couldn't take it anymore. "Sir, I don't mean to be cold, but we have to get moving. We can't stay out here like this."

The expression on the man's face was one of bitter sadness. He looked at Bishop and nodded his understanding. As they walked away from the display, Bishop noticed he looked back several times as if committing the image to memory.

They hadn't traveled far when Bishop heard the rhythmic pounding of running footsteps. In a blur, Bishop pivoted, grabbed the president, and roughly pushed him into a doorway. Bishop squeezed into the entrance with him, just as two men rounded the corner. Both of them were looking over their shoulders, as if they were being chased by a crazed T-Rex, searching for a meal. For a moment, it looked like they were going to pass by without even noticing the two travelers, but one fellow was out of wind and stopped right in the middle of the street to catch his breath. The exhausted runner stood bent over, his hands resting on his knees while drawing in several lungs full of air. His buddy stopped a few feet away to wait on his out of shape friend. It was pure chance that he glanced up and looked straight at Bishop and the president.

Bishop now understood why Sarah referred to these men as ghoulish. Their hair was uncut and filthy, resulting in shoulder-length manes that made their heads appear misshapen. Their facial hair was in no better condition, which added to the effect. The untrimmed beards made the dark circles under their eyes even more prominent, sunken, and hollow. Their foreheads had been darkened by the sun and were streaked with dirt and sweat. The skin at the corner of their eyes was wrinkled with deep crevices, probably a combination of sun and unwashed skin as well. Bishop could see the one man's hands clearly. His fingernails were long and dirty black, resembling the claws of a bird. The combined effect was similar to what Bishop had seen soldiers do with camouflage face paint, but dark - almost evil looking. To a young girl being hunted by these guys, they no doubt did appear as ghouls.

Bishop doubted either man would've been first prize at his high school prom, even when bathing and haircuts were commonplace. Now, given Deacon Brown's church controlled the water supply in the area, they more closely resembled pictures of Neanderthals he had seen in museums. "*No*," thought Bishop, "*that would be insulting the Neanderthals.*" Bishop couldn't help himself and mentally compared the two hairy beasts to images of Sasquatch. "*No*," he thought again, "*I doubt Bigfoot smells this bad.*" These two what-ever-they-were had weapons though, and Bishop focused his attention there.

At first, the breathless man just squinted at them, probably trying to determine who they were. His friend followed his gaze, and now both of them were trying to figure it out. Finally, out of breath and unable to carry on normal conversation, they looked at each other with a gesture of "*Do you know them?*" It took both men a second to conclude they weren't looking at co-workers. Bishop noticed one of the men had on a soiled orange shirt with the faded letters "County Jail" still barely readable. The man raised his rifle, and Bishop dropped him before the weapon ever reached the man's shoulder. Bishop started menacingly walking toward the second man, rifle pointed directly at his chest. "Move on," he said in a cold voice. The guy kept glancing back and forth between Bishop and his now dead friend. Bishop repeated his message, "Move on."

Anyone could clearly see the anger starting to boil up in the man. He searched for the words and stammered, "...But...but...I can't believe...you shot my..." before his voice trailed away.

Bishop's entire focus was on the man's arms and hands. At this distance, it was unlikely either shooter would miss, and his only advantage was that his weapon was already up. His vision was so attuned to the man's arms that Bishop could have probably counted the individual hairs had he wanted to do so. *Don't do it man,* he thought, *You can't win. Just run away and live.* The man's arm muscles twitched, and the barrel of his shotgun start to rise. Bishop pulled the trigger again and again. Before the lifeless body even hit the street, Bishop spun around and began motioning for the stunned statesman to get moving. The duo ran for over a block, before slowing to allow the president to catch his breath. While the older man recuperated, his heart pounding in his throat, Bishop paced back and forth, his temper getting the best of him. "Why? Why did he do that? He made me kill him and for no good reason. Why?"

The president's answer stopped Bishop cold. "You killed his brother. Didn't you realize that?"

"How do you know they were brothers? How could you know that?"

The old politician shook his head and sighed, "The resemblance was clear. I've been observing people for years, Bishop. I may not look at them tactically like you do, but my eye is still pretty keen. Blood is thicker than water they say, and every candidate learns quickly to recognize family. I could have told you the second you shot the first one that the second guy was going to seek revenge. I was wondering why you waited so long."

Bishop pretended to be checking his rifle, but was really mulling over the man's words. He finally cleared his throat and responded, "Mr. President, taking a man's life is never easy. Before I pulled that trigger I knew I would see his face at night for a long time. I will wonder who they were, how they got in this mess, and what their future would have been. I'll think about their mother and wonder if she will ever know their fate. When you take a man's life, you suddenly create a vacuum. All he was and will ever be is gone in a split second. I waited so long because I didn't want to kill the second man – I wanted, prayed...would have even begged...for him just to turn and run away."

Bishop realized he was rambling and thought the man beside him most likely didn't understand or care. He looked around and announced, "We've got to get going," and started to move off. The president's hand shot out and grabbed Bishop's shoulder, stopping him. "Bishop, you did the right thing back there. I have more respect for you as a man because you feel this way, but never doubt that you did the right thing."

Bishop looked at the Commander in Chief's eyes, seemingly wanting to say something, but didn't. After a long pause, he mouthed the words "Thank you," and then hurried off.

Terri and Diana looked at each other and smiled when the sounds of Nick's ambush reached the compound. He had told them what to expect, and early reports led both women to believe things had gone according to plan. As the blare from the second round of shooting reached their ears, looks of concern flashed across both their faces. Concern turned to outright worry when Nick didn't return in a reasonable amount of time. Terri was in charge of the quick reaction force Nick had organized. Her first instinct was to gather up her men and go help. After waiting what seemed like hours for Nick's team to return, she couldn't wait any longer and pulled her group together. Soon, Terri was leading her fighters out of the compound with rescue on her mind.

Hawk's column was completely disrupted by the ambush. His men had scattered in all directions, with several small bands roaming the side streets of Alpha, unsure what to do next. Hawk himself seemed to be in shock at the experience and had become completely ineffective as a leader. While a few of the men banded together and stayed huddled around the now withdrawn man, the majority of his force was disoriented, disorganized and dispersed.

Smokey's group fared the encounter better. Despite his screaming for everyone to settle down and form up, several of his group had taken off to pursue Nick's men. Smokey's reaction to the confusion was to stay put. He had no idea who had just shot at them or what had happened to Hawk's group. The last thing he wanted was to have one of his men panic and start shooting at people on their own side.

It was right about then that the first stragglers from Hawk's column bumbled into the army patrol. The fog of war ruled supreme as the small cluster of five criminals opened fire on the soldiers from the parking lot of a fast food restaurant. The shots were wild and high, and the soldiers reacted with the speed and skill of an experienced combat unit. Within a minute, all five of the former jailbirds were lying dead, their bodies lined up at the drive-thru window like customers waiting on a bucket of chicken.

The small town of Alpha, Texas became a confused cauldron of swirling gunfights. All over the city, small remnants of Smokey's forces engaged with the infantry, Nick's ambush party or Terri's quick reaction force. Mass confusion ruled the field as plans had gone awry, making it difficult to distinguish friend from foe. Bishop was trying desperately to avoid all of the combatants and simply get the president to the church compound – if it still existed.

Agent Powell was frustrated. To him, it seemed like random little waves of hostile people would shoot at them without reason. When the first member of their patrol fell from a gunshot to the head, the attitude of the soldiers around him changed from puzzlement to anger. It was an unfortunate college junior that received the blunt of the soldier's aggression. The kid, semi-forced into service by Smokey's thugs, came jogging around a building, carrying a scavenged shotgun primarily designed for duck hunting. Before the runner could even bring his weapon up, the three closest soldiers opened fire, causing the young man's body to spastically jerk and fall to the ground. Powell's concern was obvious, and he warned the lieutenant to get his men under control lest they shoot the president by accident. The word, calling for restraint, was passed up and down the line.

Terri's people were crossing behind a bank, heading toward an alleyway in the rear of the building. She was covering the corner when four men approached at high speed, brandishing rifles and looking desperate. For some reason, one of her men decided to give them the benefit of the doubt, yelling for them to stop and drop their weapons. That warning produced exactly the opposite reaction. One of the sprinters shouldered his weapon and began firing, while the others scattered for a building that once housed a tax accountant's office. Sporadic shots were being exchanged between Terri's team and the skinnies, when three more stragglers from Smokey's column stumbled into the fight. Terri screamed for her people to pull back, and a running gunfight ensued for a couple of blocks. One of Terri's men kicked in the door of a home and her group rushed inside, seeking to hide and avoid the attackers. It would have worked, but the last man in was spotted by the pursuing skinnies.

Unknown to Terri, Nick was watching from across the street where his men had holed up in a veterinarian's clinic. When the men chasing Terri formed up to assault her hiding place, Nick's people opened fire and killed the attackers almost instantly. There was a stressful moment while the two different teams from the church identified each other, quickly followed by a joyful reunion. Everyone was all smiles and hugs except for Nick. He was none too happy that Terri had left the compound on his behalf. Terri soothed his flash of anger by telling him Diana had ordered her to come bring Nick's group home.

One of the men with Hawk tapped him on the shoulder and pointed. The ex-con looked over to see a man in helmet, full combat gear, carrying an AR type rifle, running down the street before disappearing from view. No sooner had that man left his vision, than another identically clad individual rose up and repeated the same basic action. When the third guy popped up and ran, it dawned on Hawk that a military unit was approaching his position. His first thought was *The army is coming to put us back in jail.*

"Let's get the fuck out of here!"

Hawk and his small band of men took off running in the general direction they thought Smokey was located. They had scampered a few blocks when they saw Smokey and a larger cluster of men gathered around an abandoned semitrailer. Smokey's men almost shot Hawk's crew as they barreled down the street, but fortunately one of the sentries recognized them.

Hawk immediately ran to his old friend and reported, "We got to get the fuck out of here. There are army guys all over the place. I think they've come to put us back in the slammer."

Smokey looked at his best man and replied, "Show me."

In a few minutes, the two leaders returned to the gathered skinnies and announced that anyone who didn't want to be arrested should move out; the army was in town. Most of the convicts decided to stay with Smokey, and the 15 men took off running in the opposite direction of the encroaching army unit.

Bishop had progressed slowly, stalking from structure to structure, dragging the president along, trying desperately to avoid contact with anyone. He estimated they were within 10 blocks of the church when two men started shooting at him from a small park down the street. Bishop would have backtracked and circumvented the contact all together, but there were all sorts of skirmishes going on behind him. He decided there wasn't any choice but to address the threat that lay directly between the compound and him. Forcefully instructing the president to stay put, he went out the side door of the house they had been hiding in and ran along a privacy fence bordering the backyard. It took him less than two minutes to flank the two men in the park. They had been so focused on watching his previous position they didn't even notice his approaching from the side. As he drew closer, Bishop saw they were only kids, perhaps 14 or 15 years old at most. He could easily shoot them right where they stood, but lowered his rifle, not having the heart. Moving just a little further off angle, he maneuvered to a position directly behind the two teenagers and charged.

The pounding of his boots on the ground alerted one of the youth, but it was too late. Bishop lowered his shoulder and literally knocked one young man into the other, both of them sprawling onto the ground in a heap. Before either could react, Bishop had their rifles out of reach and stood looking down at them with carbine at the ready.

The two frightened boys looked up at Bishop with terror in their eyes, but made no move to escape. Bishop growled, "Where are your parents?"

The older one responded in a weak voice, "They died in the gas cloud. We...we...we were hungry and couldn't find any food. The guys from the jail said they would feed us if we would fight for them."

The other boy started crying and joined in, "We didn't shoot anybody...honest we didn't. I always aimed high when we went to the church."

Bishop tilted his head slightly and made his response as mean as possible, "Both of you little shits get up and get moving toward that church right now. Don't go left, and don't go right, but head straight for that church. I'm going to be there soon. If I don't find you there, I'm going to come hunting for you." Bishop pulled his fighting knife and showed the saucer-eyed boys the blade. "If I have to come hunt you down, I'll skin you and eat you myself. NOW GET!"

Bishop had to smile as he watched the two adolescents scurry away. After making sure they crossed the gardens without incident, he turned around and took a step back toward the president's hiding place. Before his boot even touched the ground, grass and dirt erupted all around him, and he had to dive for cover behind a nearby tree.

Smokey's group had been rushing up the street when Hawk spotted Bishop. The second in command pointed the target out to three of his men, and they all fired at once. Bishop rolled behind an oak tree with a trunk three times the size of his torso. As more of Smokey's men came rushing up, a hailstorm of bullets began to slam into the oak and surrounding turf. There was no way Bishop could even poke his head around to see who was shooting at him. The only thing he knew for sure was that given the number of rounds cracking past his head, there must be a hell of a lot of them. In less than a minute, all of Smokey's men were firing at Bishop. When the boss asked what was going on, Hawk told him whom he had spotted. Smokey glanced from his man to the tree and back several times, before motioning for Hawk to follow him. The two men scooted off together, moving at an angle away from Bishop's position and having thoughts of flanking him.

Terri and Nick were working their way back to the church when a massive amount of gunfire erupted almost directly in front of them. The church's defenders moved forward to get a better view of the battle. From their vantage, they could see several men shooting at someone apparently hiding behind a tree. The church's men didn't recognize any of the shooters, and hoped that meant they were on the other side. Nick's people opened fire.

Several of Smokey's men jerked and fell on the opening volley. By the time they recovered, and went to ground, Smokey had heard the commotion and believed the army's soldiers had caught up with the group he had left in the park. Smokey hesitated, torn between going after Bishop and making his escape. In the end, self-preservation won out, and Smokey momentarily forgot all about his grudge with Bishop.

Bishop had no idea who rescued him from behind the tree, but he was thankful. When the fire directed at him changed direction, he wasted no time sprinting away, hurdling over a low stonewall fence that bordered the parking area for the gardens. He had seen Hawk and another guy split off from the skinnies and guessed they were trying to flank him. He bent down low and dashed behind the wall as fast as his feet would carry him. Bishop's mind kept remembering Hawk's blows to his head when he had been bound to the chair and his desire for revenge made him momentarily forget all about taking care of the president.

After the last of Smokey's men had surrendered, Terri decided to rest while Nick searched the prisoners. Across the street was a beautiful white Victorian home with a wide, shady front porch. There hanging from the roof was a wooden porch swing. The sight was just too tempting, and she made a beeline for the house. No sooner had she planted herself in the swing than a noise from the side yard put her on alert. She begrudgingly rose up and went around to the side of the home where thick oleander bushes lined the yard. The noise sounded again, and Terri could tell it was someone trying to hide a cough. She shouldered her rifle and made her voice sound as gruff as possible, "Come out with your hands up. Come out peaceful, or I'll shoot you in those bushes."

The voice of an old man answered her, "Okay…okay…don't shoot. I'm coming out." An AR15 rifle flew from the bushes followed by a man in an U.S. Army uniform. At first glance, Terri thought the guy was a soldier, but she quickly ascertained he was far too old to be in the infantry. She thought, "There's something familiar about his face. Where have I seen this guy before?"

Terri turned around and yelled for Nick, "Nick! I've got another one hiding over here."

As Nick hurried over, he never looked at the face of Terri's prisoner. His focus was on the man's hands and torso, searching for weapons. Nick had just started to frisk the guy when Terri said, "Nick, there's something familiar about this guy. Have you ever seen him before?"

Nick glanced up at the president's face and froze instantly. Terri was stunned when Nick took a step back from the man, snapped to full attention, and saluted. "Nick! What the hell are you…" and then it hit her where she had seen the guy's face before. Terri's reaction was a little different than Nick's. She ran off of the porch and immediately confronted the President of the United States. "Where's my husband? Where's Bishop? Was he with you?"

Nick realized what was going on and saved the president from a potential assault being delivered by the charging woman. The big man caught Terri mid-stride and raised her into the air, almost laughing as her suspended feet kept trying to move her closer to the chief executive. Terri suddenly realized her lack of forward progress and turned her ire onto Nick. "Put me down, damn it. I want some answers from this guy."

Nick held her suspended until Terri assured him she wasn't going to attack anyone. When she had regained her feet, she straightened her top and changed her tone of voice to that of a demur, well-mannered southern lady. "Mr. President, my name is Terri, and my husband was on his way to Fort Bliss to deliver a report to you. Have you seen him, sir?"

The president smiled at her and stepped forward offering his hand. "Yes, young lady, I did meet your husband. As a matter of fact, he saved my life and is around here somewhere. He left me here a few minutes ago and went to take care of someone who was shooting at us. I'm sure he is fine."

Terri smiled and began looking all around, hoping to hear Bishop make that porch swing squeak. Her spirit was dampened somewhat when Bishop didn't magically appear, but at least she knew he had made it this far.

Nick was completely lost about what step to take next. His sketchy plan had not included this event as a parameter. The commander bailed him out by suggesting they proceed to the church where Bishop was originally leading him. Nick didn't know if that was such a hot idea, but couldn't come up with anything better, so he sent some of his men ahead to scout the route.

Bishop stalked through a few blocks of homes, waiting for Hawk and the other man to fall into his trap, but they never showed up. He shrugged his shoulders and decided revenge could wait. Hawk didn't seem like the type of guy who knew a lot about field craft and would probably die badly in the desert anyway. *Maybe Hawk's buddy will resort to cannibalism while they are lost in the desert,* he thought. Bishop turned around, heading back to retrieve the hider-in-chief.

There were still random gunshots sounding all over Alpha, and Bishop had to take his time. He was just about to cross a street when he saw Hawk and the other guy run into a large, single story building. Bishop recalled that Hawk had been a spy and responsible for a lot of good people being killed. Hawk had also beaten the crap out of Bishop while he had been bound and injured. Bishop had been around the dude for less than a day, and could recount no less than five incidents that really got his blood boiling. The thought of letting that guy run loose in Alpha didn't sit well. *I need to be more public service minded*, he thought. *I need to rid the community of this vermin.*

Bishop trotted off toward the elementary school.

Nick's scouts returned and reported the next few blocks were clear. "We only saw that other guy."

Nick's head snapped up from reloading one of his magazines. "What other guy?"

The scout shook his head, "I don't know his name. He was at our church driving the crazy looking Hummer."

Terri had been standing nearby, talking with the president and heard the last statement. She pounced, "What? You saw the guy who was driving the Hummer? Where...where did you see him?"

The poor man delivering the report thought he had done something wrong, "I'm sorry ma'am...but...but...well, he ran into that elementary school down that way a piece."

Terri started to walk in the direction the man was pointing, forgetting all about everything else. Nick grabbed her arm and stopped her. "Terri, hold on. We'll all go. Bishop might be right in the middle of something and you walking up behind him isn't a good idea. Just hold your horses, and let's do this right."

Terri spun around, and Nick was taken aback by the ferocity of the look she gave him. "My husband might also be in trouble – did you think about that? I'll wait, but not too long."

Nick nodded and began issuing orders to his men. The route back to the church was altered with a slight detour via the elementary school.

~ ~

Agent Powell's mood was foul to say the least. It appeared to him that this small Texas town had gone completely insane. Over the last few blocks, they had encountered small groups of armed men moving in every direction, some of them shooting at anything that moved. There seemed to be no reason for the random violence. Sometimes the men ran when they saw the army troopers approaching, while other times they opened fire. At one point, an elderly couple had approached the soldiers, believing the government had finally come to rescue them. The pair had been carrying their suitcases and announced that they were ready to be evacuated. Another man had approached, wanting to barter for food. He was a rack of bones covered in skin, filthy and very weak. He claimed he didn't have much to trade, but was willing to do just about anything for food. He hadn't seen the president. A couple of the soldiers gave him some food and he had scampered off, laughing like a lunatic.

The sounds of gunfire echoed all over the town. Powell had no idea what was going on, but knew it wasn't just the presence of the military. If the rest of the country was like this, there was no way the government would ever reestablish order.

What really bothered the agent was the thought of the leader of the free world being caught in the middle of this nightmare. Powell was surrounded by some of the best fighting men around, and they were barely making any progress at all. The president had one man with him. *Still*, he thought, *we don't have any other alternative. We have to keep going and find the boss.*

Bishop followed Hawk and the other guy into the elementary school. The double glass doors had been pried off of their hinges long ago, no doubt by looters looking for food. He entered a long hallway lined with grey lockers. Practically every door was hanging open, and the floor was strewn with papers and books. The hall had recessed openings every so often that clearly led to classrooms. Bishop realized it would take forever to clear this building and find the men inside.

He was torn between going back and retrieving the president and killing Hawk. He could assume things were going well at the church. The battleground had obviously moved from the compound to the streets of Alpha, given the intensity of the fighting going on around him.

Hawk was like a bad case of jungle rot – he kept coming back, all the worse each time. Bishop decided the president was pretty safely hidden at the moment and ridding the world of someone like Hawk carried more weight right now.

While the school was small compared to many, it was still a sizable building with a lot of hiding places. Bishop quietly proceeded to the first classroom and saw a sign on the partially open door that read, "Mrs. Perkins 1st Grade." There was enough light leaking in through the closed blinds to see dozens of small desks randomly scattered throughout the room. Many were lying on their sides with the contents dumped on the floor. The walls were covered with children's artwork, depicting everything from cattle to elephants. The front of the room was dominated by a wide blackboard. Below the chalk tray was a cardboard train, each car carrying a letter of the alphabet. Written on the blackboard in large white letters was something that caught

Bishop's attention. "Nurse Brenda needs all shot records by Friday!"

A nurse meant the school had a clinic, and a clinic might help him with a cure for his current problem. Bishop left the classroom and cautiously continued down the hall, following the signs of a stick figure nurse and found the clinic across from the library. The looters had paid special attention to this room, probably looking for drugs or medications. Bishop carefully stepped over manila folders, medical records, reference books and all kinds of items covering the floor. He finally spotted what he was looking for in the corner next to an overturned metal cart – oxygen bottles.

Bishop avoided the looter's mess and hefted one of the small bottles. He had been shown how to operate these types of devices while his mother-in-law was dying of cancer. He used the plastic key, turned the valve, and watched the gauge's needle rise. Both bottles were full. Bishop hoisted one of the metal tubes, trying to imagine how far he could throw it. He decided he could toss it a good distance.

Bishop couldn't safely clear this building by himself. He also couldn't be sure the men he was after hadn't already left via another door. Every minute that ticked by increased the chances someone would discover the president. Yet, he badly wanted Hawk. He wedged himself in a doorway, raised his rifle to the ready, and clicked off the safety. Taking a deep breath, he yelled down the hallway, "Hawk! Hawk I saw you sneak in here. It's Bishop. I got bad news for ya, buddy – school's not in session today. You won't find any little kids in here to molest. Why don't you settle up with me like a man – or do you only fight with guys tied to chairs?"

There was no response, so Bishop moved down one set of doors.

Bishop waited a bit and then started yelling again, "Who's that with ya, Hawk? Is that your lover? Did he come to take pictures of you molesting children? Maybe he's a pervert, too? I know, I know…you and he were lovers in prison and wanted to act out your fantasies in an elementary school. Now it all makes sense."

Still, there was no response.

Bishop switched positions, crossing the hall to another classroom carrying the two canisters of oxygen. This one was void of human occupants as well, so Bishop continued his taunt.

"Hawk, I had you pegged as a cowardly fuck from the get go. Why don't you come out and face me like a man. Just me and you, Hawk – come on out."

217

Hawk and Smokey were around the corner in the teacher's lounge, just four doors down from Bishop. They had wanted to rest for a minute and talk over a plan. When Bishop's voice rang out, both men had jumped. At the sound of his name, Smokey's eyes darkened, while Hawk stood and moved to cover the doorway.

Smokey joined him and whispered, "I don't think he likes you much. He's not too smart though. We know where he is now. We don't have time to get caught up in a grudge match right now. Let's get out of here."

Smokey started to move out the doorway when Hawk's hand reached out and stopped his friend. "When we caught him before, he was carrying some serious equipment. He had food, night vision and a lot of ammo. We could use that shit now. Let's pop his ass and take the gear – we may need it."

Smokey pondered Hawk's suggestion for a moment and shrugged his shoulders, "Okay – let's get it done before the army shows up though." Hawk and Smokey whispered back and forth for a moment and agreed on a plan.

Bishop tried to put himself in Hawk's shoes. He was convinced the two men were in the building and had heard him calling Hawk out. If he were Hawk, he would be listening, trying to determine where the taunting voice was coming from and, getting ready to spring. Bishop had advanced down the hall three sets of doors. There were only three left, so he was halfway. He took one of the oxygen bottles and set it next to a door. He could hit the bottle with a round from anywhere in the hallway. He carried the other tank with him back toward where he had entered the building and waited.

Hawk and Smokey had taken up positions two doors down from Bishop. They had been tracking his voice as he advanced, but now there was nothing but silence. The two men looked at each other and Smokey waved Hawk over. In a whisper, he said, "Either he's left or wised up and is staying silent. Let's go get him. It's two to one, and the odds are in our favor."

Hawk didn't like that idea one bit. "Hold on a second. I saw this guy bust up an ambush and kick the shit out of 20 of our guys. He's no amateur. He's went silent to draw us out, and I don't think it's a good idea to do what he wants."

Smokey looked at his friend with a slight expression of disappointment. "If we stay here, eventually the army will show up. I don't know about you, but I'm never going back inside. Now, we can sit here until this asshole or the army gets us, or, we can go get him and be on our way with his gear. You saying that we have a better chance against the army?"

Hawk, as usual, couldn't argue with Smokey's logic. He nodded and moved to the next set of doors.

Bishop was about to give up. This was all taking too long, and he was worried about the man he had left behind. While the sounds of shooting had died down outside, it was getting dark quickly, and the thought of approaching the church after sunset didn't seem wise. He was standing up to leave when he heard the rustling of footsteps down the hall. "*Gotcha!*" he thought.

Bishop shouldered his rifle and waited. Hawk's voice sounded, "Bishop, you still here? I'm waiting. You spouted a lot of bullshit a bit ago…come on out and back it up."

Bishop could tell the man's voice was pretty far away. Each grade at the elementary school had two classrooms with the grades advancing down the hall. Bishop was hiding at the first grade rooms and had left the oxygen beside the third grade doors. He thought Hawk was in the hall around the fifth grade classrooms.

"I'm still here, Hawk. I'm sorry I interrupted you and your friend. Is he mad at me, too?"

Another voice rang out from about the same position as Hawk's, "I've got no quarrel with you, friend. Why don't we talk this over like gentlemen? These times are challenging enough without everyone attacking each other. Come on out and talk – you have my word we won't shoot."

Bishop almost laughed out loud. He got control of himself and replied. "I don't know you, but I have a good measure of your friend, Hawk. He's a chicken shit piece of scum. Was it your idea to have those breasts tattooed on his back?"

Bishop heard boots moving up the hallway. He leaned around the corner and fired at the oxygen canister.

The explosion wasn't that large. There was very little structural damage done to the school or to Smokey, who was about 10 feet away from the detonation. The effects were similar to a flash bang grenade. Smokey was momentarily blind, deaf and stunned. A moment was all Bishop needed. Seeing Smokey's outline in the flash of the blast, Bishop fired four rounds at the motionless criminal. Two loud grunts and the sound of a body hitting the floor told Bishop he hadn't missed.

Hawk had been moving up the hallway parallel with Smokey, but was on the other side when the tank erupted. The effect of the explosion on him was lessened by distance, and he ducked into a doorway recess as Bishop's shots rang out. His vision still hadn't recovered from the flash, but he heard Smokey fall. Hawk shook his head to clear the cobwebs and decided he had better move. He stood and turned to retreat, when an odd noise reached his ears. He thought for a moment he was hearing bells or ringing. Then the sound changed to something rolling across the floor. Movement caught Hawk's eye, and he looked down to see a small, shiny silver canister rolling down the hall toward his feet. His semi-stunned brain registered what it was and the words "*Oh shit,*" had almost made it to his throat when Bishop's shot rang out.

Bishop saw Hawk's body slammed into the wall by the explosion. He watched for a moment as the man was enveloped in flames from the oxygen and slowly slid down the wall to the floor. One of the two explosions had caught the scattered papers lying all over the place on fire. Bishop took a moment to verify Hawk's body didn't move. The smell of burning flesh reached his nose, and Bishop decided it was time to leave.

He exited the school the way he had entered and started moving back toward the place he had left the President of the United States.

~ ~

Nick and Terri had hung around for several minutes at the president's insistence, the man sure Bishop would be coming back for him. Nick didn't like being stationary in such an exposed location. There were still indiscriminate echoes of gunshots ringing all over Alpha, and he wanted to get back inside of the church compound as soon as possible. Eventually, Nick convinced Terri that with the approaching dusk, the group needed to make its way back to the compound for safety's sake. Besides, Bishop could make his way to the church on his own.

Sending a few men ahead to scout, a short column of the church's men slowly started making their way toward the compound. The park was too open to cross, so Nick chose a route that would take them around it and provide more cover. Terri stood with the president, scanning the area one last time, hoping to see Bishop. She and the chief executive eventually followed the column, last in line.

Bishop worked his way toward the Victorian home where he had left the president. In the fading light, he spotted a group of men moving on the opposite side of the park and was pretty sure one of them was the chief executive. "Shit," he thought, "I played around with Hawk too long." The fact that the men were moving toward the church allowed him to relax a little, but in the fading light he couldn't be sure he had seen the president or if the right side had found his charge. Bishop entered the house and found it vacant. He moved out quickly, thinking to catch up with the men he had seen earlier.

It took Bishop a few blocks, but he finally saw people moving in front of him. As he closed the gap, he became aware that one of the people moving up ahead was a woman. His initial thought was that Deacon Brown had joined her men in whatever they were doing outside of the compound. As he moved closer, the female's movement became more familiar to him, and he realized it was Terri.

Bishop started to call out to her, but stopped. His voice would give away his position to anyone nearby, and there was still a lot of craziness in the streets of Alpha. He decided to venture closer before announcing himself. He wanted to see the look on his wife's face anyway.

Bishop was about 20 feet behind Terri and the president, when movement to his right caught his eye. There, in the fading light of dusk was a man with an AK47.

Smokey had never been shot before. In addition to his left arm being burned by the fire, he had taken a bullet to the shoulder and another to the thigh. The smell of Hawk's burning body and the smoke from the burning papers had given him a surge of adrenaline that prompted him to get up and out of the school. His mind was clogged with emotions of anger and revenge. Hawk had been a good man and close friend. They had had a good thing going in Alpha before this guy Bishop and that bitch at the church had fucked it all up. Smokey knew that without serious medical care, he was done. The chance of infection from two bullet wounds and some bad burns was high. The chance of his dying in the desert without food or water was even higher.

The realization that he was out of options made his mind snap. Smokey transformed from a reasoning, sentient human being to a biological machine programed for a single purpose – revenge. He ignored the pain spreading throughout his body and moved toward the church compound where he sensed the target of his wrath would go. He didn't even notice the blood filling his boot or the skin starting to peel from his burned arm. He could only think of killing Bishop and Deacon Brown.

Smokey managed to cross the park at a reasonable pace. He recognized the same group of people as Bishop and started moving to intercept them. Despite his injuries, he closed the gap because he wasn't worried about being exposed. He simply wanted to kill those responsible for his failure. The dying man was hiding behind the hulk of a burned out car as Nick's men crossed a street just a few feet away. He was watching each face, looking for either Deacon Brown or Bishop. A woman's voice, speaking in low tones gave him one final surge of energy. He rose up, sweeping his rifle in a wide arch and began pulling the trigger.

Bishop was moving, but the world seemed to be going in slow motion. He was trying to command his legs, throat, and arms all at once, and nothing was working fast enough. The warning trying to reach his throat wasn't going to be heard in time. His arms couldn't bring up his rifle fast enough. The only thing that was responding to the desperate commands being issued by his brain was his legs. Bishop's focus was split between Terri and the man with the rifle. His wife was walking beside the president, talking in a low voice while looking up at the taller man. The guy with the rifle was looking right at her, swinging the weapon around.

Bishop sensed, more than felt, his foot land on the second stride. His muscles strained while his heart pumped loudly in his ears. His right foot landed at the same time he detected the shooter's arm muscles flexing his trigger finger. He could see the index finger start to pull back. Bishop's mind made a calculation. He could save either the president or Terri, not both. Bishop's left foot hit the ground, and he strained with every ounce of power he could muster. His boot rocked from heel to toe, and he launched himself into a full forward dive. He had just become airborne when the AK barked its deadly blast.

The round snapped the air behind Terri's head and hit the wall of the building beside her. So close and so loud was the noise, she froze in mid-stride. The second shot was igniting in the Russian weapon's chamber when Bishop's arms extended around his wife's shoulders. He was practically flying horizontally through the air when he grabbed Terri, rolling to his side so as not to land on top of her. The second AK bullet grazed Bishop's side right above the hip and slammed into the President of the United States. Terri and Bishop were just striking the ground when the third shot hit the older man in the chest.

Bishop and Terri hit the pavement hard, and before the momentum had bled off, Bishop was trying to roll on top of the stunned woman to protect her. His head turned to look at the threat, and he watched, fascinated, as the man's body jerked spastically like he was being hit with a surge of electric current. The sound of multiple rifle shots reached Bishop's ears, as did the screaming of several people, including his wife. The shooter's rifle pointed skyward, as clouds of red mist appeared in the air around his body. The AK never fired again, and its owner fell face forward onto the sidewalk, the rifle adding a weak rattling aftermath as it bounced free of the dead man's hand.

Bishop's head turned to the president, and he watched in horror as the man went to his knees, staring down at his chest. The chief executive fell to his side and rolled onto his back almost instantly, his eyes exposing the pain and fear that was racing through his mind.

Bishop was completely surrounded by chaos. There were dozens of voices screaming from every direction. Running boots were rushing past on both sides, as people seemed to be coming out of nowhere. Suddenly, Bishop was pulled off Terri by rough hands. His arms were pulled back and someone reached around and unhooked his rifle while his pistol was yanked from its holster. Before Bishop could react, he was on his knees with both arms pinned to his sides by two burly soldiers. He looked up to see Agent Powell staring down at him. Anger came boiling out of Secret Service man's mouth. "I saw that! You could have saved the man. I saw you let the president get shot."

Powell's attention was drawn to the president. Bishop glanced over and noticed two army medics huddled over the injured man rendering aid. Powell hurried to his boss's side, trying to ascertain the extent of the man's wounds without getting in the way.

Bishop detected a shadow in front of him and looked up to see Nick. He tilted his head in surprise, and then grumbled, "I would offer to shake hands, my old friend, but these two young men probably don't care about social amenities."

Nick shook his head, "Always the smart ass, ain't ya, buddy?" He then refocused his attention on Bishop's two guards, and his voice became frosty cold. "I'd be extra nice to your prisoner, fellas. He's a friend of mine."

About then, Terri managed to make it to one elbow and glanced at Bishop. "Well, hello there my love. You sure do know how to make an entrance."

Bishop looked at Terri with adoring eyes, "I love you, baby. You okay?"

Terri stood and started brushing herself off. She nodded at Bishop that she was fine, and then noticed he was bleeding. She started to go to his side, but a soldier blocked her path. "He's under arrest ma'am."

Terri's mind was on cognitive overload, her brain struggling to process all that was happening around her. "He's bleeding. Why is he under arrest? Let me help him. What are the charges? Don't you provide medical attention to prisoners anyway?"

The lieutenant completed his call for the helicopters to land at the park. The first priority was to get the president back to Bliss and the medical facilities there. He walked over and tried to calm Terri. "Ma'am, he is accused of kidnapping and several other charges. But I'll have his injuries checked as soon as the medical personnel are finished with the president."

Terri looked up at the tall, young officer with anger all over her face. "Kidnapping! Are you shitting me, young man? He saved that man's life…. The president told me so himself. Go ask him if Bishop didn't save his life. Nobody kidnapped anyone. This is bullshit!"

The officer was slightly taken aback by Terri's temper. He started to stammer something about "just following orders," when Agent Powell appeared.

The Secret Service man didn't care about Terri's outrage. "I ordered the arrest. I can't even begin to list the crimes your husband has committed. We are going to take him back to Fort Bliss and…"

Powell was interrupted by one of the medics, "Sir, the president wants to speak with you and that man." The medic pointed at Bishop.

Powell nodded at the two soldiers standing on either side of Bishop. They allowed the prisoner to stand, and one of the medics moved aside. The Commander in Chief was lying on his back, his army fatigues covered in blood, bandage wrappers, and assorted medical refuse. There was an IV tube in his arm, and cut-away scraps of his uniform blouse were lying all around. The man was desperately fighting for each breath and looked pale and white against the concrete backdrop of the sidewalk. Bishop took a knee, and gently cradled the dying man's hand. The president's voice was broken and weak, "Is your wife okay, young man?"

Bishop replied, "Yes sir, she's fine. Don't worry about anything but yourself, sir. Use all of your energy to stay with us. Help is on the way."

The president gasped and coughed, "No, I don't think I'm going to make it through this one, son." He paused, then managed a few more raspy breaths and continued, "I wanted to thank you for helping me understand my people. I should have done something like this a long time ago…. The rabbit was excellent, by the way." The man smiled up at Bishop and started coughing again.

Bishop smiled back and watched as the president waved Agent Powell down beside him. The chief executive reached up and pulled Powell close, whispering something in his ear. Powell pulled back and asked, "Are you sure, sir?" The president nodded, coughed, and then his eyes rolled back in his head and his breathing stopped.

The two medics pushed their way in and started working furiously on their Commander in Chief. Bishop knew their efforts were in vain. The man was gone. He took a step back, and again his arms were pinned to his side by the two guards. Powell looked up and instructed them, "The president has pardoned this man. It was his final order. Release him – he's free to go."

Chapter 18

The After-Alpha-math

In a few minutes, the helicopters started landing in the park. Nick's people were informed they were free to go. Bishop and Terri were "asked" to accompany Agent Powell to Fort Bliss and make statements. Agent Powell, ever the loyal government employee and a sworn law enforcement officer, wanted the coup attempt thoroughly documented. At first, Terri was reluctant to go, but when Bishop mentioned the hot shower and shampoo, her heart was set on Bliss. Besides, she had never ridden in a whirlybird.

The army medics looked at Bishop's wound and determined not only would the wound be fine, but he would have a great scar to show his grandchildren. The round had barely grazed his side and required a single butterfly bandage and some antibiotic cream. Bishop tried to milk it for all it was worth, informing Terri that the medics advised he take it easy and stay off his feet for a few months. Terri didn't buy it for one second, but replied that she would be happy to wait on him hand and foot - for a while. After all, she reasoned, her pregnancy was bound to require the same treatment in reverse. Bishop realized, yet again, his cause was lost.

An emotional farewell was exchanged between Terri, Bishop, and Nick, with promises of "See you soon," and "We'll stop by the church on the way back to Meraton." Bishop and Terri boarded the last Blackhawk with Agent Powell and the president's body.

Talking was next to impossible on the flight to Bliss. Terri and Bishop satisfied themselves with holding hands and looking at each other. At one point, Terri managed enough volume to overcome the noise and said, "You're not leaving me again, Bishop. Never again. I want you right beside me until the day I die."

Bishop responded, "You got that right. Wild horses baby...wild horses." His eyes told Terri he meant it.

Agent Powell, ever the observer, sat opposite of the couple without comment. Deep down inside, he realized a feeling of envy at what these two people shared. His college sweetheart had divorced him years ago, unable to handle the long hours and constant danger involved with the job. He wondered for a moment how she was doing, and had secretly hoped they could rekindle their romance when he retired.

227

The Secret Service agent also had to admit his anger with Bishop was misplaced. In reality, he was angry with himself. Even that emotion began to fade as the flight wore on. No protector ever wants harm to come to his charge, yet as Powell replayed the events of the last 12 hours, he had trouble finding fault with his actions. He remembered reading the memoirs and reports of the men charged with protecting Kennedy. They had all experienced issues with misdirected anger, followed by guilt. The best, he observed, bury themselves so deeply in the job it is difficult to handle failure. He couldn't blame Bishop for saving his wife instead of the president. After watching their interaction, he might have done the same had he been in Bishop's shoes.

Agent Powell remembered the president's last words. "He's a man of honor. He did the right thing. I would've given my life to save that woman, too. They are the future; make sure they are left alone to realize it. He has my pardon."

Powell thought about those words and concluded the president was right. It was the people like the couple across from him that were going to rebuild the nation, not the high and mighty. The solution had to come from the ground up. He thought about apologizing to Bishop. Two or three times during the flight, he cleared his throat to issue the words, but stopped. He eventually excused his inability to speak, convincing himself the man sitting across from him didn't really care and was completely focused on being with his mate.

They landed at Bliss to a waiting line of Humvees. Bishop and Terri were escorted to the same room Bishop had used before, holding hands and making eyes at each other while strolling across the parade grounds. Terri called shotgun on the shower, while Bishop enjoyed a cup of coffee.

After both of them had bathed and eaten, they realized neither had gotten much sleep for days. The aftermath of a hot shower and full meal had both of them yawning and looking longingly at the bed.

~ ~

Nick watched the Blackhawks carrying Bishop and Terri disappear. He gathered his men, and they carefully worked their way the last few blocks to the church's compound. After the appropriate signals were exchanged, the excited, but tired group of men was met by eager family members watching every face as it came into the yard.

Nick saw Kevin approaching with a look of relief, but before the boy could reach his father, Deacon Brown appeared out of nowhere and pulled Nick close in a tight embrace. Nick wasn't sure, but felt like the hug was a little more than just a casual "Glad you're home." Diana looked up at the big man, and her eyes said it all. "Welcome home, soldier. I'm glad you made it back in one piece."

Nick looked around at the gathering and smiled. He'd brought back all of his men. Not every mission ended that way, but today had been a good day. "We all made it home, Diana. That's the best part of the whole enchilada. I'm also happy to report that the skinnies are no longer a force. Their leadership is dead, and their ranks have been scattered. Tomorrow, the good people of this church can retake Alpha. You can finally start to rebuild, Diana." Nick looked back down into her eyes and added, "And I would like to stay and help, if I haven't worn out my welcome."

Diana's pulled away, and her expression becoming serious. "Before we talk about your sticking around, I'm a little curious about what took you so long? I mean, I know you're not a Navy SEAL or anything, but…"

Nick was taken aback by the comment and didn't know if the woman were joking or what. He started a comeback, "A SEAL? Did I just hear you compare me to a SEAL?" He looked at Kevin as if to verify what his ears had just taken in, but the boy just shrugged his shoulders.

Diana didn't let up, "I had always heard you army Special Forces types were high speed, low drag individuals. I guess you can't trust the rumor mill, can ya?"

Nick still didn't know where this was coming from, but he wasn't going to let it go. "Look lady, the SEALS are good…damn good…but let's not be comparing apples to …"

Again, Diana cut him off, "Nick, don't take offense. I was just a little surprised I had to send Terri and her team out to rescue you." Without missing a beat, Diana planted her hands on her hip bones in an apparent sign of disgust. "Don't worry, I won't tell anyone that a girl, sorry, a *pregnant* girl, had to go help you back to camp."

Diana held her composure for a few seconds more while father and son stood silently, facing her. Nick was digesting Diana's words and had just begun to take in a deep breath when she busted out laughing. Kevin couldn't hold his pokerface either, started with a snicker and soon was laughing so hard he could hardly breathe, bent at the waist and holding his ribs. Nick, realizing he had been had, joined in the joke.

After everyone had recovered, Diana put her hand on Nick's shoulder and apologized. "I'm sorry, I couldn't resist. This has been such a tense day, I thought we could use a little comic relief. I was so happy to see you bringing all of the men-folk home. I turned to Kevin and asked him how your sense of humor was these days, and he told me to go for it."

Kevin, receiving a dirty look from his dad, decided to count branches on a nearby tree just at that moment. Nick couldn't remember the lad ever having a more innocent, angelic look on this face and made a mental note that it wasn't going to do the boy a bit of good when he issued a payback.

Nick shook his head, "You really had me going there for a minute. Now, back to the issue of my wearing out my welcome?"

Diana's face changed to a look of pure joy. She smiled and looked around to make sure none of the congregation was within earshot. She gave Nick the killer combination of a serious look and then a wink, "You're *more* than welcome to stay – I'm really happy you want to be here. I have to warn you though; some of those stories about the preacher's daughter have truth to them."

Nick portrayed pure gentlemanly innocence, "Why Ms. Brown, I have no idea what you're talking about. What stories would those be?"

Diana took his hand and replied in a low voice, "Come with me soldier, and I'll enlighten you."

Nick and Diana put their arms around each other and casually meandered toward the church. Kevin stood by smiling, understanding fully what had just occurred. He had often wondered if his dad would ever meet anyone now that the world had changed. He liked Diana and thought the two adults were a good match. Suddenly realizing he hadn't been relieved of his bodyguard duty, he decided to tag along and be an annoyance. Smiling widely, he tucked his rifle under his arm and trotted off to catch up, wondering how long he could hang around before his dad chased him off.

~ ~

To the exhausted couple, it seemed like they had just gotten settled under the covers when a knock on the door interrupted their slumber. Bishop grumbled something about no rest for the wicked and looked at his watch. They had been sleeping for over nine hours. He padded to the door. "Yes?"

"Corporal Higgins here, sir. Agent Powell sent me to inform you they are ready to start the debriefing in 30 minutes. If you wish, sir, I'll have some breakfast brought here for you."

Bishop started to inform the good corporal that Agent Powell's timing sucked, but thought better of it. He mumbled, "Breakfast would be fine, corporal. Make sure the tray has lots of coffee," and turned to Terri who was groggily propped on an elbow.

She raised one eyebrow and said, "I'll get dressed and go with you. I'm not letting you out of my sight for a long time, Mister."

Bishop started to protest, but decided it was a waste of energy. Besides, he felt the same way. A short time later, the couple was dressed and walking toward the headquarters building. Terri was fascinated by the surroundings, having never been on a military base before. Bishop had to smile at her child-like curiosity as she peppered the young corporal with questions of, "What's that?" and "Why do you do that?" the entire trip. They were shown to the same conference room where Bishop had originally met the leader of the free world. The huge wall displays were still functioning, and Bishop pointed out a few details to his wife while they waited.

Before long, Agent Powell entered the room with another man and a female soldier. The man was introduced as the base commander, General Westfield. The woman was with the Judge Advocate General's office and would serve as the official recorder of the meeting. A stenographer's machine was soon wheeled into the room.

For the next several hours, Bishop recounted his experiences of the last few days. Several times during the session, he was interrupted by either Powell or the general to clarify a point or fact. After he finished, it was Terri's turn to describe her brief encounter with the former president.

After the debriefing had concluded, Agent Powell offered Bishop an apology, "Bishop, I sincerely regret my actions in Alpha. The man I was charged with protecting died. You carry no blame, and I should've never gone there."

Bishop looked the man in the eye and nodded, "Apology accepted. He was a better man that I thought he would be. I don't know what's going to happen now, but if you have any influence with the future president, I think he'll do a better job if he gets out among the people. That's just my two cents worth."

Powell nodded his understanding and added, "I have no idea what's going to happen. As of this moment, no one is in command. I've radioed Washington, or what's left of it, and explained the situation. They are going down the chain of succession and trying to find the next leader of this nation. Who knows what's going to happen?"

Bishop started to turn away when General Westfield stopped him. "Could I have a word, young man?"

Bishop nodded and followed the base commander to a quiet corner. The officer wasted no time, "You're good. As a matter of fact, I think you're damn good. Why don't you and your wife move here to Bliss? I can re-instate you as an officer in the United States Army with the full privileges associated with the commission. I'll be blunt son – the army needs the nation's best right now. We have one hell of a job ahead of us, and I could use a man like you here."

Bishop kept his expression neutral, "Why thank you, sir. I…well…I wasn't expecting such an offer. I don't know quite what to say."

The general nodded understandingly, "Talk it over with your bride, Bishop. I know I came out of left field with this offer. You two talk it over. By the way, I've made arrangements for her to see the base obstetrician. Can't hurt to have things checked out."

Bishop thanked the man, and then the couple was shown back to their room.

Nick and Deacon Brown stood looking at the row of jail cells. The former home of criminals, convicts, and ne'er-do-wells was now stuffed with looted goods from various stores around Alpha. Smokey had been both smart and quick after breaking free. He had known what was going to be valuable and had sent his fellow prisoners on organized raids. Even the local hospital's pharmacy had been cleaned to the bone.

Nick was watching a group of the church's women take an inventory. One lady was inside of a cell while the other stayed in the aisle with a clipboard. The woman counting would yell out something like "Three 20 pound bags of sugar," and all of the others would respond with "Praise the Lord." The amount of food and medical supplies was significant. Every now and then even Nick had to let out a whistle over the quantities uncovered.

Diana turned and motioned for Nick to follow her outside. The couple proceeded to the front of the courthouse and went out into the cool morning air. Nick started to say something but Diana held her finger up to her lips, "Shhhhhhh." The big man tilted his head and listened. Off in the distance, he could hear a female voice being broadcast over a loudspeaker.

"We are using two police megaphones we found to let everyone know those convicts are no longer running this town. We have groups of church ladies walking through the streets broadcasting our message. Some people are probably still too scared to come out of hiding, but we've already had almost 50 people show up."

Nick nodded, appreciating the results, but more so the fact that Diana seemed so happy. The tone of her voice, and the spring in her step was refreshing. It was as if a tremendous burden had been lifted from her shoulders. The Special Forces operator watched her for a moment and decided she was even more beautiful than he had thought.

"Penny for your thoughts," Diana said.

"I was just thinking what a good mayor you were going to make," replied Nick.

"Ohhhh, no. Not me, sir. I'm done with civic leadership and responsibility. You are going to be the next mayor," she replied poking her finger into his chest for emphasis.

Nick broke out laughing at the thought of someone calling him "Your Honor." After the moment had passed, he became serious. "We've got a lot of work to do, Diana. There are still a few little bands of criminals running loose around here. While there's a lot of food inside, it won't last forever. The list of critical items seems to have no end."

Diana nodded as she kicked a pebble. "I know. We'll begin to organize an election soon. Until then, I'll keep at it. I want you to know though; having you here to help is the best part. I feel like together there's nothing we can't accomplish. Thanks for staying…and Nick…I'm really beginning to think you are a very special person."

Nick smiled and pulled her close in a warm embrace. "I'm so happy to hear you say that, Diana. I felt a spark about twenty minutes after we first met. I don't know if it's because the future is so unsure or all this turmoil has me acting like a teenager again. I can say this, it feels good."

Diana nodded wisely, "I think we should take it slow for a while. I've just lost a son and gained a town. There's so much to do, and I'm sure we haven't seen the last of our problems yet. I almost feel selfish even thinking about a relationship when so many people are depending on me right now."

Nick's responded assuredly, "We've got plenty of time. I'm not planning on going anywhere. I do need to say one thing though. You've been sacrificing yourself for months now. I would advise finding a balance…taking time for you…doing some things that make Diana happy."

Diana nodded and motioned for Nick to follow her. She led him down the courthouse steps and to a side street bordering the building. In the middle of the block, the sidewalk split around the base of a large tree. The giant bur oak was about four feet in diameter, and it had obviously been a town landmark for some time. Beneath the canopy, the city had installed a park bench, and it looked like a great place to sit and enjoy some shade.

The couple sat in silence, absorbing everything that had been said. Diana finally spoke, "We may have won this battle, but the war is far from over. It boggles the mind how far we still have to go."

Nick took her hand and held it softly. "Right now, right this moment, don't think about any of that. Think about this beautiful tree and warm day. Think about how we aren't worried about somebody shooting at us or storming any wall. What's the old saying about smelling the roses?"

The Meraton volunteers, along with their Beltron Ranch comrades, pulled into town waving, and honking to everyone. They stopped in front of the Manor hotel and began jumping from the back of the pickups, slapping each other on the back and shaking hands with anyone nearby. Even though the market had long since started to wind down, word of their return spread quickly around town. Despite being a dreary, cloudy day, dozens of people quickly surrounded the arriving heroes, pelting them with hugs and kisses, while eagerly pumping hands.

Pete and Betty immediately announced a celebration in the Manor's gardens. Everyone was to bring a covered dish, and Pete's would provide the beverages. A grand party was planned for that very eve.

The Beltron boys headed back to the ranch to let the boss know the raids from Alpha should no longer be a concern. Before leaving, they had committed to bringing back a side of beef to barbeque for the festivity.

As everyone was running around preparing for the grand celebration, an odd noise was heard all over town. It took most of the residents a few moments to recognize the sound of an approaching helicopter. As all eyes looked to the northwest, a large green military copter appeared and flew directly over Main Street, slowly banking into a turn to the east.

The pilot picked a spot not too far from the main cluster of buildings and gradually landed the big machine in the middle of the main drag.

Everyone seemed to gather on the street in front of Pete's, curious about what was going on. Pete yelled out that the army must have heard about the party and wanted to join in. That remark brought a series of chuckles from the curious crowd.

Two men dressed in army uniforms jumped from the cargo bay and strode toward the gathered citizens of Meraton. Pete stepped forward to meet them. The older of the two men extended his hand, "I'm Major Donaldson, a surgeon from Fort Bliss. We understand you have a wounded colonel here, and we've come to take him to our facilities back at the base - if it's safe to move him."

Pete nodded his understanding and turned to a boy standing nearby, asking the youth to fetch the doc. After watching the excited young man run off, Pete turned to the soldiers and instructed, "Please follow me."

An hour later, the Colonel was being loaded onto the military transport along with his grandchildren and their suitcases. David and Samantha hugged Betty and Pete and promised to visit as soon as possible. Samantha made Betty promise to let Bishop know where she was so he wouldn't worry. After tearful goodbyes and promises of future reunions, the citizens of Meraton watched as the big aircraft spun up its blades and slowly lifted off.

Pete turned to the gathered onlookers and decided to cheer everyone up. He raised both hands high in the air. "Are we going to have a celebration or not? The first round is on me!"

Sophia Morgan had worked for the executive branch of the federal government through four different administrations. She had never married and was 51 years old. Her Georgetown apartment had been chosen because of its proximity to the federal office building where she worked. Sophia had entered government service as an intern shortly after graduating with a Doctorate in Constitutional Law from The University of New York and had never looked back.

She had always been shy and clumsy with interpersonal relationships, only accepting a few offers to date while in school. The experience hadn't been positive because Sophia preferred computers and libraries to people. She had two basic passions in life - research and a strong desire to feel like she was making a difference.

In the fast moving world of Washington politics, Sophia was neither attractive nor smart enough to be harvested for higher positions. PhDs and lawyers were a dime a dozen in D.C., and Sophia had never published anything or achieved any sort of public notoriety. What her employer did recognize was her dedication to the country and a remarkable capability to dig through reams of data. She was what some people called a "boiler," in that she could investigate extremely complex subjects and boil down the results into an understandable summary. Busy presidents often needed such reports crafted in a fashion they could read quickly, understand fully, and count on being accurate. She was really a political agnostic and had never registered to vote for either party. Her reports were delivered without spin or bias.

Over the years, Sophia had never shown any sign of ambition or desire to climb any partisan ladder. She arrived promptly at the office every morning, and no one could recall her ever speaking out. Her job reviews noted her dedication and neutrality. These attributes allowed Sophia to maintain her position, despite the turnover associated with a new president coming to town every few years.

Since she didn't work at the White House proper, Sophia had been reasonably unaffected when the building had been overrun. Even during the riots and anarchy that followed, she had stayed quiet and safe in her studio flat. Her neighbors across the hall were a young family of four and had asked her to keep an eye on their apartment while they were away for a few weeks visiting relatives in the Midwest. That stroke of luck had made a big difference in Sophia's survival. Always frugal, the monthly trips to the member's only discount stores had resulted in the purchase of large quantities of basic staples. Having the keys to the neighboring apartment and its well-stocked pantry had bolstered her provisions and allowed her to eat after her cupboard was bare. She had lost a few pounds, but wasn't starving.

Water had been another issue. Several months ago, the rowdy tenant above Sophia got a promotion, somewhat a rarity in the days of downsizing and mergers, and planned a wild celebration. To Sophia it seemed that every up and coming 20-something in D.C. had been there, an assumption based partly on the volume of the music and partly on the way her ceiling fan shook under the weight of the occupants. It was no surprise to her that there had been some damage to the pipes, resulting in dripping water between the tin tiles above her tiny kitchen. *No telling what those idiots tried to grind in the garbage disposal once the cops showed up* she thought. The landlord had been apologetic, providing 5-gallon buckets to catch the dripping water, and no one had ever retrieved them when the repairs were finally complete. Sophia sat the buckets on the roof to catch rainwater, and that had been a lifesaver.

Her mother lived in Florida, right in the middle of hurricane country. Sophia had purchased a hand-cranked device that was a combination radio and flashlight for Christmas. She had wrapped the gift in festive red and green paper, but left it on the counter, waiting for her next trek to the post office. After all, she had plenty of time before the holiday rush. Once the world turned topsy-turvy, Sophia depended on the device to provide her light.

Cooking hadn't been a problem at first. Natural gas seemed to be unaffected in the Washington area for a few weeks. Sophia had initially panicked the first time she turned the stove's knob and nothing happened. A few days went by with only cold meals and washing with icy water. Her biggest concern was boiling the rainwater to drink, as she didn't know how pure it was, and the surface of the water was riddled with floating insects when she retrieved the buckets from outside. Her Georgetown apartment had a small corner fireplace in the living room. She had decorated the hearth after moving in, but never even toasted marshmallows in it. Her trips home from the office soon included stopping to pick up dead branches or anything else that would burn.

Another problem was the roving bands of looters. When she had moved into the apartment, the neon lights from nearby shops had interrupted her sleep. She finally had solved the problem by purchasing a very expensive set of blinds for the windows that blocked the offensive blinking lights when closed. Those blinds had probably saved her life as they blocked anyone from seeing her candles at night.

After the first week, most of her neighborhood had been thoroughly ransacked. Sophia's building had been spared because of the unusual entrance that was via an unmarked side door. The raiders had simply overlooked the building. As time went on, she saw fewer and fewer dangerous people around. It was almost three weeks before she felt safe enough to sneak to the office, and she still took the back route with great care.

When the military had reestablished control, she simply reported for work as normal, surprised to see she was one of only a few who did so. She stood in line, waiting to receive whatever the army was passing out and made sure no one took notice or followed her home.

Despite there being no paychecks, information, or leadership, Sophia continued to walk from her apartment every day. Unlocking the door to the office space leased by the government, she had sat for weeks with nothing to do.

All of that had changed a few hours ago. Two men from the Treasury department had shown up and asked for help in performing some research. Sophia had been excited, hopefully having important work ahead of her. The men wanted a list of the individuals, in order, who were in line to succeed the President of the United States.

In normal times, that task would be beneath Sophia. The line of succession was well defined by the Constitution and subsequent law. It started with the Vice President of the United States, continuing down through the Speaker of the House, President of the Senate (pro tempore) and then various cabinet level secretaries.

With the sacking of Washington, the House and Senate hadn't convened for months. There were two cabinet positions that hadn't been confirmed and of course, the vice president was dead. The two men from Treasury were really Secret Service agents and Sophia quickly put two and two together. The president was dead, and the country needed a new leader.

This wasn't the first time in the nation's history that succession had been an issue. Starting in 1849, President Polk's term expired on a Sunday, and president-elect Taylor refused to be sworn in on the holy day due to religious beliefs. For one day, a man by the name of David Atchison, President pro tempore of the Senate, was technically acting as president. Or so he claimed.

Succession has been invoked 11 times in the history of the United States. Not all of the transfers have been smooth or non-controversial. In recent times, President Nixon's looming impeachment would have been yet another example. At one point in time, there was a vice president vacancy, given the resignation of Spiro Agnew. Fortunately, Vice President Ford was confirmed before Nixon resigned, allowing him to be sworn in without controversy.

Sophia quickly summarized there were two issues involved. The first centered on whom exactly was the Speaker of the House and President of the Senate. The Speaker was elected on the first day of every new Congress, but since there had been no elections, it wasn't clear who that person would legally be. The Senate's president pro tem was conventionally the longest serving senator of the majority party, but still required appointment. With the known death and unknown whereabouts of several senior senators after the collapse, who exactly was the third in line for succession?

Sophia informed the men that she would be happy to perform the research, but the lack of electricity and access to computer systems would make the task next to impossible. She was going to need access to several different libraries as well.

The men from Treasury were ready for that response, and informed Sophia that they would take her to a facility that should provide her with everything she needed. They even offered to escort her home so she could pack a few nights worth of clothing as she may be away for a while.

Within an hour Sophia was being driven through depressing, desolate streets of Washington on her way to a remote location in Virginia. It was there, she was assured, full access to everything she needed would be provided.

As they snaked their way through Washington's side streets, Sophia noticed several tow trucks pulling cars. She had sat and looked out her apartment window for weeks without seeing any traffic and few pedestrians. The scarce people she did observe on the streets looked like an undesirable element and she had quickly moved away from the window.

She asked one of the men in the front seat what was happening with the towing.

The agent in the passenger seat responded, "The military is trying to clear a path through the main streets and freeways. They have commandeered over 100 tow trucks and are trying to clear one lane each direction. They are taking all of the cars and trucks down to the football stadium's parking lot."

Sophia nodded her understanding and continued gazing out the window. "That should help the city get moving again, I would think. This has always been a commuter town."

The agent agreed, but shocked Sophia with his next statement. "I heard one report that even with 100 tow trucks, it was going to take them over four months just to clear the beltway."

"My goodness," responded Sophia, "why don't they just put gas in the cars and drive them off?"

The agent laughed and said he had asked the same question, "The response I received was that the cars didn't have keys, and many had been looted for their batteries or tires and wheels. The military believed it was faster to tow them away than try and fill, repair and hotwire every single car."

Sophia settled back for the remainder of the ride.
Several hours later, they pulled into the front gates of Fort Mead.

Bishop watched as Terri put on her hiking boots and laced them up. She had just finished a prenatal examination performed by one the base's doctors. The physician thought Terri was a little anemic, but otherwise having a healthy pregnancy. The lady doc had even come up with two large bottles of prenatal vitamins and given them to Terri with instructions regarding the proper dosage.

Terri was in good spirits, so Bishop decided now was a good time to talk to her about the general's offer. His wife listened without comment as he repeated the conversation. The couple was walking across the parade grounds when Terri stopped mid-stride and turned to her husband. "Do you want to do that Bishop? I didn't think you liked being in the army much. Do you want to take the general's offer?"

Bishop looked up at the gray, cloudy sky, lost in thought. He finally shook his head and said, "Terri, I don't think it's the right job for me. What I do believe is that it's the right job for you and the baby. There are doctors and medical care here. They have food and security. We could actually sleep in a bed with a real mattress. They even have shampoo!"

Terri laughed at Bishop's sales pitch and nodded her head. "I agree that life here would be a little bit easier, Bishop. But the ranch isn't so bad. We have more freedom there, and it's ours. I'm very happy there, and I think the baby will be too. When the time gets closer, we can go to Meraton like we planned, and let the doc there deliver the baby. I'm good with all of that."

Bishop smiled and said, "Are you sure? I'm glad to hear you say that, but are you positive it's the right move?"

Terri surprised Bishop, "No, I'm not sure it's the right move. I've come to know a side of you in the last few months that I never knew existed. You have this desire to help fix things, and I can tell you want to be involved and make a difference. I think that's what the general saw as well. Staying at the ranch is fine for the baby and me. What I'm not sure about is if it's the right move for you. He is offering you a chance to help with rebuilding the country, and I don't think you will have the same opportunity in Meraton."

Bishop didn't reply. He took both of Terri's hands and leaned forward, resting his forehead on hers. The couple stood like that for several moments. Bishop finally broke the silence, "You might be right. Do you know what my biggest problem with the whole thing is?" Bishop didn't give her time to answer. "I'm not sure I would be joining the right side. The more I learn and see, the more attractive the Independents become. Let's think about it for a little bit. Are you hungry?"

Terri laughed, "I'm a pregnant gal in the land of plenty. What a silly question, my love."

The two joined hands and continued walking across the grounds.

The End

Epilogue

(from the upcoming novel Holding Their Own IV: The Ascent)

The lieutenant was escorted into Colonel Marcus' tent by two burly soldiers, complete with a black cloth sack over his head. Marcus nodded at the closest guard, who turned to their guest. "Sir, it's okay – you can remove the bag now."

The stranger's arms slowly rose and lifted the cloth sack from his head. His eyes squinted for a moment as his vision adjusted to the light. "Can I offer you something to drink?" Colonel Marcus asked, almost embarrassed that the situation required such cloak-and-dagger tactics.

"No, thank you sir, I'm only here to deliver a message and need to report back as soon as possible."

Marcus nodded his understanding, "Well, go ahead lieutenant, what's the message?"

He hesitated for a moment and then took a deep breath. "Before I do so, Colonel, I need to verify – are you the commander of this military force?"

Marcus nodded and then decided to add, "Yes lieutenant, I am Colonel Marcus. I am in command here. Would you like to sit for a moment, lieutenant? I've been blindfolded before and know how disconcerting it can be."

The young officer shook his head and then caught himself, "Thank you, Colonel, I'll be fine. I wasn't quite sure how I would be received."

Marcus's gaze snapped up at the two escorts standing by the entrance to the tent. The sergeant moved his head in a motion indicating, "We didn't hurt him."

"Were you mistreated in any way by my men, Lieutenant?"

It took the officer a moment to connect the dots. He seemed anxious to clear up the misunderstanding, "Oh, no, no, no sir. That's not what I meant. Before I crossed your lines, it had been a concern. There are all sorts of rumors floating around, sir."

Marcus wasn't going to be distracted by rumors, "Good. Now...the message, Lieutenant?"

"Sir, this message is from General Peabody, Commander, Task Force Heartland. General Peabody is in command of the forces that oppose this militia. His message is as follows." The lieutenant cleared his throat, reciting from memory, "The United States Army offers a cease fire and exchange of prisoners and wounded. The terms are straightforward – neither side will maneuver or take any other actions to better their position strategically or tactically during the ceasefire. Both sides will agree to provide at least a one hour notice of any intent to break the agreement. Furthermore, the general suggests a hotline radio frequency be established so as to avoid any misunderstandings."

Colonel Marcus had been expecting this visit and had already received approval from his superiors to accept reasonable terms. The point that advocated giving the other side one hour's notice was bullshit. Neither party would honor that…. However, the radio communication was a good idea.

The commander of the Independents nodded his head, "You may return to your lines, Lieutenant, with the following answer – 'Agreed as proposed.' My aide will provide you with a radio frequency on your way out. Will there be anything else?"

The young officer thought for a moment and then replied, "No, sir. Thank you, sir."

"Dismissed."